Ciel Pierlot

TERMS OF SERVICE

ANGRY ROBOT

ANGRY ROBOT
An imprint of Watkins Media Ltd

Unit 11, Shepperton House
89-93 Shepperton Road
London N1 3DF
UK

angryrobotbooks.com
Cross the Is, dot the Ts

An Angry Robot paperback original, 2025

Copyright © Ciel Pierlot 2025

Edited by Gemma Creffield, Simon Spanton and Rob Triggs
Cover by Sarah O'Flaherty
Set in Meridien

All rights reserved. Ciel Pierlot asserts the moral right to be identified as the author of this work. A catalogue record for this book is available from the British Library.

This novel is entirely a work of fiction. Names, characters, places, and incidents are the products of the author's imagination or are used fictitiously. Any resemblance to actual events, locales, organizations or persons, living or dead, is entirely coincidental.

Sales of this book without a front cover may be unauthorized. If this book is coverless, it may have been reported to the publisher as "unsold and destroyed" and neither the author nor the publisher may have received payment for it.

Angry Robot and the Angry Robot icon are registered trademarks of Watkins Media Ltd.

ISBN 978 1 91599 830 9
Ebook ISBN 978 1 91599 871 2

Printed and bound in the United Kingdom by CPI Group (UK) Ltd, Croydon CR0 4YY

The manufacturer's authorised representative in the EU for product safety is eucomply OÜ - Pärnu mnt 139b-14, 11317 Tallinn, Estonia, hello@eucompliancepartner.com; www.eucompliancepartner.com

9 8 7 6 5 4 3 2 1

*Dedicated to
all my fellow messy
anxious bitches*

PART ONE

CHAPTER ONE

Everything is positioned precisely, perfectly, and precariously. With her trusty tape measure, Luzia marks the distance between the pieces of her small model problem comprised of forks, a glass of water, and a crumpled-up ball of tinfoil. The cramped front room smells like filtered air, and in her mind she conjures the olfactory memory of fire and ash and burning fuses. Her stage is set.

"Ready?" she asks.

"Only if you agree to do the funny voices," comes the response from the boy sitting across from her. "I'll settle for just one."

"Fine, fine, I'll do funny voices, but only if no one's dead by the end, all right?" She begins her briefing. "Okay then, let's break it down. The fallen steel beam is forty feet long with a height of twelve inches, weighing approximately twenty thousand pounds. It is currently not secured on either end and balanced only by two ropes around its midsection. The exposed circuit box is attached to a wall on the other side of the beam. In three minutes, the sparking will increase to the point where they ignite the stripped power lines below. That fire will wipe out an entire city block." She holds up her stopwatch, thumbing the button. "Three minutes starting now!"

Her nephew is on the case. The young boy's palms are braced on the table, tongue sticking out of the corner of his mouth, as he concentrates on the model. Stazi might only be ten years old but it's never too early to learn.

"Do I have my body weight or the weight of an average first responder?" Stazi asks, walking his fingers up to the fork that represents the steel beam.

"Good question, and good job thinking ahead. Your current body weight."

Most children Stazi's age would be uninterested in such games, and Luzia is infinitely grateful that she's managed to turn it into something enjoyable, something that gets him thinking about things other than schoolyard diversions. There are very real dangers that lurk in every corner of their lives, from the electricity they use for illumination to the walls that support the city stories below and above them. Most people walk past such things without thinking twice, but not Luzia. And she means to ensure that Stazi will be just as vigilant.

Stazi pokes at the model. "Are there any extra ropes or something I can use to tie up the beam better? Or are there other ways I can get to the circuit box?"

"You see a thirty-foot length of rope in the wreckage, but it will take at least forty seconds to reach and extract from the rubble, and you will be limited by how long it takes the plastic of the rope to begin melting or smoking."

"Aw... Auntie Lu, why'd you gotta make it hard? Fine, I choose to ignore the rope," Stazi decides. "I'm gonna take my chances with the beam. If I fall off, do I lose? Or is the fall short enough that I can climb back up and try again?"

This question is one she has a very easy answer to, given how many times she's seen people she works with make that exact tumble. It's depressingly easy to picture the same thing happening to Stazi. "At least five bones in your body will be broken and you'll be in agony before the fire eventually gets you, so I'm going to say you only have the one try."

"How did the circuit box fall apart?"

"Probably–"

"I wanna use Astrosi magic to fly across."

Luzia purses her lips and gives him a scolding look. "Stazi. Take this seriously, please."

But it's too late. Stazi's attention has drifted to the thought of those disruptive, mysterious folk and he will not be dissuaded from the stories of the Astrosi and their abnormalities, which, to a boy of his age, are more exciting than concerning. Luzia had that period when she was about his age as well, though she had grown out of it rather swiftly once she'd hit her teenage years. Once she'd become an apprentice and saw firsthand the damage they were capable of.

"Pleaaaaaaaaaase?" he begs, putting on his best wobbling lip and innocent wide eyes. "Astrosi magic?"

With a sigh, she puts on a silly, overdramatic tone and sasses, "I'm a trespassing Astrosi that decided to break a circuit box specifically to challenge a young boy that doesn't listen to his aunt–"

"Hey!" Stazi grins and then gasps in delight. "Oh – Oh! Was it Carrion? Pleaaaaaaaaaase?"

"What is your obsession with that madman?" she asks, dropping the voice. "Generic curiosity of the Astrosi is one thing, so long as you never encounter one, but there have been confirmed incidents of Carrion's evil actions within living memory. A single circuit box is the least of what they're capable of." She checks the timer. "Please focus."

Stazi pouts. "But Astrosi magic–"

"There are no recorded incidents of Astrosi flying," she points out, "or anything even remotely similar, for that matter. Now, the fire *is* still spreading–"

An unauthorized hand sweeps the model to the side, scattering the forks and knocking the tinfoil ball into the glass of water.

The two of them slide their gazes up to see Stazi's father standing in front of the table, arms crossed in the universal signal to cut this out or else. As much as Luzia loves her older brother, she has to admit that he can sometimes be a bit of a curmudgeon. It's not that Izax doesn't understand the importance of all this, either. He knows as well as she does that they live in unsafe environs.

"Daaaaad," Stazi whines, retrieving the tinfoil ball and drying it off with his shirt. "You burned down a city block. Thousands of people just died in a fire!"

"Sucks for them," Izax says flatly. "Now go put your shoes on. If you keep murdering people with Luzia, you're going to be late. And grab a bar before you leave! If you forget to bring lunch, you're gonna come home hangry. And don't forget to take your vitamins. And don't forget to behave for your overly paranoid aunt. And don't forget–"

"To breathe? I'll remember if you do, Dad." Stazi rolls his eyes as he slides out of his chair.

Once Stazi has vanished into the next room to grab his shoes and bag, Izax sits down across from Luzia with a tired, disgruntled, and utterly unimpressed sigh. He rolls the tinfoil ball back and forth with a petulance only exceeded by that of his ten-year-old son. "This is the third time you've helped him with his infrastructure homework and it's become a fiery death-fest. He's supposed to be learning about shit like not touching old Era One buildings. Not 'How to Save the Entire Bastion From Structural Degradation 101.'"

"That's hardly enough!" Luzia winces and then lowers her voice, unwilling to let Stazi hear them arguing. "Sorry, but the Bastion *does* suffer from a great deal of structural degradation, and we both know it."

The world of the Bastion stretches higher and deeper than anyone is capable of counting. A majesty of steel and aluminum and plastic, filled to bursting with factories and recycling facilities and the endless mass of tightly packed living units like this one. It just keeps going in every direction until you eventually reach the Fringes at the edge of the world. Even Luzia, who knows more of the Bastion than most, hasn't explored all of it. No one ever has. So large is the Bastion that it's impossible to do so even if someone dedicated their entire lifetime to the task.

Luzia views that as a challenge. One day she's going to map every single inch of the world she lives in, chart every pitfall and every abandoned train. The Bastion is *old* and the technology that must have been used to create its infrastructure no longer exists, and thus its upkeep depends entirely on how much they can learn about it. She means to learn everything, even if it does take her an entire lifetime.

Luzia leans back in her chair and gives her brother a look. "There's a reason he's coming with me for 'Take your kid to work day.'"

"Because my job is boring?" Izax replies with a sigh.

"Well, yes." Her brother directs lightrail traffic for the nearby station – an important job, albeit not one that gets a child excited. "But what I'm teaching him is important. He needs to know the world we live in."

"Let him be a kid without thinking about dying in a fire."

"If he doesn't know that there's a possibility he could die in a fire," she points out, "then he won't see any warning signs that would indicate a fire is about to start. A fire that he could then die in. Just because it's statistically unlikely to happen to him doesn't mean it can't happen. You know that."

It is Izax's turn to wince. His wife had choked to death five years ago after an electrical fire started at the water-treatment plant she worked in. That wasn't the first time Luzia had been touched by the dangers of the Bastion, not given her career, but it had hurt something fierce.

Izax pinches the bridge of his nose. "I know. It's only that just because you've decided to spend your life on fire safety duty doesn't mean you have to make him do the same. He can pick his own path."

"I'm not actually on the Fire Safety Brigade. I'm a First Responder for structural damages and hazard containment. And Stazi can do whatever he wants with his life. All I want is for him to be prepared. You want the same, don't you? This is simply a matter of different methods for the same task."

Another spectacularly tired sigh. "What this is, is an argument for another day. I haven't even had my morning caffeine pill yet. Promise me that you'll take care of him today, all right?"

"Always."

With a flurry of coats and an enthusiastically swinging backpack, Stazi skids back into the room, grinning from ear to ear. "I'm ready!" He leaps for Luzia's hand and starts dragging her towards the front door, hitting the control panel to slide it open. "Let's go, let's go!"

"And I do believe that's my cue to go to work." Luzia manages to grab her own coat and give her brother a one-armed hug around the shoulders. "I'll see you for dinner on Thursday. And, just for you, I promise I will not mention fire for the entire evening."

"You better not," Izax grumbles, but he returns her hug. "See you, Lu-Lu."

Daylight is beginning to sweep through this sector of the Bastion as the warm streetlamps automatically light up in a smooth glowing wave. Shades of blue-white and yellow-white begin to fill the entire one-hundred-and-fifty-story level, as well as the levels above and below, all lighting up at the exact same time, the ever-reliable 6:30 am. The kind of light provided by streetlamps is precisely calculated for what the human body needs. Luzia doesn't understand how it works, not really, but she knows there are things that humans get from certain types of light that a daily vitamin pack can't perfectly replicate. It's the same reason most housing units have a daylamp or two in addition to normal light fixtures.

Izax and Stazi live in the Lower Transport District, so named for the number of train maintenance facilities in the area. It's a good place to live, in Luzia's mind. Sure, there's the noise, but the ventilation systems are all good-quality Era One tech, well maintained and running smoothly. The housing units in this section are also a bit larger, which is a nice perk. Housing units with more than just a front room, sleeping room, and bathroom are always assigned to families, and of course she lives alone. She'd actually volunteered for a smaller unit, one that contains a single multi-use room and shares a bathroom with the thirty other units in its cluster. It's not as though she needs the space, given that she will have no children, and there is always someone else out there who does. Each citizen of the Bastion is allowed to have only one child to prevent overpopulation, and those who want more have to submit a request and wait for someone else to give up their allotted child slot. Luzia has always been more than happy with being an aunt. If there is something she can give up for the betterment of others in the Bastion, particularly at no real cost to herself, she will do so gladly.

Luzia guides her nephew onto the nearest janky electromagnetic train and holds him close to her side as it grinds and groans its way through the city. It's old. Everything in the Bastion is old.

"I've never been down this far before," Stazi remarks after the first twenty-one minutes, pressing his face against the plexiglass window.

"I'm not surprised," she replies. "You don't have any reason to go down more than a story or two, now do you? Your school's only a few sections away and I don't live far." She tweaks his nose. "Maybe I'll move down to the first level just to give you an excuse to make the trip."

He grins at that. "It'd be so fun if you did. Maybe we could have Thursday dinners at your new place and then I could go exploring there afterwards! Maybe I could move in with you on the weekends?"

"Your dad would kill me if that happened. Your commute would be–" She does some quick math. "–let's see, three hundred stories down at standard train speed, assuming you couldn't get priority lift access... At least forty-nine hours. Besides, you wouldn't want to live on the first. The bottom stories are rather close to... well, you know. Below."

This level of the Bastion – the third – is one hundred and fifty stories tall, making it one of the largest levels. There are eleven known levels of the Bastion. The lowest three are the tallest at one hundred and fifty stories each. The four above that are shorter at one hundred stories each, and then the final four are only fifty stories, rather short and squat and mostly away from the bulk of the major factories. There are, however, a good deal more unknown levels to the Bastion.

They aren't simply levels that belong to humanity; they belong to the Astrosi, capricious and inhuman folk, shrouded in rumors that vary from claims of immortality to those of ludicrous magics. They're as old as the Bastion, people say, and thus as old as the world entire.

If you go too far down, all the way past the first level and into the sublevels, then you will eventually come to the throneworld of the Eoi, the Astrosi of the Deep. If you go too high, into the uncharted upper levels, then you will eventually come to the throneworld of the Vesperi, the Astrosi of the Mists. And you shouldn't want to go to either, if you've a sensible head on your shoulders, which Luzia likes to think she does.

The train rattles to a stop in the bustling center of the Southwest Highvent District, so named for the large number of waste refineries in the area that require additional ventilation to keep the air clean, especially considering that the air gets thinner at the top of each level. Pressurization kicks in when transferring from level to level, but not from story to story. It's all a running list in her mind, the buildings and the streets and the levels – what's likely to break, what's particularly flammable.

"Remember," she tells Stazi as they are pushed out by the grind of passengers. "It's important that you stay close to me."

Stazi gives her a nod that's trying its very best to be as serious as possible. "Got it."

"No wandering off. Not even in my office."

"I know, I know." Stazi's seriousness lasts for about one city block before he's at it again, bouncing up and down as he asks, "So what are we doing today? Any floods that need taking care of? Collapsed walls? Power outages?"

She ruffles his hair, to his adorable annoyance. "I don't know. That's the thing about my job – I never know what my day's going to be like. Or what my hours are, which you'll care a lot more about when you get older."

The crowds of people on this block are starting to slow from a brisk walk to a slow shuffle until the foot traffic comes to a stop entirely. Whispers ripple out, grumbling complaints that indicate a lot of people packed into a small street are about to get rather angry rather soon.

"...ridiculous waste of time," someone mutters. "Can't be as bad as they say it is, and don't they know folks have jobs to get to?"

Another murmurs, "I don't like the looks of that, not one little bit."

It makes Luzia twitchy, all her instincts telling her that something terrible has happened even though she knows, statistically speaking, that it's probably nothing serious at all. Her brain trusts statistics. The rest of her, not so much. Grabbing onto Stazi's hand, Luzia pushes through the crowd shoulder first.

The entire road has been blocked off.

A chain-link fence sections off the road, and numerous signs have been thrown up declaring it to be dangerous and threatening anyone who dares enter without proper authorization. Luckily, the commuters are deterred by that and have yet to attempt to push past the barricade, as no one is really interested in being dragged to the Administrator's Office and written up on charges.

"This is statistically unlikely to be dangerous," she mutters, partly to Stazi and partly to herself. She reaches into her pocket for her identification card and brandishes it like a shield as she shoves past the onlookers and towards the guardsmen. "First Responder, coming through. Excuse me. Ma'am, there's no need for that kind of language, thank you very much. I'm a First Responder. Move out of my way."

Two guards are standing in front of the barrier and one of them holds up a hand as Luzia approaches, telling her, "Sorry, but no entry. Read the signs, please."

She holds up her identification for inspection. "Luzia N. E. Drainway, lieutenant-grade First Responder, engineering corp. At your service."

"Oh, right then." He steps aside and raises the yellow tape to allow her in, then pauses and raises an eyebrow at Stazi. "I'm not sure if the kid–"

Stazi has become far more cheerful at the promise of danger. "I wanna see!"

Luzia nods to the second guard. The good thing about Stazi being short for his age and Luzia having spent her life carrying very heavy things is that she can simply pick him up like a weightbag. While he whines, she hauls him up and then deposits him before another of the guardsmen.

"Keep him within the safety zone. Do not let him out of your sight," she tells the woman in uniform. "He'll try to run off."

"No I won't–"

"He'll also lie about trying to run off. Don't let him."

The guardsman nods and puts her hands on Stazi's shoulders to keep him in place. "Don't worry, I'll look after him."

"Thank you."

Luzia gives her nephew one final stern look that will hopefully keep him from doing anything more subversive than fidgeting and then lets the first guard usher her past the barricade into the disaster area.

Part of the road itself has been torn up. Sections of metal are lopsided, as though someone picked them up and tried to drop them back into place while blindfolded. Giant claw marks have carved up the metal as well, like some sort of heavy machinery has run wild through the street. Streetlamps have been either entirely knocked over or twisted into artistic metal sculptures. The city guardsmen have set up large light cubes around the area to compensate.

"Bloody good to see you," the guardsman in charge of it all says, wiping dust and sweat from his brow. "I called the First Responder's department less than five minutes ago. Wasn't expecting one of you lot so soon."

"I was in the area," she explains, before her mind tunes out the rest of what he's saying.

There are gouges all across the sectioned-off street. They don't match Luzia's initial impression of a bulldozer run amok. If they were caused by machinery, the patterns would have had to be deliberately designed. If the machinery in question was malfunctioning, the gouges would still be more even – straighter lines, the depths of the gouges more evenly spread out. This is too... chaotic.

She reaches into her bag to retrieve her measuring tape and walks over to the nearest wall, noting the distance between the gouges and the semi-exposed electrical lines. Not as urgent a repair as it looks. They'll have to prioritize fixing the ground first, lest it impact the floor below.

Something is buried in one of the gouges. A long laceration has cut up the ground there and there's a smudge of something unnatural in the metal. She withdraws her protective gloves from her bag and snaps them on. Squatting before the laceration, she pushes a finger into the smear of fluorescent green. She rubs it between thumb and forefinger. It's fuzzy, almost crumbly in a way that a chemical spill wouldn't be. Thicker, too, made of something fibrous. She's seen this before, though only once, years ago when she was still an apprentice.

"Astrosi..." she mutters to herself.

The guardsman blinks in surprise. "Well, yeah. But how could you possibly know?"

She holds up her fingers. "This residue is seen only after one of the Eoi has been in the area. The pattern of the gouges is too organic to be mechanical. And there's the height of them as well. I could reach all of them if I jumped, but any machinery powerful enough to rip up the ground like this would be quite large. It wouldn't be limited to the height of an average human-shaped being." She rises to her feet and dusts off her gloves. "Thus it can only be Astrosi."

Though this isn't a common occurrence in her job, it isn't entirely unfamiliar to her. All those years ago, she had seen the aftermath of a fight between the Eoi and the Vesperi, vicious enough to knock out two stories of a building, causing a chain reaction of structural collapses. The effort to fix it all had been astronomical, but what Luzia remembers most is having to drag bodies from the wreckage.

"Anything else?" she asks. She tugs off her gloves and replaces them with a fresh pair, putting the old ones in a hazard ziplock. There's very little she can't squeeze into her work bag and she prides herself on always been prepared for any eventuality. "They could have left something behind." She has been trained to never be too careful when it comes to the Astrosi. "Whatever details you've got would be appreciated."

With a jerk of his thumb, the guardsman gestures to a woman with a blanket around her shoulders who's sitting far over in a corner of the street with another guardsman kneeling next to her. She has a shellshocked expression, all wide eyes and trembling jaw.

"We had an eyewitness to the whole thing. Feel free to ask her whatever you like," the guard says. "We've gotten next to nothing out of her, apart from the fact that apparently that bastard Carrion showed up last night."

Luzia draws in a sharp gasp and inches closer. "They did?"

Carrion is the most rumor-shrouded member of the already mysterious inhuman folk. A renegade, known for having turned their back on the two Astrosi thrones and gone off to work their own mischief. Of all the Astrosi, they show up in the human city the most, always to cause maximum chaos and destruction. Luzia is not a violent person by any means, but if Carrion were to turn up dead... well, she wouldn't throw a party to celebrate, but she would certainly attend a party thrown by someone else.

"Yeah," the guardsman nods. "Couple others showed up to fight them, but all that happened was a damn three-way scuffle and a whole lot of property damage. One of the others yelled Carrion's name. That's pretty much the only thing we had to go on – that poor woman didn't see much. She tried to hide, mostly."

"Were they here for a reason? All the damage I can see is rather contained to this one street. I would expect more splash damage if it was nothing more than fighting for the sake of fighting."

"Who knows?" he grumbles. "Only thing we've got on Carrion is that they're a damn lunatic."

"All right," she says as she returns to the wreckage. "Let's get started."

Luzia begins assigning tasks to the various guardsmen, having them take down the precariously leaning lampposts before they fully topple over and move the heavy metal structures out of the way. For her part, she gets to work and begins dictating notes into her recorder as she goes over the scene.

The extent of the damage is deceptive, and she quickly becomes certain that it will require far more repair than she initially thought. She marks two places on nearby walls that will need some minor scaffolding, and then a few minutes later she finds remnants of a corrosive acid that are perilously close to an air vent. By now, a few of the guardsmen have brought out containment units, so at least that can be temporarily controlled without too much hassle, but it's a short-term patch and she knows it'll take quite some effort to repair properly.

Another First Responder shows up to the scene, a medic this time, and they begin to shuffle the shocked eyewitness away from the scene. They give Luzia a professional nod and leave behind more tools they've hauled over from the nearest Responder's office.

"Whoah!" someone shouts. "Easy there!"

Luzia's rushing off to them before they've finished their cry. A streetlamp with a slight bend in the metal pole is beginning to topple over, and the two guardsmen propping it up aren't quite doing the job.

She slides herself between them and braces the metal pole against her shoulders, the weight sinking into her muscles. "Pick it up at the base!" she orders. "If it's come loose like this, propping it up again would just leave it unstable." One of them shifts to the base of the pole and she instructs, imagining what it looks like in her head despite being unable to see it, "Unscrew the connector. It's the circular device between the pole and the ground." A pause, a scratching noise, and then the pole slumps against her shoulders. "Yes, you've got it."

Between herself and the guardsmen, they're able to walk the pole away from the rubble and deposit it on safe ground.

"Thank you very much," a guardsman says, dusting her hands off and wincing at the way the metal's weight has reddened her palms. "Damn thing was about to come down on all our heads."

"Yes, it was. Make sure there's no damage to the power line that was running to the streetlamp," she absently tells them, already heading back to the job in hand.

The choppy mess of street that marks the epicenter has been left alone. From this vantage point, it doesn't look too terrible, mostly surface-level disturbances, not as deep or dangerously placed as the gouges on the wall. She inches forward, keeping an eye on her feet and stepping over the various cracks and uneven sections.

How odd. The closer she gets, the more it appears as through the ground has been torn up from below, the street jutting upwards and outwards.

Another step and her foot lands on something wobbly. Every muscle in her body freezes up as she slowly looks down at the unsteady slab of street that is currently supporting all her weight. How far down does the damage go? *What* is below, for that matter? Many feet of support structures, or empty shafts? There's a creak of metal. A crumble of old sealant. Very, very slowly, she carefully slides her back foot away from the epicenter…

Before she can move so much as two inches, the entire slab she's standing on breaks off.

CHAPTER TWO

Luzia throws herself backwards just as it all falls down, scrambling until her palms slap onto solid ground. Heart pounding, she clings to the steady steel and watches the last of the falling wreckage vanish. All manner of commotion arises from the guardsmen and she hastily throws up her hand to silence them. She listens.

There's the noise of all the rubble shifting and falling and then... nothing. No crash. No cracks. She heard it fall and she doesn't hear it land.

"Miss," the head guardsman says quietly, holding out a hand to her. "You all right?"

She grabs his hand and pulls herself away until she can rise up onto her feet again and get a proper glimpse of it all.

At first she had thought the shadows in the center of the wreck to be a result of poor lighting, but now that much of the upturned street has fallen away it becomes apparent that the darkness is far more sinister. The bits of wrecked metal and exposed piping have tumbled down to reveal a pit of pure, pitch blackness.

The head guardsman gets a tiny bit closer, craning his neck. "How far down does it go?"

"I have no idea," she replies. "I can't see a thing, and I couldn't hear the debris land."

Alarm pales the guardsman's face. "Right then. What do you need?"

Luzia plucks up her courage and begins to get as close as she can to the sinkhole without risking another tumble. Reaching into her pack to retrieve a set of delicate pliers, she crouches low to the ground to more evenly disperse her weight and then deposits her pack somewhere safe to make herself even lighter.

"I'd need a droplight or something similar to measure the depth," she says as she gets a better look. "If I didn't know better, I'd say it goes down an entire level. But that would be thousands and thousands of feet. It's oddly clean-looking, too."

"Maybe it's some sort of Era One shaft?" the guardsman suggests.

"Could be."

The Bastion is filled with buildings that are in use and those that aren't. Most stable buildings were refurbished in Era Two, reconstructed over and over again to the point where they cannot reasonably be referred to as the original building. Then there are Era One structures that are so old that all entrances to them have been sealed up over time and are now relegated to being merely support structures for the levels above and below. Impossibly far from the center of the city are the Fringes, uninhabited wastelands of Era One buildings that have no remaining stability to them. Due to the uncertain nature of the Bastion's structural integrity, they have long ago decided to shore up these Era One structures whenever possible and carefully not touch them when not.

Sometimes walls, grates, or hatches are found, but they're usually left alone. The Bastion can be a rickety place, and breaking a rule about where not to go or what not to touch can get a person in a good deal of trouble very quickly. The world was built with Era One technology, and now they live in an age when most of it is broken beyond hope of repair and the rest is so old that the last generation to know how to use it must have died thousands of years ago.

Era One or not, Luzia finds her attention drawn to something beyond just the nature of the pit. Sticking out of the pit wall is something small and oddly shining.

"We've got an unknown object down here!" she calls out.

She readies her pliers, adjusting them to elongate the handle. Leaning over the hole in the ground, she tentatively shifts a few sheets of aluminum aside, making sure not to move anything that's currently load-bearing.

What hides beneath is almost silver in color, and it shines with an internal luminescence in the same way the light cubes do, though its light is far weaker. It appears relatively spherical in shape, and at just over an inch in diameter it's easy for her to remove it from the pit without being concerned that it might cause further collapse. After examining it to ensure that it's not damaging the pliers, she drops it into her gloved palm.

The guardsman comes up to her as she inches her way out of the danger zone. "What've you got there? It safe?"

"It doesn't appear to actively be doing anything, but I don't have any real way of knowing." She returns the pliers to her bag so that she can better prod at the object with her thick, plastic-coated gloves. "Have someone fetch a containment pod just in case. We don't know what could activate it. There's so many exposed wires and pipes here that if it starts heating up or sparking we could have a massive fire on our hands."

The object isn't perfectly spherical. It's faceted – an icosahedron, if she counts correctly. She turns it over, checking for markings.

"It looks like it might be some sort of Era One device," she remarks. Those pop up in the Bastion with more frequency than the average person might expect, sometimes when an Era Two building breaks or if they try to build something else over a dilapidated structure. "This one doesn't look so bad. It's not got a single scratch on it despite being so violently unearthed. Oh, that's interesting…"

"What?"

"There's some sort of odd pattern beneath the surface. It looks almost like circuitry."

The guardsman leans over the object and pushes up his helmet. "You think? Hard for me to tell."

"Mm, I think so. Do you see those lines? The tint of the metal? Whatever it is, it doesn't look like standard Era Two tech."

A second guardsman has shuffled over with a small containment pod in hand and she too bends over Luzia's hand to ogle. "Weird shape. You know what, though? It does sort of look like something my mother had – a stone or something on a ring."

"A stone? Really?" Luzia asks, raising an eyebrow. It looks nothing like a stone to her.

The same guardsman nods. "Yeah. It reminds me of a diamond."

"Diamond?"

"Shiny sort of thing. Pretty rare, these days."

A new voice from behind them says, "A diamond? Well now, that's certainly something, isn't it?"

Luzia whips around.

It's not a guardsman. Nor do they look like the average passerby who might have snuck under the yellow tape. They're wearing a ratty overcoat and boots that are more duct tape and string than boot. The bright light globes make the stranger's brown skin appear to glow, framing a strong jaw and a straight nose. A long, loose brown braid hangs down their back.

They snatch the device out of her hand and hold it up to peer at it.

"Excuse me," Luzia protests, hands on her hips. "This area is off limits. I'm going to need to see some form of identification."

"Oh, I haven't got any."

With an exasperated slump of his shoulders, the lead guardsman flaps his hand in the direction of the yellow tape. "No identification, no entry. Please hand over the object and step behind the line."

"Nah."

From the confusion on the guardsman's face, it's clear that he's unused to people not doing as they're told. He turns to the other members of the guard; similarly confused, they start mumbling to each other about what to do with this stranger. Even though defiance of the guard and intervention in the Bastion's infrastructure usually results in being written up on charges, they can't just drag them away. That would be unnecessarily violent, surely.

The stranger, on their part, withdraws a match from a battered box in their pocket and sticks it between their teeth.

It occurs again to Luzia that they are surrounded by exposed infrastructure of wires and piping and ventilation and chemicals. There is also a sinkhole of unknown properties that may or may not include flammable, toxic, or otherwise hazardous materials.

The guard may not be trained for such things, but Luzia is. When she was first hired, ten years, five months, and seventeen days ago, she was given a manual to read regarding the important aspects of her new job. There was a whole two hundred and thirty-eight pages dedicated to safety procedures and all the things that need to be done in case of an emergency. She'd read it back to front until she'd had the entire thing memorized because very small mistakes can add up to a very big disaster.

So instead of panicking and yelling at the stranger to put the damn match away, Luzia does exactly as the pamphlet instructs.

She rushes over to a panel on the wall, yanks it open, and hits the alarm.

"Fire hazard!"

Red lights start going off, flashing throughout the city block and turning everything an ominous crimson. A wailing siren sounds, the noise loud enough to reach everyone in the vicinity of what is potentially a very dangerous fire zone.

One thing to be said about the city's guardsmen is that they don't remain overwhelmed by shock for long. Emergencies happen in the Bastion unpredictably, but more often than people would like, and the guard is trained to react to anything from structural collapse to Astrosi threats in the event they occur.

Someone cries, "Hazard alert!"

"Clear the area!" the guards begin yelling, rushing to the perimeter to corral the onlookers, the call echoing outwards as guards further away hear the alert and shout out the message as well.

Luzia whips her head back and forth, her eyes quickly adjusting to the disorienting red lights. Where's Stazi? Her heart skips a beat when she sees that the guardsman she left him with has moved to contain the perimeter. Stazi is no longer there. Maybe he's safe and she just can't see him. He's so small, so short, it would be so easy for him to get lost in a crush of people if he did the sensible thing and ran away from the alarm.

But Stazi so rarely does the sensible thing. Luzia's stomach is churning as she runs from the wreckage towards where he last was standing.

"Stazi!" she cries out, stumbling over an overturned hunk of street. "Stazi, where are you?"

In the controlled chaos, she barely notices that the stranger has turned to lay upon her the weight of their undivided attention.

She starts running towards the perimeter only to find that the stranger has suddenly appeared in her path, their intimidating presence stopping her dead in her tracks. They toss the diamond-like object into her hands with a pleasant smile and remove the matchstick from their mouth. "Have it back if you like. Unfortunately it's not a diamond, by the way. Just some rubbish Era One tech."

"Out of my way!" she demands. She shoves them in the chest to push around them as she desperately calls, "Stazi!"

The stranger grabs her by the arm and stops her again. "May I have your name?" they ask, sweet and slow.

"Luzia," she automatically replies. "Luzia N. E. Drainway. Now move–"

"Thanks, love."

They strike the match. It crackles into a droplet of orange flame and then, casual as anything, they toss it over their shoulder.

With a great whoosh of flame loud enough to make her ears pop, the very air itself bursts into hungry, cruel fire – a solid, explosive ball of pure flame, bigger than her entire body, that burns like a white-hot furnace. She can feel the heat of it bright on her face as it knocks her back, tossing her flat on her ass five feet away.

Apparently the stranger can smell weakness and they stride over to kick her between the ribs, ensuring she stays down. The blow feels like all the air is being sucked out of her lungs.

Wait, no. That's actually exactly what's happening.

She can't breathe. The stranger's hand is stretched out in front of her as though offering her assistance in standing up again and they're… they're pulling the air from her lungs. Her head feels light and swimming, and she gasps on nothing. It's not like sticking her head in a bucket, where her lungs will fill with water if she breathes. Her lungs are working. Everything is happening right, physically, but there's simply nothing there to breathe.

"Astrosi…" she manages to mumble, for what other creature could create such magics as these?

"Guilty as charged." The stranger leans down, picks up her arm, and shakes her limp hand. "You can call me Carrion. Pleasure to make your acquaintance."

A rush of movement cuts through her blurry vision. Someone so very small and so very short is swinging a metal pipe at Carrion.

"Leave my aunt alone!" Stazi cries.

No, no, no! He can't! What a stupid, brave thing to do, and she can't stop him! She gasps, mouth gaping open, free hand tearing on the torn ground as she does everything in her dizzy power to push herself to her feet.

Carrion steps back, catches the bit of pipe Stazi has armed himself with, and rips it from his grasp. "Cute," they remark.

Useless though Stazi's efforts might seem, it breaks Carrion's concentration and Luzia finds that she's suddenly breathing *stuff* again, her blood pumping louder than it ever has before. She collapses, bent over her hands, so overwhelmed by the simple act of breathing that it takes her a crucial moment too long to get herself together.

Stazi screams.

She has to get to him, has to protect him. She promised. Cold, dry fog crawls across the ground, curling around her fingers. It's thick and soupy like smog, yet a clean, opaque white and carrying a distinct chill. The white fog consumes the street, smothering the flames. She staggers onto one knee just in time to see Carrion swoop down on her nephew. Just as she can pick Stazi up and cart him around, to his great amusement or annoyance, Carrion too grabs him and swings him over their shoulder.

"Auntie Lu!" Stazi cries out, fat tears beginning to run down his cheeks. He bangs his fists against Carrion's back, to no avail. "Lu, help!"

Carrion wiggles their fingers in a mockery of a wave. "Bye now, Luzia N. E. Drainway."

With that cruel goodbye and a whirl of their coat, they tighten their grip on the struggling Stazi and jump down into the pit.

"Stazi!" Luzia screams. But just as before, not a single sound answers her.

CHAPTER THREE

Luzia can barely see, blindly stumbling through a world of white comparable only to the worst of carbon-dioxide powder explosions.

The white fog pours down into the pit in a gentle rolling wave, beckoning her down into its depths, like a trail of crumbs left behind by Carrion. She still cannot see much of anything as she claws to the edge, but if Carrion could survive the drop then she has to at least try. Her mind runs through risk assessment – how likely she is to break a limb, how long the fall would need to be to kill her – and she forces it all out of her thoughts, pushes down the unending stream of anxieties, and fills her mind with the knife-sharp knowledge that her nephew needs her.

"I'm coming, Stazi," she mutters, and then lets herself slip off the edge.

Gravity greedily clutches at her. The moment she falls is the moment she knows, with certainty, that she has miscalculated. The fall is truly endless. The world is spinning around in her in a churning whirlwind of fog and darkness. She will die, she knows that now, organs a paste even before she hits the ground, terminal velocity swiftly approaching.

As soon as that realization hits, she... slows down.

No ground is hit, no safety net catches her. Her fall simply begins to fade from breakneck to a gently drifting descent. As she slows and blinks away the fear of imminent death, lights begin to appear in the gloom, long streaks of blue-white light in circuit-like patterns – the same as the Era One diamond. That soupy white fog is still around her, coalescing beneath her. Is it cushioning her fall?

Did Carrion *leave* this for her? Or is it a remnant of their own descent? Her fall stops, leaving her on wobbly feet but still standing, as though she has been gently set down by a giant and benevolent hand.

The moment her feet touch the ground, the fog wisps away. She squints to adjust to the gloom, making out vague shapes of a standard maintenance tunnel, the sort she's crawled around in before, except this is larger, older, and appears entirely abandoned. She blinks at something in the distance. Is that a light?

It is, she sees as she approaches. A match stuck in the ground, burning a blue flame as bright as it is unnatural. She yelps and recoils from it the moment her mind consciously recognizes it as Astrosi magic – as Carrion's magic. It doesn't seem to be doing anything nefarious, other than peacefully existing. Not that that's any real reassurance. Something is behind it – a door, perhaps? No, or at least not a usual door. It's the entrance to a priority lift. And it's been left open.

The flame flickers. She tilts her head to the side. There's something...

There are scratches in the wall above the lift entrance, nasty things that look burnt more than carved. A message. From Carrion? In sharp, scrawled marks, it reads:

I've left the passage open. Follow me ;)

Every facet of her being is screaming that this is a trap. Why else would they have left such a direct instruction if not to dare her into falling for their trap? But she can't succumb to her desire to slowly back away from this obvious setup and she can't let her anxiety win. It will not help her; it'll just blind her. That's probably what Carrion wants, if they want anything beyond a base desire for malice.

She has no choice but to follow their taunting message. She reluctantly steps into the priority lift bit by bit, inching her toes and then her foot and then her whole body inside the box. When it doesn't immediately do anything, she looks about for the buttons that would usually be inside such a lift, the too-bright blue fire still providing helpful illumination. There is a panel, she finds, but it's covered in dozens of buttons, all of which are entirely unlabeled – except one. Above the lowest button is another carven message, this time reading:

Push me

She pushes the button and the door slides closed, cutting her off from the firelight and leaving her in darkness. The floor hums. Something beeps. A sudden rush of pressure crashes into her, popping her ears open with the force of a battering ram smashing through glass. She gasps, clapping her hands over her head as though that will somehow block it out, and just as she thinks she's about to scream, it stops as suddenly as it began.

There's another beep. The door opens.

Choking back the urge to be sick all over the lift floor, Luzia stumbles out into a dimly lit room and falls to her knees, desperate to not be in that box anymore.

Something soft rests beneath her legs and winds between

her fingers. A carpet of thin and blue-green things, almost blade-like in shape, packed together so densely that she cannot see the ground beneath them. For a moment it's soothing, and then she yanks her hands away and scrambles to her feet. It could be anything, including some devious device left behind by Carrion.

No matter how far back she cranes her neck, she cannot see another of Carrion's messages, and when she looks behind her, she cannot see the lift. It's simply vanished, leaving in its wake just lit-up circuit patterns circling around, similar to the icosahedron she discovered. Is she at the base of an old Era One shaft? She takes a deep breath and the air is damp. Carrion has left her another message after all. Their fog is here as well, filling the tunnel she's now in.

When she takes a hesitant step forward, there's the sensation of something waxy brushing against her arm. She barely stops herself from shrieking.

Hidden amidst the fog are these... these cables. They're a similar blue-green as the stuff on the ground, draped haphazardly all around the lower walls of this shaft, as though waiting for someone to trip into their nest so they can strangle them. It's all so moist, too. The cables have left some sort of watery residue on her arm and the air itself is damp in a way that cannot be caused solely by the fog.

A slithering and grumbling gradually reach her ears through the haze.

"Who's there?" she demands, spinning around as she strains her eyes, desperately trying to see through the thick whiteness. "Stazi? Stazi, can you hear me?"

The grumbling gets louder.

A few of the cables shift out of the way, like a curtain being tugged on, and a figure shuffles out of the gloom. They're not Carrion. Nor, unfortunately, are they Stazi. They're a man who has the stooped and squinty-eyed demeanor of someone in their eighties but the smooth face and luxurious long hair of someone in their thirties at the oldest.

"Not another one," he mutters, rolling his eyes.

"Who are–? Never mind. Have you seen a young boy? Someone took him. They went down this way, I'm sure of it, and I have to get him back."

The man wrinkles his nose. "Loud little thing, yes. Rather disruptive. You're being rather disruptive too. Run along, won't you."

The man is painfully cantankerous, but Luzia still exhales with relief. Stazi is alive – that's all that matters.

She looks around her. She is in a new environment and thus she must orient herself. That's part of her job, and so that at least she knows how to do. There's still no visible way out, even though it would seem that Carrion and Stazi are no longer here. Logically speaking, there must be some manner of exit, but she can't bring herself to pick a direction and run off like she was told. She's no use to Stazi if she falls into an even less friendly pit or hits an electric fence or a thousand other things that could happen.

This place isn't natural. Even if she has fallen further than she'd initially thought, the very first floor of the very first level still doesn't look like this. She is about to ask the man where she is before she stops herself. She's too afraid to know and Stazi is more important.

"Where did he go?" she asks the man.

Another rude wrinkle, this time one that covers the man's entire face. "Aren't you a demanding one."

"Please, you must tell me where he–"

"Hush up, you'll frighten the *Pueraria abundatus*." He lovingly runs a finger over one of the green cables and she swears on her life that it twitches in response. "I suppose if you want to follow after Carrion, I shan't stop you." Still petting the cable, he points to the left, down another tunnel. "They took the boy that way. Go on, chase your death wish."

She is already running in the pointed direction, yelling over her shoulder, "Thank you!"

"Don't bother," she hears him gripe back.

The cables don't seem to move for her like they did for him, but she's still careful to be as delicate as she can when pushing them out of her way. It's so dark down here that she can barely see them, relying on the glowing circuitry and the way it lights up the fog to guide her.

The further in she goes, the more damp the air gets.

Strange, brightly colored spheres begin to dot the cables and the green stuff on the ground as if they're growing from it. One of the spheres is particularly bulbous and purple and she shudders at how hostile it appears. Worse still is that they cover more and more of the tunnel she's found herself in, creeping up on her until she finds herself giving every cable a nervous look in case it really will strangle her. Nothing here can be trusted.

At the end of the tunnel, at last, is a door. A metal door, a normal – if large – metal door, not unlike one that she'd see in front of a warehouse. Two people, a man and a woman, are standing guard. Both are holding contraptions that are as identical to one another as they are unfamiliar to her – a tube sort of thing, longer than her forearm, with a handle on one end and a pointed piece of metal affixed to the other.

"I am here for the boy that Carrion brought down," Luzia declares, coming to a stop before them. "Can you take me to them?"

One of the two, the woman, chuckles. "Oh, feisty."

"Please, I'm not here to joke with you! I'm here for the boy."

The other, the man, turns to his companion and gestures towards the door with a shrug. "Isn't Carrion with the queen?"

"Queen?" Luzia asks, but the two act as though they don't hear her.

"Mm," the woman hums in agreement with her partner. "They should be."

"Could just let her deal with this one, too," the man says.

"Yeah, this one's harmless." The woman, ignoring Luzia completely at this point, pushes aside a clump of hanging cables to reveal another bit of circuitry that she then proceeds to mess with. To her companion, she remarks, "Bit weird, though, innit? Carrion bringing a boy with them, that is. Didn't think they dealt with children."

The man scratches his chin. "Don't ask me. For all we know, the queen won't even take him, kids being sort of useless and all."

Luzia grits her teeth together and demands, "What queen?"

"How stupid are you?" The woman pinches the bridge of her nose. "There's only one queen."

"I don't recognize any queen. I answer only to the authority of the Office of the Administrator."

"Ain't no Administrator down here."

"I'm below the first level, aren't I." Down in the areas humans dare not go, down in the depths of… She feels unnaturally cold as she stops that thought. "This queen – she's not human, is she?"

The man rolls his eyes. "Is the queen human?" he says in a mocking tone. "Bit thick, ain't you? Queen'll set you straight. Get going. The door's already unlocked. You can enter whenever you'd like."

But the doors haven't opened. Luzia takes a half-step towards the doors and then another few, slightly more confident steps. It's as though she crosses some invisible line, for the moment she gets close enough, the doors slide open all on their own, hissing with the ease of well-maintained metal. The fog has completely faded away by now, as though Carrion's lingering influence can't penetrate this far in.

"See?" the woman says. "That'll take you where you want to go."

Luzia steps through the door only to find a dead end. She looks up and down at the dark fuzz on the walls and the neon bulbs on the carpeted floor, but there's no sign of a door or tunnel or anything. It's just an empty cylinder of space.

"What is this?" She turns back to the two guards with a frown. "There's nothing here."

With a too-wide grin, the woman wiggles her finger until it lands on a wall panel. She pushes a button.

There's a sudden lurch.

The man laughs and taunts, "Bye-bye now!"

For the second time in the past hour, the ground beneath Luzia's feet falls. She screams as the circle of ground she's standing on plunges down a hidden shaft faster than a priority-access lift, air tugging at her hair and clothes. Unlike last time, there is no mysterious fog to cushion her fall, and so she simply clings to the ground on bended knee and closes her eyes tightly shut, the biting air ripping tears from the corners of her eyes. Over the fall she can hear the rapidly vanishing sound of the guards laughing at her misery.

The lift slams to a stop, the impact making her fall over, and she scrambles to pick herself back up, then winces as bright light sears her eyes after so long in the dark tunnels.

She's always done her best to avoid imagining what the Astrosi realms look like. She wants to map out the Bastion, after all, not the lower or upper realms of the world. But she's always assumed it would be more of the same, or as dilapidated as the Fringes of the Bastion. She'd thought that it would be darker, down in the Deep. Because, queen or no queen, Luzia can be nowhere else. Not with how far down she's gone. Not with how impossible this entire place is.

She is in the perilous realm below the first level, and she is not with humans.

As she pulls herself together, she has to shield her face from the blue-white light above. Overhead, just outside of the lift platform, is a solid ceiling of pale blue light panels, similar to the fixtures turned on in the Bastion during the day. She has landed amidst an open area of more green things. And she's not alone. There's a crowd of figures in this large chamber, each of them sporting hair down to at least their hips and some down to their knees. Just like Carrion.

The people nearest to her stare at her as though she's got two heads. Careful not to touch them, she weaves her way through the surprised faces towards the front of the chamber, where most have focused their attention.

A woman she passes pulls away from Luzia and curls her upper lip. "Ew," the woman mutters. "She's all sweaty."

Between the crowd of whispering people, she glimpses the familiarly ratty coat of Carrion and, behind them, a flash of Stazi's curly hair.

"Stazi!" she cries out, stumbling forward only for someone to catch her around the waist just as she reaches the head of the crowd. "Let me go! Stazi!"

The man holding her physically hauls her back from the circle that's cleared around Carrion, his gruff voice scolding her, "Don't go yelling in the queen's court. Besides, you're liable to wake the child if you keep it up."

Wake the child?

She cranes her neck, doing her utmost to shove the man away from her. It's so difficult to see – there! Stazi is lying on the ground, slumped by the foot of someone dressed like the guards at the door. At least, mercy of mercies, Stazi is peacefully dozing as though he's back in his own bed. Uninjured, but unconscious.

Carrion, for their part, pays her no mind, their entire focus on someone seated at the head of the room. "That's that, no?" they state. "One life, as promised."

A musical voice decrees, "One life. Your debt is paid."

"Bloody finally."

Carrion makes a gagging noise. Nose wrinkling, Luzia pushes forward another inch to get closer to Stazi, only to see Carrion hork up a mouthful of saliva and spit onto the ground. Something small exits their mouth as well, a tiny round object that lands amidst the spit. The thing, whatever it is, crumbles into a small pile of dust.

Luzia has eyes only for her nephew. His chest rises and falls, steady and sleeping. How such an energetic child was put to sleep so quickly is a mystery, and she can only assume it's some sort of Astrosi magic that Carrion employed.

"How dare you take him?" she demands, her entire body shaking. "You–"

Carrion is gone.

They have vanished without a sound. Were it not for that bit of dust on the ground, there would be no evidence that they were ever here in the first place.

"Do not be alarmed," that same musical voice says. "Regrettably, and despite our best efforts, the contract they just fulfilled allows them passage from our throneworld. Rise, stranger, and speak your piece."

With Carrion no longer blocking her view, Luzia can finally see who they were speaking to. A woman sits upon rough brown cables that have been twisted into the shape of a chair. She's clad in a dark bodysuit, the metallic sheen not unlike a radiation hazmat suit, and her dark skin is desaturated as though from lack of daylamps. Most extraordinary is her hair. Uncountable tiny braids trail from her head until they reach the ground and then they too become dotted with bright orbs and skinny green cables until indistinguishable from the ground.

"With all due respect," Luzia says firmly, doing her absolute best to prevent her voice from wavering with fear, "I do not know you and I have no piece to speak to you."

A man stands near the throne, a man with long black hair and a frown that is all bushy eyebrows. "Shut up and know your place! You have the honor of addressing Her Majesty Queen Sef the Third, Guardian of the Eoi, Lady of the Deep, and most resplendent consort of all that is green."

Right. All right, okay, that's... well, that's straightforward enough. Not a surprise, surely, given that the queen the guards spoke of had to be, well, here. The queen of here. Oh, lovely. Now Luzia's own thoughts are becoming mush.

"It's nice to meet you, Your Majesty," Luzia begins, because that's only polite, even though saying it and acknowledging where she is makes her want to whimper. "Look, I'm not... It's only that... Just, please understand, I followed Carrion down here after they kidnapped my nephew – the boy they brought with them. I'm only here for him, and once I have him, I'll leave you all be. Again, with all due respect, or whichever other turn of phrase you find most polite, I don't want anything to do with the Astrosi's business."

Queen Sef, guardian and lady and consort and everything else, sounds genuinely apologetic as she replies, "Unfortunately, your nephew is now part of our business. Carrion had an arrangement in which they owed our court one life, and they have given the boy to us in exchange."

"But – but what does that mean?"

"It means he's ours," the queen states. "Now and forever."

CHAPTER FOUR

Amidst the Astrosi of the Deep, Luzia is fittingly and woefully out of her depth.

"He's of the Bastion, not of your... your court, as you put it," she manages to say, tilting her chin in a valiant effort up to muster dignity equal to the queen in front of her.

"And yet," Sef points out, "he is in my court, on my soil, and has been lawfully traded to me. I regret to inform you that the Bastion no longer has a claim to him."

"That is completely... completely *nonsensical*!"

The man next to the throne scoffs, large eyebrows rising in amusement. "Listen up, kiddo. You're here, you're under the queen's rule, you're under our laws. If you don't like it, you can leave. Just not with the boy."

A gentle gesture from Sef's delicate and fine-fingered hand stops the man's retort. "Lysander, there is no need to be impolite. This must be confusing for a human. 'Twould be unfair to insist on her comprehending instantaneously." To the man still holding on to Luzia, she adds, "If she is here to speak peacefully, then we should relinquish her. As of now, she is a guest in our court, and we do not manhandle guests."

Not even a full second after the man releases Luzia does she start running towards Stazi.

She barely makes it a yard before Lysander grabs one of those odd long cylindrical devices from his back. There's little more than a blur of motion in her vision, a whistle of it swinging through the air, and then a *thwack* as it impacts her gut.

Pain erupts in her stomach. Knees buckling, she drops to the soft ground, bent in two as for the second time that day she desperately tries to fill her lungs with air. Nausea rears up behind the base ache of the hit, and she has to choke it down until she can properly breathe again, her nails digging into the wet dust beneath the green ground.

"Right, then," Lysander says cheerfully, nudging her head with the end of that device. "You've got some fight in you, seems like. Duel for the kid, if you're really keen on getting him back."

"Duel?" Her jaw hangs open as she gasps, swallowing a mouthful of spittle. "What? N – no, I…"

He abruptly cuts her off mid-sentence with a kick. A boot colliding with her back that sends her toppling over again, her chest smacking into the ground with a dull thud.

He prods her with the device again. "Come on, get up."

"Lysander," the queen states in a tone that is utterly flat. "Recall our words but a moment ago. Cease this physical brutality."

This time Luzia is quicker pushing herself back up, eyes swimming out of focus and then snapping back in as she keeps her gaze firmly on Stazi. "I just want my nephew back," she pants. "I don't want to fight!"

Lysander scoffs, turning his nose up at her like she's a puddle of oil that's gone rancid. "If you don't fight, you don't get the kid. You ain't got any of the Bastion's protections down here. In the Deep, all someone like you has is their fists."

"If I dueled you, what good would it do?" she demands, sniffling to shove back tears. Bumps and bruises are par for course in her job, and she's not going to shy away from the possibility of being injured, but if she's hurt or killed here then who will save Stazi?

"Is *that* the strength of your conviction?" He spits on the ground. "Pathetic."

"Well, it isn't as though I could possibly win! We both know I wouldn't last two minutes before you beat me to death with that metal device, and if I'm dead no one else is going to be able to get Stazi back. And even if you decided not to kill me, I would still have lost and you'd still keep him here, so the entire thing is completely and utterly *pointless*!"

"If you're not willing to die for him, then don't waste my time," he sneers.

"*Our* time," Sef's voice softly chimes, quiet but enough to shut Lysander up instantly. "This is not your quarrel. It is her decision whether or not to duel, and she has given her answer." In a motion so smooth and elegant that it is barely noticeable, she leans closer to peer at Luzia with pitch-dark eyes. "We understand that, to your comprehension, the child was stolen unlawfully. As Carrion once struck a deal with us to spare their life, if you truly wish the child returned, we shall now give you that same opportunity."

Luzia doesn't hesitate to ask, "What do you want?"

"What do you have to offer? We are flexible in what we accept. There is no one right way of making a deal, rather a thousand ways that all lead down similar paths."

"I... I have skills. If you need any sort of structural repair work done, I could do some jobs for you in trade?"

"And is that of similar value to the boy's life?"

Luzia's cheeks flush with shame, matching the redness of her nose from her trying not to cry. "No, it's not."

"What else do you have?"

This is not a type of calculus she knows how to do. Numbers are cool, reliable, constant, not a moral quandary that she's entirely unqualified to debate. "Well, I suppose I have my housing unit and all the things inside of it, though I don't know if that's enough either. I have ration stamps?"

"We will not accept human food."

"Then…" She chokes down a sob. "I don't have anything else."

"Do you not?" Sef gives her a strange look, as though staring into her bones. "Most everyone has at least one thing of value to offer. Unless someone else has claim over you."

One life for one life, Carrion had said.

It's all very straightforward, really. Quite logical. All that matters is that Stazi is not with her, that he is in danger, and that it was her failure to look after him that has put him in this position in the first place. She can see her brother so clearly in her mind's eye, hear him ask for her to protect his son. Her tongue silently forms the reply she gave him, her promise to keep Stazi safe.

In her mind, she does the math.

Stazi is younger than her and, considering their shared genetics and the family history of his mother, they are likely to live to a similar age. His youth means he has far more years ahead of him, where Luzia is approximately two-fifths of the way through her lifespan.

Stazi needs to be raised properly. There is a great deal that he has to learn, and it is unlikely to impossible that he will learn those life skills amidst the Astrosi and whatever abnormalities are the norm in their throneworlds.

And she loves him. She cannot live with herself if she leaves him here.

Thus the conclusion. She draws in a deep breath, filling her lungs with humid air. "Take me instead of Stazi."

"Oh?" Sef tilts her head to the side. "You would trade your life for his?"

Lysander gives her a mean, narrow smirk. "Beg."

Another gesture from Sef. "Enough." To Luzia, she asks, "Why should we accept a grown human who does not respect our court over a young boy, still impressionable, mind still malleable?"

"Because," she replies, recalling the conversation she'd heard from the guards in the tunnel, "a child isn't much use, right? I'd be much more useful to you. I'm strong, I'm skilled, and I'm willing to stay here if it grants Stazi his freedom. He might be young, but he's the farthest thing from malleable and I can't imagine you'd have an easy time trying to get him to do what you want. I certainly can't manage that, and neither can his father. So no, I will not beg. You're already getting a much better deal without needing to add pointless humiliation to the mix."

Muffled whispers ripple through the assembled crowd behind her. Sef hums to herself, her eyes as intense as they are distant.

After a heart-pounding seventy-two seconds that Luzia counts with bated breath, Sef smiles and decrees, "We judge your offer to be acceptable, and I shall accept it."

Good. That is... good. Right.

Luzia takes a few steps towards Stazi, now unhindered by any manner of resistance, and finally gets a close look at his peaceful expression, at the way his face is smoothed with sleep. She kneels next to him, brushes his bangs back, and tries to memorize the color of his dark hair and how similar it is to her own. The softness of his skin, the round youth of his cheeks. There is no power in the world that can stop her from seeing Stazi again, from going back to her family. It may take days, weeks, months, but eventually.

Drops of water well in her eyes as her vision blurs and she blinks around sticky eyelashes. Hopefully one day he'll forgive her for putting him in danger.

Sef's melodic voice begins to ring out once again, but it takes Luzia a long time to pay attention. It is only when the guard begins to approach her that a jolt of adrenaline floods her veins and she clutches Stazi to her as though he will turn to smoke the moment she stops.

"You bargained for the child to be spared," Sef reminds her. "You must now allow him to be returned to the city above."

"At least wake him!" Luzia pleads. "I... I just want to say goodbye."

"It will be easier on him if he remains asleep. And furthermore, it is doubtful that you would wish for him to remember the journey out, as it would therefore also show him a way back in."

And Stazi would be brave and foolhardy enough to try to run back, if not to look for her then certainly to look for some wild and entirely imagined adventure. Sef is right. It is best for Stazi if he is allowed to wake in the relative safety of the Bastion, without a single Astrosi around to lead him astray.

Before the guard can take him from her, she presses a kiss to Stazi's forehead and quietly swears, "I will see you again. I promise."

The guard rips him from her. A cry is trapped in her

throat, unable to be swallowed down or given voice, and she remains frozen in place, forced to watch as they take Stazi away from her. Something inside her is torn out, like a piece of a vital organ, and is taken away with him.

"Let us discuss terms," Sef continues, still smiling pleasantly even as Luzia can barely pay attention to what's being said. "Lysander, if you would begin notation?"

Lysander steps over to what looks like a waist-high metal pole stuck in the ground. When he pushes something at the top of it, a holographic screen pops into existence. It's Era One tech, the sort of projected image that Luzia has uncovered once or twice during the course of her work. He rests a hand over the screen, fingers flexed as he prepares to type.

"Use her name," Sef says.

With a hint of slyness in his eyes, he turns to Luzia and asks, "May I have your name?"

"Luzia," she replies, still blinking away tears. Part of her, a tiny distant part of her mind, wonders at the fact that both he and Carrion asked her the exact same question in the exact same manner. "Luzia N. E. Drainway."

Sef clears her throat and begins. "Pull up our normal boilerplate contract for claiming a human as an Acolyte. All the usual details. Date: system based. Refer to Schematic A-Prime for jurisdiction of contract. Luzia N. E. Drainway: henceforth referred to as the Petitioner. Queen Sef the Third, Guardian of the Eoi, Lady of – oh, just copy and paste the rest – henceforth referred to as the Court."

How many times have they dragged humans into their service if they have a normal contract for it? Also, what's a system date and how is it different from a normal date? And what's the jurisdiction bit about? Ah, it seems she's missed something already.

"...contract is coterminous with Petitioner's length of life, mortal or otherwise, beginning as of this system date," Sef is saying, on and on in a steady, flat voice that punctuates nothing at all. Mortal or otherwise? And what does *coterminous* mean? "Right of Clawback: Should Petitioner default on this Contract through suicide or other unlawful means, the Court reserves its right..."

Suicide! How often does that happen if it needs to be included? Oh dear, Sef is still talking.

"...duties outlined here are not meant to curtail or supersede the rights of the Court as outlined in Section 9B of the Eoi Code of Services and Acolytes. In instances where this Contract fails to outline all specific duties, the Eoi Code of Services and Acolytes will prevail..."

There's something about arbitration and 'successors thereto' and 'disputes resolution services' and Luzia is utterly, shamefully lost. A cracked wall she understands; a mathematical equation can be done in her sleep; she was doing trigonometry when she was ten years old, for fun; and yet, in the face of Sef's calm drone, she is an idiot child struggling to print her letters.

Sef slides to a delicate halt. She waits for Lysander to finish his frantic typing, and then asks, "Is that acceptable?"

"Ah..." Luzia swallows down her embarrassment, reminding herself that this is for Stazi and that she has no doubt they would snatch him back if she refuses. "Yes."

"You must say that you accept the terms of the contract. In those exact words, if you don't mind."

"I accept the terms of the contract."

Lysander taps something on his screen and she hears a snippet of herself play back before he presses the screen again. A second of 'I accept the' and then it's gone, her voice tucked away into wherever this contract is sequestered.

The court around her titters. Sef extends her hand, and at first Luzia thinks she means for her to take it, but then she turns her palm up to the brightly lit ceiling. There is, Luzia notices, dust in her palm. The same sort of rich brown dust that Carrion had spat out, clumpy and damp. Slowly, impossibly, the dust begins to rise up. It swirls an inch above Sef's palm, twisting and contorting into a small and dense object. Exactly what Carrion had spat out.

"We thank you," Sef says with an almost hypnotic resonance, "Luzia N. E. Drainway, for the gift of your name. We shall take good care of it. From now on, you shall be Ziane, Acolyte of the Deep, under our protection."

But Luzia never gifted anyone her name! She simply provided it when asked. That can't be the same. Or is it?

Sef holds the object out to Luzia. "Come here, Ziane."

Luzia comes, step by step, until she's right in front of Sef and the oval object that is still floating above Sef's hand. It's sort of ridged, brown in color but uneven, mottled in places. Like some of the patchy colors in the green things all around them.

"What is that?" she asks, side-eyeing it.

"Our contract." Sef delicately spins her hand to pinch the object between her index and middle fingers. "It is called a seed. Take it."

Luzia takes the seed and moves to put it into her pocket.

"No. Swallow it."

Her jaw trembles as she cracks it open and tentatively places the object on her tongue. It tastes of nothing in particular, which doesn't actually help her paranoia. She closes her mouth. Swallows.

Sef smiles. "Good."

"And my nephew?" Luzia confirms. There is a distinct presence in her throat, and she can feel the seed crawling its way down her esophagus to sit in her stomach with a heavy density that its size did not hint at. "He's safe?"

"We have abandoned our claim to him and he is being returned as we speak. You may be rightly suspicious of the Astrosi, and we cannot fault you for that, but you should know that we keep our word once it is given. We shall adhere to the contract we have made, and so shall the rest of the Eoi." Were Sef human, Luzia would have expected a quirk of the mouth or a pinch of the eyes to suggest mirth, but her features remain serene as she adds, "Though not even I can work miracles and thus I can make no promises for the Vesperi."

"I don't care about the Vesperi. Will I ever be able to see my nephew again?"

"We Astrosi are not so impatient as humans, I think. Such details can be discussed further at a later time, but for the meanwhile, it will be best for you to become acclimated to your new environs." She bends to cup Luzia's cheek with a gentle and oddly waxy touch. "Dry your eyes. Even as an Acolyte, there is an eternity awaiting you here, and all the wonders of my throneworld to explore. This pain you must be feeling will fade eventually. It always does."

How can it? Stazi, Izax, Luzia's mother and father – they are her life. She lives for them. She fixes up the broken pieces of the Bastion so that they can walk the streets of the world without fear. In saving Stazi, she might as well have plunged a knife through her own heart. Perhaps that bit of the contract regarding suicide is less drastic than it sounds. What about those that lose their own children to the Astrosi? They surely suffer even more than her, endless though her current pain might seem.

"And is that something you give your word on?" Luzia whispers.

Sef leans back into her throne with a sigh. "As I said. The pain always fades one way or another." She keeps her eyes on Luzia as she commands, "Lysander, assign her to the arboretum and have her work alongside Annie. That will suit for now."

With a flick of his coat, Lysander sweeps into a bow. "Of course, my queen."

"One last thing." Sef beckons him closer, and says in a voice too low to be heard by the rest, although not so quiet that Luzia cannot make it out when she leans closer, "Carrion did not carry the diamond on their person whilst here. Either they did not find it at the site of the skirmish, or they did locate it but managed to hide it before returning to our realm. Send someone to investigate."

That's odd. Luzia's despair flickers out of the way for a moment as she takes note of that name. Diamond. Carrion had referred to the Era One tech uncovered by the sinkhole as a diamond as well. What is a diamond, exactly, other than a type of stone? What does a stone matter to these people?

Lysander nods. "It'll be done. Though I doubt that cur managed to get their mangy hands on it before us."

"Nevertheless..."

"...Check anyway. You don't have to tell me more than once, my queen, I promise you," he says with a sigh. Then, with jarring antithesis to how he looks at the queen with reverence, he glares at Luzia and grabs her roughly by the arm. "With me," he grumbles, "and stop your damn blubbering."

Part of her wants to snap back at him, to demand to know how he'd like to be in her shoes, to insist that she's not blubbering, to tell him to shut up and let her cry, damn it. The other part of her is too busy doing her very best *not* to blubber. So she lets him drag her away from Sef and her throne, the Astrosi woman's radiant presence turning to someone else as though she's already forgotten about Luzia entirely. Is it better or worse for her if Sef pays her no mind now that the contract is over and done with?

Either way, the tiny part of her that's not busy drowning is busy thinking, and right now it's particularly busy thinking that she probably should dry her eyes off and pay attention to where she is and where she's going.

So much of this place is a disorienting maze of green, dotted with pinks and yellows and blues and every shade in between. It's hard to tell if a hallway turns to the left or if it splits into two and the right passage is simply covered up by hanging green cables. Here and there are glimpses of normal metal walls, lights that aren't those flawless light panels of Sef's throne room, a floor that's not green and has the usual hard texture of steel. But those hints of normalcy are rare and only reinforce her certainty that she did the right thing. Stazi deserves to grow up in somewhere that isn't tangled with cables and colored orbs and covered in green fuzz.

A set of doors open before them, hidden behind large sheets of waxy green. Beyond is more white-blue light and a mess of color.

Lysander puts his hand between her shoulder blades and shoves. She topples forward and narrowly avoids smacking into the ground once again. He's humiliated her like that enough for one day – she refuses to let him get that pleasure anymore and she swiftly rights herself so that she can face him with a modicum of dignity.

"Want some free advice?" he asks.

Not particularly.

"Don't cause trouble," he tells her when she fails to reply. "Do what you're told, keep your head down, and fade away."

With that, he slams the door in her face.

CHAPTER FIVE

Luzia cries.

Face messy with tears and snot, her shirt pressed to her cheeks in a feeble attempt to stem the tide. She is as silent as she can be, hoping that if she can't hear her crying, it isn't happening. Crying won't help her anymore. It's a waste of energy. It's pointless. But she still can't stop herself.

"There, there," a gentle voice says. "You're new, ey?"

The soft green she is sitting on shifts as someone comes to kneel next to her. A hand rests on her shoulder, soothing and rubbing, before an arm is wrapped around her and she finds herself being delicately guided into a warm embrace. It's as though she's a child again, letting her mother hug and comfort her in the aftermath of a scraped knee or a schoolmate's insult. But she isn't, and she may never see her mother again.

The newcomer keeps holding her and rocking her like she's a baby. "That's it, let it all out. It's a bit of a shock for every one of us."

Us? Luzia sniffles and looks up at the person holding her. It's an old woman, skin paper-thin and wrinkled. The Astrosi, Luzia has noticed, all seem to have impressively long hair, but this woman's gray hair is short and pinned back in a sensible style. Is she human? Upon reflection, that shouldn't be surprising, given that there have apparently been Acolytes before Luzia.

"Who are you?" she asks quietly.

"You can call me Annie," the old woman replies. She doesn't smile with her mouth, but it's not for lack of warmth in her eyes. She rises to her feet slowly, helping Luzia up as well. "Come along. I'll make you a cuppa."

"Cuppa what?"

"Tea. I don't imagine you've had the stuff that we've got down here, and it'll do you a world of good."

Now standing on unsteady feet, Luzia sees the place she's been tossed into. If she'd thought Sef's throne room to be a splendor of green and blue-white light, this place is that multiplied by a thousand. Wild and sprawling and stretching out forever, the arboretum could be ten or twenty stories tall, but a roof made of light panels makes it challenging to measure. Spires of all different shapes and colors climb up to the ceiling, rich browns next to pale grays, bright greens twining with flaky tans.

With no flat streets or standardized buildings, she struggles to determine exactly how large the space is, her knowledge of yards and miles defeated by colorful chaos, leaving her mind stranded. The only familiar thing is a rectangular structure not too far away, about the height of two standard stories, and she is embarrassingly grateful that there's at least one thing here she understands.

Annie catches her staring and gives her another smile that's all in the eyes. "Never seen trees or flowers before, have you?"

"No." Those words are familiar to her, but as words with no association. *Flowering* she knows the meaning of. *Tall as a tree*, she's heard as an idiom. She had no idea they were things. She sniffles again and asks, "The colorful orb things. Are they flowers?"

"Some of 'em." Annie pats her hand. "You'll learn."

Luzia is led inside the rectangular structure, which turns out to be the oddest house she's ever seen. It's shaped like a normal boxy housing unit on the inside, with standard smooth metal walls and floor, only it too is filled with greenery. A bed made of flowers, furniture made of trees. Various things that she cannot name hang from the walls, complicated hooks and wires keeping these rows suspended in the rooms. There's a squat thing with rings on top and a box beneath it, and next to it is a large cauldron filled with a strange sort of dirty paste.

It's a relief to see that the sink works normally, and Annie has a kettle filled and boiling away in no time.

"Sit," she says, gesturing to a tree-chair at a tree-table. "Consider this your home for the time being, if you'd like. You're welcome anywhere in it."

She gets out two mugs and fills up a teapot with hot water. To Luzia's surprise, Annie retrieves a small box overflowing with small green bits and puts that in a strainer. Tea is made with flavor powder, not... flowers? Whatever those green flecks are.

"Tea leaves," Annie explains as she pours the tea and sets the mugs on the table. She takes a seat across from Luzia and blows on her steaming tea.

Luzia tentatively pokes at the mug, feeling the smoothness of normal metal and heat from the water. She peers into the liquid and finds nothing more than semi-transparent brownish green water, not unlike normal tea. It smells quite different, however. She can't help being a bit suspicious of it.

"It doesn't bite or nothing, if that's what you're freaking out about," Annie remarks, snorting out a rough huff of a laugh.

Luzia touches the surface of the liquid. It feels like normal tea. "But... leaves?"

"They say that's what tea was originally made of in Era One, odd though it sounds. Either way, original or not, it tastes a damn sight better than the stuff above. That's one of the good things about living here." Annie stares past her tea and into the distance. "The food and drink is like nothing you ever tasted before. Once you've had it, all other food becomes dirt the moment it's in your mouth."

"I don't care what food or drink they give me. I just..." Luzia's tongue is heavy and slow, and she struggles to speak. "I can't stay here forever without seeing my family ever again."

Annie sighs. "Did you make a deal with the queen? Life of Acolyte-ing and all that?"

"Yes."

"And did you eat the contract?"

"Yes."

"Then you're here till the queen says otherwise."

"Surely I get, I don't know, vacation? Days off?" Luzia asks. "No one can work every day of the week. Can't I visit my family if I promise to come back?"

"That's not how it works." Annie glances up at her with narrowed eyes. "Didn't you read your contract?"

"I listened to it."

"Hm. Somehow I doubt you listened very closely. If you understood any of it, you'd know that vacation isn't on the table. Days off are right out. If you're granted a short break from your duties, if you're allowed up into the human world, it'll be entirely because the queen grants you that privilege, and she don't exactly do that on a whim."

Luzia glares at her tea and blinks away angry tears at the thought of having to somehow win a right such as that. "That's cruel."

Shrugging, Annie replies, "The queen ain't cruel. She's just heartless."

As Luzia thinks on that, she takes the first sip of her tea and then promptly makes a truly embarrassing noise at the first taste of it. It was easy to declare that she didn't care about food, but that was before she'd tried this. The flavor is indescribable, smooth and light and rich all at the same time. The depth and complexity of it is beyond anything she's consumed before, turning the tea powders and flavored ration bars of the Bastion into watery dust by comparison. This, of all things, is what dries the last of her tears, the shock and delirium of having something so divine on her tongue.

Annie simply drinks in peace, one eye on Luzia's reaction but no visible change in her own expression. This must not be the first time she's seen a human have their first taste of such exquisite flavors.

"You see?" Annie raises her mug an inch in a lazy toast. "Better than anything you'd get in the Bastion."

"Well... yes. But still, I'm not going stay here forever just for good tea. I'm not a liar, and I'm not... you know, I do have honor. I'm not going back on my word. I just want some way of being able to see my family again. That's it. If I left to see them, I'd come back."

"Listen close, because if you don't pay attention to my warning, then not a single soul can help you here. If you ain't given permission to leave, don't leave. Do not, and I mean *do not* try to break your contract. Honor's great, love me some honor, but Astrosi don't expect contracts to be followed because of something like honor. They set up failsafes. If you try, you won't like the consequences."

"What are the consequences?"

"Don't rightly know myself. I've never tried to go against my contract. But I've seen what it's like for those that try." Annie's face doesn't twitch, though her wrinkled hands shudder as they're wrapped around her mug. "Some can't speak for weeks afterwards. Some are left bedridden until one of the Astrosi deigns to fix them up. And a few of them… a few of them are just never seen again."

Does the contract kill if it's broken? Admittedly, Luzia has no idea what the seed currently knocking around in her stomach really is. She has no idea if it will do anything, if it can react. A sudden bout of nausea rears up, her body wanting to vomit up the seed, and she pushes it down until her stomach settles.

Contract seed aside, there must still be some way she can bend the rules. She's not an idiot – she's not going to think that somehow she's the cleverest and bravest person to ever live, or even to ever show up here, and as she told Annie, she has no intention of breaking her contract. But a single visit? How can that cause any real harm? And a sore throat or a bit of sickness is a cheap price to pay for even just an hour with her family.

"How many others are there?" she asks. "I mean, I don't imagine a lot of people end up in the same situation as me."

"And what is your oh-so-unique situation?"

"Carrion." She grips her mug hard enough to turn her knuckles white. "They stole my nephew and sold him to Sef like he's an object instead of a person. Apparently they owed Sef a life and so I… I took my nephew's place so that he could go back home."

"Not unique after all. Oh, don't get me wrong, Carrion doesn't much show up in these things – they're usually off chasing legends and trying to make everyone fight each other – but everything else? There's more of us than you think. Some of us come to save someone we love. Some folks don't understand Astrosi magic and thought they might get a wish granted, fame or power or the like. At least you didn't fall in love. I knew a man who fell for an Astrosi lady and sold his entire life for one tumble in her sheets. She found the whole thing funny and forgot all about him once it was over. Poor bastard gets to spend decades pining after someone who's never going to look at him twice."

It's difficult to deny that many of the Astrosi are beautiful. Sef's otherworldly loveliness comes to mind. Still, to spend a whole lifetime for that is surely madness.

"What about you?" Luzia wonders. "What did you come here for?"

"Nothing special, really. My father was dying. No cure for his illness. So I came down here since it was easier than going up to the Vesperi and I begged for him to live. And before you ask, yeah, the queen delivered. Got exactly what I asked for, no more, no less."

To cure a father. If Luzia can't manage to sneak out for a visit, she'll never see her own father again. Never again get the comfort of telling him she loves him.

Annie drains her tea and gets up. "Finish and follow me. If you're to work in the arboretum with me, there are some important ground rules." She chuckles. "Heh. *Ground* rules. Hope you don't get my shit sense of humor down here."

With eyes no longer clouded by tears, Luzia is led out of the building and through the expanse of green. Annie gives her a tablet and stylus with an instruction to take notes, but

Luzia has no idea what to begin writing down. There are paths of stone winding through the arboretum, uneven and messy in a way that makes her constantly nervous that they're going to slip out of place. Bins and boxes overflowing with strange tools dot the area, and somewhere in the distance she can hear the sound of running water. Whatever logic was used in the design of this place eludes her.

It doesn't help that she barely understands one word out of three that Annie says to her. The older woman's instructions may be important, but they are clearly being given by someone who no longer remembers what it is to be a novice.

"Don't touch any of the digitalis without gloves," Annie's saying at the moment. "The Eoi breed it for potency, and digitalis overdose is nasty. Make sure you don't confuse them with symphytum either, 'cause you'll see me drinking one but not the other. Similarly, stay away from the delphinium, and the *Convallaria majalis*. A general rule of thumb is that if you puke after working, you're in trouble. Yell for me and I'll probably have an antidote."

It seems to Luzia that yelling might be a challenge if she's busy vomiting. "Right. I'll do my best."

"Oh, careful with those flytraps, by the way." Annie points out a plant bigger than her entire body that seems to gape ominously in the center. "They're stronger than they look and they ain't picky about what they eat."

"They eat people? Do all plants eat flesh?"

"Only some of 'em."

Luzia shrinks away from a tree that's leaning a bit too far towards the path for her liking. She writes down a warning about flesh-eating plants, but it won't be very helpful without further instruction. "Is there some kind of rule about which ones do and which don't?"

"Eh, not really."

"Then how am I supposed to stay away from them?"

"Ah." Annie pauses in her march through the arboretum. "Good question."

To calm herself, Luzia takes a deep breath and then promptly coughs. The air here isn't just as humid as the rest of the Deep; it's also filled with odd scents and what has to be some sort of fine powder that she's inadvertently inhaled.

"I hope you're not allergic to pollen," Annie remarks.

Luzia doesn't even know what pollen is.

The next path Annie takes her down is filled with thin, tall, and wavy plants – or, as her guide is quick to point out, grasses. She doesn't dare touch them, but they look awfully dry despite the humidity.

"Are these flammable?" she asks.

"Oh, definitely."

"How do you live here?!"

"Easily. Not like anything's ever actually burned down, least not that I've seen. The rest of the world might be slowly degrading as time passes, but here things are sturdier. Things last in the Astrosi realms. Everything is just... slower here."

How can another human be so cavalier about living in a death trap? Perhaps this all poses no danger to Astrosi, but it does to humans. Luzia knows she's more cautious than the average person, but this is just common sense. Has spending so long down here turned Annie mad?

Luzia stands completely, utterly still in the center of this violent garden, arms wrapped around her chest in a rib-crushing hug. She cannot bring herself to move a single step in any direction lest her foot land on something that will cause a venomous plant to lash out at her or something else equally terrible. Is it too late to beg Sef to allow her to work in some other part of the Deep? Or is the entirety of this throneworld a house of horrors?

Annie pauses and purses her lips. "You're completely lost, aren't you?" She doesn't wait for a reply before sighing, shoulders slumping down to the ground. "Tell you what, I'll give you my botanical – my book on all the plants here. I've got it all memorized by now, so it's not as though I'll miss it. It's got pictures."

"If you've everything memorized," Luzia asks, hoping for a way out of this assignment, "then why am I here? I'm more likely to be a burden in a place like this than anything else, and I've got other skills."

"Use your head, new girl. How old do you think I am? How long do you think it took me to learn all this? They want me to train up a successor for when I eventually kick the bucket, and the last two humans they sent my way ended up not being all that suited to the task. You can't do worse than they did, trust me."

"That's quite optimistic of you," she says weakly. "This place isn't exactly... friendly."

"I see the Bastion still teaches folks nothing useful that could apply to life down here. All right, absolute basics. Don't go off the path. And don't go into the queen's bower alone."

"Bower?"

"You'll see." Annie gives her another pitying sort of look. "That's enough for today, I think." She heads back towards the building, patting Luzia on the shoulder as she goes. "I'll start cooking up onion soup. You'll like it, trust me."

CHAPTER SIX

Luzia does like the onion soup, which tastes like a dream. She doesn't like her bed, though, which is made of flowers. The first night she spends in the Deep is filled with terror that her bed might eat her or poison her or do something else nefarious, and a constant ache in her chest from missing her own bed in her own home. That, she will never see again. Even if she manages to return to the Bastion to visit her family, her housing unit likely won't be hers anymore. She will be reported missing and an investigation will eventually be concluded, and in one year she'll be declared presumed dead, and then her unit will be reassigned to whoever else needs it.

Her second day in the Deep dawns bright and early. The lighting units are never turned off or changed, it would seem, and so the only darkness during nighttime can be found inside Annie's housing unit. Even if she'd had the usual lighting of the Bastion, she imagines she'd still wake with dried-out eyes and a pinched brow.

A haze has settled over her. Each footstep she takes through the arboretum is heavy and slow, dragging over the stone paths that are set into too-soft ground. Annie carries a tablet with her that contains her botanical, reading out names and descriptions as she marches through the paths and points to various plants. Luzia does her utmost to remember which ones, at the very least, are deadly, but her brain feels as though it's been tenderized with a brick and the information keeps sneaking out.

While Luzia knows that she should be writing down the plants that Annie is listing out, she instead finds herself sketching out a rough map of the arboretum. The winding maze of paths is disorienting, and although she has enough training to know how to get her bearings in an unfamiliar environment, if she's going to spend any degree of time down here she should really get a proper map of the place.

By now her disappearance will have been officially reported. Depending on how disoriented Stazi was when he was returned to the Bastion, it may have taken him some time to recall anything about what happened to him. He may remember being snatched, but he would have no idea where she is. Would he think she's abandoned him? How long will it take for him and her brother and her parents to realize that she's not simply missing? How long will it take for them to give up hope?

Her despair swirls around her, and she's only startled out of it when Annie unexpectedly stops what she's doing and jerks her head up, staring unerringly to the left.

"It's the queen," she declares.

Luzia frowns. "Sef's here? How can you tell?"

"There are things you pick up, or you will if you end up here for as long as me. And you probably don't wanna use the queen's name to her face. It's a bit rude, see?"

She doesn't see, but she follows after Annie regardless. They end up going towards a part of the arboretum that Luzia's not been to yet.

It's a clearing of soft grass and what Annie has referred to as wildflowers, pale pinks and whites carpeting the ground. It feels unusual in how tame it is compared to everything around it. A wooden bench is set amongst the greenery, its curved and sloped shape more elegant than anything she's ever seen before. Pillows are clustered on the bench and a blanket made of a fabric so thin and watery that it shimmers in the air has been draped over the wood. A mound covered with green grass, about as tall as Luzia, is near the bench, and steps peeking out from the grass lead down towards a metal door in the mound. Atop the mound grows a twisted tree from which red, shiny orbs hang.

"The queen's bower," Annie informs her, setting down the basket she's been carrying and rummaging inside it. Luzia marks down *bower* on her map and then writes down Annie's additional instruction of *Don't eat the apples*.

"I thought I wasn't supposed to be here?" Luzia asks.

"We're not allowed in without the queen being here."

What's inside that's so dangerous or forbidden? Luzia's about to ask when the metal door creaks and slides open. Behind the door is utter darkness. Slowly, a hand reaches out to hold on to the doorframe, and that hand hauls out an arm and a torso until the figure of Sef comes into view. The queen staggers out of her bower, the door shutting behind her. Her long hair drags across the ground as she makes her way to the wooden bench and slumps down upon it with elegant frailty. This fragility is entirely at odds with the serene yet strong aura she'd previously exuded, and it throws Luzia off.

Annie retrieves a thermos from her basket and goes to kneel at Sef's side. "Here, my lady. Drink."

Sef tilts the thermos back and sips the water inside it. "Thank you."

"Are you..." Luzia chews on her words, "...all right?"

"Ah, 'tis kind of you to ask." Sef gives her a faint, weary smile. "I am merely tired. Worry not, it shall pass in due time. I come here to renew my strength. Our Annie has seen me in such a state on many occasions."

Genuine worry has pinched Annie's brow, and she lays one of her wrinkled and spotted hands over Sef's smooth one. "Did something happen? I ain't seen you like this in awhile."

"I had a visit from the most esteemed King Ari today. He – oh, I don't mean to be rude," Sef cuts herself off, glancing to Luzia. "You would not know. King Ari is my counterpart, the ruler of the Astrosi of the Mists. To be so near him is... taxing. We are like oil in water – the strength of our very natures repels one another. But such visits must be done on occasion, when our goals align or clash in particularly noticeable ways, for the preservation of our throneworlds and our people is of the utmost importance."

She drinks more and gives a fluttering, delicate sigh. Luzia would not have expected to see such weakness from the poised queen. Heartless, but not cruel, Annie had said. Indeed, this state of exhaustion snuffs out any hatred for the queen that might have grown and festered in Luzia. She's just doing her job, isn't she? Using the strength she has for protecting her people. And preservation is something Luzia is so very familiar with.

"It would seem," Sef says, lowering the thermos, "that Carrion hasn't spared the Vesperi either. King Ari reported of a skirmish on the edges of his throneworld last night."

"Carrion?" Luzia rushes to the edge of the bench.

Sef hums in agreement. "I know not how the humans of the Bastion view Carrion, but they are a rogue and a villain, and they care not whom they harm. Nor do they target only humans, whatever you might think. They attack both the Eoi and the Vesperi in equal measure."

"If they're really that bad for you all, why did you let them go?"

Annie glares at her, but Sef only shakes her head and replies, "Because I was bound to do so. Some time ago I managed to catch Carrion and snare them in a contract that would allow me to take their life without repercussion from King Ari – we both have equal claim to Carrion, you see. As you witnessed yesterday, however, Carrion instead used the contract to buy their life with another's. I am not so arrogant to admit that they bested me. And so I, and by the terms of the contract my court at large, had no choice but to let them leave once they delivered your nephew to me in payment."

"A crafty rogue, then," Luzia mumbles to herself.

Sef's laugh is a puff of air. "Indeed. They are old, standing younger than only King Ari and myself. Time has granted them the same cleverness it has gifted to us." She pauses to drain the last of the water in the thermos and then hands it back to an awaiting Annie. "Yet regardless of their strengths, something must be done. They shall continue to run rampant, and they may very well win the search for the diamond." Diamond – that reference again. "If I cannot capture Carrion, then King Ari will. I still need my rest, but on the morrow I shall assemble a team to scour the Bastion for them."

"A team to search the Bastion?" Luzia echoes.

"Yes. Their nest is somewhere amongst the humans, and we have no choice but to find them first."

Heart in her throat, she pleads, "Send me! I know the inhabited areas of the Bastion like the back of my hand. I can help your people get in and out of tight spots. I can search faster and better than them."

Sef's eyes bore into hers as they had yesterday, that same piercing and emotionless stare. "And what would you ask for in return? As much as I would not be so rude as to doubt your willingness to obey our contract and serve as commanded, this is not something I would have demanded of you. Why this particular excitement?"

"I don't want Carrion to keep interfering with human lives," she answers honestly. "And if I capture them, if I do that for the Eoi, for you, I want you to let me visit my family."

"You are so forthright, aren't you?" Sef's voice is soft, and yet there's an undercurrent there that's not so pleasant, a hint of pity beneath the gentleness. "You will never lie to me, but to others you may wish to be more careful with your candor."

"Will you agree?" Luzia presses. "If I help catch Carrion, will you let me leave for a visit? I'd come back. I wouldn't break our deal, I promise. I don't even need you to make another contract – I don't want to bother you with that," she assures her. "Just... would you let me?"

Under her breath, Annie mumbles out a curse. "Fool," it sounds like.

Sef holds out a hand to silence Annie. "If that is her request, then that is her request." To Luzia, she says, "Very well. If you capture Carrion for me, I'll allow you a visit to the Bastion to see your family. Will that make you happy?"

"Thank you," Luzia says with all sincerity, barely able to contain her relief and excitement. "I swear, I won't let you down."

"Honest and honorable," Sef muses. "Annie, would you fetch me an apple? I truly do need my rest."

Annie scrambles to her feet. "Of course, my lady."

The tree bearing the red orbs has its branches at a convenient height to be just low enough for Annie to reach up and pluck one – which is, Luzia assumes, an apple. Upon closer inspection, the thing isn't entirely red. Its skin is a mix of rich reds and soft oranges, spots and streaks of yellow running through it. A single drop of condensation glistens near the wooden stem.

Sef takes it and bites into it, pearly-white teeth piercing the skin and digging into pale flesh. She has taken barely two bites before her eyelids begin to droop and her shoulders slump. By the time she has swallowed a third bite, she sinks into the bench and its pillows and blankets, eyes shut and slack with sleep. Her arm slides off the edge of the bench, the partially eaten apple rolling out of her hand and onto the grass. Luzia scrambles away from it before it can roll towards her feet.

Annie drapes the blanket over Sef's sleeping form before quietly picking up her basket and beckoning for them to leave the clearing around the bower.

"That wasn't the win you think it is," Annie mutters. "The only thing stupider than making a contract with an Astrosi is making a deal *without* a contract."

None of that matters to Luzia. Annie doesn't understand how much her family means to her, how important it is. Maybe Annie did give herself up for her father, but that devotion must have faded with time or with distance. Getting the chance to see Stazi, Izax, and her parents again is worth any amount of time spent running after Carrion. And, as an additional win, it'll result in Carrion no longer running around the Bastion, kidnapping people and selling them to the Astrosi to save their own skin.

For the first time since arriving in the Deep, Luzia feels as though she can breathe properly again. It is as if the thick humidity and the pollen in the air have vanished, leaving behind purified air that washes out her lungs and clears her chest.

She will see her family again.

CHAPTER SEVEN

It is Thursday. That is the only thing occupying Luzia's mind as she shuffles along behind Annie. It is Thursday, and she is not sitting down at the dinner table across from her parents, next to her brother, listening to Stazi laugh as he shovels food in his mouth. She has never missed a dinner before, not once, not in the entire ten years and three months they've had this tradition. Even if, by some miracle, Sef were to appear before her right now and grant her freedom to leave, even then Luzia would not make it home in time.

Instead of walking into the warmth of her parents' residential unit, she is being led through the confusing halls of the Deep towards... well, she's not actually sure. She has her tablet with her again, and she keeps sketching out the routes she's taking in the hope that eventually she can make a proper map and walk around here without getting lost. It's more challenging than orienting herself in the Bastion, that's for certain, given the excess of plants that coat nearly every inch of the place and the fact that the humid air still makes her constantly uncomfortable.

"Here." Annie comes to a stop in front of a set of doors and pushes a button on the wall to make them slide open. "Go on in."

Whatever Luzia had been expecting, this isn't it. Inside is a large open chamber, no plants on the walls and no grass on the floor, the illumination panels overhead projecting the same type of light as street lamps in the human levels. Racks filled with those cylindrical weapons that the Eoi use are hung from the walls, and on one side of the room are a series of rubber dummies not unlike the ones that Luzia used when she was learning how to do the fireman's carry.

Only one person awaits her inside: Lysander. Her stomach begins to ache from just the memory of the hit he'd given her.

Upon seeing her enter, he rolls his eyes up at the ceiling and mutters, "I can't believe I agreed to this." Then he sighs, properly approaches her, and gives her a distinctly unimpressed look. "You had better understand just what a damn sacrifice I'm making here. If you had been the one to request this instead of her majesty, I'd have laughed in your face and kicked you out by the ass."

Luzia swallows, puts her small tablet away into her pocket, and straightens up. "Then thank you for agreeing to this."

"Don't get cheeky with me," he warns. He glances at Annie for the barest fraction of a second, and his lips contort into a pained wriggle. "Get out," he mutters, turning away from her as fast as he'd looked at her in the first place. "Leave me to this impossible task."

There is a careful and deliberate blankness in Annie's face and eyes. She says nothing to Lysander, and to Luzia remarks only, "Good luck."

Once it is only Luzia and Lysander in the room, she cannot help but ask, "Do you have a particular dislike of Annie, or–"

He swiftly cuts her off by throwing a cylindrical weapon at her, and she barely manages to catch it before it collides with her head. Going by the flash of disappointment on his face, perhaps he'd been hoping for it to hit her, which, her mind insists, would surely have given her a terrible bruise or potentially a concussion or even create a blood clot that could trigger a stroke. That does seem unlikely, but she would have not long ago labeled being stuck in the Deep surrounded by Astrosi as 'unlikely'. And anyway, a person can never be too cautious.

"This," Lysander begins, grabbing a second weapon for himself, "is a bayonet-rifle. I can't imagine you'll have seen one in the human realm before, but down here and up above in the Mists, they're the Astrosi weapon of choice."

She looks down at the thing. "What does it do, exactly?"

"Are you really looking at a long piece of sharp metal and asking what it does?" He rolls his eyes again. One day they're going to fall out of his sockets. "It stabs people. *That's* what it bloody does. This switch here," he adds, pointing to a slider next to what she thinks is the handle, "adds a nasty little electric current to the blade. In case an extra kick is needed." He points to a gauge on the side that's showing nine blue bars out of ten. "That's the charge meter. If you let it run out, shove a fucking charge pack in there or find a charging station real fast. And the barrel – this long part, since you seem to have trouble figuring out even the simplest things – shoots."

"Shoots what?"

He points the bayonet-rifle at one of the dummies and pulls a trigger that's attached to the handle. There's a high-pitched *vshhh* and for a split second a bright beam of light extends from the barrel and hits the dummy. Then that split second is over and there is a smoking hole in the dummy's chest.

"See?" Lysander rests the rifle over his shoulder in a manner that oozes cockiness and smugness.

"Well, yes, but that doesn't answer my question," she replies, frowning at the matching rifle in her hands. It's rather heavy, actually, and the weight gets more noticeable the longer she's forced to hold it. "I can see that it does, in fact, shoot, but what exactly *is* it shooting?"

He pauses. "How should I know?"

"Is it a chemical compound? Laser-based? Is it stable inside the weapon when it's not being used? Does it have any radioactive properties? Does it leak? Does it ignite? Is it safe?"

"It puts holes in people," he says slowly, as if she's a child. "Of course it ain't safe."

Her hands twitch around the rifle and she very nearly drops it before realizing that dropping it might cause it to activate, or perhaps explode, or something else unfortunate.

"Drop it and I strangle you," Lysander warns, noticing her fumble.

"I'd prefer it if you didn't, if it's all the same to you," she replies weakly. "This is very interesting, but all that aside, why does it matter? We're going to be tracking down Carrion, aren't we? Shouldn't I be involved in, well, strategy discussions for that or something else?"

He blinks. "You're going to learn to use this, you idiot."

She looks down at the rifle again. "No, thank you."

"What?"

"I'm not going to use any weapons or *fight* anyone."

"Tch. Too cowardly to manage it?"

"Actually, I've always found that violence is the recourse of those with so little confidence in their convictions that they know they can't win anything without resorting to fists."

Lysander's temples twitch as though he is about to have a stroke. He takes a deep breath and for a moment she wonders if he's going to swear at her some more, as it seems he dislikes her moral principles. Then he exhales and returns his rifle to the rack he retrieved it from. There's some sort of clunky stand near the rack and he presses a button on it to extend an even clunkier panel filled with various dials and switches and an old projector screen. It's not unlike the thing he used to record her contract with Sef.

He types in a brief set of commands before asking her, "Know what a hologram is?"

"Well yes, but that sort of Era One tech is not all that common, so I don't encounter it on a daily basis–"

"Well then." With a smile that's as pleasant as broken glass and a deliberate press of a button, he says, "Sucks for you, hilarious for me."

Before she has a chance to ask what he means, Lysander looks over her shoulder and hears footsteps behind her. Only that can't be right – she didn't hear the door open. She turns around, half expecting to see Annie grumpily stomping in, but it is not Annie. It's someone who makes her heart skip a beat and then race with a rush of overpowering adrenaline.

Carrion stands before her, a cruel glint in their eye and a bayonet-rifle in their hands.

An infinitesimally small corner of her mind whispers that this is a hologram, that this isn't real, that it would be impossible for Carrion to have snuck this far into the Deep without being spotted, that if it were Carrion then Lysander would be doing something beyond just standing there. But that corner of logic is drowned out by fear, and the moment Carrion swings the rifle at her, she drops to the ground, covering her head.

The rifle goes straight through her with a flicker of static, and then the hologram fades. Even with it gone, it takes some time for her heart rate to fall back to normal, a bead of cold sweat gathering between her shoulder blades.

"That was *pathetic*," Lysander remarks.

She winces, pushing herself up onto her knees and staring at where Carrion was standing a mere second ago. "I – I wasn't expecting…"

The irritated groan he makes is truly impressive. "You signed up to hunt that bastard down. Begged for it, even, if what I heard's right. And now you don't have the guts to so much as clock them in the face? You really think they're just gonna surrender peacefully? You think they ain't gonna kill you if given half the chance? You know that they don't care if they hurt humans, and trust me when I say that they don't care if they hurt Astrosi either. They just want blood and power, and they ain't gonna find your pacifist act cute."

She cannot avert her gaze from where the hologram was as she indignantly replies, "I can do better, I swear. But I'm not going to get in some fistfight like you want me to."

"You don't have a fucking clue, do you? If you want to be anything other than dead meat, you'd better get your shit together and sort yourself out." He yanks her rifle from her arms, glaring at her. "Because as it stands now, I'm going to toss you at them as bait the moment I get the chance."

When she scrambles to her feet, he merely kicks her legs out from under her, sending her sprawling onto her back with a pained cry.

"Stay down," he growls.

She has no intention of staying down, but by the time she's staggered back upright he's already gone. Despite finding him a deeply unpleasant person to be around, she cannot deny that the sight of the door sliding shut behind him rankles. It's not that she cares what he thinks, particularly. It's just that she's *not* completely useless as he seems to believe and she *can* contribute to this search for Carrion, human or no.

Eventually, after she begins to shiver in the cold training room, she has nothing else to do but slink back to the arboretum with her head drooping. Her mood continues to fall as she gets lost twice along the way, and even consulting her map and adding to it as necessary doesn't provide much reassurance. Just another reminder that she doesn't belong here.

It takes her some time to find Annie in the labyrinth that is the arboretum, especially considering the number of detours she has to take every time she encounters a particularly menacing plant. Fortunately, when she comes across her, she is around only one of those menacing plants, and one that Luzia thinks she knows how to avoid. Annie is in the queen's bower once more, tending to the apple tree. So long as Luzia doesn't eat one of those apples, she thinks she'll be safe. Or as safe as she can be here.

"Went well, huh?" is all Annie says as she sprays a liquid of some kind onto the plants. "Stop looking so miserable, girl. Your face will freeze like that."

"That's statistically very unlikely," Luzia mumbles.

The only noise Annie makes is a *hrmph* before she continues with her work. There is a peaceful sort of silence for a while, or a silence that would be peaceful if Luzia were capable of ignoring all the circumstances surrounding her. A vague nausea has risen up to the back of her throat. Disappointment has turned her stomach into a roiling mess, and worst of all is that she cannot tell who she is disappointed with – Lysander, for failing to even give her a chance, or herself, for failing to meet even his lowest of expectations.

"He gave me a rifle," she eventually confesses. "I wouldn't shoot it. Then he knocked me down and told me I was dead meat. Is he always so..."

"You can call him a dickhead. I'm not going to gasp in outrage or nothing. And no, he wasn't always like that." Annie opens her mouth as though she's about to say something else, then gives up on that and simply shakes her head. "Still, if you wouldn't shoot the thing, I can't blame him. How'd you feel if I wandered up to the Bastion, told you I could definitely do your job, no problem, and then refused to pick a single piece of rubbish up off the ground? Hunting Carrion down ain't child's play, and to Lysander you're disrespecting what he does."

Luzia's cheeks flush in even further embarrassment. "I... I suppose I hadn't thought of it like that."

"Didn't think you had." Annie shrugs, casual as anything. "Eh. You'll try again tomorrow, won't you. Next time, I suggest you shoot the damn rifle. I never took to it – couldn't hit a wall two feet away to save my life – but I've heard it ain't hard."

It's not the difficulty that matters; it's the principle of it. When Luzia began working as a First Responder, back when she was still bright-eyed and bushy-haired, so to speak, she'd taken an oath to do no harm. Despite not being on a medical team, she still encounters the injured more frequently than she'd like. She still works every day to ensure that lives will be saved, whether that's pulling a child with a broken leg out of a crack in the street or shoring up a building so that it won't collapse the next week.

Save lives. Do not harm. Putting holes in people, as Lysander so crassly put it, is out of the question.

CHAPTER EIGHT

It's dark. Hot and dark, like a humid ventilation shaft. Sweat is dripping down Luzia's brow, catching in her eyebrows and tickling her nose where a bead of it clings above her mouth. Black, formless shapes twist at the edges of her vision, laughing and dancing out of sight when she tries to look at them. Something else moves between the shapes, something solid and made of color.

A human shape, albeit a small one. A child's back.

"Stazi?" she calls out, but her voice is swallowed up by the blackness. "Stazi, is that you?"

The child begins to turn just as the floor begins to shake and she is grabbed by invisible hands that drag her away from him.

"Ziane!" someone is snapping at her. "Wake up!"

An exhausted groan vibrates in Luzia's throat as she forces her bleary eyes to open. Something is in fact shaking her, only it's Annie instead of mystery dream forces. In her groggy haste to wake up, Luzia accidentally inhales a flower petal before sneezing it out, her eyes watery and her nose runny. Whichever of the Eoi conceived the idea to make their beds out of flowers was clearly touched in the head.

Annie, apparently deciding that things are moving too slowly, pulls Luzia up and rips the thin blanket off of her. "You're being summoned. Look alive." She pauses, blinking at Luzia's somewhat dribbly nose. "Huh. Guess you *are* allergic to pollen. That's rough, buddy."

Luzia wipes her face with her sleeve, straightening up and quickly sliding into full awareness. Being summoned. That's familiar, at least. She's not unaccustomed to being woken in the middle of the night for a job, although usually it's via the static-laden coms panel in her living unit. Being physically jostled by a somewhat aggressive gardener wasn't standard. She gropes around for her jacket and tugs it on, nose wrinkling as she does so. It's the same clothing she'd been wearing when she came down here, and it's beginning to show.

The moment she's up on her feet is the moment Annie grabs her by the arm and starts tugging her out of the living unit. Sudden brightness assaults her senses as she steps into the arboretum, the unceasing daylight panels cheerfully beaming down on her crusted and tender eyes.

"Where am I going?" she asks, forcing her feet to start working properly as she half runs through the arboretum.

"Just follow me," Annie grumbles. "I don't got the time to give you directions."

Perhaps that's for the best, considering that Luzia quickly finds herself incapable of keeping track of the corridors Annie takes her through. She may be skilled in elementary cartography, but the Eoi realm is made more of living, moving architecture – walls that are seemingly entirely plant life and appear to move when she isn't looking directly at them. Frankly, she's a little confused as to how Annie can get around so well. The Eoi's easy ability to navigate she can attribute to their strange and inscrutable magics, but all her logic tells her that Annie should require a very complicated map to avoid getting lost.

The room she's dragged to is similar in size to the training area where Lysander so thoroughly kicked her around yesterday. Unlike yesterday, it's filled with a half-dozen other Eoi, all wearing thicker, more durable clothing and carrying their own bayonet-rifles. More than a few confused looks are directed at her as she stumbles inside, and when she turns back to find Annie the woman has vanished.

Lysander's voice barks out, "Get in line, Ziane!"

It takes Luzia a second to remember that's the name Sef decided to give her, and another second to figure out where in line she's expected to stand before awkwardly settling at the end by herself.

"We got word from one of our scouts that Carrion's setting up a new hideout," Lysander begins, all business and, for once, with no abrasive smugness. "Seems like they're looking to settle there for a while, so if we can get there in time, we should be able to catch them before they leave and then drag their sorry ass back down here. If you see the diamond, that's your new priority. And remember, we want Carrion alive. They can't talk if they're dead. Questions? No? Good. Move out!"

Even Luzia has to admit that he's admirably efficient.

The Eoi soldiers begin to file out in quick and orderly succession. She's about to follow them when Lysander grabs her arm, pulling her back and shoving a bayonet-rifle into her arms.

"Ah, I really don't think I need–" she tries to protest.

"Let me make this simple for you." He glowers at her, forehead pinched in a dozen angry wrinkles. "Take the rifle or I shoot you with it. Got it?"

She takes the rifle.

"And one more thing," he adds. "Our queen's orders are for you to follow my directions and instructions to the letter. You are not just obeying me for the duration of this mission; you are obeying *her*. So when I tell you that you're not to even *think* of fucking off back to your human life, *she's* telling you that."

"Why the specificity?"

"Because technically she holds your contract, not me. And whatever you think about me, I'm not a *complete* bastard. You need to know that disobeying me triggers your contract penalty. Regardless of how much it'll hurt you if you disobey, I ain't wasting my time and energy on keeping you alive if Carrion's feeling in a particularly murderous mood."

"I understand," she replies.

"You'd better."

With that all said, he stomps past her, shoulder-checking her on the way out as though daring her to do anything about it. Perhaps he thinks his hostility will convince her to back out of this. If that's the case, he'll have to try much, *much* harder. He can do whatever he wants to her physically – she can take that. She'll put up with a punch from him every day if it allows her to continue on this mission, to fulfill her bargain with Sef, and to see her family again. What's a smack on the shoulder or a punch in the stomach in comparison?

Lysander leads her and the other Eoi at a breakneck pace through the halls. They don't pass by many others, only two Eoi wearing what look like lab coats. What do the Eoi *do*, exactly? Half of them seem to be soldiers, the others appear to be scientists of some kind.

Eventually, they come to a section of the Deep that's just

an open circle of space. Lysander once more grabs her by the arm and drags her into position, arranging her next to him as though she's a child that needs to be babysat. Interestingly enough, however, after the initial confusion the rest of the Eoi haven't looked at her twice. They've just accepted that she's here. Do they truly have that much faith in Sef's decisions?

To seemingly no one, Lysander says, "Engage executive priority. Authorization: Code B-00-2."

Luzia jumps as though struck with a live wire when an emotionless, robotic voice from nowhere replies, "Code accepted. Prepare for launch in three, two, one–"

The floor rumbles.

If she'd thought the breakneck decent into the Deep had been unpleasant, this makes that earlier plummet seem like a walk in the park by comparison. Gravity slams her down onto her knees as the floor – no, the *platform* – rockets upwards faster than even the priority lifts she's taken in the Bastion. There's a painful pop in her eardrums that could very well have cracked her jawbone and a wave of nausea that she struggles to push down as her fingers scramble to find purchase on the metal platform beneath her.

None of the Eoi bat an eyelash at the violent ascent and once more she silently curses herself for her own weakness. She's been in rough spots before; surely she can get through this without much trouble. Surely.

There's a hand on her shoulder, much gentler than the way Lysander carts her about like a beat-up suitcase. One of the Eoi soldiers, a tall man with a faint smile, helps her stand up. He props her up against him while she gets her feet properly underneath her, holding her rifle against her chest so that she doesn't drop it again.

"Thank you," she mumbles once she can properly speak.

His smile widens a tiny bit. "No worries. The first time going up to the human realm is always the hardest. Especially if you don't have our resilience."

"It's certainly... jarring."

"That's an understatement. What do they call you, new girl?"

It takes her a minute to remember that she's been given a new name along with her contract. "I'm Ziane. If it's not too rude, may I ask..." She frowns, trying to think of the best way to phrase this. "Every Astrosi I've met so far has been quite specific in asking for my name. You haven't. Is it a cultural norm that you deviate from or just happenstance explainable by my admittedly limited conversations with your kind?"

"You're a wordy one, huh? It's pretty simple. The queen asked for your name. You gave it to her. That makes it hers, see? Think of it as a first come, first served sort of situation."

"Oh." She doesn't quite see, but it's information she can dissect later. "Thank you. Um, in that case, what do they call you? Did I ask that properly?"

He laughs. "You did. Don't get your panties in a twist over it. They call me Essten."

"Nice to meet you, Essten." She awkwardly rearranges her grip on her rifle so that she can shake his hand. "And thank you again for the assistance. Is this your first time going after Carrion?"

"Not by a long shot. That bastard is always popping up when you least want them to. Frankly, I think we're all pretty grateful that the queen has decided to focus on taking them out."

"I thought we were supposed to bring them in alive."

"The queen's hoping to interrogate Carrion to see what they know about the diamond. No one here will go against the queen's wishes, but let's just say that we won't be pulling punches either."

Fair enough.

There's a hum of electricity as the platform slows down and eventually comes to a complete stop. It all looks just the same to her, but then part of the wall slides open to reveal that it was actually a door all along.

Lysander strides out, gesturing for the rest to follow. "All right. Second level, floor seventy-one. We're not too far from where our scout reported the sighting."

"Second level?" she remarks incredulously. "That shouldn't be physically possible. How do all entrances to and exits from the Deep traverse up and down the Bastion at rates that not even the fastest priority lifts can manage?"

"Don't worry so much about time, Ziane," is the only response she gets from him. "This way."

Luzia trails out of the lift after the rest of the Eoi and gets her first breath of clean Bastion air in what feels like years. The inescapable damp of the Deep is gone, replaced by the dry and pure air of the Bastion's Era One air-filtration system. There's not a whiff of dirt or flowers and her stuffy sinuses clear up in an instant. There is neither the gloom of areas shaded by plants nor the infinite light panels of unending whiteness. There are *normal* daylamps set to *normal* brightness levels and it makes her chest ache with longing.

There's a noise from behind her. The lift door shuts, leaving behind nothing more than a blank wall, as though it's capable of an almost organic camouflage.

Oh, she knows this area. That realization is a warm blanket of familiarity around her. They've entered the lower basements of a water-processing facility, the high-ceilinged chamber filled with rows of tanks – a series of digesters that filter various contaminants from various different water sources. The ones they're currently walking through are designed to create anaerobic digestion by introducing oxygen into the water, letting the bacteria break down the solid waste. She's been here before, although only once. When she was a trainee, she'd shadowed a superior through this area on a routine inspection.

Rifle raised, Lysander takes point as the Eoi spread out through the facility basement. Luzia trails along behind Essten, more preoccupied with taking in the familiar surroundings. She knows this area better than they do, surely. It would be so easy for her to slip away and go through the long process of sneaking her way back up to her home and to Stazi and Izax and…

A rough cough forces its way out of her throat and she covers her mouth, wincing. No, she can't. She wasn't lying when she told Annie that she meant to keep her word. If she follows her bargain with Sef, she can see her family again while still being honorable and honest.

The sheer scale of the facility means that it takes them some time to reach where Lysander is leading them to. An odd place to go. It's just storage closets back here. Nothing dangerous or interesting, no switchboards that could be messed with or stashes of toxic chemicals or even a direct connection to the water filters themselves. She's about to ask what they're doing in this area when Lysander rips the door open to reveal the closet itself.

A pile of ratty blankets is shoved into one corner, the fabric torn and frayed and stained to the degree where she has no idea what original shape or color it's supposed to be. Dented canteens and ration-bar wrappers are scattered about, a lumpy bag of who-even-knows-what tossed in a corner. Someone's been living here. In a *closet*? That's so... depressing. Somehow she hadn't expected Carrion to be *depressing*.

"Well, that's the bastard's nest all right," Lysander remarks, upper lip curling in revulsion at the sight.

"Looks like their things are still here. Do you think they're coming back? Or did they get wind of our arrival and run?" Essten asks.

With a shrug, Lysander moves away from the closet and starts scanning this corner of the facility with an even sharper eye than before. "If they know we're here, they might cut their losses. Besides," he adds, another sneer twisting his expression, "their stuff is just a pile of crap. Not worth coming back for. Spread out and see if there's anything else they left behind. That or we can find a vantage point to ambush them from if they return."

Luzia sets her rifle against the wall and enters the closet, kneeling next to the items within. She picks up one of the canteens and tilts it up. Bone dry. Odd, considering that they were living right next to the freshest source of water in the Bastion. No actual food, only remnants.

It is indeed a pile of crap, but it's a confusing pile of crap. If she were always on the run, she wouldn't set up near fresh water and then abandon all containers that could carry it.

As carefully as possible, she starts to move the items out of the closet. There may be a method to this madness, as it were. Some reason why Carrion has placed these things in a way that resembles... well. That resembles *bait*. But bait for what, exactly? To get the Eoi to think that Carrion will be returning? What does that accomplish, other than keeping them around while they set up a very deadly ambush that would surely be a struggle for even Carrion to escape?

The floor of the closest is made up of four slabs of steel. One of them, she finds upon removing the final threadbare blanket, has had half a centimeter shaved off the center edge. In that tiny sliver of blackness there is a single, cheerfully blinking, bright red light.

Luzia has been in this water-processing plant before. Last time, there were no blinking red lights anywhere in the facility.

She puts the blanket down. She rises to her feet. And backs out of the closet.

"Lysander!" she calls, continuing to back away as carefully and quickly as she can. Red lights could mean a lot of things, all of them ominous. A dramatic ominous as well, one that she imagines might be exactly the sort of style Carrion prefers. "Lysander, there's a red light under that floor! The nest, the items – they're all bait. This is a trap!"

He whirls around, cursing under his breath and hitching his rifle over his shoulder. "Ziane, get away from there!"

The rest of the Eoi start running, but to her surprise Lysander rushes towards her, hand outstretched and expression for once absent irritation. She reaches out to him, fingers slipping against his before he grabs her by the arm, and it's still just as rough as before, yet this time it's also somehow comforting.

He pulls her in front of him as though his back is her shield right before the bomb goes off.

CHAPTER NINE

The force of the explosion knocks both Luzia and Lysander off their feet, swatting them over effortlessly and sending them crashing to the ground. Smoke and dust fill the air, turning what little Luzia can see into a haze of ugly gray that makes her eyes water and her lungs burn. At least, some tiny and extremely distant part of her mind thinks, it seems Carrion went for a flashy bang over actual damage. She and Lysander had been close enough that a bomb designed to maim or kill would have torn them apart.

The echo of the explosion still fills her ears as the overbearing weight of Lysander rolls off her back and onto the ground next to her, coughing up dust. She's still far too winded to even consider moving. He gets an elbow underneath him, pushing himself up a scant foot or so, and yells out something that she can't make out, the words lost in the ringing in her ears.

Behind him she can see the blurry shapes of the other Eoi staggering to their feet. No visible injuries. It does appear to have been a relatively minor explosion. Almost more of a warning than an actual attack, as though Carrion's intent had just been to tell the Eoi to leave them alone. But for all she knows, they could simply prefer the chaos of this.

Lysander is the first to manage to stand, and then of course he promptly nudges her with his boot. Her ears have settled enough that she can hear him hissing, "Get up!"

When she tries to reply, all her lungs allow her to do is spit out ashy gray saliva. If the pain in her chest is anything to go by, she might have bruised her ribs. Or cracked them. Or broken them into tiny pieces – well, no, not that last one. The pain would be excruciating if that were the case and it would be likely that a tiny shard of rib would have pierced her heart and in that case she'd be dying of internal bleeding right this very second.

"Stop freaking out, you bloody idiot," Lysander snaps at her. "Keep your head or lose it."

A few yards away, Essten is picking up one of his fellow Eoi, helping the man stand just as he'd helped Luzia earlier. "Should we try to search for more traps?" he calls out to Lysander. "Doubt Carrion's stupid enough to think one measly fireball is enough to discourage us."

Lysander picks up his rifle and dusts it off. "No. They ain't. Watch for–"

Someone screams.

There's a second of high-pitched terror. Then it is cut off with a wet, definitive gurgle. Luzia cranes her neck up to the source of the horrid noise, stomach sinking even further into the ground.

The soldier farthest away from everyone else has the blade of their own bayonet-rifle sticking out the center of their chest, the metal tip bursting out through their sternum. Ugly thick blood dribbles down from the wound and trickles out of the corner of their mouth and their wide eyes bug out in shock and terror. There's another wet noise of the rifle being ripped out of them and then their body falls with a plain and simple *thud*.

Carrion is standing behind the dead man, casual as anything.

"Morning everyone," they say, waving the stolen rifle in one hand. "Honestly, I've no clue why you all like these things so much. They're so *messy*."

With that, they toss the aforementioned weapon over their shoulder as though it's trash. Like the first stone falling before a collapse, as soon as the rifle clatters against metal the Eoi spring into action. One shoots those laser-like blasts at Carrion, another comes at them with a wild swing, and it's all a blur to Luzia, a whirling dance that her human eyes, still fuzzy from the explosion, cannot keep up with.

She hears Lysander growl, "Stay down if you know what's good for you, Ziane. You just saw what'll happen to you if you don't."

And then he too is rushing towards Carrion, rifle blazing.

For all that Luzia had begged to be allowed to do this, for all that she had been desperate for Sef to accept her deal, she does not think she understood even a fraction of what this would entail. When Carrion had stolen Stazi there had been a fight, yes, but there had been no death. A few guardsmen had been knocked around and Luzia had been briefly choked with those Astrosi magics of theirs. Stazi hadn't gotten so much as a scratch, when all was said and done. Foolishly, she'd thought that hunting Carrion would just be more of that.

Though her heart is pounding in her ears, she forces herself into something approaching the focus she needs in her line of work. Step one: get up. Step two: check the detonation site. Step three: relevant only after completion of prior tasks.

She gets up. Her legs might as well be made of jelly for all the stability they provide her, but at least she's standing, and her steps get more confident as she stumbles back to the closet where the bomb had detonated. Behind her she can hear the sounds of combat, the noise of the rifles and the sounds of–

No. Focus.

Not only did the explosion tear up most of the ground beneath where the closet was, it also took out a small section of the wall. She checks the wreckage for any exposed structural elements that might be an imminent threat and finds none. Similarly, a series of taps and knocks on the wall inform her that this section fortunately isn't load bearing. It'll hold.

Which means it's on to step three.

She turns around just in time to see Carrion snap someone's neck. One of the Eoi soldiers she doesn't know has been caught in their grip, used as a shield between them and the others, and the only reward was a swift *crack*. Carrion throws the body at someone else, knocking them out, and then they turn to Essten.

Luzia starts to run.

Essten ducks under Carrion's punch and slices at them with his bayonet-rifle, the blade nicking their coat and sending a single button scattering. Though Luzia knows little of combat beyond occasionally having to break up fisticuffs, she knows enough to see that Carrion is putting more effort into enjoying themself than they are into the fight. They don't seem to take Essten seriously for even a second. Then Essten attempts to maneuver them towards Lysander, and that must be too much for whatever sick satisfaction they get from this.

They weave around Essten with all the fluidity of water until they get a leg twisted between his. A single yank knocks him off balance and sends him sprawling, and then, for good measure, Carrion jumps on his leg like a child jumping onto a mattress. There's a *crack* of bone and Essten cries out, curling in on himself and clutching the broken limb.

Before they can finish him off, Lysander smashes his way between the two, snarling and snapping, as he swings his rifle. The strikes don't hit, but that's not the point. In barely a handful of seconds he's gotten Carrion far from the now-defenseless Essten.

"Lysander!" Carrion grins, twisting to the right when Lysander slashes to the left. "It's been too long. Honestly, we never get to catch up like this anymore. I'd offer you a beer but..." Another slash and they slide to the right, still grinning. "So, how's the job? How's the family?"

Lysander's roar is overflowing with sheer fury, and this time when he shoots it doesn't miss. The shot grazes a red line across Carrion's arm, nasty and feverish-looking. There's a burning smell.

Burnt flesh. Nauseating and almost sweet, depending on what's burning first. When the hair catches fire first, it's more putrid. When it's the skin, it mostly reeks of dirty, warm ash. When the entire body alights and all that blood is boiling and burning, then the copper smell of cooking iron fills the air with the atrocity of what's happening. No, she's not responding to a fire alarm. This is different.

Focus.

Carrion's foot collides with Lysander's chest and the man skids backwards until he collides with one of the tanks.

"Maybe if you kept your damn mouth shut," Lysander growls, dropping down onto one knee and curling his free hand into a fist, "you'd learn how to kick someone like you *mean it* instead of pussyfooting around like an overdramatic prick."

"Isn't it customary to talk shit only *after* winning?" Carrion counters.

Lysander's glare curdles into something smug and, with impossible strength, he slams his fist into the tank, cracking the metal with such force that water bursts out and begins to flow in a steady stream. He rips his fist out and Luzia can only stare in incredulity as the jet of water bends at his command, twisting and turning, mixing with brown dirt from his wristband, coalescing into a green rope.

No, not a rope. A living vine curls around his wrist and he whips it out, lashing Carrion with it over and over, forcing them back step by step. Is this the sort of magic that the Eoi can use? The vine rips open a gash on Carrion's upper arm, blood splattering over the stone. Another lash slices off a few strands of their long hair, which they seem more annoyed about than the actual injury. They have no choice but to put actual effort in now, ducking and weaving and throwing themselves to the ground to roll underneath a particularly fast and brutal swing.

They reach into their pocket and retrieve something that Luzia recognizes all too well. A single match. Given what they did with it last time…

"Lysander!" Luzia cries out. "They've got a match, be careful!"

Lysander raises his arm up high and brings it down to slice Carrion's fallen form in two with the vine. But they must have been expecting that for they twist around it and come up kneeling, pinning the vine beneath their weight. Carrion flicks their wrist. Water is ripped out of the vine, all of it sucked out and evaporated in an instant, and then they strike the match against what is now dry tinder. Flame turns the vine into a scorching vector surging directly towards Lysander's arm. He throws the vine away from him as fast as he can, but there is still that horrible burning smell and tattered bits of fabric on his sleeve.

The pain doesn't throw him like it did Essten. Eyes burning to mirror the fire, he charges Carrion. The lingering ash from the explosion and the haze of the smoke make it difficult for Luzia to see, and from the way Lysander is beginning to strike blindly, that's true for him as well. He cuts off a retreating Carrion, throwing his weight around to stop them in the knowledge that if he can properly pin them, his superior body weight will win out. She coughs, covering her nose as she tries to make her way towards the pair locked in combat, unsure what she can do to help, exactly, but knowing that she has to do *something*.

She reaches Essten and kneels at his side. "How bad is the pain?" she asks quickly, looking at the nasty break in his left leg. "Can you walk?"

"Nng…" He winces and bites down on another cry of pain, gladly accepting her offered arm and letting her help him sit up. "Don't think so."

The fire won't spread once it's consumed the dehydrated remnants of the vine, but the further he is from this fight, the better. She eyeballs his height. Guesses his weight. "All right, listen. I'm going to help you to your feet. You don't need to stand, I promise. You just need to trust me. I know what I'm doing."

"I sure hope so," he mutters under his breath.

Using his one good leg and her own strength, the two of them get up him upright. He's utterly reliant on her support to remain that way, and when he attempts to put any weight at all on his injured leg, she shakes her head and adjusts him. She wraps her arms around him, getting her leg between his.

"Ready?" she asks, tensing her muscles.

"Let's say yes and I can change my mind later."

She drops down, grabbing his legs and holding on to his arm when he tries to flail, and then swiftly stands back up, slinging him over her shoulder as she goes.

Whatever material his clothing is made out of is dense, for he's a lot heavier than she'd anticipated. She moves as quickly as she can, taking long and hopefully even strides away from the fire and the fight. He makes the occasional noise of protest, but she doesn't stop moving until they've reached a safe distance – or as safe a distance as they can, all things considered. She kneels again and helps Essten gently roll onto the ground, now in no danger of stray sparks alighting on him.

She's considering what she can use to bind his leg with when he politely pushes her hands away. "I'll be okay from here," he assures her. "Go."

"All right."

She starts running back towards Lysander and Carrion, stooping to pick up her fallen rifle as she goes. It occurs to her that Essten's instruction hadn't been very precisely worded. Had he meant for her to go towards Lysander to offer assistance, or go *away* to protect herself as well? She is supposed to follow instructions, but what if she got it wrong?

That dilemma makes her pause for a split second, and in turn that split second gives her the time she needs to see that Carrion is baiting Lysander. They're smiling as he slams his fist towards their head, still smiling as the punch is an inch away from them. At the last second, they drop to the ground and Lysander's momentum causes him to slam his hand into the tank that Carrion has positioned behind their back.

Lysander barks out a swear. "Bastard!" His entire arm has sunk into the thin metal. He yanks and pulls and claws at the tank with his free hand, but to no avail. He's stuck in the tank up to his shoulder.

Carrion dances out of his reach and kicks his rifle far away. "Maybe you'll be in more of a mood for a friendly chat next time, huh?"

"Tell me one thing," Lysander demands, spitting out the words like bile. "Did you come here for the diamond?"

"Now that's for me to know and you to find out."

His jaw drops an inch. "You son of a– Where is it?!"

Carrion merely gives him a teasing sort of shrug before waving goodbye and sauntering off towards the facility exit. "See you around, Lysander."

"Get the fuck back here!"

He might be in no position to give chase, but Luzia is and she does.

Whatever this diamond is, the Eoi seem to want it desperately. If she finds it or can learn where it is, then surely Sef will be grateful. Grateful enough, perhaps, to allow Luzia to return to her family for a visit or even, if her luck holds, dissolve her contract entirely. Anything's possible if she can get this prized object. She might not be able to stop Carrion, in fact she's certain she cannot, but that doesn't mean she can't get an answer from them.

She runs after Carrion as fast as her legs can carry her, skidding out of the far side of the facility with her heart pounding from fear and hope both. Either they've not noticed she's following them or, more likely, they don't care, for they don't bother to change their pace as she runs after them. They're not heading for the strange lift that took her and the Eoi up to the Bastion. Instead, they're casually making their way through unused maintenance corridors. If her memory is correct, the only thing in that direction is an Era One train station that hasn't been in use for likely centuries.

Out of use, yes. Disconnected from the rest of this floor? No. Carrion leaps onto the train tracks and slides along the magnetic rails like they're iced over, skating a solid few feet until they give her a jaunty wave over their shoulder as though curious to see if she'll give chase. She does, jumping up onto the broad train tracks and rushing after them.

Once she runs past the metal gates that separate the Era One station from the rest of the railway network, she instantly finds her ears assaulted with noise that she hasn't heard in what seems like years. The sounds of the *Bastion*. Of *people* – humans, not Astrosi – random citizens of the world instead of impossible beings from hidden depths. People who have just about as much ability to deal with Carrion as she does – which is to say, next to none at all.

The station next to the water plant is out of use, but she's listened to Izax complain about his work as a lightrail director too often not to know that the next station is a junction – and it is *not* out of service. Even now, as the train tracks begin to stretch out over the large gap between the towering buildings that make up floors fifty-eight through seventy-one, she can hear the distant rattling of a nearby train. Carrion is running towards the lightrail station.

A worker is attending the junction and startles as he sees Carrion.

"You can't be here!" he cries out, stepping toward the tracks and waving his arms as though this is nothing more than a mistake. "Get to the nearest platform before the train arrives and wait for the bloody guard to show up!"

Carrion grabs him by the scruff of his shirt and throws him onto the opposite train tracks. The man's head smacks into the metal with a painful *crack* and his limbs go limp, sprawled out over the rails as the sound of the distant train gets louder and louder.

There's a control stand on the junction platform. Luzia runs to it, pulls open the protective plastic covering, and hits the emergency seal-off button. A red warning light flashes and a siren starts to wail as the tracks leading to the junction lurch out of alignment, cutting this station off from the approaching train. She ignores the running Carrion and instead rushes to the fallen worker and kneels at his side.

She shifts her rifle to one hand so that her fingers can press against his wrist. A pulse. She leans her head over his and can feel his breath. Uneven, but it's there. It doesn't look good, but she cannot see any external bleeding, and if the man is alive for now there's a chance that swift medical attention can keep him that way.

"You know," Carrion's voice says, "that wasn't the cleverest choice."

They're still here? She scrambles to her feet and away from the unconscious man. If Carrion decides to attack her, she doesn't want to put him in even more danger.

"All I mean is that I could have been well on my way by now, and you were pretty damn committed to chasing after me," they say, light and calm as anything. "I wasn't expecting to see you on Lysander's little team, by the way."

"I... was a new addition," Luzia finds herself stuttering out.

"Ouch, that's bad luck. Still, it is nice to see you again. I'd say 'it's been awhile', but for you I guess it hasn't been. Nice move, by the way. Rerouting the train and all that. Very stylish."

She doesn't get much closer than another three steps precisely. Though they've not attacked her yet, if she gets too close she'll put herself at risk of being killed as quickly and as brutally as the Eoi they've murdered. "Where is the diamond?" she asks.

They shrug. "Damned if I know."

"But... what you said to Lysander..."

"Messing with Lysander is a very enjoyable sport," they reply. "Do it as often as I can, really. But love, when I find the diamond, trust me when I say that you'll *know*. Everyone will."

Terrifyingly ominous.

"Now," they continue, putting on a show of examining their nails, "did you have anything else to do or say, or were you going to just run along back to whatever human family you have? Seeing as how all your supervision is dead, knocked out, or stuck," they add with a sly and inquisitive glance. "I'd certainly take the opportunity."

Could she? As they said, Lysander isn't around to stop her. No one would even see her leave and it would be easy for them to assume that Carrion killed her, especially considering how many others they've killed today and how her dying instantly seems to have been Lysander's assumption from the start. She knows where she is, and she knows the Bastion better than the Eoi do, surely, so even if one of them got back up and started pursuing her, they'd not have the knowledge to follow her.

A route is already beginning to form in her mind when she feels another sharp cough overcome her. The dust from the explosion must still be in her lungs. She coughs again, bending over at the waist as her lungs spasm.

"Ah, well. That answers that question." Carrion approaches her, taking advantage of the fact that she's too busy coughing to move more than a few stumbling steps. "Let me guess. You were told to not even think about it? Those technicalities aren't to be underestimated, you know."

They keep walking until they reach the control stand. She can't stop coughing. Why can't she stop coughing? It's unusual that she'd experience only those mild symptoms right after the blast and now have them get so much worse. She would have thought her mad run across the tracks would have dredged up any lingering residue more than just standing around would have. What's left in her lungs to cough up? How much ash did she inhale?

A loud *crunch* emanates from the control stand. Somehow Carrion has ripped the entire thing up off the ground, a few dangling wires sticking out the bottom. She tries to ask them what they could possibly be doing, but that cough still won't go away and she doubles over, dropping her rifle and clutching at her mouth, checking to see if there's any residue on her hands that might explain this.

Something impacts the backs of her knees.

Carrion has kicked her. She collapses, faceplanting onto the ground between the rails, so out of breath that she's a hair's breadth away from fainting. A silent cry claws its way out of her throat when Carrion plops the control stand down onto her back, pinning her in place. No matter how much she squirms or claws at the ground, she can't move even an inch.

Black spots swim in front of her eyes as Carrion crouches down in front of her.

"I'm curious," they say, perfectly pleasant in tone, as though this were a conversation at a kitchen table. "Did you seriously chase me down just to ask if I had the diamond?"

She can only gasp wordlessly.

"Oh, right, that." They slap her cheek and demand, "Focus on me. Think about me and nothing else, got it?"

Why should she listen to them? They've done nothing but destroy her life since she first ran into them. They're the reason she is now tied to the Deep, they're the reason she's pinned down on a set of damn lightrail tracks, and they're the reason that multiple people have died today. She opens her mouth to say so and... her cough is gone. As soon as she stops thinking about her family, the cough vanishes in a second.

"Better, right?" Carrion smiles at her. "Anyhow, be a dear and answer my question."

"Yes," she grits out. "I chased you to ask you about the diamond."

"Ask? Don't you mean 'kidnap and then torture'?"

"I wouldn't have tortured you. I just... I thought I could..."

"You saw what I did to everyone back there. You can't have thought you stood a chance. You can't be *that* stupid. Were you just going to ask and hope I was in the mood to cheerfully waltz with you into Sef's tender embrace?" They gesture to her rifle, the weapon lying out of her reach. Not that she's actually tried to reach for it since dropping it. "You never even pointed that thing at me, let alone shot it. Did big mean Lysander send you out here without so much as showing you where the trigger was?"

She glares up at them. "I know how to use it."

"Then why not shoot me?"

"I don't believe violence is ever a meaningful solution. It's only temporary. Pacifistic solutions are actually long lasting."

Why is she even talking to them? It's not as though any of this has a point, and they've already beaten her – quite easily, for that matter. She cannot get out of this on her own, not without help. And yet there's something about the amiability they're projecting that has her answering every question and readily replying.

Carrion blinks at her in surprise. "Seriously? You were *seriously* just expecting to ask nicely? I gotta say, shooting me is a much surer bet. If you'd killed me, it would probably have made things a lot easier for you, no? Also something-something, 'right thing to do' and all that."

"If I killed you then there would still be a killer loose in this world," she retorts. "I would just have to be the one bearing that shame."

They tap their chin thoughtfully. "But what if you killed *two* killers?"

"What?"

"If you kill me *and* some other killer, then you'd still be down a total of one killer. Or what if you killed me to stop me from killing a hundred people? Then you'd be up ninety-nine."

"That's not how it works!" A furious blush burns her cheeks. "Lives aren't exchangeable with that kind of simple mathematics. These are serious ethical equations, not a kindergarten math lesson!"

"So your argument is that every life is a sort of... unique variable?"

"Yes, exactly!"

They grin at her, and there's no mockery in it, nothing but genuine enjoyment of a good conversation. "Your moral code is fascinating. Does it actually work for you, or do you find yourself running into these types of roadblocks often?"

Considering that she's not spent much time amongst Astrosi yet and that this is her first time actually in a life-or-death fight... "It's too soon to reach a definitive conclusion."

"Would it help if I killed more people to give you more data?" they ask. "What's the conversion rate for you between Astrosi lives and human lives? I mean, there *is* a great difference between the two in terms of longevity and power. Does your morality system weight them the same or is one more valuable than the other? I could definitely kill a variety of people for you if it helps you figure this out."

"What? No!"

"You sure? It wouldn't be any trouble–"

They are cut off by Lysander's pounding footsteps and his scream of, "Get back here, you fucking bastard!"

He followed them. Oh, she could kiss him from sheer relief. Well, she *wouldn't* literally, but that's beside the point.

Carrion rises up and leaps back from Luzia. "Oh, come *on*," they whine. "I was in the middle of a stimulating philosophical debate. Can't you at least let me finish?"

Lysander shoots at them. But Carrion has already dodged, though she's not sure how much use that will be given that Lysander is still charging towards them like a battering ram. As they did before with the vine, Carrion reaches out, a single finger pointed towards Lysander with an unsettling calm. They drag that finger to the right and something begins to happen.

That time spent trapped in the water tank has soaked Lysander to the bone, and now all the water that's seeped into his clothing is beginning to leave it, drawn out of the fabric drop by drop, only to turn to mist in the air. Within moments, everything around the three of them is just damp, white fog.

"Damn it," Lysander curses, his voice coming from about two feet to Luzia's left. "Can you see them?"

Not in this mist, that's for certain. She shifts her head as much as she can to face the direction she thinks he is. "No. But they said they didn't have the diamond, for what that's worth." She winces at the weight of the control stand still keeping her pinned down. "Um. If you don't mind, I would appreciate a bit of… assistance."

He gets a bit closer and now she is treated to an unobstructed view of the scathing disappointment on his face. "You," he says flatly, "are *hopeless*."

She presses her eyes tightly shut until she can see red spots, hoping that the sudden itch in the back of her throat is just a remnant of whatever had started her earlier coughing fit and not the prelude to tears.

CHAPTER TEN

After Lysander begrudgingly pries the control stand off Luzia, he drags her back to the water-treatment facility in silence. They help the Eoi that Carrion defeated get back to the mysterious lift and retrieve all fallen weapons. As for the Eoi that were killed, Lysander states that he will remain behind to collect the bodies and bring them back. And so Luzia has to stand alone, head bowed with shame, as the lift takes her and the injured back to the Deep.

A couple of Eoi, also wearing lab coats, are there to greet them when the lift arrives. Luzia is given a cursory lookover by these people, who she presumes are the Astrosi equivalent of medics, before being essentially dismissed. She lingers behind as the soldiers are helped to another room – a medcenter? Someone points her towards a bench in the hall outside and so she sits down, silent and contemplative and, now that all the adrenaline is leaving her, uncomfortably cold.

Logically, she knows the failure was not her fault. The Eoi soldiers she was with were experienced and yet were unable to defeat Carrion. Even if she had decided to discard that moral code they had seemed so interested in, she still wouldn't have been able to do anything substantial and they would simply have killed her for the attempt. Not to mention the issue of that strange cough. She couldn't have anticipated that. Still, that does not mean it doesn't hurt. She could have done something, anything more. Carrion had been willing to chat with her in the end. Could she have talked them down instead of just letting them lead her on a merry dance of a conversation?

Eventually Lysander arrives. He gives her a glare, speaks not even a full sentence to a medic, and then leaves. Were she capable of withering like one of the plants in the arboretum, she would.

Not long after that, the door opens and a familiar figure hobbles out.

"Essten!" She leaps to her feet. "How are you?"

A thick cast, reinforced with a wooden brace, covers his leg. Tucked under his arm is a crutch made from the same sturdy-looking wood as the brace. Though he clearly isn't in the best of shape, she's seen worse. He's breathing, he's walking, and there's a smile on his face, albeit one that's slightly strained.

He makes a vague gesture to his new apparatus. "Well, I can't say I've never been better." He pats her on the arm with the hand not maneuvering his crutch. "You did good."

"I achieved nothing."

"You noticed there was a bomb, not us. And best of all, you're alive." He shrugs. "I'm gonna be honest, a lot of newbies would have run or kicked it. Not even taking into account the fact that you're human, which just makes the whole thing even more impressive. Also, I'm not coughing up a lungful of smoke right now, and I owe you for that one."

"Oh, well." She's never been very good at accepting praise. "I was just doing my job. Seeing you alive is all the reward I need."

"You always this nice, or am I just special?"

"Um… I'm not certain how to answer that question," she replies awkwardly. "Can I just give you an implication-free 'maybe'?"

He laughs. It's a whole body laugh, the kind that crinkles the eyes and shakes the belly. "Aight then, an implication-free 'maybe' it is. Come on then, Miss Maybe. Let's go get a drink and a hot meal. Dinner's in full swing right now." He limps off down the corridor, looking over his shoulder and waiting for her to follow. "Don't worry, the others are gonna be out in a bit. We've got better meds down here than in the Bastion, plus they hit us with the good drugs."

"What are the good drugs?" she asks as she follows him. "Do you have the standard acetylsalicylic acids down here?"

"Nah, we've got other stuff. Whole variety of 'em. Not as much really crazy stuff as they've got up in the Mists, mind you. Those Vesperi really know their chemical cocktails," he remarks, almost longingly. "What I wouldn't give for a taste of their smokes… But anyway, nah, we've got some stuff that's like dried leaves, there's something that comes from a type of poppy, and there's these absolutely amazing mushrooms. The doc gave me the poppy stuff, so if I'm a bit loopy, that's why."

Unsurprisingly, the route he takes her on isn't one she's traversed before. If she's ever burdened with an abundance of free time, she decides that she will begin the endeavor of mapping out the Deep. When she isn't working or otherwise occupied, her mind has a tendency to eat itself alive like a madman that cannot resist scratching their own skin off. Work and family have always been what she fills herself with, and when she returns at the end of the day to her own small living unit, she is tense and tight inside until around others once again.

She takes out her tablet again and notes the hallway that Essten is taking her down, using the lift that they'd originally used as an orienting marker.

"What's that?" Essten asked, peering at the map that's barely even beginning to come together.

She shrugs nervously. "I can't seem to get a decent sense of the layout of the Deep, so I figured that I'd try to draw up a map for myself."

"Huh. You're a smart one, too."

Scratchy music and the sound of jubilant conversation are the first sensations to reach Luzia. Then comes the smell of mouthwatering food, even more tantalizing aromas than the soups and teas Annie has made for her over the past couple of days. She no longer needs Essten to lead her – she is drawn towards the smells and sounds. Not even her nervousness of the unfamiliar can break through.

Up ahead, wide open doors welcome her into a massive chamber. Tables and benches made of carved wood are spread out inside, a carpet of grass and flowers beneath her feet, vines and blossoms curling up the walls until the only normal part of the room visible is the sparkling daylight panels overhead. Groups of cheerful Astrosi are sprawled at the tables, laughing and drinking. And everywhere is food – platters piled high with things she cannot name that steam from heat and dishes that are dotted with cold condensation.

"Oh hey, it's Leneat," Essten says, pointing to a woman nursing a drink. She was one of the people on the mission as well, Luzia recalls, although she doesn't remember how the woman was taken down. "Come on. There's nothing like a beer with friends after everything's gone to shit."

"Beer?"

He laughs and slaps her on the back. "You're gonna love the stuff, trust me. I always forget that the Bastion can't ferment things."

Without any further ado, he steers her towards the lone woman and plops down on the bench opposite her. Leneat puts her drink down and grins at her new dining companions, looking oddly chipper for someone who got beaten earlier and watched people she presumably knew well die. Actually, Essten is acting much the same, isn't he? Is that the effect of whatever poppy thing they're both under?

"Hey there." Leneat has the sort of voice that suggests she's spent her whole life speaking just a little bit too loudly and is now suffering a rasp because of it. "Oh, it's the new girl. Sit for a spell, won't you? Have a drink. Hunting that bastard is thirsty work."

"That's what I was just telling her," Essten says, reaching across the table for two mugs, also made of wood.

Luzia sits and looks into the mug that he's passed her. There's a bit of frothy white stuff on top of a golden-ish liquid, perhaps a color similar to some of the tea Annie has made, although the mug is cold to the touch. She takes a sip and it is absolutely not tea. It's... well, she doesn't know what it is. All she really knows is that it's apparently fermented beer, whatever that could possibly mean. Is beer a thing that they ferment or is it a product of fermenting?

She continues to drink, trying with each sip to determine if she actually *wants* to keep drinking, and as she does so Essten and Leneat chat with the easy ebb and flow of long-time friends. They drag a couple platters of food closer to them and start eating, tossing bits of food between them and tearing things in half to share. Luzia has no idea where to even begin.

"What I wanna know," Leneat remarks, chewing on something purple and juicy, "is where they go when they're not on the hunt for the diamond."

Essten shrugs. "Maybe they just spend all day every day looking for it. Might be how they manage to keep up with us and the Vesperi, given that both our sides have the numbers advantage and they're just the one person."

"See, that's what I woulda thought, but then why do they bother nesting down?"

"Even a maniac's gotta rest their head once in awhile."

"I dunno, I think there's more to it than that." She drains her mug, wiping the foam off her lips with the back of her hand. Resting her arms on the table, she leans all the way forward and says, as though sharing a conspiracy, "I think they've got a base of operations. We've got the Deep, Vesperi have got the Mists. We all come and go from our homes. I think Carrion's doing the same. I think that we're just finding... It's like tree roots, right? I think we're just finding the thin little far-away roots, but somewhere out there is the base of their tree."

He scratches his chin. "Where would they be permanently holed up, though? I know, I know, it's somewhere in the human part of the Bastion, we *all* know. But where? Where would the humans never find them?"

"There are a large number of areas that have been sealed off for safety reasons," Luzia chimes in, glad to finally have something to contribute. "We keep watch on those sorts of places, but we don't exactly patrol them at all hours of the day. An Astrosi as reckless as Carrion likely wouldn't care about getting hit by a falling pole if it gave them a safe place to settle down. And that's not even taking into account the areas that we no longer have access to or the Fringes at the edge of the world."

"Maybe." He scratches again and then shrugs, playfully nudging Luzia's shoulder. "Ah, let's forget about it for now. Somber talk's for the morrow, and all that. Now's for *living*."

"Not to be rude, but… well, it's just…" If only there were a tactful way of saying this. "I didn't know anyone on the mission today. I'd never met any of you before. But you all must have known each other quite well. And two of your number *died* today. Why are you acting as though this is some sort of celebration?"

Leneat's smile is sad and sympathetic. "We celebrate the life we still have. And besides, it's not as though they're truly gone. Their bodies will decompose in our soil and breathe life into the earth, and then once we harvest our crops they will become part of us once again." She picks up a piece of fruit and sinks her teeth into it. "You see?"

Is that where Lysander deposited the bodies today? Did he bury them in the ground beneath the arboretum? Will Luzia walk past the dead when she returns to sleep in Annie's little dwelling tonight?

"Lighten up. It's not nearly as morbid as you think." Essten plucks something red from a platter and holds it out to her with a teasing look. "Here, try this. It'll clear out those thoughts in an instant."

"What is it?" she asks.

"Called a pepper. A ghost one, since we're talking about the dead and all."

She's about to take it when Leneat slaps it out of Essten hand. "Hey now, don't torture her," she laughs. "Bastion doesn't have spices or anything. You give her a ghost pepper to start with and you're going to burn her face off." To Luzia, she promises in a low drawl, "Don't worry, I'll get you something way better than that. This is your first time here, right? You deserve to start with something nice and relaxing and *sweet*."

"The tone in which you said that sounds vaguely sexual," Luzia automatically replies before she can think better of it.

Leneat snorts in amusement. "It wasn't meant to be, although I've never turned down a good time." Before Luzia can try to conjure up a response, Leneat hands her a sort of brownish square. "Give that a try."

It's a bit oily in Luzia's hand, the brown stuff caking a little on her fingers when she prods at it. It squishes easily too, although it does, as promised, smell quite sweet. When she bites into it, she makes an embarrassing squeak of a noise. There's a richness to the sweet, a bitterness to it, something that's absolutely divine. Instead of just being the round, plain candies that are occasionally rationed out to children in the Bastion, this is chewy and dense and packed with flavor. She polishes it off in four bites.

"That's... incredible," she says, licking the residue off her fingers. "What are they? What are they made of? Can I have another?"

"Sure. They're brownies, by the way. I guess you've never had chocolate before either, huh?"

Leneat hands her a second one and she scarfs that down just as quickly. That bittersweet flavor gets stuck between her teeth and coats her tongue, giving her the pleasure of tasting it long after she's finished the treat itself. She finishes the rest of her beer afterwards, which washes away the last of the brownie taste and leaves her craving another. The third one is just as good as the first two.

"Um." Essten clears his throat, stopping Leneat from automatically giving her a fourth. "I, uh, I think you might wanna... slow down."

Leneat looks down at the brownie and then back up at Luzia. "Oh, right. You're human."

"How is that relevant?" Luzia asks.

"Means your tolerance for certain things might be a *biiiiiiit* different than ours. Don't worry, we're gonna take great care of you. Just relax and enjoy the party. There's more food and drink to try than you can possibly taste in only a single evening, but that's no reason not to get started."

CHAPTER ELEVEN

A deluge of icy water drags Luzia violently from her slumber.

"Wakey-wakey, dumbass," Annie says, standing in front of her with a now-empty bucket propped on one hip. "Now, what lesson did we learn, hm?"

Luzia has never before craved the sweet release of death, but there's a first time for everything. A hammer is cracking her skull open and her skin is cold and clammy, bathed in a thick coating of sweat that not even the water managed to remove.

Flashes of last night return to her, images of all manner of horrors – faces melting and the Eoi turning into formless creatures, and through it all she'd been so certain that the entire world was stalking her. Now she can recall Essten and Leneat promising her endlessly that it was all in her head, but the tremors still linger in her hands. Carrion had been in her hallucinations too, slipping between dancing Eoi to laugh and wink at her, as though trying to lure her into chasing after them.

"Hnng," is the only pained sound that manages to escape her chapped lips.

"The lesson is," Annie says in the pointed and enunciated manner in which one speaks to a child, "never consume the food or drink of the Eoi. There's a reason I do all my own cooking, you know."

Luzia can only groan again in response.

"Well? Get up! We have work to do and the day will start even if you don't want it to." Clearly Luzia looks just as pathetic as she feels, for Annie stares up and the ceiling and some of the grumpiness slides out of her posture. "This was your mistake and I ain't gonna baby you, but... Eh, it's not like anyone warned you. I'll make you some soup."

Soup sounds nice, she thinks miserably.

The soup *is* nice. Unfortunately, her mouth is dry as dust and she cannot taste even a single spoonful. The moment her bowl is empty, Annie drags her sorry ass out of the living unit and once more into the unpleasantly bright arboretum.

How does Annie keep time down here? The lights never change as they do in the normal, wonderfully non-hallucinatory, human Bastion. Perhaps Annie has simply become accustomed to it. How long has she been here, actually? She said she'd come here to save her father's life, but that doesn't exactly give any indicator of time. She's been here long enough to become highly skilled, but Luzia also doesn't know how fast a learner she is.

Only once they're walking through a section shaded by tall trees does Luzia have the capacity to croak out, "Annie?"

"Hm?" Annie shoves a handful of dead plants into the heavy disposal basket she's had Luzia carry. "What? Spit it out, I ain't got all day."

"When did you leave the Bastion? That is to say... how long have you been down here?"

Annie's shears pause mid-snip. "Those are two different questions," she says, oddly calm. "Pick one."

"Um." Luzia doesn't see how different they could be. Unless it took Annie awhile to reach the Deep after leaving the Bastion. "The second?"

"I've been in the Deep for seventy-one years, five months, and twenty days," she says, still too calm. "Give or take."

Luzia's eyes widen. That number is far higher than she would have guessed, even in her most generous of mental estimates. "You've spent your whole life down here? You must have been a child when you came."

Annie shrugs and finishes cutting the dead flower from the bush, albeit with a rather aggressive snip. "I was ten. I wanted more than anything to save my father, but that doesn't mean it was a rational choice. Children are rarely rational."

Just as she'd imagined new faces onto the Eoi last night, now too does she see a different face superimposed over Annie's. Only this time it's Stazi, with his cheeks still round with baby fat and the horror of his eyes shrouded with the same jaded annoyance that Annie carries around with her at all times. Does she even remember the Bastion at this point? Would Stazi have forgotten the world beyond the Deep as well, had Luzia not been there to trade places with him?

"Can I ask... how did your father take it?" she asks tentatively. "I don't even want to think about what it would have felt like if Stazi had given himself up for me."

Annie laughs. It's not a sound that fits her. "Let's just say... he changed a lot."

"I'm sorry. At least he lived?"

Another bitter bark of a laugh, and that's the only response Luzia gets.

The better part of an hour is spent in tense silence, with Annie simply handing her things or having her trail along as a mobile trash bin. She can't really get mad about it. It *was* a rude question, all things considered, although selfishly she is glad to have gotten an answer. Annie is the only other human down here that she's spoken to, after all. The only one who could understand what Luzia is going through.

Unlike the past times Annie has taken Luzia on these rounds, today the arboretum is not empty. A few Eoi wearing those notable lab coats are standing around a cluster of fruit trees, muttering amongst themselves while they take various measurements and notations. For whatever reason, Annie seems determined to avoid them, instantly turning about-face and marching off in the other direction upon seeing them.

"Are those scientists doing anything particularly dangerous?" Luzia asks, her paranoia finally strong enough to break through the awkward silence.

Annie shakes her head. "No."

"Then what are they doing?"

"Ugh. If you *must* know, they're just developing a new breed of what they're referring to as 'apricot grapes'. Pretty much every single one of the Eoi is working on some project like that or another. Tweaking and perfecting every grain of wheat or patch of moss. No clue why, so don't bother asking me. The queen doesn't order 'em to do it and it's not like there's a shortage of food down here. It's like they have a bloody compulsion for it or something."

"Everyone's like that?"

"Not everyone. Only most. Some do other kinds of production and some are soldiers..." Annie trails off to look at something behind Luzia. "Well, speak and one shall appear, I guess."

Essten is walking up to them, bearing a sheepish wiggle of a smile. To Luzia's shock, he is no longer leaning on a crutch and the brace on his leg is entirely gone. He doesn't even acknowledge Annie beyond a quickly aborted glance in her direction. Instead, he speaks to Luzia and Luzia alone.

"I just wanted to say sorry about last night. Leneat and I got carried away. It was our bad. How're you holding up?"

"Currently existing," is the most generous assessment she can give.

"Eyouch."

"What *happened* to your leg?"

"I'm Astrosi, ain't it? We heal fast. Very fast." He clears his throat before sticking his thumb behind him. "Okay, I didn't come here *just* to apologize. Lysander is asking for you. He looked pretty unhappy, so you might want to hustle to see what he wants."

"Oh." An angry Lysander doesn't sound pleasant, especially not while she's feeling so poorly. "Where is he? I'll go at once."

"In the throne room. He said he'd be there, with the queen. I can take you, if you haven't finished mapping out the lay of this place yet."

"Thank you."

Somehow, despite the brevity of their conversation, Annie has already shuffled off by the time Luzia turns back to say farewell. What caused this strange aversion Annie has to the Astrosi? There's only one exception to this trend, and that is the affection with which she treats Sef.

Essten is sheepish and relatively quiet as he leads Luzia through the halls of the Deep, only speaking up to point out the occasional landmark, for which she is more than a little grateful. The arboretum, she learns, is nine hundred and thirty-eight steps and twelve corridors away from the entrance to the dining hall she was in last night. The endless vines covering the walls make it a challenge to remember visual cues, but her map on her tablet grows nonetheless and starts to resemble something more useful than not.

When she's ushered into the throne room, it's just the same as it was when she'd first fallen into it, the only difference being the absence of people. She can only assume that last time everyone had been dying to catch a glimpse of Carrion, either to wish the bastard dead or out of twisted curiosity.

Sef sits upon her throne once more, her delicate hands folded on her lap and her long hair trailing down into the grass until it appears to vanish into the carpet of greenery. Before her stands Lysander with a deep-set scowl that only gets worse when he catches sight of Luzia. Despite requesting her presence, he clearly isn't happy about having to do so.

With an elegant sweep of her hand, Sef gestures for Luzia to stand before her. "I thank you for your hasty arrival. Essten, you may leave us."

Essten bows low and quick. "Yes, my queen."

When it is just the three of them, Sef begins, her smooth and melodic voice soothing on Luzia's lingering headache, "In our efforts to remove the threat posed by Carrion, we have reached out to attempt to fill in the gaps. To see when they began their quest of terrorism. Once, uncountably many years ago, they served in King Ari's court, little more than a mere foot soldier. And then something caused them to snap, to send them down their current path, something powerful enough to change them down to their core."

"I still say they're enough of a bastard that they were always like this," Lysander grumbles.

"You are too young." Sef's tone is just as amiable as always, and yet there is something about that sentence that feels like a slap on the wrist. "You do not recall who they were in times long past. They may not have served in our court during this time, but *I* trust King Ari's assessment of their past character."

He bends to her reprimand at once. "Of course, my queen. I apologize. I didn't mean to question you."

"'Tis all forgiven. The task I have assigned is one that I believe only the both of you must undertake. Indeed, additional forces would be a detriment in this. In our attempt to uncover King Ari's secret, numbers will serve us ill. One human and one Astrosi may have a chance, should fate and skill align. Ziane, King Ari has humans amidst his court, as do we. Walk amongst them. Learn what rumors the Vesperi's loose tongues may have dropped."

Just the two of them? Luzia may trust in Lysander's skill, but she doesn't know if she can trust in her own. She's not a spy, and she knows that with him menacingly breathing down her neck it's more than likely to throw her off her nonexistent game. Having a buffer in the form of Essten or Leneat would be more than welcome. Even after everything that happened the previous night, they were still better company than Lysander, and Essten *did* apologize.

"I don't mean to be rude, and of course I'm glad for this chance to fulfill our deal, but if you need a human capable of blending into the background of an Astrosi, erm, realm or court, whichever term you prefer," she tries, tripping over the words, "then wouldn't it be a better idea to send Annie?"

"No."

The utterly flat and stone-cold rejection doesn't come from Sef. It comes from Lysander, and it comes instantly.

Luzia sucks in a breath and murmurs, "All right, then."

"We are only doing as you requested," Sef reminds her, almost softly. "You pleaded so ardently to be allowed to hunt down Carrion in exchange for familial visitation. Do you not think it contradictory to protest being given this specific opportunity?"

"No, you're right," she admits, staring down at her feet. "I'm sorry. I do, I really do, it's not that at all. I want this, I *truly* want this. I was just... confused."

"Confusion is understandable," Sef graciously allows. "Lysander..." Here she sighs, as though speaking the words pains her. "We are in reluctant need of further salts. Your mission is thus twofold: to trade for our court and to distract from Ziane's efforts. You know King Ari's habits, you know his personality. We trust that you will make the needed opportunity."

Lysander bows his head. "It will be done, my queen."

"Then go with our blessing."

He grabs hold of Luzia's arm on his way out, practically shoving her out of the throne room head first. Once the doors have slid shut with a hiss of air, he turns to her and opens his mouth, but for once she beats him to the punch.

"What did the queen mean by 'salts'?" she quickly asks. "Does this mean that there is established trading between both of your, um, courts? Just surprised, since it all seemed rather more hostile to me. And what precisely is the implication of 'making needed opportunities'? By definition, an opportunity results from lucky circumstances or chance, not deliberate design, so that's a bit contradictory–"

"Ziane," Lysander cuts her off, "shut the fuck up."

She closes her mouth.

"Better. I'll pack my kit and meet you by Lift Zero, got it?"

She opens her mouth again.

"One question!" he snaps, angrily jabbing a single finger at her. "You only get the *one*!"

"Is there somewhere I can get new clothes?" she decides to ask. It's a lower priority, but if she's trying to not stand out like a sore thumb, it is an important one. "Only I've been wearing the same thing since I arrived and it's beginning to show."

"Fine. New clothes, whatever."

"Also I don't know where Lift Zero is, so it would be quite a challenge for me to meet you there."

"Of course you don't," he mutters. "Just follow me, then."

At least this time he allows her to scurry along behind him without physically dragging her. She appreciates the concession to her dignity.

Lysander leads her through the halls with a fury, making more than one Eoi leap out of his way and, she notices, one human – or so she assumes by their short hair. The room Lysander takes her to is not unlike a supply depot, albeit smaller and with walls covered in curtains of bright flowers.

He tosses a bundle of cloth at her. "Here. You smell like shit."

"Sorry." She quickly begins stripping off her human clothing with gusto. It doesn't really matter to her that she's not alone as years of changing into various hazard suits in front of her fellow First Responders has given her a near total immunity to the embarrassments of nudity. "If my smell bothered you, why didn't you offer me new clothing without my requesting it?"

He throws a container of some kind into a satchel with excessive aggression. "I'm not your fucking babysitter."

"Of course not." She pauses in the middle of tugging on a clean shirt as a deeply depressing thought worms its way into her head. "Although in some ways I am entirely reliant upon the Eoi for nearly everything I require to survive. Food, water, clothing..."

"Don't be such a wet blanket. You were entirely reliant on other people up in the Bastion, too. It was just the Office of the Administrator or whatever the fuck system you humans use to determine who gets how much of what. If anything, you're better off now than you were up there. Here, you can go personally ask our queen for more if you're really that fucking desperate, instead of dealing with, like, a hundred different stupid humans with a hundred other stupid humans working for each of them. So suck it up."

"That's not precisely an accurate description of how the Office of the Administrator functions—"

"Ask me if I give a shit," he replies, rolling his eyes.

She just holds up her hands in surrender and backs off. After another couple moments of tense preparation, Lysander strides out of the room, beckoning for her to follow him, scowling when it takes her more than half a second to do so. Something about the direction he currently leads her is different than before, and it takes her a moment to realize what it is, but when she does, her curiosity – and anxiety – are piqued. There are no Astrosi in lab coats or humans dressed in casual garb as Lysander takes her up to a higher floor. The only people she sees are soldiers, and they don't mill about so much as stand stiffly at guard posts or march from one area to the next with purpose.

Though Lysander is in no way a beacon of safety, she finds herself shuffling a bit closer to him regardless. At least she knows that he's not about to cause her serious bodily harm, and the rest of these intimidating faces are unknowns. If she so much as breathes incorrectly, who knows what they might do.

Eventually, their path ends before a set of double doors that are not entirely unlike a lift entrance, albeit one that towers above her and has a truly intimidating number of security locks and stabilizers hooked up to it in a web of regal cables.

"Going up," Lysander says to the two guards standing at attention by the entrance. "Our queen sent over instructions, hm?"

One of them nods.

In silent unison, the two guards turn to wall-mounted control panels and begin to punch in codes. Slowly, with a hiss of released pressure and a *ka-chunk* of metal, the various locks and barriers around the lift entrance release and slide apart. The doors open, and before Luzia can muster enough courage to enter, Lysander shoves her in.

"Close it up!" Lysander orders, striding in after her. "Launch when ready."

Luzia manages to straighten up just as the doors slide closed. From outside, she can hear the faint whirring of mechanisms as the locks seal them in, a clicking of the stabilizers as they prepare for activation.

A hand is shoved at her and she startles, looking up at Lysander with a pinch in her brow.

"Shut up and take my hand," he grumbles. "Might wanna close your eyes, too."

"Why?"

"You know how you were able to walk down to the Deep? I'm assuming that bastard Carrion left the way open for you. Otherwise, your pea-sized human brain never would have found it. But apart from a couple of... enthusiastic responses from our guards, you were pretty much fine."

"Well, yes, I suppose."

"If you walked up to the Mists the human way, it probably would be the same, or thereabouts. I don't know," he adds with a shrug. "Not like I've ever bothered to go up there the slow way. But think of going up or down like sticking your hand into a pool of water. Easy – you just get a bit wet but your hand goes right in. Now imagine falling into that pool from thousands of feet up. Not so soft anymore, huh? This lift has got to punch through the barriers between our realms and the Bastion. It's all water, but we're taking the violent route."

She gulps and then asks, "Barriers? What barriers are there, other than distance?"

"Ask our queen if you're that desperate to know. I couldn't explain it if I tried."

"You don't know?"

"I don't need to. All I need to know is they're there." Another whirr and he extends his hand with a glare. "Before you get any ideas, I don't *care* that it'd be unpleasant for you. But you can't be holding me back and I don't want your pathetic human ass passing out on me the moment the lift starts up. So shut up and accept my help."

Under other circumstances, she'd be more inclined to believe that *he'd* be the one making things unpleasant for her, but she can't deny that it would be of great inconvenience to him were she to faint. Although she likes to imagine that she's got a stronger constitution than that. Perhaps not, however, if these unseen barriers are truly as potent as he claims, and she's quite tempted to ask more about–

He shakes his hand again and she in turn shakes the questions from her head. There's no time.

She grabs onto him just as the lift floor lurches.

The phrase 'ears popped' is a very useful one. With most priority lifts she's taken, her ears do indeed pop – first a tightening pressure in her jaw and eustachian tube, then its distinctive release. This is not that. For a second, just a split second, a bare blink of an eye, her eardrums stretch to the point of bursting. It's as though the flesh and muscle and sinew is being rent apart, torn and ripping and cracking her jaw into sharp shards of bone, and then...

And then it's gone.

Reedy, rough vines have snaked out from under Lysander's sleeve, curling around their entwined hands and latching on to her wrist as though barely repressing the desire to bury into her flesh. And yet, despite the certainty of bruising, she feels no pain. Like pus from a wound, the pressure in her ears and the weight of the lift rocketing upwards drain away, leaving her simply... existing. There is calm, at first. Then an ache in her stomach, a gnawing starvation that lashes out with defensive fury, demanding and sobbing.

Her knees tremble, every inch of her body teetering on the edge of being swept away in the timelessness of that vacuum. It's utterly foreign to her, so... it's coming from Lysander, not her. It's his emotion, his sensations, his torment. He lives like this?

With a smooth *whrrrrrr* of noise and a gentle shudder, the lift comes to a stop. The moment it does, Lysander yanks his hand away, ripping the vines and the sensations from her skin.

"We're here," he grumbles, turning his head to face the now-opening door. "Don't talk to anyone who's not human, don't give anyone your real name, and for the love of our queen, don't smoke a single thing they give you. Apart from that, welcome to the Mists, home of the Vesperi. Now let's go. This place is fucking shit."

CHAPTER TWELVE

At first glance, the Mists couldn't be more different from the Deep. No plants carpet the floor. No vines dangle from the ceilings. Even the light fixtures seem dimmer, a gloom having settled over the place. The Deep can be dark in places, but there are so many rooms filled with light designed to coax various plants to grow faster or stronger. Luzia isn't really sure on the details; all she knows is that the result is a place filled with light and patches of warm darkness. This place is filled with a grayed-out haze, a hushed and stifled silence, a wet chill that permeates her very bones.

And yet the more she looks, the more she can find similarities. While the Bastion is old, always requiring repair, and filled with more than a few buildings in the middle of being shored up, the Deep is not. It doesn't look new, not exactly, but there are no cracked lights, no damaged walls, no sense of decay. That same cleanliness is present here, the same maze of corridors instead of proper streets, as though the space up here is smaller somehow.

If she hadn't felt the way the lift rocketed them upwards, she thinks she'd be forgiven for thinking she'd just wandered into a new hall of the Deep.

"Stop gawking," Lysander snaps.

"Sorry."

She follows after him as he begins to make his way through this dim hall. As the name implies, a thick carpet of mist covers the ground, making it difficult to see anything below her knees. It's hard for her to say exactly why, but something about this mist feels unnatural. Maybe it's the way it clings to her limbs as she walks, or the heaviness of it, like a weight around her ankles. It reminds her of the mist that she'd waded through on her first trip to the Deep, when she'd followed Carrion down.

"I think Carrion can create mist like this," she realizes. "I don't know how, but…"

"Of course they can," Lysander replies, like she's an idiot for only figuring that out now. "The bastard was originally one of the Vesperi before they snuck out from under Ari's nose and fucked off to cause trouble in our queen's throneworld. You don't lose your talents when you go rogue. Regrettably."

How do their talents work, exactly? So much of Luzia's knowledge of the Astrosi is rumor and gossip, and what she has learned from her time in the Deep isn't sufficient to explain all that they can do. She's so tempted to ask, but if she prods Lysander with one more question right now he's liable to toss her back into that odd lift and leave her to suffer on the ride down.

"The first security gate is right around the corner." Lysander takes another long stride to properly walk in front of her. "You're supposed to be my attendant, and that means you keep your head down and that annoying mouth shut, got it?"

"Loud and clear," she agrees.

Slowly, a figure becomes visible. A person is sitting on a stool by a door similar to the ones that lead up to the Deep. However, unlike the witty guards Luzia encountered in front of the Deep, this man doesn't seem the least bit concerned with the fact that two strangers are approaching.

He slouches over the stool like a well-worn blanket, a sleepy, heavy-lidded glaze over his eyes as he looks at Luzia and Lysander. Pinched between two of his fingers is a short, slender glass tube filled with a grayish gas that swirls around its confines like glittery soup. The man puts one end of the tube between his cracked lips and inhales. On the fluttering exhale, pale pink smoke pours from his lightly smiling mouth.

"Oh..." He does something odd with his lips and the next puff of pink smoke comes out in a circle that drifts teasingly towards Lysander. "If it isn't Sef's baby goon."

Lysander swats the pink smoke ring away from his face and retorts, "You're not important enough for me to know who you are."

"Fair 'nough." The guard peers at Luzia. "Who's she?"

"She carries my bags."

"That's nice. Would love one of those myself." After taking another puff on the glass tube, the guard lazily waves them forward. "Go on. Door's open."

As Luzia is not allowed to speak, she simply gives the guard a polite nod as she and Lysander pass, hoping that it does the same job as a thank you. Beyond the gate lies another lift, not unlike the one she had been pushed into by the Eoi guards when she'd initially stumbled into the Deep. This one, however, seems perfectly normal and not at all likely to be used to terrify a random human, and so she doesn't have any issue getting in next to Lysander and letting him operate the thing.

"I thought there would be more... well, more *security* at the security gate," Luzia remarks once the door has slid shut and the lift begins to peacefully drift upwards.

Lysander is even tenser than normal as he replies, "They don't need it. And they know who I am, more importantly."

The lift hums as it slows to a halt and Luzia is shortly thereafter shoved out by Lysander and then shuffled into his shadow.

Where the entrance to the Deep had opened up into an atrium bursting at the seams with the overwhelming lights and colors of every growing thing, dropping Luzia directly into the gateway of Sef's throneworld, into the court that she held and the realm that she ruled, this entrance to the Mists is a rush of gray haze and cacophonous sounds. A thick, almost tangible smell fills her nostrils, the astringent scent of chemicals and rubbing alcohol, and she can feel her nose attempt to crinkle back into her skull.

She and Lysander are standing on a balcony that seems to wrap around the vast chamber, every inch filled with Astrosi – or in this case, Vesperi, leaning against the railing or lounging on piles of cushions or observing whatever is going on below with great interest. Many of them puff on glass tubes similar to the one the guard was using, thin and dainty cylinders filled with smokes of varying colors and consistencies. Surely Lysander would have mentioned if those were dangerous, right? He'd warned her not to smoke anything they give her, but is it still possible that the fumes they're exhaling could somehow harm her? She tries to ask, only to get a very sharp glare from him in return before she can even fully open her mouth.

From below, cutting through the constant noise of this place, is the telling *vshhh* of a bayonet-rifle going off. A second later, half the crowd cheers, Vesperi sticking their necks out over the railing and craning to get a glimpse of whatever is happening down in the pit. Some sort of announcement is made, though Luzia can't make out the specific words.

Lysander points at a spot on the ground, waits for her to get in place and stand there obediently, and orders, "Don't cause any trouble. I need to let Ari's little fucking jester know I'm here."

Luzia plants her feet right where he demands, though she's a bit too close to the railing for her liking. "Jester?"

"Jess. He'll let Ari know I need an audience with him." He eyes the nearby Vesperi with acidic suspicion. "Remember, keep your fucking head down and don't go anywhere. And take this." He pulls a pocketknife from his coat and shoves it into her hands. "This shouldn't get violent, but if it does you had fucking better not die, because it'll be on my head if you do. I'll be back before you can get any bright ideas."

With that, Lysander abandons her amidst the Vesperi, his footsteps stamping against the metal grate floor as he pushes his way between chattering clusters of people.

Instinctively, Luzia shifts her weight from one foot to the other, getting a sense of the balcony's stability, the thickness of the metal beams, the size of the gaps in the grate. Her eyes flicker from person to person, inhuman Vesperi to Vesperi. They're similar to the Eoi in certain aspects, at least, with the same overlong hair and eccentric clothing, as though dressed in whatever washes up from the Bastion. The chief difference is the prevalence of their smoking devices and, she notices, more prominent musculature.

A *bang* rings out from the pit below, cutting through the haze that obscures sight and sound alike.

Luzia jumps, momentarily forgetting Lysander's instructions to stay right where she is in favor of taking those last few steps to approach the railing and join the Vesperi in peering over the edge into the fog. Down below is some kind of arena, all white floors and white walls, in better condition than most of the Bastion despite the constant mist that would normally cause rust. In the middle, two figures circle each other, one with a tight braid that swings like a pendulum as they walk and the other with their hair loose down to their knees. Both hold bayonet-rifles. Even in the mist, the lights are glaring enough to make the blades glint and the barrels flash as the combatants stare each other down.

Someone rests their arms against the railing next to Luzia. The newcomer is a man, probably in his fifties going by the strands of gray in his short hair. Short hair – human.

"Who's your bet?" he asks, looking down at the two Vesperi.

Is she supposed to pretend as though she's an Acolyte to the Vesperi, or is she supposed to go along with what Lysander said to the guard? She chews on the inside of her cheek and ends up saying, "I don't think I have enough information to make a decision on that one. Who are they?"

"Fair enough." The man points to the one with a braid. "She's one of our king's newest gladiators." His finger turns to the other. "He's untested – no wins under his belt just yet."

Luzia nods, as though she understands more than just the gist. "And, um... who's your bet, then?"

"My vape's on the glad. Our king wouldn't have let her get through all those gauntlets unless she was capable."

"Doesn't that make it an unfair match-up?"

He laughs. "Does it matter? The only thing on the line is a brief second of ego."

There's another *bang* and, down in the pit, the two combatants rush at each other.

The woman slides forward to come up on one knee and aims three quick shots at her opponent, three fast *vshhh* bursts of the laser aimed at legs, chest, and head. With a move so fast Luzia's eyes can barely track it, the untested combatant holds his rifle up to block, the lasers making no dent in the blade. Fascinating – whatever material it's made of must be from Era One if it's capable of withstanding something that smoked a target dummy so effectively. He's smart enough not to let the woman get off another series of shots, closing the distance to swing out with his rifle, using it solely as a knife, and the two meet with a clash of steel.

"Vesperi can do odd things with mist," Luzia wonders. "Why are neither of them…?"

"It's banned, innit?" the man next to her says with a shrug.

Below, metal clangs against metal.

The woman takes a swipe at her opponent that pushes him out of their close-quarters engagement, forcing him to leap to the side or else get gutted. She follows it up with a shot to his feet that makes him stumble. He doesn't fall, instead jumping backwards and shooting right at her head. It nearly hits her straight between the eyes, were it not for the impressive way in which her spine bends backwards right before the shot goes off, reading his aim in a way that makes Luzia audibly gasp.

She cannot help being reminded of the effortless way in which Carrion killed. "Aren't they worried they'll kill each other?" she asks her fellow watcher.

The man laughs. "It takes a lot to kill one of the 'strosi, and a bit of a scratch-up is just character building. You're new here, ain't you? It took me a bit to get used to this too. I've heard that the Eoi aren't as quick to fight, but here they love a good scar or two."

"Yes," she agrees, not technically lying. "I'm new."

"Keep your ears open and your head down, that's my advice," he tells her. "And don't let them talk you into getting down in the pit – *oh*!" He winces as the crowd cries out. "That looked nasty."

The untested man down below is bleeding profusely from the nose and staggering back from his opponent. After a moment of clutching at his face while the woman stands before him with her bayonet rifle still at the ready, he taps the ground and yells something that's quite distorted by his injury but is unmistakably a call of surrender. A cheer rings out, and there's another announcement of some sort coming from a Vesperi on a mid-level balcony holding something not unalike a megaphone.

"Bad luck, there," the man next to Luzia remarks. "He should have wagered for more shots. He only had half a clip where she was running two full magazines."

Did the two not enter the arena with the same amount of charge in their bayonet-rifles? It seems quite unfair if they didn't, and she would have thought that, with the Astrosi's insistence on contracts, they would have some sense of fairness. Although perhaps there's a different sort of contract at play here. The man did say that the two were 'wagering' for it. Perhaps that's the bargain. You get only as much as you're willing to give.

A door slides open on the edge of the arena and Luzia's heart immediately sinks.

Gasps ripple through the crowd as a Vesperi shoves Lysander through the door and sends him sprawling flat on his back into the pit.

CHAPTER THIRTEEN

"An Eoi?" The man next to Luzia whistles, low and surprised. "Wonder what they're doing here."

One of the nearby Vesperi has apparently caught a snippet of what the man said and leans over to explain, "That's Lysander. He's Sef's pet. No clue why he's up here, unless it's to bargain with our king. Whatever it is, he shouldn't have pissed off Jess."

Luzia looks back into the pit to see a man stalking into the arena after Lysander. Lysander takes the humiliation of being knocked over for only a second before he's flipping back onto his feet, shoulders squared and chin held up in a way that's clearly designed to try and grab at dominance. The other man – Jess – is shorter and skinnier than Lysander's bulky frame, but that doesn't seem to be any deterrent.

"You arrogant son of a bitch!" Jess snaps, and the fog seems to curl around him, as though drawn to his anger. "You really think you can waltz in here like you own the place and insult our king? You think to demand his time, as though you are somehow more important than his duty to his throneworld?"

Lysander draws himself up to his full, intimidating height. "Get off your fucking soapbox, you pathetic little jester."

Jess snorts. "That's rich, coming from a dog like you."

Luzia's mouth twists in curiosity and she asks, "What's a dog?"

The Vesperi next to them just shrugs, fiddling with their glass tube. "It's just an old insult. Think it comes from 'dogged', you know?"

Should Luzia keep her head down and stay where she is, as instructed? Or should she try to help? She can remember the strange coughing and suffocation that had overcame her the last time she tried to disobey orders, but technically speaking Lysander ordered her only to stay out of trouble, not to stay where she is. It had been implied, but not stated outright. That seems to be the sort of technicality that rules over the Astrosi throneworlds more than Sef or the mysterious King Ari do.

Down below, the insults have continued to fly, with Lysander unable to control his temper, Jess all but smoking at the ears, and more and more Vesperi drawn in by the unexpected commotion. The most concern any of them show is mild confusion, and that is overweighted by jubilant grins and enthused chatter.

Jess flings out his arm to point to the Vesperi that's been making announcements. The Vesperi's head bobs up and down in an overeager nod, and he activates some sort of wall-mounted mechanism that Luzia can't see in all the mist. Two circles appear on the arena floor, sliding aside to allow a pillar of some kind to rise from each. Both are about waist high, with a container on top and a bayonet-rifle holstered inside the stand itself.

"Money where your mouth is, motherfucker," Jess snaps.

Lysander spits at his feet. "I win, and I get to waste all the fucking time I like with your damn king."

"I win, and I flay you before kicking your sorry ass down to the Deep."

The blood flees from Luzia's face. "Oh, *shit*," she mumbles under her breath.

This is absolutely not what Sef asked them to do, and if Lysander gets kicked out, Luzia will either have to reveal herself to get kicked out too or risk making her way back to the Deep alone. No doubt if she fails to return when Lysander does there will be some kind of consequence, even if she doesn't really understand the what or how of it. And also, on a selfish level, if Lysander pisses off everyone here, there's no way that Ari will give them even a shred of information about Carrion, and Luzia will be no closer to fulfilling her bargain with Sef and seeing her family again.

Jess reaches for the pillar and withdraws a small knife. "Make your wager."

There looks to be a matching blade on the pillar next to Lysander, but he doesn't take it. Instead he reaches for his hair and seems to pluck a couple of strands. He places the hair in the container and there is a faint light. Then a hum. Then a tiny smidge of blue, only barely visible, appears on the bayonet-rifle's charge gauge.

The announcer in the lower balcony cries out on their megaphone, *"One of ten! Lysander of the Eoi lowballing it this time, folks!"*

The man next to Luzia widens his eyes. "That's a downright *rude* wager."

Down below, Jess uses the knife to cut off a full, thick lock of hair from behind his ear, easily four feet long. He places it in the container and it disintegrates into nothingness a second before there's the hum of the charger. A far thicker line of blue light appear on his bayonet-rifle's gauge. A number of the Vesperi in the crowd whistle and applaud, presumably complementing a much more impressive wager.

"*Six of ten!*" the announcer cheers. "*Now that's a sure victory for our Jess if I've ever seen one!*"

Lysander and Jess face each other. The pillars slide back into the ground, leaving the arena ready for a fight. Lysander holds his rifle in two hands in that solid soldiers' stance that he employed both in training Luzia and in the fight against Carrion. All business, all anger. In contrast, Jess rests his own weapon over his shoulder, limbs loose and limber and ready to lash out.

The announcer presses the megaphone right up against their mouth as they shout, "*Match: Break!*"

No time wasted by Lysander, as he barrels forward like a battering ram. Jess proves himself to be as lithe as he looks when he twists out of the way, letting Lysander rush right past him. He finally takes his rifle off his shoulders and fires off a quick shot at Lysander's exposed back. The laser beam barely grazes Lysander's side, singeing a bit of fabric but no more, because even though he's bulky, he's fast, and he's already turning on the balls of his feet and moving out of the way before the shot can fully hit him.

With such a low charge on his rifle, he can't afford to start shooting and hoping, so he instead attacks with the rifle's blade. He sweeps out to cut at Jess's torso and then a moment later follows up with a slash to the head. Those two quick strikes don't make Jess so much as blink, and the Vesperi meets Lysander's next attack with his own blade, metal clashing. It's not even. Of course it's not. With every clash of the bayonets, Jess gets off a shot or two, keeping Lysander dancing on his toes, the bright flash of lasers leaving thin, burnt lines across Lysander's thighs, arms, and chest, each so close to being lethal if it weren't for Lysander's quick reflexes. Just being able to hold his ground without shooting is impressive, but impressing the watching Vesperi isn't the same as winning the fight.

In one swift movement, Lysander goes low and sweeps his leg across the ground, kicking Jess's feet out from underneath him, and as Jess stumbles, Lysander shoots. Luzia holds her breath, hands clasped in front of her mouth. Lysander's shot is true, the beam steady and straight – and then Jess drops to one knee just in time for the shot to sear over his head and miss.

"That's empty for Lysander!" The announcer's roar is only barely audible over the crowd's. *"Is it the end for him, or will he wager up again to stay in the game?"*

Despite the fury in both combatants' eyes, they begrudgingly return to the positions in which they started. Those pillars rise up from the floor again, awaiting further offerings. Jess checks the charge on his rifle, stows it, drops a few more strands of hair into the container, and takes back the recharged weapon.

Lysander is holding onto the knife with a death grip, veins of his jaw popping as his pride refuses to surrender on either front – the fight itself, or the relinquishing of his hair.

"How do I get down there?" Luzia asks the man next to her. She's already mapping out the direction Lysander had first walked off in, figuring out the quickest way down to the pit that doesn't involve jumping to her death.

"Uh…" The man frowns at her. "Why'd you *want* to get down there–"

"Never mind, I'll figure it out."

Luzia runs. Amidst the throngs of excited watchers and the haze of mist, she takes off in the direction Lysander had gone, scanning for stairs or lifts or ladders until she practically runs off the edge of a stairwell. She flies down the steps, skidding to a stop at the bottom, nearly knocking over the Vesperi leaning against the low balcony there. This level is only a few feet above the arena, and it affords her a better view of the fighters, of the way in which Lysander stares at the knife in his hand with frozen, stubborn anger.

She still has the small pocketknife that Lysander gave her. It's a basic thing, something similar to the one she carried in her standard First Responder kit. The blade is sharp and undamaged, and with one smooth cut she shears a clump of hair from behind her ear. Her fingers curl into a fist around the hunk of dark curls.

Mumbling an apology under her breath, Luzia shoves a couple of Vesperi out of her way and sticks her arm out over the balcony.

"Lysander!" she screams over the cacophony. "Lysander – here, take it!"

At that last shout, he thankfully hears her and turns around. His mouth opens, probably to say something derogatory, but she just shakes her arm again and his eyes narrow. He's close enough to this balcony that he only has to take a few steps to get to her, and then he just reaches up and snatches the hair from her hand without a single word of gratitude.

The announcer pumps their fist in the air as Lysander drops Luzia's hair into the container and charges up his bayonet-rifle. *"And Lysander is back in the game!"*

There's a chorus of cheers and boos from the crowd, and one of the Vesperi near Luzia shakes their head and gives her a dirty look.

"Nothing in the rules against it, folks! Although unusual, it's as we always say: If it ain't banned, it's a banger! Now, on your mark…"

Jess's features are half slack in surprise and half wrinkled in disgust. "You let a human wager for you? I knew the Deep didn't duel often enough, but that's fucked up, Lysander."

"Get set!"

"If it ain't banned," Lysander snaps back with a sneer.

"Aaaaaannnnnnnd… BREAK!"

This time, Lysander doesn't simply rush in head first. He paces, claiming the center of the arena as his own space, eyeing up Jess properly instead of with blind anger. It is Jess that makes the first move. He opens with two quick shots, one to Lysander's feet and the other to his shoulder, as though his goal is just to test Lysander, to see how quick he is on his feet after the brief wagering period. An evaluation, designed to make Lysander dance.

Anger sparks on Lysander's face, the twitch of his jaw visible to Luzia even through the lingering fog, and that's when his patience snaps. It was a nice change of pace while it lasted, she supposes. He opens fire, a series of short, quick bursts of the bayonet's laser, the extra charge from Luzia's hair letting him be more aggressive than before. With each shot, he takes a step forward, closing in on Jess but unable to pin the man down properly. The blade on Jess's bayonet lights up with a crackling aura of electricity that catches the lasers, sending sparks of energy flying as he flicks them aside like they're nothing.

Jess is stronger than he looks. But how, exactly, does the hair factor in? Does someone decide how much is worth what and grants charge accordingly?

When she leans closer to get a better look, a pair of strong hands slaps her back and someone else shoves her over the railing. She has enough instinct to tuck her shoulder in and turn the fall into a roll, but the arena floor is hard and unforgiving and the impact sends a wave of pain through her bones. An unpleasant ache lingers in her muscles as she pushes herself up, fingers slipping against the ground as she sputters and drags in a breath of heavy, soupy air.

"It's your fight too!" one of the Vesperi on the balcony cheers.

Another whoops in excitement and chimes in, "Your hair, your wager!"

The vibrating hiss of a laser rings in Luzia's ears and she freezes, eyes sliding up to see a smoking hole in the ground before her. Jess has his bayonet aimed at her, the tip still glowing from the shot. With that threat, she doesn't dare protest as he grabs her by the wrist and hauls her up, holding her in front of him with her arm painfully pinned behind her back.

"You ain't a part of this," Jess warns. For once, he isn't all anger and irritation, though he certainly glowers when he yells up at the crowd that pushed her, "Now which of you dumb motherfuckers thought that tossing her in was—"

Lysander tackles him mid-sentence.

Jess's hand on Luzia's wrist is ripped away and she staggers forward as he is thrown backwards. The two fighters crumple to the ground a foot and a half away. Wild punches and kicks are thrown between the two of them, their bayonet rifles too long and barely usable in such close quarters, both of them trying multiple awkward and failed attempts to stab one another. As fast as she can, Luzia puts a good few feet of distance between the two of them, her hands empty of anything she could possibly use to pull them apart, and nothing in the arena that could help her.

Out of desperation, she turns to the announcer in the hopes of begging them to stop the fight, but they are not looking at the roaring crowd or the scrappy melee. They're instead looking at a screen on the wall, pale-faced and nodding their head rapidly.

Luzia's half-decided to run to them for help regardless when they grab their megaphone and hastily yell into it, *"Fight's over! That's it – it's done, it's been called!"*

The second the announcement is made, Jess goes limp and uses Lysander's surprise to wriggle out from underneath him. Jess leaps back like he's been burned and holds his hands up in a show of nonaggression. It takes Lysander a moment to realize that he's no longer fighting anyone, then he slowly stands up, glaring at Jess, Luzia, the announcer, and even the arena walls with great suspicion.

At the far end of the arena, a door slides open and two soldiers march in, one moving to flank Lysander and the other looming over Luzia. They're armed, too, and she can't help noticing their rifles are at full charge. She immediately raises her hands in surrender and silently pleads for Lysander to do the same. He doesn't, that same stupid stubbornness keeping his hands fisted at his sides, but at least he doesn't attempt to fight the guards. And when the guards order them out of the arena with sharp gestures of their rifles, Lysander follows behind Luzia without starting anything.

Boos and jeers from the crowd boom in Luzia's ears until the arena door slams shut behind them and the sound of the pit is reduced to a distant buzz and vibration beneath her feet as the sheer volume of the noise ripples through the thick walls.

"Where are you taking us?" she asks one of the guards, her mouth dry.

Out of the corner of his mouth, Lysander hisses, "Shut. *Up.*" He stares straight ahead at the lift that they're being led to. "We're getting what we wanted."

They are ushered into the lift, the two guards standing ominously behind them like statues. It doesn't rocket around like the unique lift to get up here did, or like many of the other lifts that Luzia has used since going to the Deep; nor does it jolt and jerk as the lifts do in many parts of the Bastion. This one is slow and smooth and silent, and if it weren't for the wall panel showing the floor number ticking up, she might not have been certain it was moving at all.

When it comes to a stop, the guards nudge them out of the lift and into the dark chamber ahead.

CHAPTER FOURTEEN

In stark contrast to the noise and ruckus of the great room below with its central pit, this chamber is just as quiet as the lift. The air is still thick, perhaps even thicker, and it softens the only light sources in the room. At the far end is a chair and in front of that a terminal, and above it a massive array of hundreds of screens, each glowing with faint blue light that flickers and moves as the images on the screen do. When she squints, she can see through the fog that the screens are feeds from what must be security cameras, as more than a few of them display the area around the pit from dozens of different angles.

Someone rises from the chair, a dark silhouette outlined by the blue radiance of the security screens. Their most striking feature is their hair, shiny and black, piled upon their head in an elegant wreath and yet still long enough to brush the ground. After seeing the way the duels below had been determined by wagers, Luzia has a better understanding of why all the Astrosi have such long hair. It's not merely a sign of their unnaturally long life, but a warning of how much they can spend if they so choose.

"You may leave," the figure says in a hard baritone.

At first Luzia worries that they're being kicked out, but then the two guards salute and step back into the lift, the doors closing behind them.

The man, who can only be King Ari, takes a solitary step forward. His skin is pale and cool, his eyes are light as glass, and a dark tattoo is emblazoned upon his forehead like a crown. Those white eyes run up and down Luzia and Lysander, examining them with a forensic detachment. Then he raises a thin, sharp eyebrow and asks, "Did you really think that instigating a fight with one of mine would be a wise decision, Lysander of the Eoi?"

Lysander tries to sound tough, but his voice isn't as strong as it was before. "Got me an audience with you, didn't it? Jess wanted to stall, so I–"

"I was utterly uninterested in your petty squabble," Ari says, cutting him off with more efficiency than a bayonet rifle's blade. He points a narrow finger at Luzia. "What I *am* interested in is *you*, human. Why did you interfere?"

"Hey," Lysander tries. "She ain't–"

"I'm speaking with this human, not you." He stares down Luzia and she swallows, trying to bring up the confidence that she has when she does her job, the same confidence that lets her crawl through a burning building and climb over a collapsing train track. "I shall repeat: why did you interfere?"

Luzia clears her scratchy throat, the heavy mist oddly soothing. "I don't fully understand the rules of these fights, but it looked like Lysander needed to make a better wager, so I thought I'd help."

"But *why*?" Ari demands. "You are human."

"I don't see how that matters. He needed more charge to stay in the fight, so I gave him that."

"Are you in love with him?"

Lysander makes a retching cough.

"Absolutely not," Luzia replies immediately. "Why would you ask–"

Once more Ari pushes on, seemingly interested only in the answers to his questions and not in any elaboration or her broader opinions. "Were you ordered to assist him in such a manner?"

"No. I mean, we were assigned to work together, but it's not as though Sef – er, Queen Sef – demanded it."

"So, if you were not driven by affection or by command or obligation, then why did you help him?"

"...Because he needed help?"

Ari makes a rough noise, part thoughtful hum and part gruff dismissal. "I see." In the span of a blink, he snaps back to Lysander. "Why did my counterpart send you here?"

"Salts," Lysander reluctantly grinds out.

There is a long moment of silent deliberation before Ari inclines his head a fraction of an inch. "I have no reason to deny my counterpart's request on this matter. Inform her that I shall be expecting a double shipment in return, as compensation for the... *disruption* you have caused today."

"My queen won't be–"

"Your queen will do as I have said. She understands that it is the scarcity of the Mists and our need for her crops that allow her Deep to flourish and grow." Ari presses a button on the terminal and a panel opens, spitting out a large, cylindrical container. "Tell me, human, had you one word to describe the Deep, just one, what would it be?"

Luzia automatically blurts out, "Terrifying."

"Ziane!" Lysander snaps, cheeks burning red. "Stop being so fucking rude!"

"Sorry, um, I suppose..." She tries to think of something that won't continue to agitate Lysander and that will also appease the heavy gaze of King Ari. "The Deep is... well, compared to the Bastion, it's full of things that grow. I suppose a good word might be 'alive'?"

"Alive," Ari muses. "Yes, that is quite the word for it."

Slowly, as though moving through water, he raises a hand above the empty container that rests before him. The heavy fog that the chamber is suffused with begins to shift. His index finger twitches. A thin tendril of vapor thickens and turns white, drawn from the corner of the chamber towards him. A twitch of his thumb. Pale, chalky threads of mist are pulled up from a vent upon the floor. A twitch of his ring finger. Darker mist, closer to ashy smoke, is tugged down from near the ceiling. With focused, silent elegance, he twists his wrist and the tendrils of air and smoke and mist and fog coalesce above his palm, being pulled in on themselves over and over again, the insubstantial coaxed into solidity.

When Ari speaks, the intensity makes Luzia hold her breath. "Though the Deep is indeed filled with growing things," he says as the air itself slips and slides around her like fabric, "it is not as alive as it appears. The experimentations of Sef's folk, the yield they demand from their arboretums, the ways in which they take, and take, and *take*... all this drains the life from their soil and their endlessly recirculated atmosphere. The flora of the Deep provides what the Astrosi need in terms of food, drink, even clothing, but they need *us* in ways that your friend Lysander would turn blue before admitting."

The swirling haze above his palm grows whiter. Not in the colloquial way where white is an absence of color but in the realm of science and fractals and light, where white is all color at once. It all becomes denser and denser until a single tiny sphere, not unlike a large grain of salt, breaks away from the mass and drops into the container. Like the first creaking beam before a structural collapse, that first little orb heralds the fall of the rest. A series of *plink-plink-plinks* chime as the container becomes filled with the chalky white grains.

"Nitrogen," Ari explains. "We all are so focused on the need for oxygen that it is so easy to forget that nitrogen is just as crucial. The human world of the Bastion has its air filtration systems, but it is we of the Vesperi who breathe life back into the Deep's dead soil."

The final grain falls. He lowers his hand and seals the container, and it's only once the mist stills that Luzia lets herself breathe again. When she first met Carrion, they had stolen the breath from her lungs. If Ari can pull nitrogen from the air, then Carrion must have done something similar, pulling oxygen out of the air around her. That too explains their ability to create fire from nothing. Suffusing the air with an excess of oxygen would allow anything flammable to ignite at the first strike of a match. For all she knows, Ari may even be filling the air with flammable chemicals specifically for that purpose.

Ari holds out the container and waits with patient apathy for Lysander to walk up and grudgingly take it.

"Right." Lysander clears his throat with a rough cough and shrugs his shoulder in the direction of the lift door. "Well, I guess–"

"I have not dismissed you," Ari reminds him, in a tone sharper than a whip. "This is not the first time you have been sent as trade envoy by your queen, but it is the first time that a human has accompanied you. Why? You clearly neither planned nor anticipated her assistance in your duel, and she left your side shortly upon entering my throneworld. That suggests that you wanted to keep her relatively unobserved, but for what purpose?"

Lysander, to his credit, stays stone-faced. "She's here to carry the salts. Why would I do the hard work when I could get a human to do it for me?"

"Lie to me in my domain again and I will burn your tongue from your mouth."

"I was supposed to look for information," Luzia blurts out. While there's no love lost between her and Lysander, she's not going to stand by and let him be mutilated because of his stubbornness. "About Carrion. Queen Sef is trying to track them down, and I'm part of the team assigned to do it."

"A human? Tracking down Carrion?" Ari frowns in disbelief. "Has my counterpart truly resorted to such desperation that she must send a human after that rogue?"

"I asked to do it."

Once more, Ari demands, "Why?"

"Carrion kidnapped my nephew," she admits. "They were going to sell him to Queen Sef to get out of a contract they'd made. I took my nephew's place. But I want to make sure that they're stopped before they can harm anyone else. I've seen them kill other Eoi; I know they're dangerous. So I asked – well, begged really – to be let on the team that's hunting them down. This was my assignment, though I'm hardly much of a spy…"

"I see you have heard the rumors of Carrion's time in my court."

"Er, well, yes. Queen Sef said that something here caused them to snap, and that's where it all started, for them."

Ari's eyes bore into hers. "I see. What is your name, human?"

"Lu–" She stumbles, remembering at the last second Lysander's orders. There's that itch in the back of her throat as well, the same rough choking that cuts off her words the moment she begins to accidentally disobey. "They call me Ziane."

There is a long moment of silence. Ari seems to like that, as though he wants to make them sweat while he deliberates. "Come with me, Ziane," he decides. "Lysander, you will remain exactly where you are until I return and give you permission to leave."

"But I–" Lysander tries.

"That was not a question." He beckons Luzia forward with a single sharp flick of his finger and repeats, "Come with me."

A bead of sweat trickles down her brow. She inches towards him, one careful step at a time. There isn't really a choice. As Ari has pointed out, this is his domain and he makes the rules here. And if there is any information to be gleaned about Carrion, she needs to find it.

Ari turns on his heel, long hair flaring as he does so, the shine of it flashing in the blue light. He leads Luzia away from the screens and off into a shadowed corner of the chamber. On the far wall is a hidden door, so perfectly flush with the wall that she only can tell it's there when Ari opens it. Behind it is more darkness and more mist, but she can make out a stairwell as each step has a tiny emergency guidance light on the edge. Without further comment, he begins to ascend the stairs, forcing her to hurry after him.

"Where are we going?" she asks. "I assume this has something to do with Carrion?"

Ari makes an agreeing hum. "This is where they came, all those centuries ago. Before, when they were just another member of my court."

The stairwell stops in front of a door with heavy-duty security bolts on all sides and a keypad in the center of it. Ari punches in a ten-digit code, scans his handprint, and then leans in for a retina scan before the bolts finally slide away with a creak of metal and the door slowly swings open. It shuts behind them, preventing anyone else from sneaking in.

This room is strange. It's utterly empty and perfectly circular. The walls are a clean, untouched white, the lights similarly bright. The only noticeable thing is that the ceiling has a slight curve to it, a barely noticeable dome. In that domed ceiling is a circular set of doors, not unlike the Era One blast doors that protect a few of the Office of the Administrator buildings in the Bastion. No mist lingers here, and that, more than anything else, tells Luzia that this place is utterly and completely off limits.

"This," Ari explains, "is the highest point of the Mists."

And the Mists are already the highest point above the Bastion. She didn't really know if the Mists or the Deep ended or not. To her knowledge, and the knowledge of the Bastion, the two Astrosi realms are all there is above and below, and the dilapidated Fringes are all there is on the edges of the world. Does the Mists... *end*? Or is there more of that realm above that Ari simply doesn't know about?

Ari presses a button on a wall panel and the blast doors overhead slide away.

For all the dramatics, Luzia wasn't sure what to expect. Something grand. Something impossible or terrifying. Instead, there are just smooth panes of colored glass. She tilts her head further up. The first layer of thick glass is clear, and beyond that is a reddish-orange pane. It's pretty, to be sure, but not anything particularly special. Not anything that is worth going mad over.

"I don't understand." She moves to the center of the room, examining the glass from every angle that she can see.

Part of her wants to get a pair of gloves and touch it, to see if there's anything strange about the material, but it looks perfectly normal. "*This* is what made Carrion go rogue?"

Ari's sigh is drawn-out and resigned. "I cannot comprehend it either. Perhaps you, with your odd little dedication, will find a way to explain it."

"But it's just glass."

"I know."

She chews on the inside of her cheek. "How is this the top of the Mists?"

"We've not found a way to travel higher. Whatever is beyond is thus not part of my throneworld, and so I would be arrogant in the extreme to claim it as my own without setting foot in it."

"What's beyond?"

"Presumably something akin to the Fringes on the edges of the world." After another minute of letting Luzia puzzle at the glass, Ari closes the blast doors. "If you wish to inform your queen of what you have seen here today, I shall not attempt to stop you. And if you ever wish to decipher the mystery of Carrion, feel free to return to the Mists. I would welcome any information you acquire." He steps aside, letting her exit the strange room. "You may leave now. And do take Lysander with you."

The image of that red-orange glass lingers in Luzia's mind all the way down the stairs and is still consuming her thoughts when she reunites with Lysander.

"So?" Lysander demands the moment she returns. "What the fuck was all that?"

She shrugs and says honestly, "Just glass. Plain red glass."

"That can't be it. There's no fucking way."

"That was it. Just glass."

CHAPTER FIFTEEN

Sef doesn't share the same outraged disappointment as Lysander when Luzia returns to the Deep and breaks the news. Indeed, such violent emotions don't seem to be something that Sef is willing to display, if she's even capable of them. Instead she simply nods, slow and contemplative, and then dismisses Luzia and Lysander. Though Lysander is quick to salute and stomp off, Luzia stays behind, shuffling from one foot to the other as she waits to be alone with Sef.

For someone currently sitting upon a throne, Sef in no way gives the impression of looking down on Luzia. Instead, there is only curiosity and openness in her peaceful countenance. "Is there aught I can do for you, Ziane?" Sef asks. "You shall not be forced away if you wish to speak."

Luzia steels herself. Back straight, head high. "Can I be granted some kind of leave to go see my family?"

"You cannot."

"But I've done everything you asked," Luzia points out, rushing over her words. "I went after Carrion at the water-treatment plant, I went to the Mists – I'm not trying to brag, but I got the information from Ari when Lysander got on his bad side. Surely that's worth *something*. I'm not asking to break my contract, as I've said. I just want to see them."

Sef opens her mouth, and her voice takes on a cadence that is not her own. It is Luzia's. "'If I capture them, if I do that for the Eoi, for you, I want you to let me visit my family.'"

"But I–"

"Those were your exact words," Sef reminds her. "That was the contract you made. I am not here to impose petulant restrictions upon you, nor do I wish to trick you into forfeiting what you have rightfully earned. All I shall do is obey the terms of the verbal contract that you set forth, that you *offered*." That last word rings out through the room like a weight being dropped. The memory of Annie's warning rings out with it. "Carrion has not been captured. I shall indeed praise your actions in the Mists, and I am not ungrateful for them, but they do not satisfy the terms of your contract."

She's not cruel, Annie had said. *Just heartless.*

For all that Luzia had been welcomed to a riotous and, frankly, off-the-wall party with Essten and Leneat, and for all that the Vesperi had been fixated on the chaotic duels in the pit, this, Luzia realizes, is the part of the Astrosi that she doesn't know if she can hold out against. At her old job, she'd dealt with plenty of hectic situations, dangerous situations, but it was a puzzle, like the sanitized game she'd had Stazi play. It's a series of calculations. How much weight this will hold, how long this fire will burn, how many people are in danger, how old is the building. It was all math; it all made *sense*. She'd thought the worst part of the Astrosi was that they were willing to accept a child in place of a criminal.

But this, the emotionless scales of the Astrosi contracts, is the real threat. The wagers of the Vesperi's duels, where you get exactly what you give and no more. The joking way the announcer had stated that only that which was explicitly banned would not be allowed – the absolute adherence to preexisting rules. The way Sef was willing to give Luzia a chance to see her family, and now will not bend on the hastily established terms.

Sef *is* heartless. Any plea for leniency would be more effective against a wall.

Luzia presses her stinging eyes tightly shut. "I understand," she says, because there's nothing else she can say.

"Is there anything else?" Sef asks, in a way that is neither kind nor unkind.

"No. Thank you."

With a delicate sweep of her hand, Sef gestures to the door. "I shall call upon you when next Carrion shows themself. Given their tendency to hide in the human realm of the Bastion, I imagine it will not be long for us before we hear of their presence."

Luzia's feet are heavy as she trudges out of the throne room. By now, her well-trained sense of direction has begun to learn even the twisting and homogeneously green halls of the Deep and she only makes two wrong turns before ending up outside the arboretum. Someone is waiting for her, however, and even though she had hoped to crawl back to Annie's little corner of humanity, she doesn't want to snub one of the few people who has been kind to her during her time amongst the Astrosi.

Essten is lingering by the door, a smile on his round, cheery face. "I heard Lysander's grumbling return," he says by way of explanation. "Did it go that badly?"

"It's hard to say how it went," she tells him honestly. "But Lysander wasn't successful in the way I think he'd hoped to be."

"Well, so long as the only injuries were to his ego. Want to grab a drink?"

She shudders. "That didn't go very well for me last time."

He laughs and awkwardly scratches the back of his head. "That was probably the amount of cannabis and opioids in the brownies we let you scarf down. Just beer on its own shouldn't really mess you up any."

"No offense, but I'm not interested in risking it."

"What about juice?" he offers. "No alcohol there. Just fruit. Or I could mix you up a great mocktail?"

It would be nice to down a glass of cold liquid, to wash the clinging haze of the Mists out of her throat. While she'd prefer above all else to be drinking the clean, processed water of the Bastion straight from the tap in Izax's kitchen, she knows she needs to eat and drink to survive, and she can't snub everything down here. Alcohol, whatever chemicals he said she consumed, all those she is happy to avoid, but she can't let herself die of dehydration by avoiding *everything*. No wonder Annie only eats and drinks what she herself prepares. It must make things a lot safer for her in the long run, as she wouldn't have to risk cross-contamination with whatever insane concoctions the Eoi prefer to consume.

Taking her lack of further protest as acceptance, Essten cheerfully leads her away from the doors to the arboretum and off through the halls of the Deep. She's not sure where he's taking her, and after a few twists and turns they end up in a smaller dining hall where the carpet is a blue-green grass and bright pink, bell-shaped flowers grow around the light fixtures. He leaves her at a table that's more of a tree stump with chairs around it than an actual table and returns a minute later with two metal cups. To his credit, he doesn't comment as Luzia finishes up the additions to her map, noting the existence of this room and the way to it from the arboretum, and he just smiles when she puts her tablet away.

There's a sweet-smelling yellow liquid in Luzia's cup. She takes a single sip, tries not to melt at how delicious and fruity it is, then puts the cup back down. "I'll wait ten minutes before having any more," she declares. "Just in case it *does* effect me."

Essten blinks at her in befuddlement. "It's just pineapple. I promised you no alcohol, and there's no alcohol in plain pineapple juice."

Even if there isn't any alcohol, she doesn't trust it to not affect her adversely. Everything about the Astrosi is hostile.

"So..." Essten takes an awkward, slurpy sip of his own drink. It takes him a couple attempts to successfully make eye contact with her. "What, uh. What did you and Lysander learn? About Carrion, I mean. If you're allowed to tell me that, of course, I don't want to step on the queen's toes."

She can only shrug. "I don't know."

"You didn't learn anything?"

"Well, not exactly. We got some information from Ari, it just doesn't make any sense. I tend to believe that all data is relevant in some way or another, but this might not matter at all."

He leans in an inch, hands wrapped tightly around his cup. "So what was it?"

"I don't know," she repeats. The words feel so heavy on her tired tongue. "Ari showed me something that apparently made Carrion snap, but it was just a ceiling with a sheet of red glass in it. Nothing that seemed all that extraordinary."

"Huh. I wonder what Carrion took away from that, if it contributed to their madness."

"I really, *really* don't know."

"Right, you said. Sorry. It's just confusing, is all."

She shrugs again. What else is there to say about the glass ceiling? None of it makes sense. "It is. Essten…" she pauses before continuing, "There was something else that Ari said about the room with the red glass. He said that it was the highest point of the Mists, and, well, the Mists are the only thing above the Bastion. Does the Deep have a lowest point as well, or…?"

"Oh, yeah," he says with a nod. "I don't know if you've seen the queen's bower in the center of the arboretum, but from what we know, that's the lowest point of the Deep."

"So what's beyond it? Does anyone know?"

"Not a clue. Presumably more of the same, or something like the Fringes at the edge of the Bastion. Just can't claim it as the Deep cause the queen's never been down there, you know. We've never been able to figure out a way further down. There's a lot of dirt, but then you hit solid metal. Era One stuff, really strong. We can't find a way around. Might have been deliberately sealed off, if the Fringes below are enough of a mess that they'd be dangerous even to Astrosi."

About what she expected, then. It does make sense. Era One tech was built with methods that have since been lost, and the Bastion hasn't discovered any means by which an Era One wall could be destroyed. While Era One structures degrade over time, and need to be shored up on occasion, actively tearing one down is beyond them.

"Does it bother you?" Luzia asks. "Not knowing, that is."

"Nah." Essten's response is quick and casual. "Why would it? It's not like we need anything that we can't already get from the Deep – or the Mists," he adds begrudgingly. "The queen says the diamond isn't below the Deep either, so it's not as though we need to search for it down there, and that's about the only thing we want that we don't already have."

"I suppose... Essten, what *is* the diamond? I've not gotten a straight answer about it."

He frowns, mouth scrunching into a squiggle. "Not rightly sure, to be honest. A source of power. We can't let Carrion get their hands on it, that's for sure."

"That's all a bit vague."

"Hah. True enough. I'm sure the queen knows more about it, but if she's decided that we don't need any more info, then we don't need any more info. Simple as that. We get it before Ari does, and we keep it from Carrion, and that's that."

Footsteps approach the table, and Luzia looks up to see Leneat walking up to them, holding a tray in her hands. Exhaustion has left dark circles under her eyes and her shirt is stained with what looks to be an oil smear.

Essten lets out a low whistle. "You're a wreck."

"Ugh." Leneat slumps onto a wooden stump and deposits her tray on the table. "Our queen sent me to scout the Bastion for Carrion. It's been *ages* and damn am I tired. No offense to you humans," she adds to Luzia, "but up there just ain't nearly as pleasant as down here. Wears you out, you know?"

"You've only been gone for a day," Luzia points out. "Surely it can't have been that bad."

Leneat blinks at her. "I was in the *Bastion*," she repeats, as though that's supposed to mean something. "Anyway, I hope you lot get some decent sleep tonight. I changed out shifts before heading back and it looks like we might have a lead on Carrion. They're sniffing around one of the human Administrator buildings, but they keep vanishing before we can get a solid lock on their position."

"The Office of the Administrator?" Luzia draws in a sharp breath, the shock of that cutting through her depressed haze. If Carrion attacks any of the Administrator buildings, that would be devastating to the Bastion's security, to its ability to respond to danger, to its very capacity to provide resources to the people. "Why would they be there, of all places?"

"Who knows?" Leneat says. She grabs a piece of something from the tray, a curved piece of yellow fruit, and shoves it in her mouth, chewing as she talks. "Could be anything with them, really." She holds out a piece of fruit to Luzia. "Pineapple? There was a fresh harvest of it earlier today, apparently, and it's damn good. Ain't even added anything to it, so it shouldn't fuck up a human any. Er, sorry again about last time, by the way. Honest mistake."

So far, the juice doesn't seem to have had any effect on Luzia, so it's likely the fruit is safe to eat for her. Especially if the Eoi haven't added any additional enhancements to it. She takes the offered piece and bites down. Flavor bursts on her tongue, sharper and fresher than the crushed juice, and the fruit is oddly fibrous, strands of it getting caught in her teeth. It's undeniably wonderful, somehow cool and refreshing despite being served at room temperature. She finishes the piece and takes another.

"See?" Essten raises his own glass in a toast. "Perfectly safe. What'd I tell ya?"

"In my defense, it didn't go all that well for me last time." She turns back to Leneat. "Has Carrion indicated that they're going to attack the Office of the Administrator? Or are they just laying low in that area?"

Leneat shakes her head. "We honestly don't know."

"Yeah... I know what that feels like."

"Well, I just wanted to give y'all the heads up. It won't be long before we're called out to detain Carrion, I suspect." A shadow flickers over her expression. "Let's hope it goes better than last time." With a tired sigh, she pushes herself up onto her feet. "I'm gonna go get some shut-eye. Enjoy the fruit, and get some sleep."

Luzia and Essten finish the plate of pineapple in relative silence. A few other Eoi filter into the dining hall, mostly those wearing white lab coats, who murmur to each other and gesture to various diagrams on their tablets. One soldier comes in, nursing a mug of beer and a plate of something green. Eventually, Luzia murmurs a goodbye to Essten and heads back to Annie's.

The arboretum is circling through a nighttime cycle, the bright ceiling lights turned down to a softer, dark blue glow. Annie is still awake inside her little house, sitting on a wooden chair and sorting a basketful of flowers into two separate piles, occasionally pausing to make a note in her botanical guide.

"Welcome back," Annie says gruffly as Luzia enters.

"Ah, thank you. How, um. How was your day?" It feels so odd to ask something so normal, but Luzia's not sure what else to do.

Annie lets one shoulder raise and then slump. "Same as always. You?"

"Not great," she admits. She takes a seat on her bed of moss and flowers and blankets that still makes her nose run when she sleeps for too long. "You were right, by the way."

"I often am. About what?"

"Queen Sef. She's not cruel, just heartless. I asked her to see my family, given how much I've worked to catch Carrion, and she denied it. That's not how my contract was worded. She wouldn't budge."

"Mm-hm. Don't say I didn't warn you."

"I know." The corners of her mouth start to itch as she talks. She scratches at it, and tiny drops of blood come away under her nail. "What the– I'm bleeding!"

Annie doesn't look particularly worried and just sighs. "What did you eat?"

"Just pineapple."

"Wow, you've got shit luck. Allergic to pollen *and* sensitive to pineapple." She waves a dismissive hand. "Pineapple ain't toxic, before you freak out, but it does have an enzyme in it that can break down proteins. In a way, it digests *you* while you digest it. Doesn't really do much to most people. Some are just weaker to it than others. Sucks for you."

Luzia licks her lips, tasting iron and trying not to freak out about it. Pineapple is going on her list of things she will never again consume, along with any alcohol. "Everything the Astrosi deal with is dangerous, isn't it?"

The look Annie gives her is a mix of pity and condescension. "Get used to it," she says sincerely. "Don't forget – you're stuck with the Eoi for the rest of your life."

CHAPTER SIXTEEN

A good deal of time passes, more than Luzia would have expected. She spends her days following Annie around, her knowledge of the plants that grow in the Deep expanding every day. This place becomes less and less unsettling as time passes, as she becomes accustomed to the ways in which the Deep is different from the Bastion. She adjusts, and part of her wishes she wouldn't, that she would spend every day on edge, that the unnaturalness down here would never become familiar.

It takes a few months for the hunt for Carrion to resume.

The call to mobilize comes first thing in the morning. Luzia fortunately is already awake, dressed, and breakfasted, and just about to start doing the rounds with Annie when the Eoi arrives with the message.

Lysander is waiting at one of the lifts – Luzia has no idea which one; it isn't one she's been to before. There are a few soldiers that she doesn't know either, but Essten and a tired Leneat are amongst the small group and she can feel her tense muscles relax a smidge. They tighten up again when Lysander shoves a bayonet-rifle into her hands. The group is also given small portable communicators, slim and lightweight versions of the wall-paneled ones that dot the Bastion, small enough to be tucked into a pocket.

The group marches into the lift and after Lysander has punched in their destination and they're on their way, he begins one of his short briefings.

"Listen up," he says over the faint hum of the lift moving. "For the past few months, we've been tracking Carrion's movements in the Bastion. The bastard's been busy. Far as we can tell, they've got a base in the Fringes set up, and we mean to catch 'em with their guard down. Carrion was seen leaving the Office of the Administrator and heading in the direction of the Fringes of the Bastion by our scout an hour ago down here. They might've left the Fringes again by the time we get there, but if our last attempt proved anything, it's that they tend to linger in an area for awhile before moving on, if only to try and fuck with us. This time we'll be ready for a trap. Pursue them, capture them. You know what to do."

The Fringes? But if Carrion has only just left the Office of the Administrator, right in the heart of the Bastion, a mere *hour* ago, then there's no way they could make it to the Fringes before the high-speed Eoi lifts get there, and Carrion certainly wouldn't have time to sense the Eoi are coming and get away. Luzia is tempted to ask, but Lysander's perpetual glower is even more cloudy than usual and she imagines he's still sore about what happened in the Mists.

"And keep an eye out for the diamond," Lysander adds. "They're a lunatic, but there's always a slim chance they've beaten us to it."

There's a murmur of agreements and nodding.

"Where along the Fringes?" Essten asks.

"Near the Runoffs," Lysander replies, double-checking his rifle. "Second level, first floor. Shouldn't be any humans around there, before *anyone*," and here the sharp word is clearly directed at Luzia, "gets picky about 'em getting in the way."

The Runoffs. An area that, according to older records, was used to store any recovered Era One technology. As time passed and Era One tech became increasingly valuable and necessary, it all got moved to a location closer to the center of the Bastion so that it could be properly utilized. Luzia has never been there before; she's never had the need. That said, she knows Lysander is correct. The area *is* off limits except to authorized personnel, and no one has any need to go there anymore.

Given the speed of the lift, it doesn't take long for the team to arrive on the first floor of the second level. She does wonder at the precision of the network of these lifts. She knows that there are tunnels and shafts from Era One that the Bastion doesn't bother with, but it appears as though somehow they connect to the Deep, with the lifts being able to go sideways as well as vertically to be able to deposit passengers at nearly every corner of the Bastion. How much do the Astrosi rely on Era One tech? And, more curiously, how has it degraded over time in the Bastion yet seemingly not at all in the Deep and the Mists?

Her train of thought is sharply cut off by Lysander ordering, "Move out. We'll be losing sight of each other in this place so keep your tact-coms clear. Let's get the bastard."

And that is all the direction they get. Once more Luzia is sharply aware of just how out of her depth she is here, as the rest of the team spreads out in an orderly manner and begins to scan the area. She's done similar as part of her work before, but it has been in a way she understood –

move around unstable structures, check collapsed sections for trapped people, make sure there are no water pipes punctured or electrical lines exposed.

In some respects, the Fringes are similar to the rest of the Bastion: tall buildings, lamp fixtures, standard streets, the remnants of rail tracks – all the facilities needed to sustain life. That is where the similarities cease. Not a single building is fully intact. The passage of time has resulted in walls crumbling, buildings leaning against each other in a perilous series of harsh diagonal lines that clash with the perfectly straight towers of the Bastion. The street is completely torn up in many places, leaving behind pits of darkness that lead to who knows where. Light fixtures and street lamps are smashed, unlit, as power was cut off to the Fringes who knows when. There are signs, rusted and tilted, stamped with the seal of the Office of the Administrator, declaring the place off limits, placed here who knows how long ago.

No one knows. Anyone who has gone too far into the Fringes has never come out.

Luzia struggles to take so much as a single, inching step on to the dilapidated streets. For all that it is a wreck, it does hold her weight, and the Eoi seem to be having no issue with traversing the outer edges of the ruins. She passes another warning sign and a shiver runs down the back of her neck. Even the air here is unnatural. There's a lack of the clean, recirculated air that pumps through the Bastion at all times. Instead it is heavy, musty, sour. As though the Fringes themselves are warning people away.

For all that she is an outsider in the Deep, she has never been more certain that she is being ejected from a place than she does now, here at the edge of the world.

Someone rests a hand on her shoulder and she jumps. Then she realizes it's just Essten, with a sympathetic sort of scrunched smile on his lips.

"Hey." He gives her shoulder another friendly pat. "It ain't that bad. Just give a yell if you're in trouble and I'll be there to help, all right? Remember why you're doing this, and keep that in mind – I know this place can be creepy as all get-out, but if you're focused on something besides the shadows, that'll make it at least a little bit better."

"...Right," she slowly replies.

Remember why you're doing this. Help with the unnatural Fringes or no, she hasn't forgotten the odd choking that had overcome her the last time she went after Carrion. The way it had risen when she thought of her family and running off to see them regardless of what she'd been ordered to do, and faded when Carrion forced her to focus on them. She can't risk collapsing again in a place like this.

"Here."

She startles to see Essten holding something out to her. It looks like a pair of handcuffs, except with the same clean appearance as the technology of the Deep and the Mists. There is a series of blinking lights on the side and the metal is oddly thick.

"They're cuffs," he says, which is rather self-explanatory. "Era One tech, a holdover from some of our earlier skirmishes with the Vesperi before Carrion became... well, a priority, I guess. I know you don't like using that thing." He points to the bayonet rifle in her hands. "Get close enough to Carrion and slap these babies on their wrists, then press that little button on the side. It'll activate the same electric field that we use on bayonet blade, and that should suppress their abilities. They're unpredictable enough that I don't think these cuffs would hold them for long, but it'll buy you some time for us to get there."

"I…" The cuffs are heavy in her hands, heavy and cold and reassuring. Hopeful. "I don't know what to say. Thank you."

Essten grins. "Just glad I could help. Keep a calm head on your shoulders, all right?"

"I will," she promises with a nod.

The longer she holds onto the cuffs, the warmer the metal gets, even as Essten walks off to fall into position with the rest of the soldiers. She rotates them, getting a feel for the weight of them, and then clips them onto her belt, letting them hang against her hip. It's something she can actually see herself using, whereas she cannot imagine herself truly trying to hurt someone with the wicked bayonet rifles. Not even Carrion, despite what they've done.

Bolstered, Luzia forces herself to take a step further into the Fringes, and then another, then another, until she is properly walking into the shadows.

A chill begins to seep into her skin, not merely caused by her trepidation. Although most areas of the Bastion are kept at a consistent temperature, it's clear that no efforts have been made to heat the Fringes. With no one living here, it would be a waste of energy that could be far more effectively utilized literally anywhere else. As she slowly goes deeper in, ducking under doorways that have semi-toppled over, goosebumps spread up her arms and her fingers stiffen around the bayonet rifle.

Occasionally her new tact-com will buzz and someone will report in, always with a stoic "Clear south" or "Nothing south-west."

After a good five minutes of walking, she realizes that she's been an idiot. She stops where she is and leans her bayonet-rifle against a nearby crate after testing to make sure that it's stable. Then she takes out her tablet and stylus, opens up a new file, and sketches out the path she's taken. This territory is more hostile than the Deep, but it can still be mapped. Indeed, mapping it will probably be easier than mapping the Deep, as there won't be any Astrosi magic making the paths difficult to traverse. All she has to deal with are the ordinary pitfalls – chasms, collapsed walls, crumbling ceilings. This is at least something she has been trained for.

With it all beginning to be laid out before her in a flat series of lines, she can see that there is a pattern to at least this section of the Fringes. It reminds her of residential areas of the Bastion, the similar layouts of apartments and streets and heating units tucked between walls. Of course, it's difficult for her to tell that at first glance, or even on second, given how dilapidated everything here is and how fallen beams and missing sections of street have interfered with the lay of the land.

Could any of this be repaired, or has it all been out of use for so long that there's nothing to be done for it? Or is there another reason that these areas were abandoned besides structural degradation?

Despite the confusing paths of the Fringes and the way Luzia finds herself getting turned around quite often, her map lets her keep going in a relatively straight line, using her growing draft to reorient herself whenever a building is thrown in her path or a street is blocked off. She ducks under a crumbling archway and pulls back a tarp that's been strung up like a door. Odd. Perhaps it was added before the Fringes were abandoned, as part of a last-ditch attempt to stabilize the area. But the tarp looks new…

Behind it is a wide open room that is absolutely *not* abandoned.

Luzia takes a deep breath, pulls out her tact-com, and activates it. "Lysander? I think I've found... *something.*"

"Remain where you are," Lysander instructs. *"I'll ping your tact-com's location and come to you. Don't do anything stupid."*

The line goes silent, and Luzia can't help but walk inside. Nothing in it appears outwardly dangerous. In comparison to the dilapidated areas of the Fringes outside, this place is remarkably clean, as though someone has swept up dust and debris and moved any rubble out of the way. As was the case in that previous nest of Carrion's, there's a pack lying slumped on the ground against a wall and a makeshift bed of a tarp and a ratty blanket has been made up. Although her mind keeps reminding her of how the last nest had been a trap, this time she doesn't think that's the case.

In the center of the room is a device, and she doubts that Carrion would risk destroying it with a bomb. It is some sort of scanner or tablet, set up atop a tripod from which a pendulum silently swings back and forth, an inch of movement at a time. The device has a light slowly blinking as it works away. What truly makes it valuable is the neat blue glowing lights and smooth, unblemished white surface that reminds her of all Era One technology. Whatever this is, it's Era One, it's active, and there's no doubt it belongs to Carrion. Who else would be out here, of all places?

There's a crinkling of the tarp and Lysander rushes into the room, aiming his bayonet-rifle at the corners to ensure that Carrion isn't hiding in one of them, ready to pop out. Then he gets a proper look at the device and his rifle drops to his side. "What in the fuck is all this?"

"I don't know," Luzia replies. "It was set up like this when I got here, but if the only person out in the Fringes is Carrion, then it must be theirs."

Lysander briefly says into his tact-com, "Possibly got something at my location. Don't converge, but stand by." Humming, he puts down the com and circles the device before peering at the screen with a suspicious glare. "Looks like a scanner."

"Yes, that's what I thought. What is it scanning?"

"Not sure. That bastard Carrion has it set up all weird. Hmph. It's picking up something, that's for sure, but nothing solid." He leans closer and starts poking at the screen, flipping through what she thinks are scan results. "It's murky all right. But these readings…" His eyes widen and he swears violently under his breath. "I know this radiation frequency. The fucker is using this to try and track down the diamond!"

It's at that moment that the tarp is pulled back once again and Carrion shuffles into the room, holding a cup of something steaming hot and yawning.

"The fuck?" Lysander spits out in surprise.

Carrion blinks. "Damn. Aight."

"You fuck," Lysander repeats, this time with his customary venom. "You're tracking the diamond, you son of a bitch."

With a tired sigh, Carrion puts their cup down on a nearby crate. "I was really looking forward to drinking that, ya know. And yeah, obviously I'm tracking the diamond. Please don't do your normal wild punching-and-wrecking-things bullshit, Lysander. I've had that tech for a long time and it's got sentimental value."

Lysander shoots.

As if in slow motion, Luzia watches Carrion drop to one knee, the beam going over their head and right through the tarp and into the crumbling archway behind it. All her instincts kick in. She knows what's going to happen, and she moves before she hears the cracking of old hinges and the shifting of metal. A shower of dust falls into the room and then the entire archway is disintegrating, smacking into the walls as it topples over and bringing them down too, causing a cascade reaction of collapse.

Luzia is already running, heading straight for the Era One scanning device. Lysander leaps towards Carrion, but Carrion has moved at almost the exact same time as Luzia and they too are going directly for the scanner.

She and Carrion reach for it at the same time. The tips of her fingers brush against the scanner's cool metallic surface. Then Carrion smacks her wrist out of the way and wraps their hand around the scanner, ripping it from the tripod set up as they dash past her. It might just be her imagination, but she could swear they wave at her as they run to the far side of the room and vanish behind another hanging tarp.

There's another creaking and groaning of metal and she glances behind her to see that Lysander has used Eoi magic to grow thick, twisting pillars of wood that plunge up from the ground beneath him at the same time as dirt pours from a bag at his hip, strong enough to keep the roof from completely coming down on the two of them. His arms are held upright, muscles straining under the weight of the entire ceiling, the wood starting to splinter.

"Don't let them get away!" Lysander orders. "I'll deal with this bullshit and be right on your heels!"

No need to tell her twice. Her feet slam against the fracturing ground as she nearly throws herself after Carrion, ducking through the tarp and finding herself in another street, the buildings around her shuddering from the still-degrading archway. Up ahead is a flash of Carrion's coat and she locks onto it, her boots sliding over rough pavement as she turns a sharp corner to follow them.

She forces her body to keep moving, to push past the anxiety of knowing that there's a collapse behind her, past the fear of the Fringes, past the desire to stop and reorient herself. They vault over a fallen wall and she's right behind them, leaping over it with less agility but just as much efficiency. When they jump into a pipe and slide down like a child on a playground, she throws herself in right after, skidding her knees and thighs against the metal, and when she lands she rolls upright into a run and doesn't let them out of her sight.

They're fast, that's undeniable. But the Bastion is Luzia's home, and even though she doesn't know the Fringes, the patterns are the same. She can tell which streets are safe to run on, which beams will hold her weight as she hurdles over obstacles. Carrion rolls under a service hatch and she knows exactly how tall it is at a single glance and knows how tight to the ground she has to be to dive through after them.

The ground turns to metal grating as the two of them run into an old drainway street. A narrow gateway cuts off the far end of the alley, the only way out for Carrion. Luzia's heart jumps up into her throat the moment she sees the gateway and the lever attached to the wall. No electricity out here, no power-based safety measures, but if this is anything like the drainways in the Bastion, that's a manual floodgate release. No power needed. So long as the mechanisms inside haven't fully deteriorated, then…

She leaps to the lever, grabs it with both hands, and throws her entire body weight into yanking it down. With a mighty groan of rust and age, the floodgate is released and a solid wall of metal drops down to block the gateway.

Carrion skids to a stop before they crash into the gate. If they're surprised, it doesn't take them more than a second to recover, for they immediately drop to one knee and spread their palm out onto the metal grate. Thin tendrils of green vines run down from beneath their sleeve, curling around the back of their hand. Whatever they're preparing to do, Luzia won't let them get away this time.

She draws the cuffs Essten had given her from her belt, flips them open, and lunges towards Carrion. One moment she's about to snap the cuffs onto Carrion's exposed wrist, the next they've spun around, grabbing her forearm and yanking hard. Momentum carries her forward and all she can see is Carrion drop to the ground and pull her down with them. Pain aches in her knees as she hits the metal grate and something cold and hard clamps down on her wrist, her arm uncomfortably stretched.

"That's better," Carrion says, stepping back and dusting off their hands.

Luzia stares down in dismay at her own right hand. The cuffs are latched around her wrist, one ring on her, one attached to a rung in the metal grate below. She pulls and twists and tugs, but to no avail, the durability and strength of the Era One materials too much for her to hope to overpower. An angry red line begins to form around her wrist from where the cuff has dug into her skin and she slumps down, breathing hard from exertion and fear.

Carrion stands in front of her, stuffs their hands into their coat pockets, and says, all casual ease, "I admit, I wasn't expecting y'all to crash my party. Sure, I *did* set up shop in the inner Fringes – mea culpa on that," they add, as though those words are supposed to mean something. "Shoulda gone for further out, but you know how it is, it gets a bit chilly. I'm curious – did you find my setup or did Lysander?"

"I did," she admits. "Does it matter?"

They scratch their chin. "Well, only in that I'm surprised someone found me. Figured most people would get turned around by all the mess out here. How'd you find me, anyways?"

Perhaps she might have been turned around, if she were one of the Eoi she'd come here with. She tries to think, but when she opens her mouth, a burning question comes out instead. "I'll answer that if you answer one of my questions."

Carrion blinks and then looks pleasantly surprised. "All righty, then. Shoot."

"Lysander said that we saw you leaving the Office of the Administrator and heading in this direction an hour ago. Getting from there to here would take at least two days with priority lifts and non-stop trains the entire way, and you don't have access to either. Not to mention the fact that *someone* would have stopped you. There are checkpoints for these kinds of things, and you do not have clearance. Even if you started traveling as soon as you were spotted near the Office of the Administrator, which is statistically unlikely, it would take a lot longer than an hour at most. The math simply doesn't work out."

"I walked," they reply simply.

"That's even more impossible! Did you take one of those lift systems that the Eoi use to get around?"

They wag their finger. "That's two questions. I answered the first but I won't answer the second. So go on, then. You know how deals work by now, yeah? How did a human like yourself, who's probably not that experienced with the Fringes, get to my setup, and how'd you get there so quickly? Come on, fair's fair."

"I started mapping the area out. I need to bring you to Sef," she says, feeling like a useless feedback loop. "I thought that making sure I could navigate this area without getting lost would help me find capture you."

"Well," they generously allow, seeming rather cheerful, "you *did* get closer this time. Nice idea about the cuffs, by the by. A great alternative for someone who doesn't want to shoot me with a rifle. So... come here often?"

"What?" she sputters, blindsided.

"This your first time out here? In the Fringes."

"...Yes."

"First time for everything. This place can be a real home away from home if you get used to it. Let me see that map of yours."

A burst of adrenaline runs through her as they reach towards her, and again she tries – and fails – to scramble away. But they don't do anything nefarious, even as she instinctively flinches the moment they touch her. All they do is reach into her pocket and pull out her little tablet and stylus and the map that's still on the screen.

Carrion lets out a thin whistle. "Neat map." They twirl the stylus and start to draw over the map.

Her heart skips a beat and she draws in a breath that's too small and sharp to fill her lungs. "Don't ruin it!"

"Relax," they drawl. They don't seem to be doing much, just writing something down. "This isn't half-bad work. I'm not going to ruin it. Think of this as... a door. If you ever feel like walking through it." They bend down and set the map in front of Luzia, just out of her reach. Then they straighten back up and wink. "Let's see if you can impress me, Luzia N. E. Drainway."

CHAPTER SEVENTEEN

There is truly nothing Luzia can do beyond watch as Carrion creates a sturdy crowbar out of some strange type of wood like Lysander did, and uses it to pry the rusted bars open. They have nothing further to say to her, apparently, and simply leave in silence, sauntering away as though they have all the time in the world.

And then it's just her kneeling on the grate, shame making her curl in on herself and the rotten taste of failure sitting in her stomach like acid.

Is it even *possible* to capture Carrion? The first time she had been part of the team to do so had been at the water-treatment plant, and Carrion had cut through that team with what seemed like minimal effort. While she has only just realized that the most terrifying aspect of the Astrosi is their skill at bargaining and deals and the way in which they can weave words, Carrion managed to twist their bargain with Sef around their little finger until they could buy their own life with a child's and walk away safely. Even this time, when she and Lysander had clearly caught them by surprise, they'd somehow managed to work things to their advantage by setting Lysander up to take himself out of the fight right away and dodged Luzia like it was nothing. If one thing has become clear, it is that Carrion is a master of beating the Astrosi at their own games.

If Luzia can't so much as keep up with the Eoi, what hope does she have of beating Carrion?

Eventually Lysander finds her. He doesn't say a word, merely undoes the cuffs with an expression so sour it could grow mold on water. She picks up the cuffs and her tablet with its marked-up map and shuffles along behind Lysander as he stomps away, her head hanging and her cheeks flushed with shame.

The two of them reconvene with the rest of the group on the edges of the Fringes, near the lift they'd first taken.

"Welcome back," one of the group says. "Did you find Carrion?"

Lysander makes a gruff noise. "Yes. But the fucker got away. They're long gone by now, probably moved on to their next little nest. Head back to the Deep – Carrion or no, I got some new info to give to our queen."

The Eoi fall into step and head off after Lysander back to the lift. Essten is slower and slides alongside Luzia, walking with her while she lets everything Carrion's said and done turn over in her mind until it's all an endless, meaningless slurry.

"So," Essten makes the facial expression equivalent of twiddling his thumbs. "What did you all find out there?"

She shrugs. "I'm not really sure. Carrion had some sort of scanner set up, apparently tracking some kind of radiation. Lysander thinks it's how they've been searching for the diamond."

"Suppose it's not all that shocking, when you think about it," he admits quietly. "We knew that they were after the diamond, and we knew they've gotten close in the past – or at least, we think they've gotten close. It's not like we've ever beat them to it. It makes sense that they'd have some way of searching for the thing beyond just guesswork and luck."

"What would they even *do* with the diamond that they can't already? I know it's some sort of power source, but they can run circles around the Astrosi without even breaking a sweat and that's *without* the diamond."

Essten stares off at the rest of the group, gaze a thousand miles away. "Imagine everything they've done," he says, "and then imagine it hundreds of times worse."

"That's a rather vague thing to imagine," she says, though she shivers anyway.

"Trust me. We can't become lax for even a moment when it comes to the diamond. Not to mention the fact that if Ari gets to Carrion before we do, he'll probably be able to salvage whatever Carrion's using to scan for the diamond and beat us to it anyway. I know you're still new to all this, Ziane, but even humans won't like it if Ari gets the diamond instead of us. I know you probably think that us Eoi are all crazy, but the Vesperi are more violent."

"When I was in the Mists, I saw that they had a dueling pit. Everyone was watching it like it was entertainment."

"Oh yeah, the Mists does do that. We duel here too, when we need to settle things that way, but they do it casually, for sport. Supposedly, that's how Ari became king. He fought his way up to the throne in the dueling pits." Essten nudges her and tries to laugh it off. "Don't go challenging Ari to a duel, eh?"

"I was not planning on it."

They enter the lift behind the rest of the Eoi and Lysander runs through the controls, sending them back to the Deep. Although Luzia would in no way call herself accustomed to this method of transportation, given how jarring it is and how she still isn't certain she fully understands how it works, she has had enough experience to no longer be startled by it, to keep standing straight without having to grab a handrail or someone's shoulder. She's glad of that right now. It affords her some measure of dignity after her crushing failure.

Once they arrive in the Deep, Essten gives her a supportive clap on the back before he and the rest of the group peel off. Lysander, on the other hand, grabs her by the scruff of her shirt before she can even think of leaving.

"You chased 'em," he reminds her, "and so you'll be coming with me to the queen."

This time, however, Lysander doesn't lead her to the throne room. He instead goes to the arboretum, pointedly refusing to so much as glance in the direction of Annie's little house, and beelines to the queen's bower.

Sef appears to have only just arrived amongst the shaded boughs, still in the middle of taking her seat upon her bench as Lysander and Luzia approach. A bright red apple is clutched in her hand. "Ah," she says, looking up with tired eyes. "I had barely left my throne before being informed that you have returned. 'Twas a swift sojourn into the Bastion, was it not?"

"We were up for a good number of hours, my queen," Lysander reports. "And we were able to find Carrion, although Ziane over here let them get away when she was the only member of our squad able to pursue."

"Carrion's knowledge of the Fringes is not a thing to be underestimated." At that, Sef turns to Luzia and asks, "Did you learn aught of Carrion in your pursuit?"

Luzia shakes her head. "Just that, like you said, they know the Fringes better than I thought possible. I tried to map out what I could while I was there, but they clearly had the place memorized."

"As expected. To beat Carrion in the domain that they have spent so long traversing is a difficult thing to ask of anyone, let alone one who has been amongst us for as short a duration as yourself. It will not be held against you," Sef adds, and though she doesn't face Lysander, it's clear the words are directed at him. "I sense you have more to say. What else was unearthed in that desolate and forsaken place?"

"We found Carrion's nest," Lysander reports, the veins at the side of his jaw popping as he grits out the words. "They... they've got some way to scan for the diamond. Got this Era One scanner and configured it to pick up on the diamond's radiation trace. That's how they've been looking for it, and I don't know if any of our own scanners are ready to outperform a piece of Era One tech."

Sef lets out a long breath of air, the most delicate of sighs. "No," she admits. "We have yet to recreate anything that can compete with the designs of Era One, no matter how well we replicate them. The materials from which they were created simply no longer exist. Still, we shall do all that we must to achieve a scanner of the highest quality any Astrosi is capable of. There are remnants of Era One devices that can be repurposed to our needs."

So even though both the Deep and the Mists are realms where Era One tech exists in far greater abundance than it does in the Bastion, there's still a roadblock to recreating it. How could the materials just... stop existing? In the Bastion, everything comes from something. Everything is a recycled form of something or another, from air to clothing to food to electricity. It's conservation of matter, really. Things don't cease to exist; they just change shape. Did whatever was used to make Era One tech simply change shape too many times?

"What do we do?" Lysander asks. "We've got to beat Carrion to it, I know that much."

Sef closes her eyes for a long, thoughtful moment of silence. "Indeed," she finally agrees. "We must. There is no choice, it would seem, but to dissolve the task force hunting Carrion and instead to focus all our efforts on reaching the diamond before them."

It didn't seem possible for Luzia's heart to sink further, and yet it does. "But…" She nearly swallows her own tongue amongst her sputtering words. "But if we're no longer hunting Carrion, then our bargain…"

"There were no conditions set in our bargain," Sef reminds her. "As stated, you may still have a chance to capture Carrion should they happen to appear. That is all I may grant you. Once more, I implore you to remember that it was you, not I, who set forth the terms." Something in her eyes softens, a mere flicker. "You may, if you so wish, scout the Fringes for any remaining traces of Carrion. If you have begun to map the Fringes, then I shall not force you to squander that effort."

If that's the only mercy Luzia will get, she'll take it. "I'll do it," she declares desperately. "I'll go right away. I'll find something or I'll capture them or… I don't know. I promise I'll be back and I'll bring back something that will let us find Carrion."

Sef nods, a single tilt of her head. "You may leave when you are ready. I must rest, but I shall impose no limit on your time save that you must return once I wake."

"You mean to send her up there for that long?" Lysander protests. "My queen, she's refused to be trained, she won't use a rifle, she's a walking corpse if she spends that long in the Fringes on her own."

"I have made my decision," Sef states, with no room for further argument. How long does Sef even sleep for, if her nap will give Luzia an apparent excess of time to search? "Now I must ask the both of you to leave me to my rest."

Lysander bows. "Of course."

When Luzia hurries out of the bower, she turns to Annie's house to grab something to eat and a cantina of water. If she's going to be out in the Fringes for a few hours at minimum, it would be best to have some provisions while she's mapping. She's in the middle of snatching up a peach when Annie walks in.

Annie simply looks at her, puts down the basket she's been carrying, and asks, "What now, girl?"

"I've been given permission to go the Bastion by myself," Luzia tells her, a nervous, twitchy enthusiasm creeping into her voice. She doesn't dare let herself think what she's truly hoping to do, but it lingers in the back of her mind, in the same little corner that the worst of her anxieties occupy when she's trying not to pay attention to them. "I don't know how long I'll be gone. I just have to be back before Sef wakes up. She and Lysander seem to think that'll be ages, I guess."

"Well," Annie says slowly, "you *will* be in the Bastion. *You* might have days to search. Just…" She moves as though she's about to reach for Luzia, but lets her hand drop. "Even if you pay attention to nothing else I tell you, remember this: The world is no longer *your* Bastion."

What is that supposed to mean? "I'll be careful," is what Luzia ends up promising, mostly because she's not sure what else to say in response.

Annie purses her lips and then jerks her head in the direction of the door. "Go on now."

No need to tell Luzia twice.

She's out of the arboretum as swiftly as possible, tracing her way back to the lift that she'd taken to get to the Fringes. The guard stationed by the lift entrance lets her pass without comment. As she rockets up through the network of lift tunnels that the Deep has strange access to, she is all but vibrating in place, shifting her weight from one foot to the next. All her despair at losing Carrion fades into the background, sliding off her like water off waxed plastic.

In the Bastion without supervision. In the Bastion without any real orders other than to check out the Fringes and get back before Sef wakes from her nap that apparently lasts for long enough to worry Lysander. She doesn't think about what she's going to do once she gets to the Fringes, to the Bastion, to her world.

When the lift spits her out on the edges of the Fringes and she finds herself once more looking up at the decrepit wasteland, she is no longer afraid. All the fear is shoved down, her chest filled instead with a bubble of hope. Although she might not have been to the Fringes before, she knows where she is, and she knows that if she keeps going away from the Fringes and towards the inhabited areas of the Bastion, she will find priority lifts that will speed her away into the human world. When Sef had given those orders, she had said that Luzia *may* scout the Fringes, *if she wishes*. She'd given Luzia leave to go, and had, presumably in her exhaustion and distracted by her desire for rest, not given direct instruction to Luzia. Luzia hasn't been ordered to go into the Fringes, and she hasn't been ordered *not* to enter the Bastion proper.

Although Luzia is no master of the wordplay that the Astrosi use, she is capable of learning, just like with any other skill.

She lingers for a moment, staring up at the floors and floors and floors of barren structures that go all the way up until presumably the next level begins. What could Carrion possibly want here? Sure, it provides a good place to hide, but they'd implied that they couldn't get good readings on the diamond from out here. What else is out here? What would make them linger? What would draw them back to this wasteland?

Luzia retrieves her tablet from her pocket and opens up the map that she'd been working on. Beyond the small area that she'd drafted – far, far beyond it – Carrion has drawn a line right across the entire page. And on the other side, they've written, in the same scrawling handwriting that they'd left behind to pave her way to the Deep that very first time, three nonsensical words:

HIC SUNT LEONES

CHAPTER EIGHTEEN

The message Carrion left is meaningless, and Luzia pushes it to the back of her mind as she rushes away from the Fringes and towards the Bastion proper.

It takes time, a lot more time than she would like, but she eventually finds an old priority lift. Her clearance codes still work, although she has to try multiple times to get the computer to accept them. The lift is far slower than the ones the Eoi use. It's a familiar sort of slow, however, the top speed at which things in the Bastion can move, and although the lift is somewhat cramped and the trip takes hours, she still does not regret what she's doing. Without priority lift access, going from the first level to the third takes over two days. With that access, it takes about ten hours of going straight up to reach the third level, though the speed makes her nauseous. If she has potentially days before Sef wakes, she can make it as long as she's quick.

Once she gets out of the lift, her legs stiff, she finds that the Fringes are nowhere in sight. They must begin further in on the first level than on the third. Right. Next transport.

She keeps walking. She finds a train. It's so strange, being surrounded by humans again, even just strangers going about their day, nothing special or important happening, just the average trappings of life in the

Bastion. There aren't that many people on the train, but that doesn't stop her from jolting each time someone brushes up against her or gives her a polite nod as they pass. When the train reaches the end of its line, she gets out at the far busier station and transfers to a direct line, using her clearance as a First Responder to get on a train that will skip the dozens and dozens of stops that the normal train will make.

It still takes almost a full day, and she has to stop partway through to get food and water from a supply depot. How much time does she have left? How long will Sef keep sleeping for? 'Days' could be one, or two, or three, or... The back of Luzia's throat begins to itch, and she cannot tell if it is because her throat is dry or a repeat of that strange cough that had previously overcome her.

At last, at *last*, the train stops at the Lower Transport District, and Luzia jumps off it with a spring in her step that hasn't been there in ages. A smile begins to tug at her mouth as she walks through streets she knows better than the back of her hand. The streets do look different, somehow, but she cannot figure out in what way, and it is probably just how her time in the Deep has affected her. She coughs twice. The itch in her throat begins to grow.

The bubble of hope in her chest is a glowing thing by the time she finds herself in front of Izax's front door.

She presses the door chime.

She waits.

After one minute and seven seconds exactly, the door slides open and Luzia finds herself staring at a man that she's never seen before in her life. The bubble of hope freezes.

"Good morning," the man says. He's got the same brown skin as Luzia, though his hair is gray. From age, given the number of wrinkles on his face and the spots on the backs of his hands. Something about his eyes strikes her as familiar. "Can I help you?"

"I…" She coughs on the word and feels something in her stomach twist. "I'm looking for Izax and Stazi. Where are they?"

The man pauses, an old sadness working its way into those oddly familiar eyes. "If you're from the Office of the Administrator or something, I think you need to update your system. Your records are clearly outdated."

"So they moved?"

"Dead, actually." It is as though the blood in Luzia's very veins ceases to circulate, her heart stopping its beating, her lungs freezing mid-breath. And still the man keeps talking. "I'm sorry, I can't remember off the top of my head when my grandfather died – I was pretty young then. But my dad died last year. I, um. I still have his ID if you need it to update your systems, but apart from that, I can't help you."

"Your dad."

"Stazi S. Trandistrict. Do you need that ID, or…?"

"How did…"

"Old age," the man says as though it's obvious, as though it's not an affront to the very fabric of the world that Stazi is… "He was getting up there, you know. Look, I don't mean to be rude, only I'd really rather not spend ages talking with a stranger about my dad's death, all right? I can get you that ID if you want, or I can schedule an appointment with the Office of the Administrator to help update your system, but that's all I can do."

"I would like the ID. Please."

The ID is fetched and the man hands it to her. A face stares back at her from behind the thin plastic card. Stazi's face. Stazi's face without any baby fat, without any youth in his formerly round cheeks, with lines pinching his eyes – the same eyes as the old man in front of her. His hair is shot through with silver and his mouth has smile lines carved into it. The date of birth is correct. The blood type is correct. The system identification number is correct.

"Is that it?" the man asks.

Luzia's arm is made of lead as she hands back the card. "Yes." Her throat burns. "Thank you. Sorry."

"It's all right," he says.

It is not all right. It will never be all right again.

The door closes and Luzia is left alone on the street.

Annie had warned her that it would not be her Bastion when she returned. Sef and Lysander had said she would have so much time up in the Bastion while Sef simply naps. Leneat was gone for only a day while she scouted the Bastion but she and Essten acted as though it had been ages.

It is nice to see you again, Carrion had said at the water-treatment center. And then, *I'd say 'it's been awhile', but for you I guess it hasn't been.*

Time passes slower in the realms of the Astrosi.

People walk past Luzia. There is chatter and the hum of air filters. Street lamps shine down daylight, so much older than what is seen in the Deep and in the Mists. Beneath her feet are scuffs on the ground that weren't there before. No wonder the computer had taken multiple attempts to accept her clearance codes. They would be old by now. This is not *her* Bastion. Not anymore.

No family. No job. No friends. No home. As far as the world is concerned, she is long dead, and everyone she ever knew has passed, dead and gone, as though they were just a line in the dirt that has been smoothed over and erased.

It takes a very long time for Luzia to move. When she does, she returns to the train station. She returns to the direct line, to the slower outer train, to the priority lift, the time passing in a fugue state until she is once more standing on the edge of the Fringes. Whatever hope had been inside her chest is as dead as everything else, as barren at the wastes that stretch out before her into infinity, into nothingness, until Carrion's line and Hic Sunt Leones and the edge of the world.

Where else is there to go but back to the Deep?

The eternal emptiness of the Fringes follows her down, a shroud insulating her from the world of the Astrosi as much as it insulates the Fringes from the world of the Bastion.

When she reaches the Deep, she just keeps going and going, body unsure of what to do when it actually stops. Stazi gone, Izax gone, her parents gone, her friends gone, her coworkers gone, the neighbors that she only saw once a day and never really spoke to gone. In the Bastion she is a ghost. At least here she is a person, even as a lowly Acolyte and human that can't keep pace with anyone around her. At least there are people here who know who she is. At least she is real.

Eventually her feet step onto the cool green grass of the arboretum. The overhead lights are still on the same setting they were when she left, the same time of day, the same chores being managed. Were she to go back inside Annie's house, the old woman would still be sorting through her basket and the hours upon hours that Luzia has been gone for whittled down to nothing at all, her absence a mere blip on the timeline of the Deep.

Tears are running down Luzia's cheeks by the time she enters Sef's bower, scalding and freezing at the same time, stinging her eyes and dripping down onto her shirt. Her lungs burn as though she hasn't breathed in hours and by now she has been awake for so very long, her entire body worn down into nothing. Shock, a very distant and clinical part of her mind tells her. Shock is so rational, such a formal diagnosis. She is being cracked through the very center of her being, and shock would be a blessing in comparison.

Sef is gone – her bench is empty – but there is still the grass mound, and the apple tree above it, and the metal door that rests in its roots. The door is open and the solid wall of blackness within it beckons, the emptiness of it calling to the void inside Luzia. Blackness so deep that it could whisk her away from everything. Her steps are a slow, drudging march. She walks down to the roots of the apple tree, to where the soil is rich and the tree overflows with soporific life. The darkness is thicker than a solid curtain and when she crosses the threshold it swallows her.

There is nothingness. Nothing more than the cracks in her heart and a warm sensation wrapping around her chest, tugging her forward. Guiding her in the endless night.

Then, in the heart of darkness, there is light.

Though it is blurry through Luzia's tear-filled eyes, there is still an unmistakable glow that grows ever brighter the closer she gets until it is right before her. A large orb hovers in the darkness. It is a rich gold, like the deep color of the sap that glistens on tree bark, amber swirling like water in a stream. Luzia's legs finally give up on her, and she sinks to her knees below the gilded sphere, bathing in its light as she cries ugly, scratchy tears.

"Oh, my Acolyte…" Sef's voice drifts through the night and the queen appears before Luzia, stepping into the glow, her cold skin radiant with golden warmth. "What ails you so?"

Luzia chokes, salt on tongue and trembling in her fingers. "My family." Her eyes ache as she stares into the light and no matter how much she blinks away the tears they don't stop falling. "They're... they're all..."

"You disobeyed our covenant." There's no anger or even annoyance on Sef's face. The heartless queen is above such things. "You returned to the Bastion not to search for Carrion, but to seek out those you left behind. And now you are burdened with the knowledge of the Deep's secrets, of the fate that befalls all humans who come to live here. Your nephew may have been missing for but months during his brief time in my halls, but you have felt the sting of time's passage far more keenly."

Of course Sef knew all along. And she bargained anyway. "You knew I never stood a chance," Luzia blurts out. "You knew."

"'Twas you who made the bargain. I but accepted." Sef's eyes hold no sorrow, nor do they hold any malice. There is not a single sharp edge in her gaze. "Oh, my Acolyte," she murmurs again. "I never wish to see those under my care suffer. Tell me, what can I do to alleviate your agony?"

Luzia's fingers dig into her shirt, knuckles pressing into her chest. "My heart," she sobs. "It *hurts*. I just want it to stop."

"I can grant that wish," Sef promises.

The queen turns to the golden sphere and runs a fingertip along its surface. Though it appears solid, the moment she touches it, she is able to pull a wisp of light from its depths, like swirling amber sand that clings to her fingers. She manipulates it, forms it, and the wisp of light takes shape until it is a single golden rose, thorns and all.

Sef comes to kneel before Luzia, bending down with all the grace of a sweeping willow. "As you have asked," Sef says softly, her free hand brushing away Luzia's tears, "so shall I answer. With that which is granted to me, I shall ensure that your heart never hurts again."

Energy leaves Luzia's body all at once and she slumps over into Sef's arms, as a weeping babe cradled by her mother. Her hand falls from her chest, her fingers no longer strong enough to cling to her shirt, her body no longer able to do anything other than let her tears run dry. Sef places the golden rose above Luzia's heart and its petals, delicate and sharp all at once, begin to glow. One by one, the petals fall, burning holes into her shirt and then turning to soft light as they sink beneath her skin.

When the final petal falls, Luzia N. E. Drainway breathes her last breath.

PART TWO

CHAPTER NINETEEN

A steady hum of life inhabits every grain of soil, spreading out into every blade of grass, every root of every sturdy tree, spilling into the ripe fruit, full to bursting. Sap pulses beneath tree bark in a beat as sturdy and steady as a heart pumping blood. Leaves stretch up to the ceiling, reaching for the overhead illumination to embrace the vitality of the light, letting it seep beneath the thin membranes and enrich the branches with warm energy. It breathes. It grows. In minuscule increments, it rises from the spark of life in a single seed and soars up into its final shape.

"Wake," someone commands. "Wake, she who is called Ziane, Eoi of the Deep."

Life flows into Ziane's still body as though pure light kisses her brow. Yet, as she rises from the soil, she is cold. Everything is faint. Everything is distant. She curls and uncurls her fingers and it is fuzzy, vague, not her. As though she is viewing the world from behind a curtain.

Before her stands Sef, her queen. Sef proffers an elegant hand to pull Ziane from the dirt. "How do you feel, my new child?"

Ziane coughs. There is something in the back of her throat, yet when she turns her attention to it, it fades away. "I am... fine," she says. She does not know what else to say. "I am... awake?"

"Are you in any pain?"

"No."

"Full glad am I to hear that you are no longer so burdened." No gladness appears on Sef's serene countenance, but her voice is not devoid of gentleness. "Have you any memory of what came before?"

Flashes of sights and sounds and scents wriggle through Ziane's mind. They too are faded and distant and barely hers at all. Images through a looking glass. She was human, once, though the humans that she believes were once around her are little more than blurred-out faces with no emotions attached to them, like dolls set up to adorn a scene. How long has she been down in the Deep? For how long has she walked its green halls? And, clearest of all memories, how long has she hunted Carrion?

"I'm called Ziane," Ziane states slowly. "And I have been living with Annie. I hunt Carrion."

Sef touches her cheek, a bare brush of her fingertips against Ziane's skin. "I see," she murmurs to herself. "So much and yet so little. Never are two journeys the same."

"What do I do?" Ziane asks. It doesn't seem like there is anything else she should be asking.

Sef pulls away after a scant moment and straightens up, her long hair shifting like water where it meets the grass. "Long have you slept. There are those that would see you once more, those that would speak with you and learn of you once more. Now you are of the Deep, and its halls and secrets are yours to dwell in without restriction. Seek fulfillment in whatever manner calls to you most, as that is the fate I wish for all those who are under my care."

Does anything call to her? Is she supposed to feel something?

As Sef glides away, Ziane is left standing in a circle of trees with white bark and pale green leaves that droop and sag. She is naked, she finds, and the grave dirt from which she has risen dusts her bare flesh. Her toes curl in the soil, seeking the warmth that does not permeate her own body. This is not the arboretum, with its high ceilings and wandering paths and menagerie of flora. This is somewhere else in the Deep, somewhere that Ziane cannot recall seeing previously.

Behind her is an arch of those ashen trees that leads to a doorway. She walks out through it and feels no desire to ever return. When the door closes, it is as though the room disappears, fading from her mind like smoke.

Someone is waiting outside. It is Annie, holding a blanket in her arms.

"Hm." Annie drapes the blanket over Ziane's shoulders and stares into her eyes, the lines on her face more pronounced than ever. "Well now. I suppose I should ask what you got in return, but I suspect that I already know what you wanted taken away. Not weakness, not illness, not the curse of mortality. All that effort you spent in service of one damn favor and you just bargained it away, didn't you?"

What *did* she bargain away? She is not sure what she has gained or what she has lost. Though the scales are presumably balanced, to her sight they are empty. "Annie," she asks, focusing on the clearest and most recent of memories that she can conjure up, "why do I want to stop Carrion?"

There is something sad in Annie's voice when she replies, "They hurt someone you cared about."

Oh. Of course. "They killed Eoi when we tried to capture them in the water-treatment plant."

"...Yeah," Annie says eventually. "They did." And then she asks, "What were their names?"

"Sorry?"

"The names. Of the Eoi that you watched Carrion kill."

Ziane has no idea. She can recall the event, but the details, the emotions – it's all gone. Did she forget their names, or were they always nameless strangers to her, even as she watched Carrion cut them down? "I... I don't know."

"Right." Annie clicks her tongue and shakes her head. "Thought so. That seem strange to you at all?"

"Not really."

"Come on, girl. You had a big brain up in there, you fool. Use it. Don't that seem strange?"

"No," Ziane insists. Why can't Annie just stop asking her? Isn't it that simple? "No, it doesn't. Carrion was hurting people and it's important that they are stopped."

"Well, that's something, I guess." Annie shakes her head again. "Come on, then. You've not got a stitch on you and I ain't planning on staring at your scrawny ass forever."

Ziane is no warmer with the blanket than she was without it, but perhaps proper clothes will help with that. She follows Annie back through this unfamiliar section of hallways until they reach the arboretum. More than one Eoi passes them as they go, and while they all ignore Annie as per usual, most have smiles and nods for Ziane, as though she has somehow achieved something that is deserving of additional geniality.

In Annie's home, Ziane dresses in the same trousers as the other Eoi that had been tracking down Carrion – thick fabric, large pockets, and tucked into boots with heavy soles. She pulls a shirt over her head and once more looks down at her hands, wondering if she will appear different now that she is fully clothed. She doesn't. It's the same, faraway skin that doesn't seem to fit her.

"Queen Sef said that I should find fulfillment of some kind," Ziane says as she finishes lacing up her boots. "What did she mean by that?"

Annie shrugs. "Some of the Eoi are called to muck about in the gardens, some spend all their time coming up with weird new crossbreeds, some like sitting around on guard duty, and some go on up to the Bastion and do their little soldiering." Ah, right. Essten had said something similar. "Suppose our queen is hoping for you to figure out which of those is singing your name."

"What if none of them are?"

By now, Annie has started making tea, and she sets the kettle down with a clack of metal and turns to stare Ziane down. "Listen here, and listen good. I've said it before and I'll say it again: You ain't unique. You think you're the first one that can't figure out what they wanna do? Hundred others have struggled the same. You think you're special cause Sef awoke you? You ain't. That's how the Astrosi keep on surviving. Most humans that become Acolytes end up bargaining it away and wake up as one of 'em. Not saying this to be mean. But what'll happen is you'll go tearing off after Carrion, and you'll think you're somehow special, and you'll get your fool self killed for it."

"I don't think I'm special," Ziane replies honestly. What's special about her, really? What makes her any better than anyone else?

"Good." Annie picks up the kettle again. "Remember that."

Eventually the tea is poured, and Ziane cradles a steaming mug between her cold hands, and that too does not break through the chill in the core of her. She drinks, and her stomach is warm and her tastebuds enjoy it, but the feeling is empty and it fades and then is gone completely.

What did she give up in exchange for becoming Astrosi? Did she even ask to become this, or was it just a thing that happened as a result of whatever she asked for? She bargained something away for this, and for the life of her she cannot remember what. It must have been important, if it was balanced out by such a powerful revivification. And yet how important could it have been, if she gave it up for something that feels so empty? There had been such life, such vibrancy, such collective organicity when she had first woken beneath the soil, a connection that she has never before experienced and that is now gone, leaving her barren.

There is a knock on the door and then Essten pokes his head in.

"Hey there." He's grinning, nervous and twitchy, and looking at Ziane as though he's not quite sure what to make of her yet. It is still a grin, and that has meaning. "Leneat and I have been waiting ages for you to wake up. You were out for a good week while the queen fixed you up. Was thinking you might wanna go get some drinks to celebrate your awakening, now that you've got the same tolerance for everything that we do."

"All right," she agrees, putting down her cup of tea and following Essten out the door. She does not look back at Annie as she leaves. "I apologize for keeping you and Leneat waiting."

He waves it off. "Ah, no worries, we knew you might take a bit. Some awaken in an hour or so, some have taken months. A week isn't that much in comparison."

Essten takes her to the main dining hall, and to her surprise it is overflowing with people. Leneat is at the forefront, holding a mug of beer and grinning, but behind her are more familiar faces. Not anyone that Ziane knows by name, but she knows their faces, has worked side by side with them in the various groups sent to hunt Carrion. People that work in the arboretum and have given her a nod or two in passing, though they don't acknowledge Annie. Absent are Sef, who of course would not attend such things, and Lysander, who apparently never attends these things either.

"Fellows and gentlefolk!" Essten gestures to Ziane with a dramatic flourish. "I give you… *Ziane*!"

Some applaud, some cheer, some, like Leneat, let out a raucous hoot, pumping their fists in the air. And then Ziane is guided into their midst, with pats on the back and playful nudges against her shoulders and even the odd high five that she awkwardly returns. Most of the other Eoi offer her congratulations, ushering her into the middle of the party as though she belongs. Doesn't she belong now? She's one of them. That means she belongs, right?

"Hey, hey, all right," Leneat says, cheerfully pulling out a wooden bench for Ziane. "Take a seat, have a drink! You've earned it."

Someone across the table hands Ziane a mug of beer, clapping her on the wrist as they do so and offering a smile at the same time. Ziane takes a sip and it is rich, a gentle yellow-brown, the froth cool and light. She is Eoi, and this will not harm her. When Leneat drinks deep, so does Ziane, and there is no bitterness or bite to it as there was before.

"So," Leneat continues, pausing to grin at someone walking past. "A whole week, huh? Not bad, not bad."

One of the passers-by snags a plum from the table and remarks, "Could be worse. I was out for almost a month. Nice and quick, Ziane! If that's a sign of anything, I bet it means you'll be as good as the rest of us in no time flat."

Leneat waves them away. "Yeah, don't think hard on that one. It ain't a sign of nothing, not really. The queen would know, but what's the point in asking? It is what it is." She holds out a peach, skin bright pink and orange, fuzzy and ripe. "You've got our constitution now. Try this. It'll give you just a little trip. Nothing big, nothing like what's in those brownies you scarfed down that one time. Just a bit of fun, something you'll easily come out of after a short while."

The peach is juicy when Ziane bites into it, an explosion of flavor on her tongue. "How long were you… out for? When you became…"

"Ach, I was out of it for almost a whole month. Like I said, don't put too much stock in it."

Essten's voice rings out as he teases, "You're only saying that cause I had to wait around for your ass to finally wake up." He slides into the bench on the other side of the table with a plate of bread in his hands and adds to Ziane, "I got juiced up before she did. Felt like she'd never wake up. Fuck, I nearly got up the disrespect to bug the queen about it."

The still surface of the beer reflects Ziane's features when she stares into her mug, the amber liquid showing her a wavering image of what must be her reflection. Her curly hair is loose around her face – presumably her hair tie vanished along with the rest of her clothes. Her skin looks a little waxier than she thinks it was before, a little closer to Queen Sef's skin. She stares at her own blank expression and feels nothing whatsoever. If her heart beats in her chest, she cannot feel it.

"What did you bargain away?" she asks Essten and Leneat. "What did you give up to become this?"

Leneat's hard mouth sharpens into a confused frown. "Give up? Didn't give up anything, did I? This was a gift. I worked hard as an Acolyte and harder as a soldier's assistant and Sef balanced that out by gifting me this."

A gift. Is it? Ziane looks to Essten. "And you?"

He shrugs and looks down at his hands, absently tearing off a chunk of bread. "Don't remember. I can't recall if it were a gift or if I bargained something for it. I was here before Leneat and way before Lysander, so neither of them know. By now I've lived so long in this life that I don't really care what I was before. Can't remember nothing of it, and I wouldn't want to be a human again anyway. A lot of us can't remember what was before. It's not that uncommon."

"What about Lysander?" Ziane prods. "If he awoke after both you and Leneat, then what did he give up in exchange?"

Essten and Leneat exchange an awkward glance. "Lysander…" Essten says carefully, picking each word slowly, "isn't a standard case. Someone else bargained for him, and I don't even know if they meant for him to be awoken."

"It was stomach cancer of some kind," Leneat mutters. "Not sure what. So bad it was killing him, and they say that the queen had to replace the organ completely with thistle to stop him dying. That's why he don't eat with us." That would also explain the strange stomach pain Ziane experienced when he linked hands with her to help her stand the trip to the Mists. No wonder he deals with that day in and day out, if there is just thistle within him. Is there thistle in Ziane's chest? Or something else? "He took a full month to wake up." Leneat guffaws and shakes her head. "It don't mean nothing, but he acts like it does."

"You don't gotta like him to know that he's good at what he does and he's devoted to the queen," Essten points out. "I'm not chomping at the bit to have a drink with him, but I ain't gonna complain if I'm under his command. The man found his purpose like *that*." He snaps his fingers. "Faster than most of us. Now that does mean something. You got any idea what you're gonna be doing now? Our queen tells us all to find fulfillment when we wake. Some of us know what that'll be sooner and some know later. It's fine if you don't know yet."

What *does* Ziane want to do? Will anything bring fulfillment? What does fulfillment even feel like? Is it an objective and measurable metric, or is it an emotional state that she has to keep waiting to hit her?

"I think…" There is someone out there who she cannot forget. In her mind, behind a flickering shadow of a child that she doesn't think too hard about, is one figure, slouching over with their hands in their pockets and a too-sharp look in their eye. "I think my purpose is to hunt Carrion."

Leneat raises an eyebrow. "We've been ordered to pursue the diamond."

"I know. But I don't know what will bring me fulfillment, and I can't think of anything else other than going after Carrion."

There is simply nothing else. There was once, she thinks, but it was before, and she cannot remember it. Now there is just Carrion, the sole person that comes to mind when she tries to think of having a purpose. Whatever she's looking for, Carrion will have it. That, she knows.

CHAPTER TWENTY

"Aim," Lysander says.

Ziane takes aim at the practice dummy.

"Shoot," Lysander says.

Ziane does not think as she pulls the trigger of her bayonet-rifle. The beam flares out and burns a hole through the dummy's head before she removes her finger from the trigger and the laser dies.

"Holster," Lysander says.

Ziane lowers her rifle and slings it onto her back, the weapon's strap sitting securely across her chest.

With a sigh, Lysander walks forward to inspect the dummy and judge the precision of her shot. There's still plenty of room for improvement and she knows it. Compared to Lysander, who's had a bayonet-rifle in his hands for probably longer than Ziane has been alive, she's barely competent. Still, she has no choice but to improve, Lysander's criticism or not. If she wants to catch Carrion, she'll need to learn how to fight on their level as quickly as possible. After regular training sessions with Lysander, she is improving, and that is something at least.

Lysander doesn't look impressed, but he looks less irritated than his usual, so she will take that as a compliment. "Your aim is still off," he chides. "You can't keep being this shit if you want to get Carrion."

"I'll do better," she promises. "But what about–"

"Our queen has said she'll teach you what else you need to know," he cuts her off. "Pick up on it all quickly. Techs have said that our own scanner is almost ready to go. Once it is, we're going after the diamond. And before you open that fucking mouth of yours, we have good reason to believe Carrion will be there too and that our scanner works the same as theirs. You'll get your shot to hunt the bastard."

She nods. "Good."

Lysander's eyes narrow as he stares at her. "Hm."

"What is it?"

"Everyone changes, I guess."

"Did you?"

"Shut the fuck up, Ziane," Lysander snaps, before unceremoniously yanking her rifle from her and shoving her out the door.

So dismissed, Ziane returns to the arboretum to await the queen's summons. It is a bit surprising that the queen herself would agree to instruct her personally, but perhaps it is something that Sef does for all new Eoi. There's a lot to being Eoi that Ziane doesn't know yet, that she doesn't understand, and she knows that in order to stand on an even footing with Carrion, she shall have to master more than just the bayonet-rifle.

As she walks through the arboretum to Annie's house, she bends to brush a finger against a nearby tree. There is that spark of life tingling beneath the bark, a spark awaiting ignition, and she can feel the way in which it resonates with her, the warmth that runs through the bark like firelight. The warmth that still does not permeate her, no matter how long her touch lingers. She remains cold. But as she pulls away, the tree quivers and a thin, newborn branch creeps out from the bark to reach for her hand, chasing her resonance.

A shudder runs through her and she moves on before it unsettles her further. If she learns how to do it deliberately, to control it, then perhaps it will no longer be so disturbing.

Annie is not at home, and so Ziane retrieves her tablet and once more turns her mind back to her map. Earlier today she had taken a new path through the Deep, so she dutifully adds it, going back over much of her earlier scratchy marks with clean, certain strokes of the stylus. Then there is the map of the Fringes that she doesn't know what to do with. Carrion might continue lurking out there, but she isn't sure when she will next pursue them out there in that collapsing labyrinth.

The door slides open and Annie steps in. "Back so soon?" she asks.

Ziane nods. "Lysander dismissed me. He said the queen would finish teaching me later."

"Hrmf. Well, you either did something very wrong or very right if he kicked you out that early. Don't matter, I suppose. Are you sticking around for dinner, or are you off with those friends of yours again?"

"Essten and Leneat haven't invited me anywhere, so perhaps I shall be here."

"Right then." Annie leans against the counter as she sets down her basket. Her fingers shake as she begins to remove herbs from it. "Cuppa?"

"Please." Ziane watches as Annie slowly makes her way to the kettle. "Are you... all right?"

Annie rolls her eyes and grumbles, "Don't waste your time fussing over me, girl, or I'll wallop you over the head with my botanical tablet, Eoi or no."

"Sorry." Ziane taps her stylus against the map of the Fringes. If only she had more information about the Bastion's layout beyond what she learned doing her job when she was a human. After all, the maps she'd had previously did not include the Deep or the Mists, and they'd barely touched the Fringes. "Annie, do you happen to know if there's a completed map of the Deep somewhere? Or of the Bastion?"

Annie puts the kettle on. "Not a bloody clue. Doubt there's one of the Deep. Everyone sorta just knows their way around down here. For the Bastion... Hm. Tough one, that."

"There are numerous partial maps," Ziane explains, "and I've seen a few of them, but even First Responders aren't expected to be trained on areas outside of their districts. It would be too much information to try to memorize if everyone was forced to learn the layout of the entire world, of course. Perhaps there's a way to obtain all the partial maps and manually combine them."

"If there is, I'd say the best place to find 'em would be somewhere in the Office of the Administrator."

Outside of her first day as a First Responder, back in her human life, Ziane has never been to the Office of the Administrator, and even then she had been in there for only a short while, mostly in just one room, going through an orientation process. But there are large databanks, maintained by self-replenishing Era One batteries, held in the Offices. Those would certainly have the most complete maps available. Perhaps even some that detail the Fringes, although they may be outdated. Still, she will take whatever she can get.

Ziane gets up and tucks her tablet into her pocket. "I should go."

"Our queen ain't summoned you yet," Annie scolds. "You wait for your lesson with her the same as anyone else."

"I'm not going to the queen. I'm going to the Office of the Administrator."

"You nuts? Don't you remember the last time you went up to the Bastion without getting the queen's express permission beforehand?"

Has Ziane done that? "No. Did something bad happen?"

The thousand-mile stare Annie gives her is incomprehensible. "Depends who you ask," she eventually answers.

"If I do anything that violates our queen's direct commands, then I'll know once I start coughing," Ziane reasons. "That's what always happens if I disobey, and it stops once *I* stop, so I can simply head back to the Deep in the event that I cough. Until then, it isn't as though I've been ordered *not* to go to the Bastion. And besides," she adds, "any information I get about a map of the Fringes will only aid in hunting down Carrion. It will help, and I don't want to bother the queen about it, especially considering that even hours spent searching in the Bastion will be no time at all down here."

I don't want the queen to stop me, she thinks, traitorously.

"Can't stop you then, can I?" Annie says flatly.

Ziane shakes her head. "This is the right thing to do."

"Well. At least you've got that still."

"What is that supposed to mean?"

"...Just go on."

Though Ziane's memories of before she was Eoi are fuzzy in parts, she could swear that Annie has gotten more cryptic and odd recently. Annie simply watches her as she slings an empty pack over her shoulders and steps out, and even though she is half waiting for Annie to say something, the old woman never does.

Ziane hasn't left the Deep since she became Eoi, but she knows where most of the lifts are, and she makes her way to a confluence of them, the various lift entrances wreathed in pale, faintly glowing yellow flowers. A few guards are stationed by the lifts, and when she inquires about which will get her to the Offices of the Administrator, they point her to a lift with a plant hanging above it that oozes sticky sap. Clearly not a lift used often. Not that surprising, she supposes, as she doesn't imagine that the Eoi would have all that much reason to wander into such a hub of human traffic.

This lift is one of the normal too-fast Eoi lifts, not the one that took her and Lysander to the Mists and punched through barriers. It takes longer to reach its destination than the others she has taken, however. Eventually it slows to a halt and the doors open.

Filtered air fills her lungs. Not the earthy, faint damp of the Deep. Not even the tangible fog of the Mists. A sharp, visceral memory flickers into her mind, and she can recall so clearly the last time she was in the Bastion, the same air, the same dry and pure air, and it hurts as it flows through her nose and into her chest and burns around her heart, and then... the memory is gone. The air is just air. Her chest is just cold.

The very tip of the toe of her boot touches the hard ground of the Bastion. She shouldn't be here. She *should* be here.

She rests her weight on her foot. She steps out. Behind her, the lift doors peacefully slide shut, the outline of them fading into the wall, the clean interior of the lift replaced by a dingy, dirty metal surface, dented and scratched from the passage of time in the same way the rest of the Bastion is dented and scratched. Another door is right in front of her and there's an old cleaning unit lying against a nearby wall. It would seem as though this lift has spat her out into a storage closet. When she exits, she finds herself in the maintenance halls beneath a train station, a faint rumble overhead indicating that a train has just passed by. Along the hall are bright light fixtures next to clearly marked signs pointing in various directions. Nothing at all like the maze of the Deep. Orderly, despite how old it is. Well maintained, well loved.

Ziane touches one of the painted signs and it is warm. No strange resonance, no living sensation. Just plain and simple metal, heated from the machinery that's humming in the station and keeping the trains running. Another moment passes and the warmth is gone. She draws in a sharp, lung-rattling breath and shakes off an odd shiver. Best to be heading off. Following the signs, she strides out of the maintenance halls to the access stairwell and walks up into the human world.

There are so many people, such a rush of humanity. Chatter of conversation as people stand around waiting for their trains, groups hustling off in various directions, the tall buildings overhead bright with the specific light frequency that means morning. A bustle of commuter traffic. Ziane follows a couple out of the train station and into the busy pavilion outside of the sweeping tower of floors and rooms and units that make up the Office of the Administrator, a pillar in the heart of the Bastion.

She sets off for the main entrance. No one stops her as she walks with her head held high as though she has every right to be here.

Two large doors, each seventeen feet high and forty-eight and a half feet wide, are open to all during business hours. A steady trickle of people flow in and out. A teacher with a gaggle of schoolchildren stands outside, instructing her charges to behave on what must be a field trip. A man carrying a stack of boxes carefully makes his way out, checking constantly to make sure he doesn't trip. A woman with a First Responder security badge pinned to her front enters, walking past Ziane as though she isn't even there.

As on Ziane's past visit to the Offices, her attention is inevitably drawn by the monument in the center of the foyer. Within a protective glass case rests a plaque on a plinth. It's very, *very* old, despite the efforts to preserve it. It's a relatively unassuming plate of golden-tinted metal with words stamped into it, partially scratched out but still mostly legible.

The Office of, it reads, before a scratch cuts through it, and then it continues *Admi*, another scratch, *Bastion*.

The Office of the Administrator of the Bastion.

According to all methods of dating materials that humanity has, this single plaque is from Era One. Some even claim that it is from before Era One, or right at the beginning of it, the first piece of the world that they have.

Dragging herself away, Ziane walks to one of the many help desks that are scattered neatly through the foyer. A man stands behind the desk, tapping away at his information screen, a tablet in front of him buzzing happily with an influx of new messages.

As Ziane approaches, he gives her the sort of polite smile that becomes ingrained in anyone who works in customer service for long enough. "Good morning. How may I assist you?" he asks.

"I'm looking for architectural data storage," Ziane informs him. Unlike speaking to Annie, talking with this human stranger feels rather awkward. "Maps, specifically."

"Clearance code?"

She enters her old First Responder code into his computer.

"Don't tell me that they're recycling codes again," he says with a tired sigh. "One moment, please. It needs an extra few seconds to process." The screen lights up. "There we go. Everything looks in order, although I would suggest you speak with your division leader to scrub your code – the previous user's information is still in the code's metadata and it may cause issues going forward. Now, you're going to want to go down the hall to the left, take the lift to the eighth floor, and keep going until you see the sign for Navigation Databanks."

"Thank you very much," she replies with a nod.

At the lift, more than a few others shuffle in alongside her and she almost jumps out of her skin when a human woman's shoulder brushes against her own. Murmuring an apology, she keeps her head down, her eyes fixed on her feet, and waits to arrive on the eighth floor.

Navigation Databanks is quite far into the depths of the eighth floor, past small offices dedicated to individual administrators and their various assistants, past the larger sections for architectural permits and evaluations. Inside Navigation Databanks are an old school Era Two series of storage towers, the terminal lights flickering faintly as they whir away. A woman wanders from tower to tower, pressing the occasional button.

"Hello there," the woman says to Ziane.

"Good morning," Ziane replies, because that's simply polite. "I need as many maps of the outer districts and the Fringes as possible, completed or uncompleted, and I'm not particular about when they were originally dated."

The woman shuffles to the front and holds out a hand. "Got a tablet or stick for me to put that on?"

Ziane passes over her tablet. "There should be plenty of storage space."

"Well now, that's a well-maintained tablet if I've ever seen one. You keep it quite clean." The woman hooks it up to a terminal and starts transferring over the data, the fans inside the tower whirring away like its life depends on it. "I must say, this is a rather strange request. Get plenty of people looking for specific sections that need upkeep, but not the Fringes. May I ask what it's for? Just research, or…?"

The woman returns the tablet, dozens of new file notifications filling the screen. Ziane clutches it to her chest, self-recharging battery still warm from the data transfer, the heat leaching into her flesh for only a moment before it fades. "I think," she tells the woman, "it is to achieve my purpose in life."

"Huh." The woman is clearly taken aback. "Well, erm… That's a tall order. Not really anything in the Fringes that can grant something that big."

Oh, there's *something* out there, in that wasteland. There is Carrion, and there are their secrets.

CHAPTER TWENTY-ONE

It takes Ziane a while to reach the Fringes.

She could have gone back to the Deep and taken the other faster lift to the Fringes, but for some reason she had found herself on a train before she could even think of doing otherwise. It's as though part of her wants to spend more time in the Bastion, sitting on trains next to humans that interact with her, even though it is only for brief seconds at a time, a trickle of 'excuse me' and 'sorry to bump you' and 'can you scooch over'. As though she is part of the human world, even in this slight capacity. For the life of her, she cannot figure out why she would want such a thing. It isn't as though she is human anymore. This is no longer her world.

As the Office of the Administrator is in the center of the Bastion, it is equidistant from all edges of the Fringes. Thus, after four days of non-priority travel, Ziane returns to the same place she had been before, the very same place that they had last found Carrion. Unlike some of her fuzzier memories, as she stares up at the stories upon stories of crumbled walls and exposed beams, she can remember with crystal clarity the way that she had chased Carrion only to be pinned in place with her own cuffs.

She pulls out her tablet and opens up the maps again. A sea of images and files and notifications fills the screen, quickly sorted into neat categories by the helpful software, blinking cheerfully up at her. She selects the files for this area of the Bastion's edge and begins to line them up with her own sketchy map, resizing and rotating as she goes until it matches up. The official maps go a bit further than her own, although they do not get close to Carrion's line. With these maps, she can't reach that boundary. But she can get closer.

Now the only question is, does she dare?

She takes half a step forward into the shadows and then thinks better of it. No, no she shouldn't. Not now. Later. Now she's been gone for too long, even with the time difference in the Deep. She cannot miss Queen Sef's summons, and it's too soon anyway, she doesn't have a plan, she doesn't... Her chest is pounding and she doesn't know why. Her breath sputters, her lungs ache, and *why*? It doesn't break through the cold within her; it is simply like ice injected into her veins, sudden and freezing and... and terrifying.

Before, she knew what fear felt like. Or, at least, she remembers knowing what it felt like, remembers that there had been a steady whisper of anxiety, of what-ifs that ran through her mind. Since she woke up, however, she hasn't felt any of that. Why did that change? Why now? Is it because she is afraid of encountering Carrion? Surely not.

Or is it because she fears what might be out there, what is lurking in the depths, what hides at the edge of the world?

Ziane flees.

She doesn't run – she's not that mad – but she remembers where the hidden lift back to the Deep is, and she returns to it as swiftly as she can, crossing the stretch of warning signs and empty space with long strides, stuffing her tablet back into her pocket as she goes. The lift rockets downwards and she stands stock still in its center of the small space, as though if she moves, the floor will crack open and swallow her like the decrepit roads of the Fringes.

Even once the lift opens its doors and she is greeted by the damp air of the Deep, she is still twitchy, her eyes darting from corner to corner, her muscles tense and strained. Did she always live like this when she was a human? There was that anxiety, yes, but was it always this taut, this thin? Did it always feel like a shadow in the back of her mind, lying in wait to cannibalize her own brain the moment she stops actively repressing it? This cannot be how she continues on now that she is Eoi, now that she has her duty to the Deep and to the queen, her duty to track down the diamond for Sef and Carrion for herself.

When she returns to the arboretum, Annie is still in the house, still flipping through her botanical with her basket of greenery, just as she had been when Ziane had left her. The only indication of the passage of time is that the kettle must have boiled, as a cup of tea rests next to her, thin threads of steam wafting up.

"Well now," Annie says as Ziane staggers into the room. "That was longer than I thought you'd be. Took your time, did you?"

Ziane just nods.

"Got what you need?"

Another nod.

"Think I preferred you chatty," Annie grumbles. She points to the second chair. "Sit there and help me sort through this mess. Some of them Eoi are breeding a new type of *Papaver somniferum* and we gotta check the size and color of this batch."

As instructed, Ziane sits and begins to go through the plants with their thinner stalks and bulbous tips. She goes through the motions without thinking about it beyond placing things where Annie tells her to. It is peaceful work, interspersed only with Annie muttering measurements to herself as she writes them down, her wrinkled fingers occasionally fumbling both plants and pen.

Hours pass in a quiet that is neither comfortable nor uncomfortable, quiet that simply *is*, before Annie stops, raises her head, and declares, "Queen's here. Bet it's for that lesson of yours. Go on, girl. Go meet her outside her bower."

One day, Ziane is going to have to learn how Annie always seems to be able to tell when the queen is in the arboretum. No wonder she had originally been assigned to learn from Annie. The old woman is an endless bowl of knowledge and secrets. With a murmur of agreement, Ziane places the last plant in its place and shuffles out into the bright grassy field. She makes her way to the queen's bower and waits just outside the circle of trees, far from the mound with its darkness below and its apple tree above.

Sure enough, Queen Sef soon approaches, her long hair trailing behind her in the grass. "'Tis good to see you again, Ziane," she says in greeting. "What has your training with Lysander yielded?"

"It's been two weeks and five days," Ziane replies swiftly, "and I do not think I've learned enough. My aim is still off and I'm not doing well enough in the hologram obstacle courses he has me go through."

Sef rests an ethereal hand upon her shoulder. "Such skills take time. Do not trip in your haste to run."

"I know. It's just…" How to explain the itch under her skin, the scratching in the back of her mind? "Not being able to go after Carrion or the diamond is irritating, that's all."

"Then I shall teach you what I can to aid you in your quest." With a wispy gesture, Sef leads Ziane not inside her bower, but instead to a field of pale pink flowers not too far away. "As Eoi, we are blessed with gifts beyond mortal abilities, beyond even mortal comprehension. Magic, you may have heard it called. So too are the Vesperi blessed, though their domain is of the air and the elemental properties that enrich it. Our domain is of the earth, of that which is green and growing."

Coming to stand in the center of the field of flowers, Sef gestures for Ziane to stand opposite her. The flowers around them appear to lean towards Sef, only slightly, as though magnetized to her presence. *Asclepias syriaca*, or common milkweed. One of the notably harmless wildflowers that Annie had told her about, though she hasn't been in this particular field before. Amongst their waxy, oval leaves are stalks tipped with puffs of light pink and delicate lavender conical blooms. Though they do not cling to Ziane as they do to Sef, there is still once more that resonance.

Sef raises a hand to the ceiling and the flowers grow up, stalks thinning and roots sprouting from the soil as they rise. The resonance sings, echoing through Ziane's blood like a vibration, a single piece of dust falling onto glassy water.

"Describe what I have just done," Sef says once she ceases her display and the flowers stand tall.

Ziane swallows and licks her lips. "I suppose… it's magic."

"No." The reply is as emotionless as a rock. "You are newly Eoi and you retain the misconceptions humans have about our people. Purge your mind of magic and mystery, for this is neither. What we do is science, and it is lawful, quantifiable, comprehensible. It is rearrangement. It is balance. It is the spark of life. We cannot drain what we cannot replenish, we cannot bend what is not within our boundaries, and we cannot take what does not exist."

In combat against Carrion, Lysander had made vines from the dirt he carried and the water in the tanks. Carrion had pulled water from the vines, but they hadn't made anything new. They had ignited air, but they'd needed a match. Ziane looks at the broken soil around Sef, broken because it has been used to feed the flowers' growth. She thinks of the wagers placed up in the Mists, hair given for energy. None of them can make something from nothing.

"On your knees, Ziane," Sef instructs. "Plunge your hand into the soil and feel the life that teems within."

Ziane kneels and slowly sinks her fingers into the soil, further and further, until the dirt is up to her wrist, warm from the light fixtures overhead and soft from recent tilling. Vibrating and welcoming, the resonance reaches out to her. Is that life?

"Everything is the sum of its parts," Sef tells her. The more Ziane focuses on the ground, the more distant Sef's voice becomes. "Sense the atoms of the soil, the vibrations of the roots, the sound of life. Let it in. Do not fight it. Sense the way in which the base elements could be tweaked, the way in which the particles of the soil could be drawn into the stems, the way the color sings and changes. Listen to it. Feel the pulse of it. Imagine the map of it in your mind's eye."

Everything is particles. Everything is atoms. Maps and math, the things that make the most sense to Ziane. Her eyes flutter closed and she can *see* the map of the soil, her fingers running over each atom, delicately strumming them like strings, letting the flowers and the roots and the trees in the distance sing to her. She can see what needs to go where to change the equation, what shapes to rearrange the matter into. She plucks an atom from here, a molecule from there, takes from the soil across the field and draws it all into the base of a single flower, and within all of that, there is a new pattern, a new map. Equilibrium.

Inch by inch, petal by petal, one lone milkweed curls up and up until it stands far above the rest, matching the height of Sef's work.

Sef's face is serene but Ziane thinks the queen is pleased. "Now you see the scales. *Omnia mutantur, nihil interit.*"

Ziane's head snaps up. "What did you say?"

"'Tis but an old saying, in a language none now know. Translated, they say it means, 'Everything changes, nothing dies.' Sense what is missing from the soil, what you took to make that flower grow. That is the balance, the price paid." Sef bends over to pluck the flower and then it crumbles into dirt in the palm of her hand, a rain of soil falling back to the ground to nourish the next thing to grow from it. "We can only take as much as there is to give."

When Ziane pulls her hand out of the soil, the connection does not snap. It feels instead as though it goes dormant, ready to reach out for her again. But whilst she was connected, when she was balancing the equations, it was enough to suppress the whispering anxiety stalking her mind. Not enough to remove it, yet just enough to distract it.

"Please," she whispers. "Please teach me more. I... It was all so even. So clear."

Sef slowly shakes her head. "You have found the connection. That is what matters. Were I to instruct you further, I would take you down a path that leads to neither the whiplash speed of combat maneuvers nor the precise calculations our botanists use to crossbreed, but instead to a place of control. Of dominion. I would be teaching you how to guard the borders of my throneworld, how to balance the scales on a grand level, and that would not help you on any of your quests. Find what you wish to use this knowledge for and seek masters in that field. That shall aid you far more than I can."

"But Lysander doesn't seem to want to teach me."

"Is he truly the only one you know that has found their calling as a soldier?"

The 'yes' is on Ziane's tongue before she stops. "Essten and Leneat. They're soldiers, and they're both older than Lysander. Do you think they would teach me?"

Sef gives her a pale smile. "You have but to ask them to receive an answer."

"I will." Ziane gets to her feet and brushes the dirt off her knees like shedding little flecks of embers. Then she pauses, and that breath of hope fades away, as everything seems to these days. "I... haven't been a very good friend to them, have I? They've reached out to me, and I don't think I've ever actively reached out to them."

"You have all the time in the world to change that," Sef reminds her. With that, she leaves, each slow footstep silent on the grass, the only sound that of her hair dragging through the flowers. Before she steps out of the clearing, she looks back over her shoulder and asks, "Are you truly certain this is your purpose, Ziane? Eventually, one way or the other, Carrion shall be brought to justice and the diamond shall be retrieved. What shall you do when all is said and done? They cannot be your fulfillment forever."

In her mind, Carrion is simply *there*, a fixture of the world. For all that she knows she has to capture them, she cannot envision what she will do with herself when they are no longer there to chase. When did hunting them become the only thing that she could see herself doing? It is difficult to remember, but she thinks since they were the one to bring her down to the Deep. They were the first door to her new life, for better and for worse.

When she does not answer, Sef eventually walks away, vanishing into the wilderness of the arboretum.

Ziane looks down at the tiny specks of soil that have clung underneath her nails and between the creases of her palms. When the wall had collapsed in the Fringes, Lysander had grown slabs of wood to stop it falling. Does that mean that she can take this with her even into the darkness of the Fringes? Can she bring that spark of life to the edge of the world?

She goes to find Essten. It takes her a good half-hour to locate him, and she once more has that twinge of shame at realizing that, despite his friendship, she has no idea where he would be or what he would be doing on a day-to-day basis. She doesn't even know which of the many personal dwellings in the Deep is his. When she does find him, he's in one of the smaller training rooms that she's not been to before. He's positively tearing through a holographic combat program, hitting target after target.

"Woah – end program!" he calls out once he spots Ziane.

She hovers at the edge of the room, uncertain if he'll be willing to do this for her. At the time, Sef's words had been reassuring, but in hindsight they hadn't been a certain yes or no. "I'm sorry to interrupt," she says.

He hangs his bayonet-rifle up on the rack and cheerfully strides over to her, brushing his hair back from the thin sheen of sweat on his forehead. "Eh, don't worry about it. Not like I'm progressing through the levels all that much anyway. So what's up? You look a bit dirty. You all right?"

"Oh, um, yes. I was wondering if I could ask for a favor." She takes a deep breath and gets out, "The queen taught me the basics of what we Eoi can do, but she said that if I wanted to learn how to use those skills in a way that would help me take down Carrion, I would need to ask someone who's good at combat. I was hoping... I was hoping that you might be willing to help me. I know it's a pretty large request, and of course you're free to say no, but I would be honored to learn from you."

Essten blinks at her, and then grins from ear to ear. "Fuck yeah!" He claps her on the back and ushers her out the door. "Come on. I know a place with a ton of fresh soil and pre-crafted seeds that'll be a great starting point."

That's really it? No questions, no hesitation? "I'm grateful, really I am, but... why are you always so willing to help me?"

Essten's grin doesn't falter. "I've been here awhile, Ziane. All of us, and I mean *all* of us, take a long-ass time to adapt to the Deep. I generally give folks a good few years of figuring things out before I make any final judgement calls on their personality. And you, you've been nice and polite right from the start, even if you're always a bit in your own head. That means a lot more than you think it does. You're one of the most skittish people I've ever met, but, you know." He lets out a long sigh. "I was there, the day you first bargained with Sef. It was a damn brave thing you did."

That first bargain. Carrion, she remembers – the way they'd twisted out of the Deep on a technicality, skirted the most vicious trap that the Astrosi have, the trap of words and contracts – yet Ziane cannot recall exactly what she had asked for. "I think by now you remember it better than I do," she admits.

That smile fades, and Essten stops in his tracks. "Oh," he says slowly, realizing. "So *that's* what you bargained away."

"What was it?" she asks, before immediately regretting it. Even reaching out to try and decipher those fuzzy memories feels like being shocked with static.

"If you wanted it gone," he says slowly, "then I won't undo that. Deal's a deal, bargain's a bargain."

She flinches and decides, "I don't want to know."

"Good call." Then he adds, "We only take what people are willing to give."

The balance of the equation.

Leneat is relaxing in one of the many dining halls when they find her, her feet up on a wooden table, in her hand a mug of beer that she sips at every so often. When she sees Ziane and Essten, she gives them a sharp wave.

"Interested in helping me teach Ziane?" says Essten, plopping down in a chair across from her.

"Oh, fuck yeah." Leneat gives Ziane a proper once over and remarks, "You've grown your hair."

Has she? Ziane reaches up to her curls. For all her adult life, she's simply tied her hair back as tightly as she can and kept it relatively short, a style she had not deviated from during her time in the Deep. Yet now it is indeed longer, the curls puffing out around her head and as far down as her shoulders. With everything that has happened to her since she arrived in the Deep, cutting it simply never occurred to her. There was always something more important to do than sit down with a pair of scissors.

She pats down her curls and asks, "Does it look… bad?"

"No." After a moment, Leneat sighs and elaborates, "It looks Astrosi. Which is good. That's all I meant."

"Oh."

"You gonna keep it this way?"

"I hadn't thought about it. It might get in the way if it gets longer."

Essten laughs and replies, "We all have long hair and none of us let it get in the way." He gestures to his own blond braids and then to Leneat's dark ponytail. "Pick a style, any style. Though maybe not what Lysander's got – leaving your hair totally unbound like he does is kind of a big dick move. Implies you're confident enough that you ain't worried someone will grab it in a fight. It's a skill thing."

Although Ziane hadn't really wanted to let her hair down regardless, she permanently scratches it off her list at that remark. "I definitely am not that skilled."

"Sure ain't," Leneat bluntly agrees.

With an embarrassed handwave, Essten tries to smooth it over. "Well, you could be. One day. Skill is learned and all that, you know. Besides," he adds, patting her on the shoulder, "you don't want to be like Lysander. The man ain't even got a hobby. There was something Queen Sef told me when I was new: reinvent yourself as many times as you want, just don't waste time trying to be someone else. One day we wake up and we're Astrosi, so if you want to wake up every day as someone else, that's fine by her, so long as you're not trying to live your life imitating someone you'll never be."

Good advice it may be, but as Ziane continues to feel her too-long hair, she has to wonder who she even is. She's Astrosi, no longer human. She's technically a soldier, though something deep within her rejects that as an identity outright. She's a mapmaker, yet lacking in the expertise needed to call herself a proper cartographer. That emptiness inside her yawns wide once more, and she has that creeping discomfort of the thought that she was something to someone else, once. An identity held deep to her chest, hinging on her relation to someone that she cannot remember.

Leneat raises her mug. "Want a drink before we get started? Training is thirsty work."

"Damn right," Essten agrees with a laugh. "Vintners have got a new wine I'm dying to try."

Ziane thinks on it. Wine. Grapes fermented until the sugar turns to alcohol, the process releasing carbon dioxide that then gets funneled into the Deep's photo-generators, where various trees convert it into oxygen. Everything changes, nothing dies.

CHAPTER TWENTY-TWO

"Fucking waste of fucking time," Lysander grumbles under his breath, shaking the device he's holding with a growl.

Ziane closes her eyes and lets the disappointment wash through her. Not *again*.

This is the sixth time they've gone up to the Bastion in search of the diamond, armed with the theoretically powerful new scanner that the scientists in the Deep have fixed up. While Ziane doesn't know much about the way the scanner that Carrion had used actually works, the techs have assured Queen Sef that what they've concocted is, if not identical, then similar enough for the differences to be unnoticeable. It is designed in the same way, to detect the specific frequency of radiation that the diamond produces and provide as accurate a location as possible. Yet every time the same small squad has to gear up and take a series of lifts that spit them out in increasingly odd locations, they simply end up standing around for hours while the scanner gives inconclusive readings. The only pro of the entire situation is that Ziane has been able to spend plenty of time in the Bastion over the past month, but the bitter taste of failure is quickly burning through.

Next to her, Leneat mumbles a curse or two. "Starting to think this scanner is piece of junk."

Though the technology itself has the same clean lines as all Era One devices, Ziane can't help but think she's never seen Era One tech that works so poorly. The bits and pieces that wash up in the Bastion at least have the excuse of being neglected. Something restored by the Astrosi for a specific purpose doesn't get any leniency from her, nor from any of the other Eoi on the squad.

A static-heavy whine emanates from the device and Lysander snarls in frustration. "This bloody useless motherfucking..." He jabs a finger at the rest of the group. "All right, fan out anyway. Tenth level ain't busy at this time of day, and in this district there ain't much area to cover before we leave the scanner's range. For whatever that's worth. Ignore humans or kick 'em out of the way, I don't care. Stay on tact-coms. Keep an eye out for Carrion." He pauses to look up at the ceiling and adds, "And watch out for Vesperi. We're closer to their domain than ours up here, and who knows what they've got to track the diamond." He pulls a small seed from his pack and tosses it in his mouth, swallowing it down like a pill. "Prep just in case."

The rest of the group does the same, fishing around in their packs for their own tiny seeds. Following suit, Ziane grabs her own and swallows down the small oval object, feeling it latch into her throat and rest there, dormant.

"If we've got any luck, the Vesperi have got something even more shit than we have to track it," Essten says under his breath, loud enough for Ziane and Leneat to hear but quiet enough that Lysander misses it.

Ziane shrugs. "The Vesperi have yet to show up during our tracking excursions. I don't see why they would now."

There's a frown creeping across Leneat's rough features. "I don't know," she says. "Sure, we don't know if the Vesperi are focusing on Carrion or the diamond. That don't mean we can count on it being the former. Ari doesn't send his folk out often, but when he does, he strikes hard."

Essten laughs and gives Ziane a comforting pat on the shoulder. "Well, if Ari's folk do show up, we'll teach 'em a thing or two about fucking with the Eoi, ey Ziane?"

"I've never fought the Vesperi before," she points out.

"You've been doing great, seriously. And we'll have your back. Even Lysander will, if it comes to a fight."

"He once told me that I was dead weight and he would leave me to die."

"...Yeah that sounds about right. Still, that was probably before you were Eoi, yeah? It's different when you're one of us. Our queen gives Acolytes leeway and chances and all that, but being Eoi means she's decided you're worth it, and Lysander won't go against her opinion. He serves her, she serves her people, you're her people now. Simple as that." Essten gives her another friendly nudge. "Come on, let's fan out before Lysander gives us another death glare."

After so many sojourns up to the Bastion to track the diamond, Ziane has become accustomed to working with the group – how to move, what place to take. She goes to the far left, Essten and Leneat to the right of her. This time the tracker has led them to a maintenance facility near a train station, the sidings filled with orderly rows of locomotives and carriages in need of various repairs. The station itself is still in operation, but it's being run by a limited redeye shift while the majority of the Bastion's population sleeps through the night.

During the nighttime, most of the Bastion's light fixtures and street lamps are set to a dimmer frequency than the bright day lights – all the better to help people sleep – and no one really knows if the Bastion's light cycle is designed to mimic the circadian rhythm of humans or if humans developed in a response to the Bastion's light cycle. Ziane supposes she'll never know. Either way, it's rather dim in the maintenance facility, but fortunately for them security lampposts dot the area, their cool light making sure that any off-hours worker passing through doesn't trip and fall in the dark.

Since Ziane's trip to the Office of the Administrator and her unexpected retreat from the Fringes, the Bastion no longer feels as welcoming as it perhaps once did. The air is still comforting, but she keeps glancing over her shoulder, waiting for something unfamiliar to appear, as though the Fringes are right behind her and waiting to menace if she gives it the chance. Though the maps she has procured from the Office of the Administrator were far more thorough than what she had as a First Responder, they are not complete. Large sections of the Bastion remain unknown, and not merely within the Fringes. Humanity's desire to avoid disturbing Era One structures has in this one regard worked to their disadvantage, and sectioning off such areas has led to an information void. Who knows what there might be, even here?

Ziane splits off from Essten and Leneat to cover more ground. She scans the area as she walks, but she honestly isn't sure what she should be keeping an eye out for. Everyone has always been vague about what exactly the diamond looks like, and Leneat once told her that not even Lysander has been made aware of the item's appearance. Only Queen Sef knows, and for some reason she has chosen not to share that information with anyone else. All they know is that they will know it when they see it. If the diamond is apparently a power source, Ziane's best guess is that it's some manner of Era One technology. It's uncommon, but she knows that some pieces of Era One tech have their own power supply, a battery of some kind, that isn't hooked up to the rest of the Bastion's energy-recycling system.

Something *clinks*. Ziane whips around, one hand going for the bayonet-rifle holstered on her back.

A shape moves in the shadows of a rundown train car.

She doesn't hesitate to draw her rifle, aiming at the flicker of a shadow, just as she has been taught. She has the vaguest sensation that she should be feeling something, that there should be a pounding in her chest, a strain of some muscle, but there's nothing. The mental anxiety remains yet the physical sensations seem somehow lacking.

Someone steps out of the shadow and lets out a groan. "Fucking great. It's *you*."

Her eyes widen as she recognizes that voice and the face clarifies under the blue-white light of the night cycle lamps. Trying not to be obvious, she briefly activates her tact-com, just long enough so that Lysander can pick up her next words. "Jess," she recalls. "King Ari's lieutenant."

Jess has his own bayonet-rifle resting on his shoulders, finger not on the trigger but close enough to show the threat. He's got something strapped to his waist, like a toolbelt, and attached to it is a small piece of distinctly Era One tech, not dissimilar to the one Lysander uses.

The Vesperi have their own scanner.

"So. You're Eoi now. And I'll assume from your getup and weaponry that you're one of Lysander's soldiers, hm?" Jess's gaze flicks from one edge of this alley to the next, lingering on any pockets of shadow between train cars. "Then I'll go ahead and also assume that Lysander is skulking about somewhere, along with a gaggle of other Eoi, yes? If you're searching for the diamond, then he'd have to be a moron to come without more backup than just you. He might be thick, but he's no moron."

"How do you know we're searching for the diamond?" Ziane asks, frowning.

Jess glares at her. "Don't insult my intelligence. You're not out here for a fun nighttime stroll. If you're still wandering about, you haven't found it yet."

"Well, no, we haven't. But neither have you."

"It's just a matter of time."

Slowly at first, Jess begins to walk towards her. She raises her rifle and aims it at his head, her index finger coming to lay atop the trigger. It's at full charge, the steady little blue bars blinking along the barrel. There's enough light that she has a clear shot. All she needs to do is take it. Jess takes another step towards her. *Take the shot.* He keeps walking, a thin smugness in his glare as he walks right up to her.

And then he simply strides past her. She jerks her rifle up and to the side and finally shoots, the laser hitting the side of one of the carriages and sending a shower of metallic sparks flickering down over both of them.

"Stay where you are," she tells him, trailing her rifle at him again, "or I will shoot."

"No, you won't. You haven't been one of us for very long and you don't know yourself," Jess says over his shoulder. "We don't lie. We don't need to. And we can all read a bluff from a mile away."

Another shadow moves and then Lysander is standing between the train cars, pointing his rifle right at Jess. "She might not, but I sure as shit will."

That makes Jess stop. "You don't wanna do this," he warns.

Lysander's upper lip curls into a twisted sneer. "Nah," he spits out, "I really think I *do*."

Jess sighs. "So be it then."

A thin fog has begun to cling to Ziane's boots. Then, in unison, a dozen shapes appear atop the carriages – a full team of Vesperi, all aiming rifles down at Ziane and Lysander, all ready to shoot at a moment's notice. Her breathing is shallow and twitchy, and it takes all her effort to avoid spinning around and running away. If she moves, they'll shoot. Even if she can somehow dodge the lasers, without the weapons, there's still the mist.

Despite his visible red-faced rage, Lysander doesn't move either. "You fuckers don't play fair."

"As if you wouldn't do the same," Jess points out. He glances back over his shoulder, though not at Ziane. "Come on, then. Where's the rest of your folk?"

"On their way right the fuck now, about to kick your lot in the ass."

"All right, so we've got a few minutes. Before we burn you all full of holes, answer me one thing. Your scanner. It can't pinpoint the radiation frequency properly either, can it?"

Lysander's eyes narrow into slits, but he doesn't say a word.

"How did you know?" Ziane asks before she can stop herself. "About the radiation."

Now Jess properly turns to look at her. "The scanners – *both* our scanners, at a guess – work by detecting the specific radiation frequency the diamond gives off," he explains. "You know that, we know that. If I'm right then you've been having the same problem we have. At a distance, the scanner gives you a reading, and then once you get close, it starts acting up and can't get a lock. Am I right?"

"That matches with what I've seen and heard," she confirms. "Why is it happening?"

"Well, I was hoping you lot might have an answer to that. We've noticed you moving into the levels closer to us lately. A while back, you were on the fourth level. Now you've gone up to the tenth."

Ziane nods, short and shallow, still worried that the fog or the soldiers might take her out if her reply is a bit too enthusiastic. "We started searching with the scanner on the first level."

"And us the eleventh," Jess says. "This time our scanner directed us to the sixth level, but we found you first and figured we'd cut you lot off."

"So it gave both our scanners different signals?" She frowns as she tries to reason out that difference. "Our scanners must operate differently. Or perhaps yours is set to the wrong frequency of radiation. Or ours is wrong. Or both are wrong? You started at the eleventh and us at the first – maybe the scanners were calibrating? Getting more accustomed to the radiation frequency, getting better at tracking it. But if we were being sent up to the tenth and you to the sixth…"

"Stop fucking talking to him!" Lysander yells. "Shut your damn mouth and wait for backup!"

Jess's rifle lowers the slightest of inches and he ignores Lysander completely. "You were overshot up and we were overshot down. So, what? Are we supposed to meet in the middle?"

"Maybe." No, but there's something wrong with that. Ziane thinks carefully, a thought right at the edge of her mind. "Even if we got two of our separate readings at the same time and split the difference, head to the middle level, that would only give us a vertical direction, not a horizontal one. We would be on the correct floor, but that wouldn't be enough to locate it. It also doesn't explain why the scanners start failing the closer we get."

"Perhaps the diamond's radiation isn't contained," Jess suggests, a deep wrinkle forming between his eyebrows as he thinks. "It could be leaking out to the area around it." He curses and shakes his head. "No, if that was the case, it wouldn't be fluctuating. The leaking radiation would remain traceable even if the diamond has some kind of interference bullshit going on."

That's not all, though. What else, what *else*? "That's why Carrion was in the Fringes," she realizes. Of course, of *course* they got to that conclusion first. They always get to everything first. "The scanners are accurate at range but fail the closer they get. And so the best way to counteract that would be to go to the very edge of the world."

"Nobody move!"

Ziane freezes at the sound of half a dozen footsteps rushing into this standoff. The other Eoi have finally got here. On the far side she can see Essten, only a few feet away from Lysander. Out of the corner of her eye is Leneat, the woman's rifle shifting from Jess to the Vesperi that have taken the high ground. The air is so thick with tension and growing fog that Ziane could choke on it, as the Eoi and the Vesperi face each other down, waiting for a signal to shoot, waiting for that thread to snap.

Jess has one hand held up in half-surrender. "I know this is a big ask, but if none of you could do anything *stupid* for five minutes, that'd be great." To his own soldiers, he adds, "If they shoot me, kill 'em. Until then, don't engage."

Lysander jerks his head back in surprise, recoiling as though Jess's restraint is contagious and will get on his clothes if he's too close. "What?" he demands, clearly aiming for snobbish and scathing and instead landing more in the confused territory. "Are you too chickenshit to settle this in an honest fight?"

"I am *trying* to have a damn conversation with the *one* reasonable person here," Jess grits out, the veins of his jaw popping from how tightly he is gritting his teeth. Slowly, he turns back to Ziane and lets out a short, tense breath. "You said Carrion was in the Fringes?"

It takes Ziane a few aborted attempts to speak before she can sufficiently ignore the dozen rifles ready to fire and reply, "Yes. We found them there a while back. They had their own scanner and they had some sort of pendulum or calibrator or something set up with it – I can only assume to further refine the readings."

"You've actually got Carrion's scanner?" Jess asks incredulously.

"Well… no. Not exactly. They hadn't left the area and were able to retrieve it," she admits. "As far as I know, they still have it."

"If we're right then the thing I keep wondering is, assuming they have the same sort of scanner as us," Jess wonders, slowly thinking it though, "and if they've been getting way more precise readings from the Fringes this whole time, then… why haven't they already beaten us to the diamond?"

An enthused voice rings out in the night: "That's my question exactly!"

Everyone here, Eoi and Vesperi alike, turns to face this new party. Lounging on the rusted roof of a long-condemned carriage, their chin resting on their hand as they look down at the confrontation like it's a particularly entertaining show, is Carrion.

CHAPTER TWENTY-THREE

"So, y'all got any answers?" they ask the assembled armed forces. "Nope? Aight, well, thanks for the insight, I guess."

Slick as anything, they roll backwards and vanish into the darkness behind the carriage.

"You son of a–" Lysander slices his hand through the air and orders, "Cut them off! And don't kill 'em, the queen wants 'em alive!"

At the same time, Jess tells his forces, "Do not let them escape! Shoot to kill if necessary!"

As everyone scatters after Carrion, the fear of being shot that pinned Ziane in place fades and she can focus on Carrion. Lysander and the rest of the Eoi peel off, spreading out to flank the carriage that Carrion had been resting on. The Vesperi are already sweeping the area to see if Carrion is hiding behind other units. Ziane is about to follow when she stops. It's dark enough that no one can clearly see where Carrion went, and by now she has learned that Carrion always manages to slip away.

Ziane walks three steps to the right, five steps forward, and opens the rusted door of the carriage. One of the back windows has been left open, just wide enough for someone to slip in without a trace. The door connecting this car to the next is partially slid back, and recently too, judging by the dust pattern on the floor.

Ziane walks through the connecting door to see Carrion waiting in the next car. They are sprawled out on a cracked plastic seat, their head tilted back to rest against the tinted window. At Ziane's approach they lean forward to rest their elbow on their knee, stretching out the length of their back as though trying to pop every individual vertebrae one by one. The movement is languid, casual, and somehow intimidating in the shift from slack relaxation to full, intense awareness.

With a flick of their wrist, they flip their loose brown braid over their shoulder, pushing the messy waterfall of hair away from their face to look directly at Ziane. "You know," they say slowly, "I gotta say that you've really gone and surprised me."

"It was not that difficult to find you," she explains stiffly, her hands tight around her bayonet-rifle. "Why would you run when you could hide in plain sight?"

"Oh, nah, not that." They wave off the suggestion. "I figure that if any of 'em guessed I'd just stay put and wait for them to leave, it'd be you. You're cleverer than they give you credit for. No, that ain't a surprise." They've always been so flippant, and it makes her squirm as their voice grows steady and serious. She feels as though their eyes pierce right through her when they frankly say, "What surprises me is what's happened to you. You were so... *human* when we first met. What did you trade away?"

Her tongue is dry behind her teeth. "I don't know. Why do you even care?"

"Everyone has more to lose than they think they do," they reply cryptically. "For some, this life is more of a gift that they have to pay a hefty price for. With others, it's more of a… a thing that *happens* to them. Well, if you don't know, can't be helped. Second question for you. Why haven't you called up Lysander on that tact-com I know you've got and sent him running over here?"

That had never even occurred to her. "I," she says, drawing herself up, "am here to capture you. That is my purpose as an Eoi."

"Aight then." They hop onto their feet and dust off their hands. "Capture away."

She doesn't move. This is a trap. It has to be, right? There's no way that they would simply stand here and wait for her to take them in when every time before they have defeated her with ease.

"Hm." They give her a bemused look. "Not much of a purpose in life, is it?"

Why hasn't she shot them yet? Why hasn't she gone for the handcuffs that Essten gave her a lifetime ago?

"Well, much as I love our chats," Carrion says as they turn from her, "I really gotta be heading out. Who knows when Jess or Lysander will wise up, eh?"

It's only when their back is to her that she snaps out of it and finally does what she has been training to do. Her finger tightens around the trigger of her bayonet-rifle and she shoots the ground by Carrion's feet.

"Stay where you are," she demands, "or else I'll–"

With the slightest of gestures, Carrion splatters the ground with dirt from one of their myriad pockets and they drop something into the soil below. A single seed. Ziane can feel the burst of life-warmth before she recognizes what's about to happen, and then she is scrambling backwards as a writhing mass of vines erupts from the ground like a bomb going off. The thick vines smash through the old plastic windows, tear up what's left of the carriage floor, and spear towards Ziane with terrifying speed.

But she isn't human anymore, and she has been learning. She shoots the first vine that comes at her, the laser slicing it in half, and then grabs the second, wrapping her fingers around it and digging into the thick and waxy epidermis. Her focus dips downwards into the spongy mesophyll layer and she rearranges it, twisting it and taking control of it, imposing her will upon the living structure. Using it as a shield, she smacks the other vines aside until she has a clear view of Carrion jumping out the broken window.

This time, Ziane does not hesitate to chase them. She jumps over the sharp edge of broken plastic and hits the ground running, her rifle abandoned on the ground.

Presumably the sound of combat has by now attracted attention and the other Eoi and Vesperi and presumably their backup will be on its way shortly, but she doesn't and indeed *can't* wait for it to get here. Carrion is slippery and elusive and they will get away if she stops for even a moment. They're heading in the direction of what looks like a dead end, sliding underneath a service station and dodging round a pristine locomotive. At first, she wonders why this way, and then she sees them throw aside a sheet of aluminum propped against a pillar and reveal the entrance to a hidden lift behind it.

Oh no you don't. Not if she has anything to say about it. As Carrion opens the lift door and steps inside, she picks up her pace, feet pounding against the ground, and then throws herself through the doors right as they shut behind her.

In the dim light and cramped quarters of the lift, there is perhaps a foot of space at most between her and Carrion. Her chest aches and her pulse skips.

They smile at her. "Persistent, huh?"

"Removing you as a threat," she says carefully, thinking each word through a dozen times before she voices it, "is the only thing that should matter to me – that *does* matter to me."

"Wow, nothin' beyond that? Really?"

"Nothing."

She moves, grabbing the cuffs from her belt at last and lunging at Carrion's arm. Too slowly, it would seem, as they duck out of the way just in time, hair swirling against her fingers as she misses by a mere inch. They come up behind her, practically perching against the lift walls with that smile undisturbed. She swings again and they use the wall as a springboard to kick off, tumbling over her head like an acrobat before they snatch her wrist and pin it behind her back with a painful twist. Cold steel impacts her chest as Carrion slams her against the wall, her cheek pressed tightly against it.

"Did you follow my map?" they ask, the words right against her ear.

"No. There's no point," she shoots back, unwilling to confess to that anxiety that had sent her running. "Going to the edge of the world is meaninglessly dangerous, and there is nothing that far out."

With every ounce of strength in her, she slams her head backwards and smacks her skull against Carrion's. They hiss and their grip on her wrist goes slack enough for her to wrench out of their grasp, and then she's turned and pressing her advantage, kneeing them in the chest. It's their turn to crash back into the wall, and she doesn't give them even a second to recover, jumping at them handcuffs first. Carrion tries to snag her arm before she can get the cuffs on, but their nails just scrape against her forearm, hard enough to draw blood. The cuffs snap around their wrist with a *click*. Now for the other hand –

Another *click*.

She looks down to see that Carrion has snapped the other cuff around her own hand, locking the two of them together.

"Want to play nice?" they taunt.

"No," she snaps right back. "Nothing you do or say can be trusted. I went to the Mists, and if all it took to make you go rogue was a plane of red glass, then you clearly lack the full capacity for rational thought."

That smile of theirs fades into something sharper. "So that's what you took from it all? Right then."

They kick out, their leg skating past her hip and their heel smashing into one of the lift buttons.

Ziane stumbles backwards as the lift groans and begins to shoot upwards. Once they reach the next level, she has no idea if her tact-com will still work, but when she reaches to activate it, Carrion yanks her hand away to stop her from touching the thing.

"Oh no, love," they croon. "You're coming with me."

As they had so long ago – though she cannot quite remember the details – they raise their hand and the air around her begins to thin. Their fingers caress her neck, trailing over her carotid artery. She chokes, the lightheadedness from carbon-dioxide poisoning beginning to set in as Carrion uses the magics, the sciences, of the Vesperi to reconfigure the chemical composition of the air around her. However, unlike last time, she is prepared. The seed within her throat that she had swallowed earlier blooms to life, coating the inside of her trachea with a thin film of photosynthetic moss, not enough to damage her body, but enough to turn the carbon dioxide she breathes into oxygen.

The dizziness in her head fades and her mind clears. She takes in a lungful of processed air, and Carrion's trick no longer touches her.

"Look at you, picking up on Lysander's little tricks," Carrion remarks. "And in such a short time, too. Well, probably short for you, long for me. Color me impressed."

"Stopping you is my purpose," Ziane repeats. "I will learn whatever it takes to achieve it."

They twist their leg behind her knee and *yank* her towards them, tripping her up and making her stumble. For a moment, they're pressed up against each other, Carrion's deep, almost burgundy eyes locking with her own. In the second when she staggers, they use the connection of the handcuffs to twist her arm, throwing her over their shoulder and sending her crashing to the ground on her back. When she tries to push back up, they kneel on top of her, digging a knee into her chest and using their own cuffed hand to keep her arm pinned above her head.

There is a sudden sharp pricking sensation in her thigh. Like a switch being flicked, the anxiety in the back of her mind rushes to the forefront. A long, gnarled thorn is embedded in her flesh, piercing straight through the fabric of her pants, the veins along it a sinister scarlet.

The stem is pulled out of her, and she cranes her neck to see Carrion holding it in the palm of their free hand.

"What…" A foreign sensation is spreading through the punctured limb, like the pleasant numbness that some of the Eoi's food induces. Whatever chemical cocktail was in the thorn now pumps through Ziane's blood, flooding her limbs and into her torso and deadening her legs. "What did you…?"

Carrion retracts the narrow stem until it's coiled up in their palm, and then they turn it back into dirt. "Sorry," they say without a shred of real remorse, "but it's not like I can knock you out with deoxygenation anymore, eh? Not with that little seed in your throat. Had to go about it differently."

"You…" Her tongue feels swollen and stiff. An image of Annie's botanical guide comes to mind, page after page marked up with lists of poisonous plants. "This is… one of the poisons of the Eoi?"

They scoff. "Nah. One of my own concoctions."

And that's a problem. As the poison continues to circulate through her blood, she tries to focus on it, to find exactly what it is and see if she can do something, anything at all, to counteract it. But while she knows how to latch on to the warmth of plant life and twist it around, she hasn't the first clue how to do the same for just the chemicals secreted by the plant itself. When she tries, her focus seems to slide right off it, as though there's a boundary where the plant's influence ends and the Eoi's domain fades away.

"You're going to have to sit this one out for a bit," Carrion tells her. "The Vesperi are the chemists, not the Eoi. Funny, innit? Vesperi and Eoi are designed to work in tandem as part of a bigger picture, and yet at every opportunity y'all are nipping at each other's throats. Fucking shortsighted is what it is."

Designed to work in tandem? What are they *talking* about? No one designed the Astrosi; they just *are*. A part of the world in the same way that humans are. It isn't as though they were created deliberately. Astrosi create more Astrosi, that may be true, but there can't have been some greater design behind it. Plants create more plants and humans create more humans too, after all, just in different ways.

"You're insane," she mumbles, yet it feels weak, like a frail shield.

Carrion hums. "Might be. All a matter of perspective, when you think about it." They pause for a moment, their fingers lacing with her slack digits. "But that don't matter, and you know it. Only thing that matters is that I'm right. Wish I weren't, sometimes. Sure would be a lot easier for me if I weren't."

Every word that comes out of their mouth causes the previous word to make even less sense. "I don't understand. Right about *what*?"

"Oh, only everything." Their laugh is unexpectedly bitter.

At first, Ziane is too busy trying to decipher what Carrion is talking about to notice the fact that sensations are beginning to return to her. Slowly, she can feel her hands steadying, her fingers tensing against the cold metal ground, her toes pushing against the soles of her boots. Within her chest, she can feel the poison's embrace lighten, as though something inside her is filtering it out. She tests each flicker of returning strength, flexing her hands and straightening her neck. It's not fully out of her yet, but it *is* leaving.

Carrion absently glances back down at their fistful of dirt, a small pink flower forming in their palm, its blushed petals delicate and dusted with pollen. "You recovered fast. Weird. Your heart must not be circulating blood in quite the way it should be…" They pause, tilting their head to the side and staring at her chest. "Oh, no, I see. Wow. Sef really is passing on her heartless legacy, ain't she?"

"My heart is none of your business," Ziane grits out.

They raise the flower to their lips and blow. A cloud of pollen bursts forth from the golden stamen and engulfs Ziane in a dusty haze, filling her sinuses and itching her eyes. She sneezes, again and again, until it hurts her ribs where Carrion's knee is digging into her, her nose watering and the bags under her eyes getting unpleasantly puffy. With the aggressive allergic reaction front and center, it takes her a long second to notice the faintness encroaching upon her, and by the time darkness swims in the corners of her vision, it's too late.

The toxic pollen renders her unconscious.

CHAPTER TWENTY-FOUR

There's a cold, hard floor beneath Ziane's head and raised bumps on her arms from a pervasive chill. Wherever she is, it is quiet, her breathing the only thing she can hear, too loud in her ears. What in the world has Carrion done to her? Her eyes are crusted, as though she has slept for some time, and it takes her a good few attempts before she can open her eyes and look around. The room she's in is empty as far as she can tell and perfectly circular, with clean and blank metal walls and a clean and blank metal floor, and...

She's been here before.

It's difficult to push herself up; her arms are stiff. This is in the Mists – the one part of the Mists untouched by fog and haze, the one place that no one enters save for King Ari. The room with the red glass ceiling that had sent Carrion mad. High over her, the blast doors are closed, nothing but smooth metal, hiding that glass from view.

"You bounced back quick from that," Carrion says, their voice echoing in the empty room. "Good."

They are behind her, and as her legs are still too fuzzy to stand, she can do nothing but awkwardly shift around to face them. "Why did you bring me here?" she demands, her voice sore and dusty from the pollen.

"You've been here before," they remind her. "But Ari only ever comes up here during the day. See those blast doors?" They point a finger up at the ceiling. "It's got a time lock to it. Don't open during the night. You need to override it, and Ari don't bother. He doesn't need to. Fuck, I don't even know if he knows how. To him, it wouldn't be worth it."

"What are you talking about?" Carefully, so as not to arouse their suspicion, she takes note of what she has on her. No tact-com, not anymore. No bayonet-rifle. No cuffs. All she has on her is her tablet, and that's of no use in a fight. She's got absolutely nothing that she could use to take out Carrion or even call for help. "What does it matter?"

Carrion leans against the wall next to the control panel. Their eyes are on her, but it's like they're staring straight through her at something visible only to themself. "It can seem like time passes faster in the Bastion. That's not the way it works, though. In the Bastion, time passes *normally*. It slows down in the Mists and the Deep."

Her eyes narrow. "If all Astrosi magic is science, then *how* does the time slow down?"

"You ever been to Sef's bower?"

The darkness beneath the apple tree, the sphere of light, the golden rose. "Yes."

"That big ol' orb she's got down there? The Mists have one too. Ari's got it hidden away where no one can fuck around with it, just like Sef. The orbs generate this... Think of it like an energy field," they explain. "Two great big energy fields, sectioning the Mists and the Deep off from the rest of the world, slowing time down within those barriers. Slowing everything down, really. You've probably noticed that things in the throneworlds don't fall apart the way things do in the Bastion; they don't decay. If you've ever taken a ride in the direct lifts from one throneworld to the other then you know there's that nasty barrier you gotta punch through. That's the energy fields."

Absently, she wonders what the difference really is. Why would it matter if time is normal in the Bastion and slower in the throneworlds, versus normal in the throneworlds and faster in the Bastion? The end result is the same. Isn't it?

"And so time out there," Carrion says, pointing again at the ceiling with a sharper stab of their finger, "passes the same as in the Bastion. So say Ari comes up here during the night – night out *there* – and the blast doors are time locked. Oh, well, don't matter much to him, he only has to wait a little bit before it's day again and he can take a peek if he likes. And then all he's seeing is red glass and he don't care much. To him, this place is off limits for a different reason."

What reason? Are they implying that the red glass would change? And what do they mean by 'out there'? "We're at the highest point of the world," Ziane reminds Carrion, her brow furrowed. "Why are you pointing to the ceiling when you're talking about the Bastion?"

They laugh, and there is that sharpness again, that regret, that *resentment*. Not resentment of her, she doesn't think, but as though they resent the entire world. "'Cause I ain't talking about the Bastion."

"There's nothing above the Mists," she says slowly. "Or if there is, it's just more of the Fringes. That's still part of the Bastion."

Instead of responding directly, Carrion opens up the control panel. They pull the protective casing off the wall and directly mess with the wires behind it until something sparks and fizzes, and then when they put the panel back into place, they press a button on the glitchy screen, bypassing a bright red warning that pops up. That must be the time lock. How often have they been here if they've figured out how to break the lock so quickly?

Above Ziane's head, the blast doors on the ceiling slide open. There is no red. Behind the thick layer of clear glass is a different image entirely – black, but not pure black. Black swirling with blues and greens and flashes of red and purple, an infinite black that she could drown in. And amidst the colorful darkness are hundreds upon hundreds of tiny specks of pure light, so many that when she tries to count them, she gives up almost immediately, her thoughts fading away in the distant glow.

Unconsciously, she rises to unsteady feet, drawn upwards by this strange image. It must be computer generated somehow, or otherwise manufactured. Various different colors of glass fused together, surely. She's no expert in glass maintenance or refurbishment, but she knows it's possible to get all sorts of colors into it. This must just be some type of odd abstract pattern, made by an artist that doesn't follow any standard aesthetics.

"I don't understand," she admits. It is strangely difficult to tear herself away from the ceiling to look at Carrion. "It's just glass, isn't it? Or a computer screen?"

Carrion is gazing up at the glass, their features smoothed out but their eyes heavy beyond belief. She sees them as she hasn't before, their ratty coat worn thin with no way to replace it instead of chaotically torn, their long hair tangled without a mirror to brush it in instead of roguishly unkempt. Not wild and dangerous but tired. For the first time, they look old in the same way Queen Sef and King Ari do – a dignified, dutiful old.

"Is it?" they ask, their voice gentle in the silence.

There's no conviction to her when she counters, "What else could it be?"

"Hic Sunt Leones, love," they say softly.

As if that means anything concrete. What does a line in the middle of the Fringes have to do with glass in the Mists? Is it because both are at the edges of the world? If this truly is the highest point of the Mists, is Hic Sunt Leones where the world ends and turns to nothingness? Was the line they drew the end of the Fringes?

"Night's almost over out there," Carrion tells her. "Watch."

The black begins to fade, the bright lights begin to dim, overcome by a soft pink glow to the left side of the glass. Within moments, the darkness has gone entirely, replaced by that same orange-red that she had seen the last time she was here. It must be a computer image, then, she decides, if it can change that easily. And yet. Why does that answer sit uneasily in her chest? Why the time lock? Why those particular images? Why change based on the time of day in the Bastion? And why would it have anything to do with the time of day in the Bastion in the first place if the world really does end above that ceiling?

For once, Ziane doesn't know how to ask those myriad questions, so instead all she can say is, "King Ari said you went mad after seeing this."

"Nah. Seeing this made me ask questions." Carrion gives her a knowing look, a crooked smile dancing at the corner of their mouth. "I bet you've got a half-dozen of your own."

"Are you about to tell me that you have a half-dozen answers?"

"If I just handed you answers, you wouldn't believe me. It'd be a waste of our time, and we don't have an infinite amount of that right now. If you want answers, if you *really* want 'em, you're gonna have to work for it."

"What do you mean, we don't have time right now? How *did* you bring me up here without King Ari stopping you?"

"Good question," Carrion praises her. "Lysander followed your tact-com breadcrumbs to the Mists. He's chatting with Jess and Ari right now, a couple floors below. Not in front of Ari's throne of security cameras. I know the Mists as well as I know the Deep and the Bastion and the Fringes – it wasn't hard for me to sneak up here, even hauling you around. But that lot ain't going to gab forever, and once Ari comes back up to his throne, you're going to have a bitch of a time sneaking out."

She glances at the door leading down to that dark, misty room with its hundreds of cameras that she'd been in the last time she was in the Mists. "I don't have to sneak out. Unlike you, I'm not a wanted criminal. Jess was reasonable enough during our encounter. It's not unrealistic to think that he would believe me again if I simply tell the truth."

"What, that I dragged you up here and showed you Ari's little off-limits view?"

"Yes."

They shrug. "Sure, you could always give that a try. But I wouldn't, if I were you. They might ask their own questions. If I were a suspicious bastard like Lysander, I would have a *lot* of questions for you."

"I don't lie," Ziane insists, her jaw clenched with stubbornness. "I've never wanted to and I've never needed to. Secrecy only ever complicates things unnecessarily."

"I gave full transparency a shot once," Carrion admits. She never would have thought it possible to sound both bitter and cheerful at the same time, but they manage it.

"Did the whole telling-folks-the-truth thing. Pro tip? It rarely works. When you most desperately need people to trust you, when you beg them to listen, that's when they let you down. That's when they refuse to believe you. That's when they refuse to look. *That* is when you go from being an upstanding member of Ari's court to being shunted into the role of madman. Trust me, sweetheart, secrecy is underrated."

She points a single finger at the ceiling. "Then why show me this?"

"You were trying to map the Fringes. And I don't think it was all to try and track me down. You were mapping those wastelands for your own sake, to answer your own questions." They push themself off the wall and straighten up, pressing the panel on the door to slide it open. "Welp, I need to be heading out before Ari gets back."

"Considering the low value you place on the lives of others, and the ease in which you defeated an entire team of Eoi, I'm surprised you haven't simply killed King Ari for trying to stop you."

"Are you kidding me?" They laugh. "A team of soldiers ain't nothing. Ari? Ari could beat the shit out of me with one hand tied behind his back." They scoff and shake their head. "But yeah, I'm sure your honesty and transparency will go over great with him. Good luck with that."

"You're afraid of him."

"For better or worse, I need to stay alive, and fighting Ari would be a great way to become *not* alive." Carrion pauses, then adds, "And just one more thing. Take charge of your life. You're reacting – to Sef, to Lysander, to *me*. Start *acting* for once. You'll be surprised what you learn if you do."

With that, they vanish, the door sliding shut behind them.

That's the third time now. The third time Ziane has gone after Carrion, found them, and they've walked away from her. And worst of all, this time she'd given up on the fight as soon as she'd woken up. Capturing Carrion is her purpose, isn't it? Or is it something else, something to do with all the questions they've sparked in her, and Carrion is simply a conduit for that other purpose? If that is the case, then it lessens the blow of failing to capture them again, but it doesn't lessen the shame of knowing her failure will disappoint the rest of the Eoi.

Her head is bowed in disappointment as she leaves Ari's hidden room and its mysterious ceiling, heading back down the dark and narrow stairs to the even darker throne room with its hundreds of security feeds showing every inch of the Mists. As Carrion promised, the room is empty, Ari still occupied with Jess and Lysander and the others.

Even though she does trust in the simplicity and clarity of telling them the truth, she doesn't want to stay up here. But before she can hurry out of the throne room, the main door is thrown open and King Ari strides in, a furious glower darkening his face. Behind him is Jess, and behind Jess is Lysander.

"Behold," Ari all but snarls to the two following him. "Your missing Eoi. Lysander, cease your prattling accusations. And as for you," he snaps at Ziane, "you shall explain what, precisely, you are doing here. *Now.*"

She stands up straight and says truthfully, "Carrion brought me here. They knocked me unconscious, and when I woke up, I was here."

"See?" Lysander stabs their hand towards Ziane. "I told you she wasn't some spy. Carrion's just a fucking bastard who gets their kicks messing with us. Let her go, be glad Carrion doesn't have the diamond, and we forget this bullshit ever happened."

"And would you be so unconcerned were it your precious Deep that Carrion infiltrated and deposited one of the Vesperi into?" Ari counters. "Carrion may have slipped Queen Sef's noose by wheedling their way out of her contract, but they have no such blessing of safe passage in my realm. It is my duty to uncover how they entered with an unconscious body in tow, and why they brought her here, of all places." To that, Lysander has no good or quick response, and so Ari once more turns to Ziane and demands, "Did Carrion leave you here, in *this* room?"

That question pins Ziane in place and her mind races as she debates what answer to give. Does she do as she so confidently declared she would and tell the complete truth? Or does she do as Carrion suggested and lie? It is not just Ari who will know her answer, either – Jess is watching with keen interest. Lysander will hear her words too, and there's no doubt he will report them to Queen Sef. Can she admit that she just let Carrion *talk* instead of fighting them? If she does, Ari is certain to ask what they spoke of, and then she will have to try to explain what she herself doesn't understand.

She opens her lips and the word that tumbles out is, "Yes."

Ari does not glare at her, nor scowl in the way that Lysander does to intimidate. He merely stares her down, as though his pale white eyes see every inch of her, as if his gaze is capable of peeling back her skin to stare into her mind and see right through her. There is a moment, as she tries not to look away in fear, when she knows with utmost certainty that Ari has figured out that she is lying. Carrion was one of his court before they turned rogue, after all. Ari has known them longer than anyone, and thus likely knows that Carrion wouldn't have dropped Ziane here when there is a far more tempting locale right above.

"Ceiling or floor?" is Ari's eventual question.

Floor? Was there something else below her feet the entire time she was in that room? If there was, Ari is clearly not willing to offer any details in front of Lysander. "Ceiling," she replies.

"And?"

"It's… it's just glass."

It's impossible to say whether or not he believes her. "To Carrion, it is not."

"I'm not Carrion," she says, doing her utmost not to mumble under the weight of his piercing gaze. "I don't know what it is to them."

"And yet you *do* know more than you say." Ari's eyes thankfully leave her. "I may not be able to force truths from your lips, but know this: Whatever you may think of me, Ziane of the Eoi, I hold no ulterior motives beyond the obliteration of Carrion and their chaos. My sole regret in the long years of my life is that I was the one to grant Carrion the blessings of the Vesperi, and thus it is my duty and my burden to bring them to heel, even if it should be the last act I ever perform." He strides forward and sits upon his throne, the blue light of the security screens radiating around him. In that aura of imposing authority, it is all too easy for her to believe that he is the one person Carrion is unwilling to meet in combat. "You and Lysander may leave. Inform your queen that I shall soon arrive in her realm to speak on this matter further."

Lysander grabs Ziane by the arm and drags her towards the exit without so much as a polite word to Ari.

Once they're out of the throne room, Lysander demands, "What the fuck did Carrion want?"

"I don't know," Ziane replies. To be fair, she doesn't. They had wanted to talk, but she can barely piece together the point of the conversation. What specifically had they been trying to motivate her to do, beyond just following their map? Or was that the extent of it? If so, she can't see how that would serve their goal of reaching the diamond first. "They're not exactly sane, as we well know. What does it matter?"

He doesn't look particularly convinced by that, but he doesn't press that matter. "Come on. We need to report this to Queen Sef and let her know that Ari's gonna show up. If you ask me, the queen doesn't need to be that fucking polite to Ari. The man's just pretending he's civilized, but you saw how much of a prick Jess was back there."

All things taken into account, Jess had been remarkably reasonable. And despite the hostilities between the Eoi and the Vesperi when it comes to their search for the diamond, it's clear that both Queen Sef and Ari at least understand that outright conflict is risky at best and devastating at worst. Keeping an open channel of communication seems deeply practical to Ziane, and though she hasn't personally seen the type of power the two rulers wield, if Ari is enough to threaten Carrion and Queen Sef is the king's equal then she imagines any clash between the two would be a very, *very* bad idea.

The throng of people in the Mists don't pay Ziane and Lysander any real attention beyond a few curious glances, but the handful of guards posted along their path do, ensuring that the two of them leave immediately. Lysander takes her back to that too-fast lift that they had previously used to go from the Deep to the Mists.

"I've sent the rest of the team back to the Deep already," Lysander explains. "Jess was already touchy enough about letting me come along. We'll meet them there, go over this, then talk to the queen."

Start acting for once, Carrion had said.

Ziane hesitates in front of the lift. The path she is supposed to walk is clear. React to Carrion's movements, do as the queen says, follow orders, and wait to be sent out after the diamond again. And yet there is a map in her pocket, half a dozen questions in her mind, and the dissonance between the certainty that there is nothing outside the world and Carrion's insistence on *out there*.

"I'm…" She takes a deep breath and tells Lysander, "I'm not coming."

He blinks. "Fucking excuse me?"

"I'm going to the Fringes. There was something Carrion said. It doesn't really make much sense, but I think there's something out in the Fringes that might help us against them."

"Hrm." His forehead wrinkles as he frowns. "Queen approve of it?"

"She told me to find my purpose. This is what I'm meant to do," she reminds him.

After a long moment, Lysander calls the lift and turns his back on her. "Fine. Do what you want. Just don't get your fool ass killed out there. You won't have backup this time, and I won't be there to bail you out when it goes to shit."

"I won't get myself killed," she promises.

From what she can tell, even if she did encounter Carrion again, they don't appear to have any desire to kill her.

CHAPTER TWENTY-FIVE

The Fringes are as Ziane left them: ominous and gray, shadowed and ruined. Walking in deeper is not as intimidating this time; she does not hesitate for more than a moment or two. The fear is gone, replaced by the conviction that there *is* something in here and that she *will* find it, regardless of what Carrion wants.

With her map to guide her, it doesn't take long before she reaches the hideout that Carrion had set up the last time she and the other Eoi had been in the Fringes. Considering the time differential between the Astrosi realms and the Bastion, she's not surprised to see that the lair is even more of a wreck than it was previously. The wall that Lysander's errant shot had taken out has sagged even more, and she's careful to avoid it as she delicately inches her way through the hideout to make sure that they didn't miss anything when they were here before. Nothing stands out.

She walks deeper, retracing the path she took before when she ran recklessly after Carrion, digging up every memory of the moment that she can, as she'd not had the opportunity to properly map it at the time. It takes her over twice as long to return to the scene where Carrion had cuffed her and left her for Lysander to find. She takes the route that Carrion had taken back then, exiting through the far back floodgate.

From here on out, she's in entirely uncharted territory. Her patchy map of the Bastion and the Fringes that she'd acquired from the Office of the Administrator peters out a few miles into the Fringes.

She keeps going. This place is a maze, but it is close enough to the street patterns of the Bastion that she can figure out how to avoid dead ends without getting completely turned around in the process, making sure to mark every move she takes on her own map. When it becomes too dark for her to see, she uses a handful of dirt to create a bioluminescent moss that shines a green light onto her surroundings.

Eventually she tires and has to sleep, her back against a cold wall that still isn't as cold as the void in her chest. Eventually she has to eat, and she rearranges dirt into a tasteless peach that has only the barest spark of life and a sterile pit.

Ziane had known how great the expanse of the Fringes was. She had known that there were a thousand reasons why the Office of the Administrator never sent survey teams to map the area, chief amongst them being that people died trying. But unlike moving about the Bastion, with its priority lifts and constant trains, she has no way to speed up her travel out here. Her even pacing gives her at least a semi-accurate sense of how many miles she is walking, but she can *only* walk. It is so cold and so dark, and soon her biggest issue becomes not the meager food she can create, but lack of water. For some reason, the abilities of the Eoi stop when it comes to the creation of water, and she cannot draw it from the air. The strength of the Astrosi keeps her body going for longer than a human could, yet after almost two days she begins to flag.

It is then, when she's beginning to think that she has no choice but to retreat and return with provisions, that she finds the first message. It's been so long since she saw one of these. Despite the time that has passed, she remembers it perfectly. The marks carved into a wall are large and clear and in exactly the same style as the messages that Carrion had left for her all that time ago, when they left a path for her down to the Deep.

The message is simply an arrow pointing to the left.

Her breath catches in her bone-dry throat and she turns that way, and then there is another arrow. She follows that to another arrow, and another and another and another, and then there is a ratty-looking tarp hanging up in a doorway, just like there had been at Carrion's hideout in the very beginning of the Fringes. She stumbles through the doorway and coughs on the lungful of dust that kicks up when she disturbs the tarp. It's difficult to tell with only the glow of her moss to light up the room, but she's relatively certain this place has been abandoned for quite some time. How long has Carrion been anticipating her coming through the Fringes?

Amongst the ruins are stacks of metal supply crates, and she gratefully pries one open to reveal a liter of water. She doesn't hesitate to pop open the cap and start drinking, the cool liquid soaking into her parched throat. It takes all of her willpower to stop before she drinks too much. Another crate contains ration bars, still protected by dusty wrappers. Once she forces herself to put down the water, she rips open a bar and shoves it into her mouth, barely chewing as she chokes it down.

Hunger sated, she sinks to the ground and leans against the wall, steadying her breathing and staring up at the cracked ceiling.

Ziane can't remember the last time she has gone this long without contact with others, either human or Astrosi. The emptiness in her chest eclipses any feeling of loneliness, true, yet that doesn't mean that she doesn't feel... *off*. Humans aren't made to be alone forever, and it would seem that Astrosi aren't either. These old messages from Carrion are the most contact she's had with someone else since she parted from Lysander, and they're just faded scratches on a wall.

Even though this is Carrion's hideout, she sleeps here for the night. Or she thinks it's night. It's impossible to tell for certain without the rhythm of day and night lights in the Bastion or the Deep. When she wakes, she marks this spot on her map to ensure that she can find this stash again, and then fills a threadbare sack with as much water and rations as it can hold before the seams threaten to give out. So supplied, she continues on, the trek seemingly endless. And yet turning back isn't an option, not anymore. After how far she's come, she has no choice but to make it to the end.

Her map grows, and when she finally reaches Carrion's line, she finds herself in front of a plain wall. At first it appears to be just another towering building, but it looks... different. Solid metal, not the standard mix of steel, aluminum, and plastic that make up the majority of buildings in the world. Nor are there any windows or doorways or indicators that there once were such things. A plain wall, stretching up and to the sides.

No, wait, there is something.

There is a door. Its outline is barely discernible as it sits perfectly flush with the wall. Next to it is a wrecked control panel that has almost completely fallen away. Given that she can see no way to walk around this structure, she tries the door. It's heavy, heavier than she would have guessed.

She drops her satchel, her sack, and her handful of glowing moss onto the ground and puts her entire weight into the effort, digging her fingers between the tiny crack to push it back, her nails scraping against the dusty metal. She pauses. It's not dust. Though it's difficult to tell under the green-tinted light, the stuff looks more like a red powder. Almost like sand, or chalk, or one of the other substances the Eoi keep in the arboretum. A dark, reddish brown that's caked into the doorframe and, she notices, covering the ground around it.

A strained groan emanates from the doorframe as she finally manages to get the door moving. Once she dislodges the gunk rusting at the edges, it slides easily, and she pushes it aside – and is then immediately blinded by bright, glaring light.

After such darkness, this veritable explosion of light is too much, and she raises a hand to shield her eyes while she blinks and slowly adjusts. And then there is the air. Not the damp of the Deep or the fog of the Mists or the recirculated air of the Bastion or even the musk of the Fringes. The first breath is clean, fresh, and then the second burns in her lungs. All the while, the air is blowing at her like there are vents surrounding her, tugging at her clothes and hair.

Squinting and staggering, Ziane lowers her hand and steps onto the brown floor of the room or hall or wherever this door leads.

And… it is not.

It isn't a room or a hall or a building or even an open pavilion or… She doesn't know what this is. All her knowledge of the world and its layouts and levels and floors and she has *no idea what this is*. There is dark reddish-brown rock beneath her feet that stretches out so far she cannot see where it ends; she cannot even wager the faintest of guesses at its distance, her mind scrambling to come up with a number and unable to begin to comprehend it. Overhead is an orange-red *something*, the exact same color as the glass at the top of the Mists, but as with the floor's length she cannot begin to fathom how high up it is. It just keeps going, forever and forever until it looks like it bends down to meet the floor so far away that it is a distant blur, beyond the reaches of her vision. She can't do this, she can't – she looks behind her and there is the door, but it is set in a wall that goes up as high as the eye can see and goes out to the sides forever.

Everything in the world is measurable, quantifiable, defined by limitations and boundaries. But this...

This is *infinite*.

She claps her hands over her mouth, her fingers trembling against her cheeks. Tears run down her face and between her fingers as she stares wide-eyed at whatever this is, the whipping air blasting her eyes.

Hic Sunt Leones. The end of the world.

Infinity doesn't exist, not like this, it can't, but – no. No, this isn't possible, this can't exist.

She stumbles backwards, away from the infinity, back into the darkness of the Fringes, and the second she is back inside the world, she slams the door shut with shaking arms. The moment it is closed, she collapses onto her knees, only to leap away when she sees the red-brown dust scattered on the floor. She falls painfully on her tailbone, then scrambles away as fast as she can, elbows scraping against the ground.

In the blackness of the Fringes, she has only the illumination of her abandoned moss, and though the darkness is better than the unfathomable light from outside, it does not comfort her.

She has to get out of here. She can't be here, she doesn't know what that room *is*, she doesn't know what it could do to her, not with the air sitting sharp in her lungs, her eyes still smarting from the light and the dust clinging to her boots. It's dangerous. It could be deadly. It could be *anything*. She can barely breathe, blood pounding in her ears, the emptiness in her chest straining as fear takes her, fear like she has never felt before, not even when she wasn't cold all the time, when she wasn't so flat, when she was human.

Ziane runs.

CHAPTER TWENTY-SIX

The dampness of the Deep is gentle and welcoming, yet Ziane has been on edge for days and it does not ease her terror when she staggers out of a lift, exhausted and at the end of her limits.

She has no energy to make it to the arboretum and to Annie's little residence. Instead, she barely gets to the nearest common room and passes out on one of the moss-softened wooden benches. Too-bright dreams chase her, the blasting air from the infinite shredding her skin and cracking her bones, and only when she is dying does her dream let the phantom pain pass, replaced by the towering form of Carrion. When they hold out a hand to her, the dream shifts into shadows and she is chasing the blurry form of a child, constantly reaching out to them only to have them be too far away for her to touch. The child stops only to speak a single syllable, a humming *Lu–*

Someone shakes Ziane awake.

She chokes on a scream as she jolts upright, rolling off the bench and onto her knees, every vein in her body filled with swift panic, ready to run from whatever has woken her.

"Whoah, hey, hey."

Essten's voice. She is not in the infinite, and she is not alone.

Her voice cracks as she speaks her first words in weeks, "Sorry. I didn't mean to – that is, it was just a bad dream. Essten, listen, I need to talk to you, or I need to talk to the queen, or... I'm not sure, but..."

He helps her to her feet, lays a reassuring hand on her shoulder. Or a hand that is meant to be so, as it doesn't provide any reassurance or calm her scattered nerves. "Take a couple deep breaths, Ziane," he tells her. "You're pretty out of it and you don't look good, if I'm being honest. Why don't you eat something first, all right?" He goes to grab a plate from one of the tables at the far end of the room and brings it back to her. "Here. Fresh harvest of peaches just got plucked."

When she bites, it is bursting with juice, with water, with life. Nothing like the dead version she was able to create in the Fringes. She polishes it off, her body starving and aching, and yet it sits uneasily in her stomach, too heavy and clashing with the jitters that she can't shake off.

"What happened out there?" Essten asks. "When Lysander came back and said you were heading to the Fringes, well... we were worried. You were gone for awhile too, way longer than we thought you'd be, even with the time difference. Now you're a mess, you're clearly wrecked, and you're jumpier than I've ever seen you."

"It's... hard to explain." She holds the peach pit in her hands and lets herself feel the warmth of it, the life contained within. Nothing like the dead, barren infinite. "I don't even know what it was, I don't understand it, and I don't know what Carrion meant by their message. It was nothing, but it was everything too. I think..." She swallows and stares down at her boots as she admits so quietly that she can barely hear herself say it, "I think I saw the edge of the world."

When she looks up, Essten is blinking at her, one eyebrow raised in obvious doubt and confusion. "You mean, like, deeper into the Fringes?"

"No, it wasn't – I mean, it was, but it wasn't. I don't know what it was," she repeats desperately, unsure how to word any of it. "I need to talk to the queen," she decides. If anyone will know what to do, if anyone will understand, it'll be Queen Sef. Oldest, wisest, on par with Carrion, if not greater than them in strength. "Where is she?"

"She's in the arboretum," Essten replies slowly, hesitantly. "I suppose you should be there as well, all things considered."

Ziane frowns. "What are you talking about? Is the queen in her bower?"

"Like I said, you were gone for awhile."

There is something somber and uncharacteristically flat in his voice that makes her reply with only a sharp nod before heading out the door. She'll find the queen, she'll find a way to explain what she saw out in the Fringes, she'll find an answer to this beyond the gibberish Carrion was spouting at her. There *has* to be an answer. Something that makes sense, something that will allow her to comprehend what is... *out there*. Out there, just as Carrion had said.

It takes Ziane a long time to find the queen in the arboretum. No one is in Annie's little dwelling and the usual group of Eoi in white lab coats are absent. Only Ziane's extensive time spent here allows her to make her way through the maze of paths without getting turned around.

Queen Sef is in a small glade, gentle grass beneath her bare feet and peaceful trees lining the clearing. There is nothing poisonous in sight, nothing dangerous, nothing beyond delicate blue wisteria and low golden maple. The leaves and flowers drift in the mild air cycle of the arboretum, swaying back and forth in the tranquility of the glade. The queen stands in the middle, tall and regal, head bowed with all the grace of a willow bending over to brush a kiss against the grass. Before her is a patch of freshly dug soil, warm and rich, approximately eight feet long and two and a half feet across.

Disturbing the serenity feels deeply wrong, and so, even with the panic filling Ziane's mind, she stands at the edge of the clearing and waits. What she waits for, she doesn't know. Someone else is waiting as well, and he is so still that it takes her a long time to notice him. Lysander stands in the shadow of a maple, his face hard, the anger that so often overtakes him nowhere in sight. His hands are fisted at his sides and his jaw stiff, lips pressed tightly together.

Sef's voice drifts through the soft silence. "Have you any requests? On this, I shall acquiesce to your desires."

At first, Ziane thinks that the queen is speaking to her, but then Lysander replies, voice flat, "No."

"Very well."

There is a weight to Sef's motions as she raises a hand and coaxes a seed of life through the warm dirt. A small shoot of green sprouts up at the head of the rectangle of disturbed soil, tenderly coiling and twisting until it settles into smooth branches and a low trunk, pure pink blossoms spreading out into a perfect cherry tree. Not a single bud remains curled up, the flowers in flawless, everlasting full bloom.

"She wouldn't have cared," Lysander mumbles, staring down at his boots.

Sef exhales and looks upon her resplendent creation. "In our realm of timeless life, it is all the more important to remember those that pass through, those that are extraordinary. Those that may have garnered no reverence in life oft deserve the most commemoration in death." Her eyes close, pristine and ageless features serene. "I was and am incapable of returning her love, yet that does naught to erase her decades of devotion. This may be all I can do to immortalize that." She opens her eyes and her gaze slides over to Lysander. "Out of respect, never before have I asked, and yet... did you?"

"Did I what?"

"Care."

Lysander's hands shake. "She was an idiot."

"That is cruel to say."

"She wasted her life. She could have let me kick the bucket and gone on with her life and properly lived, instead of being stuck down here with folks that weren't ever comfortable with so much as chatting with her." Lysander gives a swift and sharp shake of his head. "And for what, huh? Someone who couldn't even stop a child from making a stupid bargain, that's what. Love and service, but what did it get her? Not eternal life, that's for damn sure."

"She never asked for such a gift," Sef replies. "She never wished for it, and I do not force such things on those that beg otherwise."

Lysander turns his back on the queen and on the cherry tree. "She should've."

Those are his last words as he stomps out, and Sef doesn't attempt to stop him. She simply returns her attention to the tree, seemingly content to watch its perfection forever, her hands folded neatly in front of her. A hint of pink appears in her hair, a single cherry blossom curling around one thin rope of dark hair, joining the greenery that trails at the ends of her braids.

"You may approach," Sef eventually says, and this time Ziane knows the invitation is for her.

She steps into the clearing, lingering beneath the bough of a maple, her throat tight and closed up. Her eyes trail down the branches of the cherry tree, down to the roots, and down to the patch of upturned soil beneath it. "How did she...?"

"In her sleep." The queen sighs. "There are far worse deaths that claim humans. Humans age, they wither, they die, no matter the strength that they affect until their last breath. For Eoi, death is a return to the soil, the start of new life as much as it is the end of an old one. Humans do not view things in the same way. None shall celebrate her passing tonight. No feasts shall be held to celebrate the deeds of her life. That does not mean I do not have a duty."

Ziane struggles to speak, and she looks back to where Lysander had stormed off. "A long time ago, Annie told me that she went to the Deep and became an Acolyte to save her father from illness."

"She did."

"She said you saved him from death. No more, no less."

"And so I did. I do not believe Lysander has ever forgiven her for it, nor himself for accepting."

It takes some time for Ziane to muster the strength to approach Annie's grave. Despite the woman's age, she had always seemed to be almost immortal in the same way the Astrosi are. Strong and proud and as though she were untouchable by something as simple as death. And yet she was *not* immortal. Now she lies beneath the ground, buried in the manner of the Eoi, not processed and reclaimed in the manner of the Bastion. In that way, at least, she was not human, transcending that fate at the very end.

Eventually, Ziane asks, hesitant and afraid, "What does Hic Sunt Leones mean?"

Sef pauses. "As far as I'm aware, it means 'Here Be Lions'."

"What's a lion?"

"No one knows, not anymore. The sole record we have of such a phrase being used is upon one of the very first maps ever made. The first, and perhaps the only attempt to map the Fringes. 'Tis a thing written where maps fail, where the world ends. Here be danger. Here be creation's edge."

Ziane swallows. So it really was the end of the world. How can it be possible to enter the end of the world? "I followed the trail Carrion left in the Fringes," she quietly admits. "There's... *something* beyond the Fringes. There was a door and then... then infinity. An infinite ceiling and an infinite floor. I think it was the end of the world. I think that was creation's edge. I don't know what else it could have been. Hic Sunt Leones, like you said."

"It is a turn of phrase, my child, nothing more." Sef does not look at her, still facing the cherry tree. "Not a place that truly exists. If Carrion left a trail for you, then it is likely it was one of their traps."

"I... maybe. They did lead me there, in a way."

"You have trained with our Era One holograms, have you not? I do not imagine it would be truly difficult for Carrion to scavenge something similar, to set a snare for you to stumble across," Sef explains. Is that really it? The holograms of the Eoi are impressive, but there had been the blowing air, the burning in her lungs, the *light*. "I commend you for escaping it. They are a cunning foe. Did their trap contain any remnants of their attempts to track the diamond or anything that might be used to interpret their next movements?"

Ziane hangs her head. "No."

Why does she feel like a stupid child? Can it really be just a hologram? Was that truly all that Carrion had left for her? A hologram that would have been left running for who knows how long, that wouldn't have run out of power despite the fact that no active power lines run through the Fringes, that would be set not to mimic an existing location but instead to show something impossible? The appeal of holograms is their ability to copy real things, not make up an unbelievable scene whole cloth. Would Carrion really go to all that effort just to… what? Unsettle her? That cannot be it, right?

Infinite orange-red stretches overhead in her mind when she closes her eyes.

If she remains in the Deep then she'll be safe. She'll be away from whatever that was, hologram or not. If she remains then she can mourn Annie alongside Queen Sef and perhaps Lysander, should the man decide to care for his departed daughter. If she remains, she can believe it was a hologram and ignore *here be danger* and try to pretend that it may not be a threat to the Bastion and all who live there. Because that is the other matter at the center of all this, isn't it? It was her duty as a human to protect the Bastion, and if there is something out there, if that infinity is dangerous, then does she not still have a duty? If this is the work of Carrion, then does she not still have a duty?

She wants to stay in this pocket of safety, so far from the Fringes and the end of the world, but she can't. She has to go back. She has to *know*.

"I should have searched more carefully," she admits, though only she knows the true depth of what she's saying. "I… I don't want to stay here, I want to return to the Fringes and see what else there is to find. There has to be something, I'm sure of it."

Queen Sef inclines her head a fraction of an inch. "Very well. I cannot fault you for wishing to depart this somber place. Go with my blessing."

With one final look at the dream-like cherry tree, Ziane leaves the glade and its grave.

Out of both habit and prudence, she returns to Annie's house. It is quiet. Annie's bed with its flowered mattress and light blankets has been made, her kettle has been taken off the heater, and her basket and botanical have been neatly set upon the table, as though waiting for her to return. A tree, a grave, and an empty house. Love for a woman that is incapable of love. Never leaving, never returning to the Bastion, never seeming to have any true friends other than the handful of humans she has tried and failed to teach. The sum of Annie's life.

A cup of half-drunk tea has been left on the counter. When Ziane rests her hand against it, it is cold, abandoned, left alone while she was up in the Fringes. All that time spent making it to the end of the world, and she missed the end of a life. How many times has she been gone and missed the end of a life? Surely just Annie, and yet it feels as though she is retreading old ground. As though this has happened to her before. There is nothing in her chest, no warmth in her flesh, and still she aches, a familiar and empty ache.

"I'm sorry," she whispers to the house.

She packs a proper bag of provisions. There had been that bright and stinging light, and so she packs a pair of safety goggles. There had been that burning in her lungs from the air, and so she packs one of the rebreathers that Annie used when tending to noxious plants. If she has to trek through that desolation, then she will. She slings the bag over her shoulder and doesn't look back as she leaves.

Leneat is waiting for her outside the arboretum. "You aight?" she asks.

Ziane shrugs. "I don't know if I ever am."

"Fair 'nough. Look, about Annie…" She hesitates for a bit, not nearly as open about softer emotions as Essten is. "I know you liked the woman. Sorry you lost that."

"It was always going to happen eventually."

Leneat makes a murmur of agreement. "True. By the way, Essten said you wanted to chat with 'im? He's hanging out in a training room. I can take you to him, if you want. But if you're wanting to talk about Annie, I gotta say, don't think he'd be the right person for it. None of us ever knew her, really."

"No, I…" Ziane looks up at Leneat and asks, hoping, "Do you believe in the edge of the world?"

"What now? I mean," Leneat frowns and taps her chin, "sure, it ends somewhere out in the Fringes, don't it? And above the Mists and below the Deep, I guess. Never really thought about it. I don't go below where the queen draws her borders, you know."

"I mean beyond that. As in, do you think there's something at the end of the world?"

Leneat chuckles. "Whole point of the end of the world is that it's the end. Ain't nothing there. World gotta end somewhere."

Does it?

"Leneat, I'm sorry to be rude, but I have to be going," Ziane says, trying and failing to give her a reassuring smile. "Give my apologies to Essten as well, please?"

"You sure?" Leneat asks, giving her a concerned look. "He said you weren't looking too hot."

"That doesn't matter. I need to be going."

"Well… if you say so. Just, be careful, aight?" she adds.

Ziane doubts it is possible to be careful at the end of the world. Still, she gives Leneat a nod and heads towards the lift that will take her to the Fringes. Part of her wonders if she should bring a bayonet-rifle or anything at all that might be useful in a fight. The other part of her knows somehow, deep down, that she doesn't need to fight there. That infinity is a place of survival, not combat.

When the lift releases her at the very beginning of the Fringes, she pulls out her tablet and its map and braces herself. For another expanse of time without contact with others. For another endless trek. For another set of days in the darkness. For another glimpse at infinity.

She begins.

This time, she can move at a faster pace, having already figured out and mapped the various pitfalls and obstacles along the way. She goes further and further into the darkness, and once more has to guide herself by the light of bioluminescent moss when the distant lights of the Bastion fade away completely. When she finally, *finally* reaches Carrion's supply stash, she refills her water containers and then keeps going, pressing on to the end.

At last, the final wall stands before her. There is still the dusting of reddish granules, the faint line of light around where the door is. She stares at it, telling herself over and over again to make her limbs move, to open the door, to step out. Pushing herself through that last fear. She puts on her protective goggles. She puts on her rebreather. Once more, she digs her fingers into the doorway and slides it open, and the light bursts forth again.

Ziane braces herself, then steps into infinity.

CHAPTER TWENTY-SEVEN

Between the blowing air, the bright light, and the terror of the unknown, it takes Ziane a lot of effort to walk out. And it is only when the door eventually slides shut behind her that she gathers the courage to move more than an inch. She isn't quite sure where she's going other than the knowledge that if this *is* a hologram, it will have a limited range that it can extend from its generator, and if she keeps going, she'll be able to find where the hologram ends and see where she *actually* is. And if it's not a hologram, if it's… something else, then her plan is to measure how much food and water she has and to stop and turn around when she's halfway through the provisions, to ensure that she has enough to return.

The most crucial thing is to keep going in a straight line. She has experience of measuring distance through pacing, and thus is quite good at taking perfectly straight steps, counting as she goes. Every five minutes, she bends down to scratch a mark into the rocky floor.

At first she begins to sweat underneath the bright light overhead, and then it slowly gets dark, like the daylamps being switched to their night setting, and she gets so very, *very* cold. Her arms are tightly wrapped around her torso, her entire body shivering, her eyes firmly on her feet to keep herself from deviating on the uneven ground.

Only when she has to stop to sit and have a brief meal does she finally get a look at the ceiling at night.

What she sees pulls the breath from her lungs in the most tender of caresses. It is still immeasurably high above, and it is unmistakably the same image that she saw in King Ari's glass above the Mists. Fathomless black. Black in the way that is not colorless but all colors at once, blues and greens and purples and reds scattered across the boundless expanse. And the pinpricks of light, shining with glory that the glass had dimmed, so far that they might as well be an eternity away, and yet stretched all around her in such an enthralling dome that a childish part of her swears that she could just reach out and touch them.

A weightlessness fills her body and, even with her goggles to protect her eyes from the stinging air, she cannot stop the tears that slide down her cheeks. This is too much for a hologram, and it's this limitless ceiling that makes her truly, finally realize that this has to be the end of the world and not a creation of Carrion. No skills of either the Eoi or the Vesperi can do something like this. Whatever this is, it's real, impossible though it might be.

Ziane feels... exposed. Watched. *Small*.

Sleep eludes her, and when the blinding light begins to return, she continues her trek. The air begins to blow far more fiercely, the rocky granules whipping around her and making it nearly impossible for her to see what's in front of her or what's around her, let alone what's above her. All she can do is mark the ground and refuse to let herself topple over despite the force shoving her back and forth. The marks might get erased by whatever phenomenon is going on, by whatever environmental controls are broken out here, but she has to risk it.

Finally, after endlessly trudging along and hoping with every fiber of her being that she will not die in this air-blasted wasteland, she sees something in the dust. Something large, round, and metallic, sunken into the rocky ground. Similar in size to a small residential unit, but shaped with swooping lines and a partially missing outer frame. Dust has piled up around the sides to the point where it nearly covers the thing entirely, and only the domed top is left bare, covered in rust. Blemished though it may be, it is *beautiful*. A sign that there is something out here, that this is not the end of everything.

Stumbling towards it, Ziane catches a glimpse of something resembling a door latch and what she thinks might be the outline of an entrance. Clutching the latch like it's a lifeline and pulling with all her might, the door slides open and she manages to get inside and shut it behind her before the dust can follow her in.

Immediately she is hit with a breath of recycled air, exactly the same as in the Bastion, and just that single breath is enough to make her sink to the floor as tension is leached from her body. She rips off her rebreather and her goggles and gulps down that beautifully familiar air. Her satchel and equipment fall to the ground as she all but collapses against the door, and slowly she turns out to face this place that she has found herself in.

The walls are a clean, smooth metal, the same tempered color as the metal supports and buildings in the Bastion, albeit with rust along the edges, collecting in the rivets and at the floor. A couple of seats are propped up on the ground, with empty brackets above them that make her wonder if they were originally affixed to the walls. Computer terminals cover nearly half of the room, with those same sharp blue circuit lines running up the sides that she always sees on Era One tech. And then there are the details that are clearly later additions. A pile of worn-thin blankets, a satchel with a few scruffy items of clothing spilling out, a stack of ration bars and water canteens. Reminiscent of that hideout of Carrion's they had previously found. A janky setup of wires and connectors and ports that have hooked up a power pack to the computer terminals, the pack slowly humming away. How is there so much *stuff* here? Did Carrion cart this all the way out to the edge of the world just to hide it away?

Her hand reaches for the light panel next to the door and she turns the lights up from a mid-grade standby setting to full brightness. The moment she does, one of the computer screens flickers to life and a crackly strain of music starts to warble through the room:

Starships... were meant to fllllyyyyy... Hands up and touch the skyyyyy...

She hurries to the computer and finds the button to switch the music off, leaving just the white noise of the power pack. Despite being distinctly Era One, this technology is like nothing she's ever seen before. Even rusty, even showing signs of maintenance, visibly suffering from wear and tear, the programming is clear and clean and organized. Not in the way the Era One scanners from the Deep are a reconstructed program with a messy user interface. As though this is the original.

Buried under a mess of discarded containers is a tablet of unmistakably similar design to her own. She pulls it out and dusts it off, pressing the power button to wake it up. A small collection of files appear to be the only thing on it, and she taps on the newest file to open it.

Date: system date of 67.34.11.05. Refer to Schematic A-Prime for jurisdiction of contract. The next word is a jumble of symbols and corrupted text, entirely illegible, but it continues: *henceforth referred to as the Petitioner. Queen Sef the Third, Guardian of the Eoi, Lady of the Deep, henceforth referred to as the Court.*

Ziane's eyes widen as she recognizes the text. This is the same way that her own contract with the Eoi had begun. It's obviously not hers, and the place where a name should be has clearly been deliberately obscured, but it's nonetheless unmistakably the same. She remembers the utter confusion she'd had when she'd first agreed to her contract, and she still doesn't understand the vast majority of the text as she reads through it, struggling to puzzle out the legal terminology. There's a section detailing the terms: the promise of a life to the Eoi. This is… familiar? She doesn't remember, not fully. She knows about the bargain that Carrion had struck with Queen Sef that was designed to facilitate their capture and that they had managed to dodge by instead doing… she's not sure. They slipped through that noose. Somehow. A different life, she thinks.

She selects the oldest file this time. There's another contract in it, with the same corrupted text where a name should be, only this begins differently:

Date: system date of 51.28.01.29. Refer to Schematic A-Prime for jurisdiction of contract. Unknown name: *henceforth referred to as the Petitioner. King Ari the First, Defender of the Vesperi, Lord of the Mists, henceforth referred to as the Court. The Court has agreed to accept all mortal memories of Petitioner's life on the following Terms and Conditions of Service.*

All memories. Ziane reads that line over and over again. Carrion sold their life to Ari, committed to decades of being an Acolyte, in exchange for their memories. Unlike Ziane, who had lost some of them upon becoming Eoi, Carrion had gone to the Vesperi for the specific purpose of begging to have them removed. Much of the rest of the contract is incomprehensible, detailing duration of service – forever – and the specifics of the totality of memories to be forfeited – all save the barest essentials, including where they are and what they have done.

She keeps reading, going through file after file.

Contract after contract. Carrion selling bits and pieces of themselves, over and over again. Their head of hair for a chance to fight a duel. Their lungs for the blessing of becoming Vesperi. Their first love to glimpse Ari's glass ceiling. Their liver to Sef for the powers of the Eoi. Their sense of taste to explore the lowest area of the Deep.

"What's the *point*?" Ziane wonders to herself.

There's the groaning noise of the door being opened and she stares at the entrance as Carrion steps inside.

They have a scarf wrapped around their nose and mouth, the same sort of goggles as her, and when they strip off their gear, they don't look even slightly surprised to see her standing here, in the heart of their true lair. She's not surprised to see them either. They had invited her here, after all, and this is their home, as much as they are able to have one. Their pocket of something in the void. For one long moment, the two of them stare at one another, them looking her up and down, her still holding the tablet of contracts.

Eventually they jerk their head towards the tablet and ask, "Interesting reading?"

"What is this place?" she blurts out. "Is this the end of the world?"

"No." They toss their scarf and goggles onto the pile of blankets and head over to the computer terminal, running their fingers along the surface to properly power it all up. "But I guess to you it might seem that way. Thought the same myself when I first came out here. You saw the night sky, didn't you? The same as Ari's little window?"

Sky? "Where *are* we?"

"Outside the Bastion."

"There's nothing outside the world. There's not supposed to be anything beyond the Fringes."

Carrion flicks a wrist towards the door and tells her, "There's a lot outside the Bastion. Once this damn sandstorm dies, I'll show you what it looks like from a distance. For now, here." They step aside so that she can watch as they press a button on the computer. A hologram is projected above the terminal. It's showing an orb, slowly rotating in place, with one smaller orb stuck to the edge and moving with it. Carrion points to the smaller orb. "*That* is the Bastion. And *that*–" Here they circle the larger orb. "–is the world we're on."

How can there be another world that the world is clinging to? She chews on her lower lip, staring at those two circles. "How high up is the ceiling out here?"

"Ain't got one." Carrion zooms the hologram out and three more tiny orbs appear around the larger one. "No ceiling. A sky. Beyond that, you got these three lumps of rock that are this planet's moons. They're orbiting this big hunk of rock. And then beyond *that*," they say, zooming out again until the world-circle is a tiny speck and a massive orb appears on the edge of the projection, "is our sun. A star. Big-ass ball of fire. That's what's lighting the world up during the day. Brighter than anything you can get in the Bastion."

Her mouth is dry. The tablet drops from her hands as she takes a tiny, trembling step towards the hologram. "How can anything be that big?"

"Oh, it's *way* bigger than that. You saw the lights in the night sky, right? Each one of those is another star, with its own cluster of worlds spinning around it. They're billions and trillions and quadrillions of miles away. We're just floating around, except we're also hurtling through space – we just can't feel it. Not sure how it works." They frown at the computer terminal, giving the screen an annoyed tap and sending the hologram flickering off. "I got all that from the systems here, but they all sort of *assume* that people just already know all this crap."

Ziane collapses onto one of the dislodged seats. Nothing is that big. Nothing can be that big. What would support it? What would keep it all up?

Pity softens Carrion's expression. No, not pity. Compassion. "Did anyone believe you?"

"I told Queen Sef," she confesses. "About the end of the world. She thought it was a hologram you'd set up."

"Ooh, a hologram. That's a smart guess. I mean, totally fucking wrong. Ain't stupid, though. Sef and Ari have always been inconveniently smart. Just narrow minded. Hard to dodge. All they give a shit about is keeping their throneworlds safe, which, sure, it's admirable, but it means they don't think about anything outside of that. That and the diamond, 'cause they've gotten the idea into their heads that it's gonna finally give 'em the edge over the other and make 'em strong enough to ensure no one ever hurts their throneworlds again. Eternal cold war that they're never gonna actually win."

When Ziane had first found this end of the world – this new world, this other world – she had thought it infinite.

Even this stuff Carrion has been saying doesn't make it less infinite. If the Bastion is that small compared to the world it is on, and the world it is on is that *tiny* compared to this theoretical sun, and that sun is so very, very far away from all the other ones, then how is it different from infinity? How can it possibly be measurable if it's all impossibly far away from everything else?

Carrion sighs, sympathy softening the sharp edges of them. "It's a lot. It was a lot for me too. Want a drink?"

"Please."

They toss her a flask and she's foolishly expecting alcohol and is thus surprised to get a swallow of water instead.

Something on the computer terminal beeps. "Oh, hey." Carrion gives her a floppy sort of smile that clearly has been used sincerely so rarely that they've forgotten what it should look like. "It says the sandstorm's stopped." They bend over her seat and offer her their hand. "Wanna see outside properly?"

"No," she says.

And yet she takes their hand anyway. Their hand is just as cold as her own. Not the warmth of life when she grows something, or the heat that so many others radiate, but the same temperature. An unexpected match.

Carrion leads her outside, through the thick metal door and into the harsh light. As promised, the sandstorm has died and the air is still and calm. The light overhead, the *sky*, is shining bright and clear, and when she looks straight up and squints she thinks she can see the round orb of the sun. It appears so small from down here, but it is so bright that she cannot look at it for more than a second or two without her eyes watering. The air still tastes wrong, still burns in her lungs, and she regrets leaving her rebreather inside.

"Here," Carrion says, and they slowly reach towards her. "Oh, for– Don't flinch, I'm not gonna slap you or nothing. The wind might not be that rough anymore, but the air itself is its own problem. This'll help you breathe." She holds as still as stone while they carefully place a hand on her cheek. They poke her tightly pressed lips. "Open up."

She cracks her lips open a tiny sliver, and the moment she does so, Carrion sends a gust of air rattling through her mouth and down her throat to sit in her lungs. The urge to cough rises up only to settle down a moment later as that strange gust turns fresh and pure, and when she breathes in, she no longer tastes that dry burn. A Vesperi trick? One they must have learned on their own, given that none of the Vesperi have ever ventured out here.

Carrion lets go of her and allows her to pull back a safe inch or two. "Better?" they ask. Swallowing another mouthful of pure air, Ziane nods. "Great," they say, though it's not that enthusiastic. "Right, then. Take a look."

Ziane stops focusing on her breathing and the light, and turns to face away from the domed structure, back towards the expanse of nothingness that she had crossed. As promised, it is no longer a haze of sand and wind swallowing up any distinctive features, and she can at last properly see what is behind her.

When she had first stepped out of the Fringes, there had been that door and the metal wall behind her, and it had stayed behind her as a towering barrier until the sandstorm came and she couldn't see it anymore. Now, in the distance, over the uneven red-stone rocks and the way it peaks and valleys, sitting right where the sky meets the ground, is an impossibly large metal sphere. A dome partially sunk into the sand and rock, gleaming in the daylight. A golden glow curving around the metal, the aurora of light stretching out, the sphere casting a long shadow across the rock, shrouding almost the entirety of the landscape with its sheer existence.

The Bastion.

Carrion doesn't sound unsympathetic as they ask, "Looks different from out here, don't it?"

Her hands tremble. "Has it always been this?"

"Yeah. You've just never known." Carrion doesn't stare at that metal sphere as she does. Instead they stare at her, a long, intense stare. When she blinks at them in confusion, they cough and explain, "Sorry, I just... I've seen it a hundred times before, but I've never seen it through someone else's eyes. That's what you've been living inside. Ain't so much the whole world from far away, huh?"

Despite now being able to breathe easily, her throat is still scratchy and raw when she answers, "It shouldn't be possible for things to be this... big. And so... empty. If the entire world is inside there, then what is the point of all this out here?"

"Space is big and empty, apparently," they reply. "And I don't think there is a point."

Empty, infinite, pointless existence.

Wrapping her arms around herself as though she can squeeze out that thought, she quietly begs, "I would like to go back inside, please."

"Yeah." Carrion sighs and opens the door behind them. "That's what I wanted, too."

CHAPTER TWENTY-EIGHT

Ziane sits for a long, long time. Though the protective dome of Carrion's nest isn't safe, not by any sense of the word, it is close enough in appearance and atmosphere to the Bastion. And, most importantly, it is not the vast expanse that is the world outside. In here she doesn't need the Vesperi trick to breathe safely, the light doesn't blind her, and she is enclosed within thick walls, no longer exposed and tiny, a speck upon the rock. So much smaller than the Bastion, and yet the Bastion is so much smaller than the rest of this planet. Knowing the world is finite is far preferable to knowing the world is infinite.

In their defense, Carrion doesn't push her to speak. They instead sit at the computer terminal, scrolling through a dataset over and over, patiently waiting for her to start functioning again.

Eventually, more to herself than them, she murmurs, "I *had* wondered what was beneath the Deep and above the Mists."

"That's your answer," they readily agree. "Above the Mists is a whole ton of sky, and below the Deep is a fuckton of wrecked levels and then more of the planet's surface. That's why the Bastion is so bottom-heavy. You saw what it looked like. It's stuck way far into the ground."

Stuck in the ground. Implying that it did not grow, as things in the Deep do. It did not come from the planet's dirt, not in the normal way. "Why?" she asks, and then, "How? And what is *this* place? It appears the same as the Bastion, in aesthetics, technology. Even the air is the same, and not at all painful like the air outside."

Carrion frowns to themself, pressing a finger against their lips as they think. After a while, they turn back to the computer and activate the hologram once more. "Might be easier to explain if I show you."

The hologram hums and pops up. That planet and its sun appear again. Carrion messes with a slider before plugging in what she thinks is a date, but not a date stamp like any she's ever seen before. It's too short, for one. Once they've finished, the planet shifts to take up the center of the hologram, and the orb that is the Bastion vanishes from the planet's surface. Instead, an orb of similar size appears floating in the corner.

"That's the Bastion," Carrion confirms. "Fucking *long* time ago. You know what a colony is, right? This was, far as the records say, a colony ship."

She recalls the lines of that warbly song that had been playing earlier. "A starship."

"Damn right," they say, lighting up at her recognition. "A colony starship. Got no clue where it came from, but it was chock-full of people, folks waiting to find a planet and settle down there instead of living inside that ship forever. Every single person in the Bastion, Astrosi too, are the descendants of the folks who were on that ship. Something went wrong, though. Not sure if it was ever even meant to land here." The Bastion orb on the hologram speeds up and smacks into the planet orb. "It crashed. That's why it's half-buried in the ground."

"But it can't have really crashed," she replies before thinking about it, images of the Fringes crashing around her and turning to utter ruin filling her mind. "If it had, it would have, well, broken. That horrible air from outside would have gotten in, no matter how hard the Bastion's air filtration attempted to counteract it. We wouldn't be able to live here at all."

Carrion shakes their head. "Not quite. A starship this big, it don't break open easy. It was designed to withstand a crash. Those thick, massive outer walls? That's the *last* layer of protection between the ship's insides and the space outside. I've found the schematics for the original ship, and–"

"That's how you know so much about the Bastion's layout!" she realizes with a gasp. "That's how you can sneak in and out of both the Deep and the Mists. That's how you were able to tell my map was accurate. That's how you can keep hiding in the Bastion while avoiding humans and Astrosi. You have had a complete map of the world this entire time."

"Not the world, love," they remind her. "Just the Bastion. Don't worry, I'll give you the schematics too," they add, as a peace offering. They wink at her. "Then you'll have another of my secrets."

She is no longer certain she wants those secrets, yet the promise of a map, at least, is something that for once doesn't make her wish she could erase all knowledge of Carrion and their secrets from her mind. A map, she can handle. "Then what is this place?" she demands. "It isn't connected to the Bastion physically, not as far as I can tell, but it looks like it's from the same... *starship*."

"It is," they confirm. "It's an escape pod. It launched when the ship crashed." They stare at a spot on the ground for a moment before shaking their head. "Some poor bastard tried to get out. There were... bones. When I first found this place. Dunno how long they were able to live out here, but they would have died eventually, one way or another. If they were looking for help, they didn't find it. Don't worry," they tell her, "you're not sitting on 'em or anything. I buried the remains. But no one had disturbed this place between them kicking the bucket and me showing up here, so everything was in pretty good condition. When I got the power hooked up and running, there wasn't any of the corruption in the computer files that the Bastion had from all those years running their systems on limited server space."

Ziane runs through it all in her mind, over and over again. "The colony starship crashes. An escape pod launches. The outer layers of the ship's protection were broken, but not the last. Our ancestors survived. They never left the Bastion. The databanks degraded. The knowledge was lost."

"Just about, yeah. The systems got fucked, locked down, went into survival mode. Nothing got in, nothing got out."

"Except you."

"Except me." They give her a slow look. "And except you."

Something not unlike anger flickers in the void in her chest. "You didn't have to do this to me," she accuses. "The Bastion is closed, it is safe, nothing in this wasteland gets in. I didn't have to know *any* of this."

At that, they go still and quiet, staring off at the hologram as though it contains all the answers in the world. They sigh, shoulders slumping. "You weren't the first person, you know. I've tried before, usually with humans. Astrosi don't listen to anything *I* got to say." They gesture to themself with a flamboyant flick. "My reputation precedes me there. No one's ever even made it to the Fringes, let alone beyond, and I didn't *really* know if you'd have what it takes to get this far. Truth is, I... need help."

Only that's not true, is it? For who even knows how long, Carrion has been capable of running circles around the Astrosi and humanity, and it isn't as though she's ever been able to catch them. She isn't on their level and they both know it. "No," she says, refusing to let them obfuscate the truth. All that knowledge that they have to carry themself, the burden of that empty, infinite, pointless existence. "You want to not be alone."

They flinch as though she has slapped them. "That ain't a crime."

"It is when you condemn someone else," she retorts. "You led me to this. I never would have gotten this far if you hadn't marked up my map."

"You got very, *very* far on your own. You were making that map, you were willing to run into the Fringes after me. For all your twitchiness, you got guts."

"Hic Sunt Leones," she reminds them. "*You* told me that."

They purse their lips and then turn it into a twisted grin, and this time she can see it for the mask it is. "Aight then. Kill me. Capture me. Strike me down with all that righteous vengeance you got in you. You got more reasons than you know to hate me."

It's a bluff. They know she won't do it, and yet she's unwilling to admit they're right. "You once said that, for better or worse, you needed to stay alive." And before they can wriggle their way out of that one, she adds, "Why? The Bastion is safe. You do nothing but cause chaos while you try to beat the Eoi and the Vesperi in their cold war for the diamond. Are you truly so dedicated to making someone else suffer that you'll cling to life for it?"

"It ain't about suffering," they snap.

"Then *what*?" she demands, the emptiness in her buzzing like an overheating battery. "What *is* it about? Because from where I'm standing, you have more knowledge than anyone in the entire world and you haven't done a shred of good with it!"

They leap to their feet, pressing their hand to their heart and the tattered, worn-out coat that covers their chest. "I'm trying to *save* your precious fucking world!"

"By killing people? By ruining lives?"

"Yes," they say with a snarl. "If need be. What's a life compared to a thousand lives? What's a thousand lives compared to the entire population of the world? I do what needs doing, for all the damn thanks I get. Oh, Carrion's *insane*," they mock. "No point listening to what they have to say. They just wanna rack up their kill count!"

"The Bastion is safe – you said so yourself. It doesn't need saving!"

They burst out laughing, bitter instead of mocking. "You worked as a First Responder. You've seen how the place is falling apart at the seams. It can't sustain itself forever, not like it is now, not while y'all slowly continue to lose knowledge of how to repair it, of how Era One tech works, of what the place actually is. And even if you could. Even if humans were able to keep it in perfect condition forever, it still wouldn't matter. Not in the long run. That last layer of the Bastion's outer walls? It's being worn away. Slowly but surely. It won't last. And one day soon, those walls are gonna fall, and the toxic air is gonna get in, and every fucking person on this world is going to die." They knock on one of the walls. "Even this place is wearing thin."

Her jaw snaps shut and she swallows her retort. That cannot be inevitable, can it? "How can I trust anything you say?"

"I can show you the original schematics. How many layers there used to be."

"You could have edited those."

They tilt their head to the side and taunt, "Like how our darling Sef believed the outside was just a hologram? If you really don't believe me, you're welcome to walk the entire perimeter of the Bastion and dig up every metal slab of the outer layers that have been buried in the sand. I'll even give you a shovel."

She has to accept that would be a waste of time. They've shown before that they are perfectly willing to wait while she stumbles around and uncovers their secrets. They would likely wait while she stumbles around, digging in the sand as well. So, then... the world – the Bastion, and she shudders to think of the two as different – is unsafe. She has known her whole life that it has its perils, that it's falling apart, but to learn that it will be completely destroyed by forces outside of her control, by the crushing presence of time, is something that makes every part of her empty body tremble.

Out of the corner of her eye, she sees Carrion get up from their chair – and then they are kneeling before her, filling her vision. They place a hand on her cheek, tilting her head up. "Your fear will *not* get the better of you," they promise. "When we first met, you were terrified and you chased after me anyway. You were terrified when you watched me kill, and you still did everything you could to stop me. You were terrified of the Astrosi, and you became one. You were terrified of the Fringes, and you mapped it anyway. You adjust. You push through."

"I shouldn't be feeling any kind of fear," Ziane says, unable to pull away from their touch. "I have felt so little since I woke up as an Eoi. It's like there's nothing inside me."

"Some things get so buried in your brain that you can never totally dig them out. The emotion moves to your head, not your heart." They lean forward and rest their forehead against hers, and there's that similarity again. The same temperature, the same frequency. "I was fucking terrified too. But you can't go back. So you do what you gotta do, and you do it scared."

It had been so empty out in the wasteland during the days she spent trekking here. An expanse of nothingness, exposed and alone. As much as she had insulted Carrion for their desire to have someone to share these truths with, she understands why they had needed that. This knowledge is too big for one person. Maybe she too would go mad if she were alone for so long, with no one to listen to her, no one to believe her. She lets out a slow sigh, the air rattling around in her throat as she tries to force her body to stop trembling. She doesn't want this fear. It isn't welcome.

"How have you lived with this?" she quietly asks. "All these years, out here and in the Bastion, time passing swifter for you than it does for the Astrosi?"

They huff out a laugh, their breath mingling with hers. "Badly."

"And you expect *me* to live with it any better?"

"That's up to you in the end, innit?"

If she were still human, at least then she would die well before the Bastion collapses. She wouldn't have to live to see it. And even though the Deep and the Mists are protected by those two energy fields that slow down the degradation of the infrastructure, they aren't fully sealed off from the rest of the Bastion. The toxic outside air would creep in eventually. The Vesperi would still be able to breathe with that trick Carrion had used, if they learn how to do it in time, but with the Deep destroyed and the Bastion's food production ruined, they would eventually starve to death regardless.

If that happens, Ziane too will die, of either toxic air or lack of food and drinkable water. Unless she is actively killed, she will not die of old age as humans do, and instead be condemned to slowly suffocate or starve. Having it eventually happen is one thing. Knowing years, perhaps centuries, in advance and being unable to prevent it is a cruelty of a different sort, a mental curse that she has no choice but to carry.

She wants to glare at Carrion, but that indignation from earlier has faded. Instead, she simple feels... tired. "What now?"

"I said I needed help," they remind her.

"Help with what? Easing your loneliness?" She pauses and thinks through everything they have said again. "Or do you have some sort of plan?"

They grin, and now that she knows where to look she sees that it is all fake bravado. "Sure do. Little fuzzy on the final details – I'll figure out the tweaks at a later stage, you know how it is – but it *is* a plan. The only plan that can actually work in the long term. Because you've seen how it works out when all you do is try to prop up what's broken. It just becomes an infinite loop, a job that never gets done, and it gets harder and harder every year. If we wanna stop this, *really* stop it, we need to tear it all down and rebuild it from the ground up." They sigh and stare up at the ceiling in exasperation. "But that ain't something the Eoi or the Vesperi wanna hear, and I gotta get past both of 'em."

Needing to get past the Eoi and the Vesperi. Carrion has been working on this plan for a long time. Ziane wants to slap herself for not piecing it together earlier. "You need the diamond."

"Exactly!"

"I mean," she says slowly, trying to think it through, "I suppose a massive power source could be helpful for any number of–"

They shake their head, cutting her off. "It's not a power source. Well, it sorta is. Not really. Ask yourself this: What's standing between living in the Bastion and living out here?"

Everything. "The toxic air," she immediately replies. "A lack of water and water recycling facilities. No food manufacturing plants, and no other sources of food like there are in the Deep. No shelter, so nothing to protect people in the long run from sandstorms."

"And yet," they say, pointing a single finger to her lips, "with one simple trick you were able to breathe safely without a filter. The Eoi can coax a weed from a few specks of dirt. Couldn't they grow crops from even this wasteland? In terms of shelter, the real danger ain't from the sandstorms. It's from the wind we can't even see." They rise to their feet, pulling away from her and depriving her of their touch. Then they hold out their hand to her once more. "Come with me."

She takes their hand before she even asks, "Where?"

"Back to the Bastion. The best way to explain all this is to *show* you."

CHAPTER TWENTY-NINE

Leaving the safety of the escape pod again is a challenge. Ziane deliberately tarries in repacking her bag, fiddling with her goggles and her rebreather for far longer than she needs to. Strange and alien though this protective pod may be, at least it feels the same as the Bastion, and that illusion of security is difficult for her to put aside in favor of the sun-blasted wasteland outside. *Wasteland* is a more manageable word for what it is – the world, the planet, the emptiness – and when Carrion opens the pod door, that harsh wasteland light silhouettes them in burnt orange and glaring gold.

Ziane's legs feel as though they're made of solid lead as she puts one foot in front of the other and walks out of the pod into the exposed world. She squares her shoulders, draws in her final breath of clean recycled air, and leans into the emptiness in her chest that she hopes will chase away the twitchy fear. It feels as though the words she had shared with Carrion remain in the escape pod, wrapped up in that tiny space, and she glances back over her shoulder at its smooth metal surface as one thought lingers in her mind: *You do what you gotta do, and you do it scared.*

Without the sandstorm, the half-dome of the Bastion is clear in the distance, unmistakable, the only thing in sight that isn't red rock and fiery sky. It gives her and Carrion a clear path to walk as they begin their trek. The downside, of course, is that without the sandstorm to obstruct her view, she is constantly bombarded with the truth of how minuscule her world is, of the vastness of the wasteland.

Carrion points to the right of the Bastion. "See how there's a bit of a dip in the rock? Like a trench? Far as I can tell, that's from when the colony ship first crashed. Like skid marks. It's been worn down with time and sand and wind and all that, obviously, but the shape of it remains."

It does indeed appear to be a trench of sorts, trailing behind the Bastion and sinking further down until it meets the ship's outermost layer. If she squints, she thinks she can see glints of metal in that trench-trail. Those must be the fallen layers of protection that Carrion said once coated the Bastion. She hadn't noticed them when she'd briefly been outside before to first see the hulking form of the Bastion, but in her defense, it was rather too overwhelming to pay close attention. Frankly, it's still too overwhelming now. She simply has no choice but to carry on. To do it scared.

"I can see the outer layers you were talking about, I think," she says. When she takes another look and does her best to ignore the bright light, she can make out imperfections on the dome of the Bastion. "How much longer does the final layer of hull have before the sand wears it down?"

"Damned if I know," Carrion admits with a shrug. When she stops to peer at the dome, they wave her forward. "Come on. Keep moving. It ain't good to be out here long, even for us Astrosi."

"Because of the air? Won't the rebreathers and your Vesperi trick protect us?"

They shake their head. "Ain't the air. So the Bastion, right? It has these layers of hull, right? Keeps the air in, keeps the energy in. Even stripped of outer layers, it's still protecting everyone inside from the effects of the planet outside. Think of the Bastion's hull like a bubble. Planets that folks can live on have a bubble too, one that keeps good stuff inside and bad stuff outside. You felt how cold it was at night and how hot it is right now, yeah? The bubble keeps the temperatures normal. Keeps the folks on the surface safe. That bubble is called an atmosphere, and a planet apparently needs one to be habitable."

"This wasteland doesn't appear to have a very *good* atmosphere," Ziane replies. "The Bastion has far better temperature regulation, to begin with."

"You're right. Atmosphere here sucks ass. But it ain't its fault."

"I suppose there are a lot of things that are not the fault of anyone in particular. Some things just are."

"Well, yeah and no."

"That's a very unspecific answer."

"I mean, okay, sure, generally you're right," they allow. They wave a hand through the air as if trying to sort their thoughts, like they're not used to having someone around to watch their odd habits. "But not in this specific case. The Bastion was meant to be a terraforming ship. It was carrying a ton of stuff to make sure that it could set up shop wherever it landed. So when it crashed, a couple of those terraforming devices kicked into gear. Two of 'em, specifically. Ta-da!" They snap their fingers. "Big ol' ball of something gets shot into the core and we've got better gravity! Second one goes off and, ta-da, number two, we've got an atmosphere."

"What kind of devices were these?" Ziane asks, chewing on the inside of her mouth as she tries to wrap her head around the sheer amount of energy needed to do *anything* to a planet of this size. The Bastion couldn't even light daylamps across this entire space, let alone anything of the magnitude needed to create a bubble. "And if one did create an atmosphere, why is the one this planet has doing such a poor job, especially since gravity appears to be working perfectly fine?"

Carrion shrugs again. "Hard to explain. And before you ask, no, I have no clue how they were made. The ship's records don't say. As for the second question, an atmosphere can't sustain itself without other things backing up. Like you can build a really sweet roof, but if there's no support beams propping it up, it ain't gonna last long, right? Atmosphere needs the same thing. Just not literal support beams. Couldn't make beams that long anyway."

If it can't sustain itself, but the ship was always intended for terraforming, then... "One of the other devices was meant to provide the support for the atmosphere. But it wasn't one of the two that went off."

"I knew there was a reason I liked you," Carrion says with a grin. "Quick on the draw. You're right. There were five, total. The two that went off, two that got removed from stasis but never properly activated, and one that wasn't disturbed at all. That last one's supposed to prop up the atmosphere, along with a fuckton of other things."

"As you said, it can't exactly provide literal support beams. What does it do, exactly?"

"You know magnets?"

She nods. "Of course."

"There's something called a magnetosphere. On planets. Without one, the atmosphere slowly gets scraped away. With one, you get protection from the sun's temperatures, from solar wind, from radiation. That's one of the reasons you can't stay out here forever. The radiation will kill you eventually, and it ain't a good way to die. Hull of the escape pod and the Bastion keeps it out, but again…" They sigh and stare up at the sky full of danger. "Not forever."

To this, Ziane has no good response and thus falls silent.

Radiation is dangerous – she knows that much, though she's had little experience with it herself beyond the fact that the diamond apparently produces a specific type of it. It seems harmless enough from the diamond, compared to the stuff that can cause cancer and all manner of other illnesses. Rarely does the Bastion ever have radiation issues, but the threat of a contaminant is always a possibility, and they have limited containment devices to protect people from its effects. Her skin crawls at the thought of the radiation that apparently plagues this wasteland creeping into her body, permeating her cells, corrupting them until they suffocate her.

How many times can she trek back and forth across this wasteland before the radiation becomes too much for her, even as an Astrosi? How many times has Carrion made this journey? Is there an invisible counter, ticking up and up each time she stands underneath this all-piercing sky?

Perhaps it is merely because she has just reexperienced the controlled climate of the Bastion within the escape pod, but when night falls it feels even colder than it had on the trek here. It too pierces, the chill cutting straight through her flesh and clothing to gnaw at her bones.

Though their bodies are far more durable than those of humans, both Ziane and Carrion do require sleep, and thus once night properly arrives, they settle down to rest. It is awkward to sit on a patch of cold stone next to someone that she was determined to hunt down only a few days ago, and despite all that has happened and all that she has learned, tension still keeps her muscles tight and coiled, her eyes flickering to Carrion every few seconds. They seem entirely unbothered, flopping down on their back and crossing their arms behind their head as they stare up at the sky full of stars.

"Creepy as fuck, ain't it?" they say with a sigh. "But a view like this almost makes up for everything else."

Does it? "I feel too exposed," she admits. "As though there is something out there watching me."

"Maybe there is. Who knows, right? Maybe there were more colony ships out there. Maybe there's a whole galaxy of terraformed planets and we just happened to have crashed into an empty one. Maybe we got abandoned, or no one out there knows we're here. Or maybe there's no one else. Maybe we were the only colony ship and we're the last of anything in the universe." They hum to themself. "Can't quite say which is more comforting."

"Neither." Being alone in this vast expanse is terrifying. Knowing that there are others out there who simply have left a world full of her people to a slow death makes her... *sour* inside.

Carrion gives her a knowing look out of the corner of their eye. "You ever watched medics go into triage mode? Desperate times, forced to ignore those who are gonna die no matter what you do? Maybe any other ship out there was in triage mode too. Wrote us off as fucked no matter what. Something like that better suit your moral compass? Or is it different when it's *your* life that's getting categorized and tossed out?"

"I have never considered myself to be above any categorizations like that," she replies with full honesty. "Everyone's life is unique and valuable, but at the same time... everyone is a statistic, at the end of the day. I'm not an exception."

"Aren't you?"

Ziane turns her head to face them, their messy brown hair spread out on the rough stone, mingling with her own dark curls that have haloed around her head. "No, I'm not. It's not humility or modesty, before you accuse me of that. It's just realism. I can do everything in my power to protect the Bastion, but I'm still only one person. One person is *one person*. It's the reason the Office of the Administrator is made up of so many people, the reason the Bastion has no queen or king. If I save a hundred lives, that doesn't make me more valuable than anyone else. It doesn't make me more than one person."

"Oh, I think you're more than just one person at this point," Carrion replies with a faint chuckle, their eyes locking with hers. "You're at least two. Human – you and Astrosi – you, to start. And now there's the you that knows what the world really is."

"That's not how it works."

"Isn't it?"

All of that makes her sound like she's more important than she really is, or somehow greater than herself. "I am not you." She isn't certain if she had meant it to be acerbic or not, but the acid falls from her voice halfway through that short sentence, vanishing into the endless sky above. "You've prioritized keeping yourself alive and pursuing your goals at the cost of so many lives, and you justify it because you believe that killing a few to save the many is worth the cost. I don't know if that equation balances out, and even if it did, *I* cannot justify it. I will not think of myself as particularly greater or lesser than anyone else. I can't."

"If I hadn't prioritized myself," they point out, "then I would've died a long time ago, and no one would know that their precious world is slowly falling apart at the seams. You have no idea what the weight of that feels like."

"You aren't the only one anymore."

Their lip tugs upwards into a crooked, toothy grin. "Oh-ho, and now that you've got all this bouncing around your brain, it's fine for me to die, is that it? You think that the partial knowledge you've got your hands on is enough to toss me to Sef or Ari to be hanged or worse? Color me impressed. I didn't think you had it in you, love."

"I don't," she says, surprised by her own swift denial. "You might have done horrible things, but you had your reasons, and for that you deserve to be heard out, at least. Not killed."

"...You don't know everything I've done," they admit, so softly that she barely hears it.

What an obvious thing to say, in her opinion. "Of course I don't. You've been doing this far longer than I've been alive. I imagine that if you tried to recount every single action, we would be here for quite some time."

They give a single, minuscule shake of their head, and they turn from her, looking once more at the sky. "You don't *remember* everything I've done."

"You're the reason I became an Acolyte, I know that much," she replies, though the words are uneasy. The details of that first meeting with Carrion are so fuzzy, wiped away like so many things were when she became Eoi. "Is that what you mean?"

They laugh, a somber huff of air more than anything else. "A decent person would jog your memory. But I'm not a decent person."

"I was never under the illusion that you were," Ziane replies, just as candid, just as straightforward as them.

They hum, a low sound that's all in their throat, and repeat, "Good."

A calm silence fills the open air, floating along on the gentle night breeze and tugging her breath up towards the sky full of stars. Those lights seem peaceful for the first time, cold and distant, maybe, and yet non-judgmental. Uncaring of what happens on this planet, this world, unable to see what occurs within the Bastion. It all still radiates that sense of yawning terror, a maw of fear, but she finds herself leaning into the void in her chest to seek refuge from those unwanted, unnecessary emotions.

"I read your contract," Ziane eventually says into all that unbound air. "You traded nearly every memory of your life as a human to become an Acolyte to King Ari."

They nod, a quick tilt of their chin. "Sure did. Past-me wasn't stupid about it either. Asked to keep some basic memories, like how to talk and walk and general worldly knowledge and that sort, but everything else got washed away. Long, *long* gone by now."

"Why?"

"Why did *you*?" they counter.

A flash of a vague, half-faded dream flits through her head, of running after a child in the dark, but the image ends before the child can turn around, before she can see their face. Important? Or just meaningless, as so many dreams are, a mashup of things floating around the brain with little to no significance at the end of the day? The louder, more reasonable part of her mind decides that it must have been nothing more than the latter. After all, she doesn't know any children.

"I suppose it was a pointless question," she murmurs, before adding, "I apologize."

"For what?" Carrion's surprise shakes off their previous somber tone, pushing them back into their usual casual pleasantness. "I presumably wanted them gone, the same as you. It's not like either of us lost something that we didn't ask to lose. That's the way it works with the Astrosi, whether you're dealing with the Vesperi or the Eoi. You get what you ask for, no more, no less. I wanted my memories gone, and I got it. Whatever problem I might have had was solved. When it comes to that specific detail, we're not so different."

She swallows. "We are different. I won't kill. Even when I tried to, I couldn't, and I don't know if I'll ever be able to."

"That's really the biggest difference to you? A willingness to kill? Because if that's what you focus on, if that's where you decide to draw your line in the sand, when the day comes that you're inevitably shoved over it by some bastard that wants you dead and can only be stopped one way, your whole idea of who you are is gonna come collapsing down around you. Want my advice?"

"I don't know if I really do," she says respectfully.

They tell her regardless. "Find something else that matters. We can keep reinventing ourselves, the us-that-was-human, the us-as-Astrosi, the us-with-knowledge, but if you keep pinning your identity on things that can vanish with one single event, with one measly little murder, then you're eventually gonna lose sight of who you ever were to begin with."

All those contracts, all those pieces of themselves that they signed away. Ziane turns her head to look them straight in the eye and asks, "Is that what happened to you?"

Their smile is a broken thing. "Of course it is."

While she cannot deny that the knowledge Carrion has gained in their quest is valuable beyond belief, she is also certain that she never wants to become what they are. What hate she felt towards them is being tugged away and into the wide air, but in its place is the deep-seated understanding that, while she may not hate them, she never wants to become them. The road that she now walks is new, only barely visible, and yet she knows where it ends. She knows what she will be if she walks this road for as long as Carrion has.

"Do you ever wish it were otherwise? Or wonder what would have happened to you if you had stayed as just a Vesperi?" she asks after a long stretch of quiet.

"What," Carrion replies with false cheer, "would be the point of *that*?"

CHAPTER THIRTY

Once Ziane and Carrion return to the protective walls of the Bastion that no longer feel quite as safe as they had before she left, it takes them surprisingly little time to head through the Fringes towards the inhabited areas of the world. Although she had thought herself skilled in mapping the Fringes and in finding the fastest and most direct route through, Carrion has spent a lifetime in these abandoned parts and they know seemingly infinite shortcuts and hidden paths that allow the two of them to cut straight through the sections that she'd had to carefully maneuver around.

Once they are through, into the clean air and the regulated light of the Bastion proper, Carrion leads Ziane not towards the center of the Bastion or to the lift leading to the Deep but to a maintenance tunnel that's been marked with a very old security warning, instructing unauthorized personnel to keep out.

"This isn't safe," Ziane points out as soon as Carrion starts prying open the tunnel's entrance. "I think we should better take the lift if we're trying to get to the Deep."

Carrion laughs and wrenches the door open. "And get snatched up by Sef the moment I pop out? No thank you." They give her a cheeky bow before gesturing dramatically to the dark hole of the unlit tunnel they have revealed. "Besides, we ain't going to the Deep. We're going to the Mists."

"What in the world for?"

"Best way to show you what I'm talking about. You gotta see what Ari's hiding."

She inches closer to the entrance until she's able to look down and see no hint of a distinctive top or bottom. "How do we get up there?"

"This tunnel used to funnel carbon dioxide up from the lower levels of the Bastion to the floor right below the Mists. Vesperi can turn that stuff into oxygen just like the Deep can, and a lot of that filters down into the levels below. Not that the Bastion *knows* it, obviously, but you know as well as anyone just how many air-filtration centers have been set up on those higher floors to take all that excess oxygen back down. Humans might not know even half of what's really going on in their world, but they ain't stupid, and they know that sometimes things just *are*." They step right to the edge of the tunnel, one foot resting perilously close to the end of the floor. "Important thing for us now is that this tunnel is designed to handle massive blasts of air without breaking."

Once more she craves the full schematics of the Bastion that Carrion has and has been utilizing for years, but she has been promised them eventually, and so far Carrion has yet to prove themself a liar. Right now, on the edge of this tunnel, is likely not the best time to demand those maps.

"Are you suggesting…?" She trails off as she watches them cozy up to the abyss.

"Yep. You floated on air when I cushioned your fall into the Deep that very first time, remember? It's easy to do the same in reverse."

"Is it safe?"

"Love, if you've learned *anything* over the past few days, it should be that there ain't nothing safe."

That, she cannot deny. Her teeth gnaw at the fleshy inside of her cheek as she creeps towards Carrion and their aura of confidence. They stick their hand into the tunnel, fingers tensing and splaying out, calling up a thin thread of wind that soon turns into a controlled gale. It tugs at their hair and clothing, making the tunnel look all the more threatening and nothing at all like the gentle pillow of air that had slowed Ziane's descent into the Deep.

They have their back to the tunnel, one foot dangling over the edge and a gleeful mania creeping into their eyes. "It'll be fun," they say, as though that's a temptation too great for her to resist.

"How deep is it?" she asks hesitantly.

"Doesn't matter. You won't fall."

Mustering up the same confidence that let her step out into the wasteland beyond the Bastion, she walks right up to the tunnel entrance. This will not be as bad as what's out there. No sandstorm, no radiation, no toxic air. Just Carrion.

When they allow themself to fall backward into the tunnel with a grin, Ziane follows. The moment she's within the darkness of the cold metal tube, Carrion's wind pulls them upwards as though they're just weightbags being tugged along on a rope. She struggles to breathe through the constant stream of worry that they will fall, that the wind will give out from under her, that she will plummet down and die before she even hits the bottom, that no Eoi power she knows of can save her from that fate. And yet every breath she manages to draw into her lungs is full of oxygen, of life, of resolve.

Though the wind is strong enough to support the weight of two people, it is not so strong as to bite and sting in the way that the sandstorm outside was. She doesn't feel as though it might scrape the skin from her flesh, for starters. It is roaring in her ears, but the ascent is just slow enough to smooth out the shifting between levels. The biggest struggle soon becomes preventing her body from tumbling around and around as she flies up. It isn't a safety issue, but Carrion is perfectly calm and upbeat, grinning as they are carried upwards, cool and casual as ever. It feels rather embarrassing to be literally falling head over heels in front of them.

They shout something at her, beaming from ear to ear, and she is surprised to find herself filled with great regret that she is unable to hear them. Part of her wants to yell back, to implore them to repeat themselves, yet she knows that it would be pointless, and perhaps it would feel worse when they cannot hear her in return.

With no change in the walls of the tunnel or the wind around them, Ziane has no way to measure the speed at which they are ascending or the number of floors that they are rising through. Occasionally she thinks she can feel the change in pressure between levels, but she can't be certain of whether it's that or if it is Carrion adjusting their wind current for reasons unknown to her. The weightlessness changes her perception, making time slow down – or, perhaps as the case may be, speed up.

At some point, the wind slows to where Carrion can reach out and grab onto a security guard rail built into the wall, wrapping their arm around her waist to catch her as the air starts to die down. They lean towards a door panel, but Ziane is faster and identifies it easily even in the gloom. Her hand smacks into it and, a foot above them, an access door groans open. There is enough wind at her feet and enough strength in her arms to haul herself up and out of the access door, landing on her stomach before quickly getting to her feet. Carrion slips out behind her with far more grace, killing the wind with a flick of their hand and closing the access door behind them.

"Where are we?" Ziane asks as she examines the empty room. There's a single window, the plexiglass clearly neglected going by the crack in its frame and the lack of cleanliness. She takes a step forward, checking the banged-up computer terminals dotting the room. "There's dust on the outside of the window, but none on the inside or on the computers and floors. This place must have been sealed off for quite some time – properly sealed, not simply marked as off limits. Is that tunnel the only entrance besides the door?"

Carrion shakes their head and strides forward. "No. That tunnel goes straight up to the Mists, but it ends in a wind turbine and I ain't dealing with that. Before folks started using it to funnel carbon dioxide, back when the Bastion was still a ship, this was apparently a monitoring station to make sure that the air systems were keeping on keeping on. Once the ship crashed, the computers here got fried and this whole place was sealed off to stop people fucking with the malfunctioning tech."

"And?" she prods.

"And yeah, it's not the only entrance. No one knows about this place apart from yours truly, but it's a convenient shortcut to the Mists." Carrion hits a control panel on the wall and there is a groan of metal, part of the wall on the other side of the room sliding back to reveal a small, relatively hidden doorframe. They say cheerfully, "Hazardous waste disposal. Comfier than the name sounds."

Ziane scans the room one final time, the stretch of silent, lonely time lingering on her skin, as though it is actively calling out to her, begging her not to leave it alone again. She touches just the tip of her finger against one of the computer terminals, noting the aesthetic similarities to Era One tech, wondering for the first time what exactly Era One *was*. Were those the days before the colony ship crashed? Or were those the days before the ship even left... wherever it had come from to go on its colonization mission?

The disposal area that Carrion is waiting in front of turns out to be a small, cramped room off the main monitoring station, rather similar in appearance although with substantially thicker walls, going by the differences in the way their footsteps sound. A single access hole is built into the ceiling, which Carrion cracks open with the same practiced surety that they've exuded this entire journey. They grab onto the ledge, swing themself up with a messy grace, and then help her up afterwards, pulling her until she can scramble over the edge.

From there, they find another ancient lift that rockets them higher and higher at a speed that nearly makes Ziane keel over, reminiscent of the direct lift between the Deep and the Mists. At least, as Astrosi, these lifts that are swift enough to punch through the energy barriers that surround the Astrosi throneworlds no longer send her to her knees. When the lift stops, they exit next to a thick bulkhead door that Carrion unlocks with a code swiftly punched into the door panel.

Ziane frowns at the bright red lettering on the door, faded over the ages until the color is barely visible. "Radiation containment?"

Carrion wiggles their eyebrows. "Ten guesses what kind of radiation?"

"Not the diamond," is the surest answer she can give. Carrion has no idea where it is, of that she is certain, but the diamond is the only thing she knows of that produces radiation they could be alluding to. Era One objects wash up in the Bastion and occasionally they produce radiation, mild and containable, yet those would be of no interest to Carrion.

"Nope." Carrion pops the *p*. "But you're closer than you know."

The bulkhead door creaks and complains as it opens. Beyond it is a metal room with a series of panels above, all of which appear to have been blocked off save one, where the metal plating has been filed back as though with a cheap rasp, leaving behind rough edges and a set of small holes. Carrion stands on their tiptoes and slides their fingers through those holes – a perfect fit. They remove the panel, quietly setting it on the ground, and above this new entrance is the bottom of a ventilation grate, the bars casting odd shadows in the containment room. Through the grating, Ziane can see darkness and faint blue flickering light, as though from a hundred computer screens.

"We're directly beneath King Ari's throne room," she realizes, craning her neck closer to the entrance. "This is how you brought me here before, the secret entrance you have to get into the Mists undetected."

"Sure is," Carrion replies. They haul themself up, hanging from the grate with naught but the strength in their wiry arms. After a moment, they announce, "Ari ain't home."

With a huff and a shove and contortion of their body, they flip the grate open and swing a leg up over the edge. They sit there for another moment, scanning the room, while Ziane waits below, half-expecting to hear the distant sounds of Ari returning at any moment, the sound of Vesperi guards yelling at Carrion, the noise of bayonet-rifles being fired. All she would see would be Carrion's body tumbling down to land at her feet. Nothing of the sort happens, despite her bracing for it, and Carrion eventually leans down to help her climb up into the cold and sparse throne room.

Ari's throne itself stands empty, with the hundreds of screens still powered up, still displaying those endless security-camera feeds, awaiting the return of their king's surveying eye. When she had last been here, it had been against her will, dragged unconscious by Carrion. Now she's allowed herself to be peacefully led here by the very same person, and standing beside Carrion instead of across from them as they enter the throne room is uncomfortable in how natural it feels.

Carrion goes to the hidden door that leads to the room with a glass ceiling and starts to open it with whatever code they've stolen from Ari.

"Last time we were here," Ziane recalls, running through the thousand possibilities as to why she might have been brought here, "you said that the viewing glass room above King Ari's throne was off limits, but not because of the glass. You said he had a different reason to keep it safe. Now we're back here, and both of us have already seen what's on the other side of the glass. There's something else here, isn't there?"

"Stop guessing *all* my secrets." Carrion flashes a grin over their shoulder as the door opens and they begin to ascend the steps, trusting that she will follow them. "Eventually you're gonna rub off all my mystique and then what'll I have?"

"I thought you wanted someone to ignore the preconceptions that the Astrosi have about you? Surely rubbing off all your mystique only helps there."

They make a retching noise in the back of their throat. "Ugh, that makes me sound so pathetic."

Ari's viewing-glass room has not changed since Ziane was last here, and yet it appears all the more unfamiliar. New not because *it* is different, but because *she* is. Behind the protective barrier overhead looms a sky full of stars and a truth a part of her still wishes she didn't know. A lump wedges itself into her throat as she looks up at the closed ceiling, the burnt orange sky she knows is out there filling her mind, the memory of the sandstorm rough on her cheeks.

"Out of the center," Carrion tells her when she moves to step into the middle of the circular room. "Yep, that's it, just back up a foot."

They flip a switch on the control panel and a tremor runs through the floor, faint but unmistakable. As Ziane watches, the glass overhead is revealed as its panels peel back, and below it a massive circle in the middle of the floor slides back as something begins to be raised up. Even beneath the steady, clinical lights, the object slowly breaching the room is blindingly bright, so bright that Ziane can barely look at it, so bright that she is overcome by the sudden sensation that she should not be here, that she should be running far away as fast as she can.

With a hum of machinery, the platform stops creeping upwards, and the object comes to a halt, hovering in the center of the room, the endless sky shining down upon it and it meeting the radiance of the night like a reflection of those distant stars.

It is an orb, identical to the sphere of gold beneath Sef's bower, only blue-white, silvered like steel. Beneath the smooth exterior is a wavering swirl, similar to water, casting rippling refractions of unnatural light, and when the water curves, thick mist follows in its wake, a trail of pure cloudy white. Beautiful as it is, it is cold and regal where Sef's prize was warm and enticing. Repelling. There is an air to it that warns Ziane away, a bite of chill creeping towards her fingers and nose.

She leans back, finding herself right next to Carrion, the faint warmth of their body that is a perfect match to her own reassuring in the face of this icy sphere. "I don't think we should be here."

"We're fine," Carrion promises. "It's pushing you away, innit? I felt the same when I ran into the secret beneath Sef's bower. It repels the opposite, like magnets. I was Vesperi, so Sef's orb wanted to kick me out. You're Eoi, so Ari's wants you to get gone."

Long ago, Sef had mentioned that speaking in person with Ari taxed her, strained her, that their status as king and queen were counterparts. Ziane had not felt that standing across from Ari or Jess, but then again, she doesn't have a fraction of the power that Sef does, and she was not faced with the raw source of Ari's strength. To her relief, Carrion does not force her closer to the sphere, nor do they abandon her to approach it on their own.

"This," they explain, "is one of the partially activated terraforming devices. Its original design was to generate an air-and-water cycle for this world, to mash up air molecules into oxygen and water and let it rain on a scale way beyond just sprinklers putting out a fire. If it gets properly activated, it can set up real air circulation, with a way to recycle water that don't need all the treatment facilities we need right now."

All water in the Bastion is carefully controlled, measured, regulated. To have a natural, free system of water recycling would be revolutionary, so much so that, as the implications fill her mind, she finds herself teetering towards the orb despite the discomfort. So many people who spend all their time managing water would suddenly be free, no longer having to put in that endless effort day after day. Districts dedicated to treatment facilities, to overflow management, to… drainways. Her body stills. Living by drainways. What does…?

Carrion continues to explain and she has no choice but to listen carefully, unwilling to miss a single tidbit of their secret knowledge. "Sef's orb is the other partially activated terraforming device," they say. "The place it's in was a seed bank, from Era One or even before then. It's supposed to turn all that ground out there into land that we can actually use to grow stuff in without the Eoi doing all the work. Land that don't need them guiding the process of life. Can you imagine that?"

"It would change everything."

"That's what these things do. They change, transform, but on the size of *planets*. Using it on people is way too much for a human body to handle, not without changing themselves, giving up part of themselves to make way for all that power juice."

"Will it kill us?" Ziane asks. "Eventually? If even someone as strong as Sef had two of her predecessors die, then surely they can't *both* have been killed in combat. Surely we must have some way of dying beyond being actively murdered."

"Dunno. Sef, Ari, and myself are the oldest, and I can't say any of us haven't felt the weight of that over time."

Perhaps it was too foolish to assume that they've been granted – or cursed with – true immortality. "And yet they keep making more of us. Not many, but…"

They laugh and add, "Think of the look on Sef and Ari's faces when everything they do suddenly becomes totally pointless. Get their two devices up and running and *bam*. No more need for Sef and Ari. No more need for any of the little spats between Vesperi and Eoi, even though they can be good fun."

"Fun? People have *died*."

"Wanna stop it all?"

The question is so sudden that it takes her aback. "You want to fully activate Queen Sef and King Ari's spheres."

"That would stop a whole lot of things, conflict being just one of them." And then, with hope creeping into their eyes, they prompt, "What else?"

"You don't care about conflict. You want to finish what the terraforming devices started. You want..." Radiation. Radiation... *Think*. What is she missing? Why does radiation here matter? Why would it be something she already knows about? She's been so unsettled, so thrown off, that she hasn't been thinking clearly. "You said there was a fifth device that's so far remained completely undisturbed. If Queen Sef and King Ari gain their power from their spheres and have no knowledge of their true purpose, then they would assume that anything similar is also a massive power source. A power source that produces radiation, a radiation that I assume is different but not dissimilar to the radiation produced by their spheres." She meets Carrion's gaze, and finally makes the connection that she should have made earlier. "The fifth device is the diamond."

Carrion is right in front of her, and she is suddenly aware that they could lean forward just six and a half inches and that would be close enough to kiss her. "Exactly," they say, the word a thrilled exhale. "*Exactly*."

She attempts to clear her throat. "How do we activate the last three devices?"

They blink. "You're really willing to help with all this?"

"Of course."

"Even though it's... *me*?"

"It's not about you," she says, a bit of confidence returning to her voice. "It's not about me. It's about the Bastion, and I will do whatever it takes to keep it safe."

CHAPTER THIRTY-ONE

Once Ziane can no longer stand the opposing presence of the sphere and Carrion has presumably finished their examination of the thing, the terraforming sphere is at last returned to its vault beneath the viewing-glass room.

Carrion begins to pace. "It's all about the scanners," they say, gesturing wildly with their hands. A manic energy buzzes in every step they take, seemingly invigorated by Ziane's willingness to work with them. She's not quite sure why, as it's not as though her agreement has magically produced the diamond. "I've got one, Sef's got one, Ari's got one. None of 'em are fully working and ain't none of us can figure it out. Without the scanners, we ain't got a chance of finding the damn thing."

Ziane does not pace, but she finds herself picking at her nails. "Are there other ways to track the diamond?"

"None," Carrion says with a sharp shake of their head. "Well. Not that I know of. Suppose there could be others. The schematics I have don't show its location, if that's what you're asking."

So all they have to work with is a specific type of radiation and three scanners, only two of which they can access and none of them actually functional. "Refine the scanners?" she suggests. "Or perhaps there's an ideal location to scan from, since we know from what we learned at the trainyard that the readings are more accurate at range. Maybe there's an ideal distance that we can calculate?"

"I've tried thousands of measurements," they tell her. An irritated frown twists their mouth. "Trust me. If there was a correct distance, I'd have found it."

It seems statistically impossible to have truly checked every single area of the Fringes for a signal, but Ziane doesn't press them. It wouldn't be of any use. "Why do the non-corrupted schematics not show the diamond's location?"

"Dunno," Carrion replies. "They don't show where Sef and Ari's spheres are either, and we actually *know* where they are for sure."

"Give me the schematics, please?" she all but begs. It's all that she has wanted for so long, for as long as she can remember, even with certain details blurred out. "Maybe I can figure something out."

Carrion retrieves their tablet from their kit. "Here."

She catches it when they toss it to her, clutching it to her chest, treating it as the treasure that it is. A faint, suppressed excitement tingles at the edges of her mind, fighting against the echoes of fear and worry and wonder. She retrieves the map with the softest stroke of her fingertip against the smooth screen.

A perfect, complete, utterly unblemished map of the Bastion appears before her as a hologram, the image projected from the tablet in a way that she's never seen a tablet capable of doing before. With a caress of the image, it begins to slowly rotate, showing her not just the floors and levels of the Bastion that she knows so well, but the pristine, undamaged sections of the ship that she knows only as the dilapidated Fringes, and beyond that are the layers and layers of thick hull, steel and aluminum and plastic reinforcing each other in perfect harmony. And yet, there's something not quite right. She can't pinpoint what, precisely, and so she pulls out her own old and worn tablet. When she opens up the map she has, the sections she has charted and acquired from the Office of the Administrator's records, it immediately becomes clear.

"The schematics you have don't line up with the Bastion's schematics." She turns the hologram this way and that, checking and double checking. "It shows areas that the Office of the Administrator doesn't even know exist, but there are a few sections that are both fully mapped and don't match up. For all that you can sneak in and out of the Deep and the Mists, enough of this… starship," the word is difficult to get out, and she nearly trips over her desire to call it by the name she has always known the world by, "has been damaged by time that certain areas are completely different."

Carrion stops pacing. "So?"

"There aren't many," she says, pointing to three specific sections. "However, these sections that appear in perfect condition on your map have clearly collapsed or otherwise fallen apart on the Bastion's current version. Neither of us have been working with fully completed, updated versions of this map. And just replacing yours with mine won't work, as it's very possible that new revisions have been made to the Bastion's map since I last saw it, given the difference in the passage of time."

"You've got to be fucking kidding me." They smack their palm into their face. "Of all the obvious things to–! Fine, fine, whatever, we mash up maps. Even a mashed-up map doesn't fix the scanners, so it ain't like that will solve all our problems. I can mess with the data, I can rescan from the Fringes, I can–"

Quietly, uncertainly, Ziane says, "You can stop acting as though you're working alone. With two of us, we can work twice as fast."

"Well, we can't scan multiple locations at once, we've only got the one..." Carrion trails off, a gleeful twinkle in their eye. "Aight. Okay. We'll head to the Office of the Administrator so that we can get the newest map they've got on hand and use my schematics to find the quickest route out of the Mists. Easy." With a flurry of sudden movement, they rush off down the stairs back to the throne room.

Startling, Ziane runs after them, taking the stairs two at a time to keep up with their swift gait.

"I can use all the security feeds downstairs to check we've got a clear exit," Carrion says. "I'll be right behind you."

"What if King Ari notices that someone has tampered with the recordings? He would certainly be suspicious enough to trace it back to you."

"Just cause he knows it's me don't mean he can do anything about it. And if Ari tracks me down, then I'll turn around and run the fuck away. He can kick my ass blindfolded with both hands tied behind his back, but I know more than him about how to sneak out of places and I can give him the slip. Usually. Hopefully. Look, if I've gotten good at anything over the ages, it's saving my own skin." Their grin turns softer, teasing but somehow heartfelt. "But I'm touched that you worried about me, love."

"I–" She trips over her words. "I don't want to be alone in this either, you know."

Carrion heads to Ari's throne of security feeds and lounges in the stark chair as though it belongs to them. They plop their feet up on the computer, flicking through the cameras, the blue light dancing across their features. Ziane lingers on that image for a moment before she makes herself turn away, tucking both tablets into her kit and returning to the hidden room below that they had used to enter.

A moment later, Carrion is jumping down after her. From there, the two of them follow the map.

It leads her through areas she didn't even know existed, lifts that she thought long abandoned but have been marked as safe for use, along lightrail tracks that have been since scrubbed from the Bastion's records, down buildings that are corrupted blips of pixels on the Bastion's map as the computer systems sacrificed non-essential information files in an effort to slow the degradation of their limited data-storage space. Carrion has left tracks down many of the paths as well, obviously not intended for her considering the age of the marks, but instead guides for themself, arrows pointing in the right direction, signs of them having shored up structures that would have blocked a convenient tunnel or doorway. She had always known that it would take lifetimes to fully map the Bastion, and Carrion has had more lifetimes than she suspects they are willing to count.

Once they get close enough to the Office of the Administrator, they take a lightrail train the rest of the way and she manages a short nap during the ride before hopping off at the very same station she had used when she'd gone to retrieve her map. She gets an odd look or two for her clothing, the rough cargo pants and polyester shirt dirtied from the sandstorm and her endless trek, but no one actually comments and she isn't stopped while she loiters in the wide open courtyard that leads up to the office buildings.

Carrion stares up at the complex of buildings that make up the Office of the Administrator and whistles. "Damn. Been an age since I've been here."

"Lack of reason or worried that you wouldn't be welcomed?" she asks. If the guards ever recognized Carrion, it wouldn't end well. For anyone.

"Honestly? Haven't really thought much about the Bastion's info in awhile," they admit. "I got what I needed from this place a long time ago."

Or so they had thought. Though Ziane is no longer human, a faint stirring of pride twinges in the corner of her mind at the knowledge that the Bastion has something that Carrion needs after all. She scans the area for guards. Carrion is also getting the occasional odd glance for their attire, but no one comments or looks about to report them.

"All right." She checks the entrance again before walking towards it, her stride even and measured. "Last time I was here, my First Responder clearance was still active. The clearance level I possessed was high enough to allow me to bring an additional guest with me, so I should be able to use that to get you in as well. Have you ever been in areas of the Bastion where there were security cameras that may have captured your face?"

Carrion shakes their head as they fall into step alongside her. "They've caught me, but I've been careful not to let 'em see my face. It ain't something I can change."

It has been years, in the Bastion's time, since Ziane was last here, walking through these two doors, still precisely seventeen feet high and forty-eight and a half feet wide. Outwardly, little has changed, though there is a new polish on the walls and entirely new faces manning the various desks. She approaches the main greeting desk and waits patiently for the worker to notice her. The middle-aged woman gives Ziane a curious once-over and Carrion a frowning twice-over.

"Good afternoon," Ziane greets before the woman can ask any potentially prying questions. "Here for Navigation Databanks, please."

The woman pauses for a moment before habit presumably kicks in and she turns to her computer. "Level of clearance and identification code?"

"First Responder and guest." Ziane proceeds to rattle off her ID number.

"Hm." The woman narrows her eyes at the screen before turning that skeptical look to Ziane. "When was your code last updated?"

"Quite... some time ago."

The woman stands up and gestures to the foyer. "Wait here, please. I need to check with my supervisor."

"Ah, of course."

It would seem that the luck which had carried Ziane through before has since run out. Once the woman has scurried off to her higher-ups, Ziane steps away from the desk and takes a deep breath. How long before her code is flagged, her entrance denied? How long before an alarm is sounded? How long before a guard decides to act on her and Carrion's unusual appearance?

"Plan B?" Carrion starts to wander into the center of the foyer, gaze darting from hall to hall, desk to desk, guard to guard. "I mean, I'm happy to wait for her to come back and deal with this another way, but it doesn't seem like your style."

How far can they get if they aren't approved to be here? Can they make for the right office without being stopped? "I'm... thinking."

"Right then."

She surreptitiously looks out the foyer until she ends up in front of the one thing that hasn't changed at all since she was last here: the scratched-up plaque of the Office of the Administrator of the Bastion, kept safe beneath its protective glass.

When Carrion sees what has drawn her attention, they laugh under their breath. Tablet in their hand once more, they ask, "Want another missing piece of the world?"

Without waiting for her answer, they click on an image file and a photograph pops up on the screen. It shows a group of people in matching uniforms, smiling at the camera, some with their arms around an older man in the center. A couple of others are cheerfully pointing at the plaque that is proudly displayed above the older man. It's a golden plaque, the shiny and pristine version of what stands before Ziane now. New, untouched by time. Undamaged. Until now, she has only ever seen the partial words, the same as anyone else. This image is legible. In clear, clean, condemning lettering, the plaque declares:

The Office of Admiral Jean-Luc Bastian.

Carrion's voice falls softly on the fuzz that has filled her ears, "The whole world. Even its name is just a broken half-memory."

Is any of this world real? Or is it all just a collapsing pile of forgotten truths and ruined fragments of a past so long ago that time has erased all traces of it, scrubbed it away like dirt beneath a streetcleaner? Is it possible to bring back any of this knowledge, to fill the Bastion's databanks with the truth until everyone understands the world, the danger, the necessity of the diamond? Or is it too late? Has too much time passed? The Bastion has repaired itself and repaired itself so many times that it is only the bones of the starship that once fell from the sky. All else is of its own making. Does Admiral Jean-Luc Bastian matter anymore, when all that anyone cares about is the Administrator of the Bastion?

Ziane retreats. "Let's head to the Navigation Databanks. Please."

"Aight." Carrion puts the tablet away, to her relief. "We're running for it?"

"I've been to the Navigation Databanks before and I'm certain I remember the way. I don't know if the desk worker is coming back."

"After you, then." They sketch a small and cheeky bow. "I *knew* you had the perfect expertise for all this."

"For breaking and entering?" She's almost insulted.

They smile, like they can't help themself. "For everything that needs to be done."

To that, she has no idea how to respond, and thus simply heads towards the correct corridor, trying to project a confidence that is flagging with every official and assistant and guard that the two of them pass. They go up to the eighth floor and down past the other offices and finally to Navigation Databanks.

As with last time, there is someone stationed at the front desk. "May I help you?" the man asks.

Ziane clears her throat and hopes this goes smoothly, even though she is nearly certain it won't. "We're looking for the most recent maps, please. Whatever changes have been made over the past few–" she guesses, a knot in her stomach, "–decades."

The man nods and then asks the dreaded, "Clearance code, please?"

Before Ziane can blink, Carrion swings themself across the desk, claps their palm over the poor man's mouth, and gathers enough Vesperi magic around their hand to render the man unconscious in a matter of seconds.

They let the body fall. "Oxygen deprivation, 'fore you ask. Only gonna make him sleep for a bit. You're welcome."

"Thank you," she responds automatically, before adding, "I appreciate your restraint."

"Don't get *too* used to it."

Ziane heads straight to the map databanks that she recalls from last time. From there, Carrion uses their superior skill with the computer systems to pull up the most recent changes, dropping the new data into their tablet before holoprojecting the three maps side by side: the original starship schematics, Ziane's partially homemade map, and the Bastion's latest discoveries. The differences are small. Additional buildings have been marked off limits. Part of the Fringes on the second level has expanded, abandoned completely and left to the ruins.

Some areas that were blank in her previous version of the map have since been discovered and detailed, however, and she pays close attention to see if those deviate from the original schematics. A warehouse basement that's marked as lost on the old schematics has been found, and an old street has recently been converted into additional housing units. One new addition in particular is two dozen floors beneath the Office of the Administrator complex, a section of circular tubing that's been designated as Era One and sectioned off accordingly.

She is about to mention this when Carrion anticipates her, pointing to the area and remarking, "Weird that the humans finally stumbled onto that area. Thought they'd never find it."

"What is it?" she asks, tilting her head to examine the strange torus-shaped tunnel. "It's quite large, for a structure that appears empty."

Carrion shrugs. "I popped my head in there once and checked – only got a quick peek, I was running from Lysander at the time, and it's kinda annoyingly close to major dense human population areas, but it was totally dead in there when I looked." They draw her attention to four other similarly shaped structures that she hadn't noticed before, ones only visible on the ship schematics. "Whatever it is, it repeats. I was able to walk the entire length of all these others, though. Some of them more than once, just cause I felt like it. It's quiet in there, great for talking to yourself. They were all empty too."

"Don't you have any suspicions for what they were used for?"

"Navigation, maybe. Or a kind of flight stabilizers. Could even have been storage," they guess with a shrug. "Can't say one way for sure."

"Wherever the diamond is, it can't have been anywhere outwardly visible or humans would have discovered it by now, considering the amount of time that has passed between the starship crashing and now. It may be moving, but it's moving somewhere out of sight. There are only so many places in the Bastion that aren't visible, and if it wasn't moving in a repeatable pattern, it would have run out of hidden locations ages ago." She stares again at those torus loops. "Are you *certain* all of those were empty?"

"Pretty sure, yeah. You think it's in one of 'em? Cause I checked those," Carrion insists. "All of 'em."

She shakes her head. "No, you told me that you checked *four* of them and found them empty. But the fifth, the centrally located one, you only looked at briefly because you were running from Lysander at the time. If the diamond is moving through that torus tunnel, then you easily could have simply missed it when you were down there. It makes sense. They're a loop," she replies, "and they're out of sight. It could be an easy pattern for the diamond to follow, although I suppose with the scanners not giving precise readings, we have no idea how big that pattern is or how fast it's moving."

Carrion gives her a pointed look. "If it's going fast as fuck, we could get *crushed* if we get caught in its path. Or we could spend forever walking around in circles trying to find it."

"...I would prefer it if that didn't happen. So how do we get a better lock on it, then?"

A creak. Ziane tenses. The door is opening.

In unison, she and Carrion whirl around to the sight of a secretary entering the room, freezing in their tracks, and staring at the unconscious man at their feet in abject horror. There is a clatter as their tablet falls from slack hands.

"He isn't dead," Ziane calls out immediately, her pulse skipping.

If anything, her reassurance sets the secretary off and they begin to scream, the sound crashing out to the rest of the office floor.

The only thing Ziane can think to do is turn to Carrion and ask, "Plan C?"

Carrion is already poised to run, their hand grabbing hers and dragging her after them. Not towards the door and the escape it could offer, but to the plexiglass window at the back of the room, past rows of computer storage towers. Footsteps begin to pound behind them – she measures the sound, guessing fifty feet away at most. She doesn't look back. Vesperi wind starts to thread around them, summoned forth by Carrion's sheer will, rushing along before the air pressure blasts forward.

"Ever heard of intruder window?" Carrion laughs, bright and sharp.

"I don't think this is a good—"

Her protest is lost as Carrion snatches her by the waist, uses the wind to smash the glass, and jumps through the shattered window.

To her credit, Ziane does not scream. The scream can't escape her clenched jaw, her locked muscles, her frozen body. This is far from the swift yet sturdy ascension to the Mists, instead a frantic plummet more akin to her tumbling fall the first time she entered the Deep. She clings to Carrion for dear life, her stomach slamming up into her throat and her eyes watering. For a split second, between the leap and the landing, she sees the entire plaza of the Office of the Administrator laid out in its neat grid. An admiral is such a small thing in comparison.

Barely half a second before the two of them would have turned into an unfortunate splatter, Carrion creates a cushion of air thick and dense enough to slow their descent. As soon as her feet touch solid ground, she stumbles out of Carrion's embrace. She does not, however, release their hand.

An alarm sounds. Every guard stationed around the plaza is staring directly at the two of them, and hundreds of visitors, administrators, and passersby are all stopped dead in their tracks.

"And now we run," Carrion pleasantly declares.

Hand in hand, the two of them run with the speed of a sandstorm blasting across infinite rock.

CHAPTER THIRTY-TWO

Every time before now, when Ziane has stumbled into one of Carrion's nests, it has not been pleasant. The water-treatment facility where a bomb lay in wait for her and the other Eoi. The dilapidated building where they had their sensor rigged up. The supply cache they had in the Fringes, a point of tainted respite before her understanding of the world was ruined irreparably. From the way the Eoi spoke of Carrion, she got the vague impression that they had lairs all over the Bastion, stashes of supplies, nooks where they could hide away and lie in nefarious wait.

Now she finds herself side by side with Carrion, settled down on a stash of worn-out clothing, blankets, and other rags that may be ugly and slightly dirty but are still oddly comfortable. They are sprawled out next to her, legs crossed and head tilted back as they watch the hologram maps slowly rotate overhead, their tablet humming away. Ziane is not so relaxed, her body still strained from their precipitous escape and the subsequent chase which ended only when Carrion led her down a hidden hatch that the guards were unable to discover. It's all so surreal. And after everything that has happened since she last left the Deep, the opportunity to pause and collect her scattered thoughts is a rare, valuable thing.

Carrion turns the hologram around in lazy circles. For all that they were a whirlwind of motion back in the Office of the Administrator, they now seem content to take their ease. Ziane cannot. Carrion may have lived an excessive number of lifetimes with the knowledge that the Bastion is condemned to inevitable decay, but she is not capable of accepting a slow pace. Who knows when a crack may form in that final layer of the starship's wall? Certainly not Carrion, and she doesn't even know how to begin guessing.

"Stupid of me," Carrion remarks out of the blue, their attention on the hologram.

Ziane draws back an inch in surprise. "I thought our escape was rather effective, despite the unplanned and reckless nature of it. I'd really rather not repeat it, but I can't say that it would have been better to be captured by the security guards."

"Not that. Rather proud of that escape, all things considered."

"Then how were you stupid?"

"I spent way too long focused on what Sef and Ari were doing. They're my competition, ya know. The only folks out there who know what I'm really after in terms of what the diamond *is*, even if they ain't got a clue as to the why of it. The only two who could actually stop me from saving this ungrateful little world. So there I was, being an idiot, completely ignoring what the humans have been up to."

When she had been human, she had ignored what the Astrosi were doing. Although she's spent far longer as a human than an Eoi, and thus is biased towards acknowledging and respecting the accomplishments of humanity, she can't truly judge Carrion for making the same mistake she did in reverse. "I think," she says slowly, "it's easy to be so focused on the immediate threat that you cannot think of a broader picture. That... primal worry, perhaps, is a challenge to shake off."

Carrion hums and remarks, "Tunnel vision. Anxiety. Stress. Keeps the mind narrow." They snicker, though it's not with any malice. "We're both a bit neurotic, ain't we?"

"We are not the same," she says. It sounds less and less convincing to her own ears every time she says it. "My paranoia has always been reasonable." She pauses, and then corrects, "It's not paranoia. It's just reasonable suspicion."

"You saying my paranoia ain't reasonable?" they tease.

"I... suppose it is," she admits. She has always been paranoid of the Bastion falling apart. The difference between her and Carrion is that they *knew* it was going to fall apart. It takes a good deal of her effort not to get up, not to pace, not to count the seconds like the methodical, steady, constant numbers will somehow calm her. "It doesn't matter, does it?"

They shrug. "Not to me."

Somehow, that is a reassurance. "Well. Um." She clears her throat. "To work, then?"

"Bunch of tunnels." Carrion opens up the hologram again. "Potentially deathly fast diamond. Fucked-up scanners."

Her mind narrows to just the hologram, to the invisible lines between locations, to the possibilities that have presented themselves. "The scanner has been giving us straight lines across the Bastion, showing the diamond's current location before losing the signal. But the Bastion is a three-dimensional space. One scanner giving one straight line isn't the most accurate way to locate it." *Think.* "But there are three scanners. If we set each of them up at different points in the Bastion, we can get a much wider field of view and use them to triangulate the diamond's position."

Carrion wiggles the scanner in their hand. "One out of three."

"It might not work." She bites down on her lower lip. "And even if it would, we are still down two scanners."

"Good thing we know where the others are, then."

"I doubt that you'll have an easy time taking the Eoi's scanner from Lysander." And for that matter, Ziane doesn't want to betray the Eoi. She... doesn't even know if she can. Not killing Carrion is one thing, but actually stealing from the Eoi is likely going to be a direct violation of the contract she made with them when she was human. "And I don't think that the Vesperi would be any more likely to relinquish theirs. Isn't there some other option? If we make our case to Queen Sef, perhaps she'll listen. She might have thought the outside world was a hologram before, but maybe this time we can be persuasive enough."

The look they give her is one of faint amusement. "You're too clever to really think that'd work."

"We should still *try*."

They close their eyes, jaw grinding, unable to look at her for a long heartbeat. "Fine," they grit out eventually. "Fine. We *try*. But I've got one condition."

If it gets them to find a peaceful solution... "Name it."

"If we try, and we fail, then Sef can use your contract to shut you down instantly. Before we make our case, as you put it, we break your contract. I," they declare, "am *not* losing you to Sef. I ain't doing this alone."

Something in her chest twists. "I... I don't know how realistic that is." Even to her own ears, she sounds meek. Small. Helpless. "I do not even remember the full terms of my contract. There was something–" Fuzz, again.

"There was something distracting me, I think, at the time I agreed to service as an Acolyte. And I don't remember the details."

"I can get your contract."

Her jaw hangs open and then she forces it closed. "I'm sorry?"

"I know how to get your contract," they repeat. Back drawn straight, head held high, customary slump absent. "I can get 'em, I can read 'em, I can break 'em. It's what I've been doing forever, and I can do it for you."

"You would really do that? For me?"

"Like I said, I ain't doing this alone."

Suffering shared is suffering halved, she'd once heard. Perhaps it has some truth to it.

Carrion begins to grab their things up, stuffing various devices back into their ratty coat and its numerous pockets. "Right then," they start, returning to their usual casual drawl and slightly manic energy. "We'll need to space the scanners out if we wanna triangulate the diamond with any real accuracy. Actually, we might not even need to *take* Lysander's scanner. I can program it to feed its results back to mine. We hook up Jess's scanner in the Mists, we get Lysander's working in the Deep, and then we settle into the center of the Bastion with mine and watch all three sets of results show up from the comfort of, uh, this." They gesture to the ragged nest around them with its piles of bits and bobs. "I can whip up a couple of hacking bugs with what I've got on hand here. Little things. Just slap 'em onto a scanner and it'll zap its way into the system."

"Are you certain returning to the Mists so soon is a good idea?" she asks. King Ari's wrath is not to be underestimated.

"Convincing Sef is the bigger risk. We save that for last. And once we rip up your contract, she might not be so keen on letting you waltz off without a care in the world. Can't speak for you, but I'd rather not try to sneak into the Mists with a team of pissed off Eoi running after us."

"That's fair enough."

Once the two of them have packed up their necessary things, they begin the journey back to the Mists.

The ascent is different than the route they previously took. How many ways into the Mists does Carrion have? Though she has by no means traversed as much of the Bastion as Carrion has, by now her boots are beginning to feel more worn than they should be. They have trod across more of the Bastion than she'd dreamed she would have been able to as a human, and across more of the world than she'd imagined possible even as an Astrosi.

Eventually the two of them end up in an air-filtration facility, waiting by the side entrance. Carrion kneels, twisting the air into something pale and thick, sending it into the next room via the cracks between the sliding doors. They silently count down on their fingers while Ziane presses her door to the ear and listens. A faint *thunk* emanates from the next room.

"Clear," Carrion declares.

Ziane opens the door to see a guard from the Office of the Administrator passed out on the ground, snoring away without a care in the world.

Carrion saunters through the doorway while Ziane sneaks out into the cavernous facility right behind Carrion, surveying the area for any hidden pitfalls or dangerous objects. There aren't any immediately visible to her, though that doesn't mean they aren't present and simply hidden from her eyes. There don't appear to be other guards either. She examines the rust on the metal piping that runs across the high-up ceiling, hears the way the tanks and loops of processing coils rattle in a familiar background hum. This place isn't high priority for humans. It's likely more of an oxygen- or hydrogen-storage area that slowly cleans and processes the gas back into the Bastion's air systems while other facilities deal with the carbon dioxide.

"We're in the final few floors between the Bastion and the Mists," Carrion explains, jabbing a finger upwards. "Couple of ruined floors that humans have left alone, and then Ari's throneworld properly starts. We should start to hit the time-change barrier soon, and if you've got a keen eye, you can spot where the Bastion's rot ends and the perfect little preserved world of the Mists begins."

A nervous shiver begins to crawl up Ziane's spine. The hairs on the back of her neck stand straight up. She's felt this suspicion before, so often during her days as a First Responder, her subconscious picking up on signals her mind is still racing to detect, a twinge right before a wall starts to crack or a pipe begins to leak. This facility might be older, but there should still be more than just the one guard patrolling the air, maintaining the tanks. And there is not.

"Carrion..." she tries to warn, her tongue heavy with something that is the memory of panic, doing its utmost to get past the emptiness in her chest.

Her new companion freezes mid-step, but it's too late.

There are footsteps behind them.

"You shouldn't have gotten so close to the Mists." Jess's voice rings out, echoing in the open facility. "Twice in so short a time? Damn big risk you took there."

Ziane's body tenses, her fingers curling into her palms, as she turns to face Jess. He is standing perhaps thirty feet away. While there are no soldiers behind him, when her eyes dart to the wire balconies around the area, she sees two shadowy figures shifting forward, and she cannot imagine they area anything other than two snipers preparing to take out her and Carrion.

"This doesn't have to be a fight," she tries, because she has to. "We aren't on our way to the Mists to hurt anyone."

"Oh, I was definitely gonna hurt Jess," Carrion mutters under their breath.

It was quiet enough that Jess couldn't have heard them, but that doesn't seem to matter. Though Ziane could beg and plead for this not to come to violence, it appears that Jess has already come to that inevitable conclusion. "King Ari has given us full permission to kill you," Jess declares, hand twitching to the bayonet-rifle on his back. "And trust me, it's gonna be my *pleasure* to carry out that order."

Carrion tilts their head to the side as they consider it. "I could take you."

Another set of footsteps. Another sinking of Ziane's stomach. Even before she looks in the direction of these newcomers, she knows who it is. She knows those footsteps. Three sets of them, three sets of familiar gaits. It would seem that Sef may not be as willing to hear her out as she had hoped.

Lysander stands across the facility, a blank-faced Leneat to his left and a slumped Essten to his right.

"You can't take all of us, you son of a bitch," Lysander snarls. "And the fucking traitor at your side ain't gonna be nothing but a hunk of dead weight." His narrow eyes burn into Ziane's. "You should've thought of that before teaming up with this damn madman and selling us out, you motherfucker."

Jess is more smug that Ziane has ever seen him before as he declares, "You were spotted by one of our scouts during your little break-in of the Office of the Administrator. I figured that it would be best if we sent a message to the Deep, letting them know that one of their own has turned traitor." And with the speed of the direct lift between the Deep and the Mists, both factions could have easily beaten Ziane and Carrion to the punch. Time is, as always, her enemy. "They're here to retrieve you, and to drag you back to Sef to face the music." And to Carrion, they add, "Honestly, I'm surprised you didn't see this trap coming."

"Yeah," Carrion says with a sigh, looking right at Ziane before pressing their eyes tightly shut. "I am too."

CHAPTER THIRTY-THREE

Back in the train yard, a dozen lifetimes ago, Ziane had fought against Carrion. All she'd done had been ineffective against them, and no matter what she'd told herself at the time, no matter the new emptiness inside her, she'd still been unable, unwilling, to take lethal action. All her weapons training, all her new convictions, were nothing in the face of that deep instinct carved into the bones of her: Do no harm. Take no life. Preserve. Protect.

Against a single, albeit formidable, opponent, she had barely been able to hold her own in a short brawl. Against six opponents, she does not stand a chance. Carrion may be confident that they can take Jess and Lysander, but can they match both? Can they hold out with two snipers in the wings? Can *she* stand aside and let them fight, perhaps *kill* Essten and Leneat? She knows the answer to the last before she has even finished thinking the question. They will come to no harm. They will not die.

That flash of an echo of a dream comes to her once again. A child with his back turned, face hidden. She will not lose anyone she is close to. She will *not*.

Lysander raises his bayonet-rifle, aiming directly at Ziane's head. Though he speaks to Jess, he doesn't take his eyes off her for even a second as he says, "The traitor is ours. Do what you want with Carrion."

Ziane holds up her hands in clear surrender. "Please, just listen. Jess, you were reasonable before, you were willing to hear me out, you–"

"That," Jess interrupts, hard and unyielding, "was when we shared an enemy. You brought this on yourself."

"The world is being *destroyed*," she implores them all. "It's–"

Lysander takes a few measured steps forward, on the prowl, body shaking with unbridled fury. "Yeah," he agrees, "it sure is being destroyed. By the bastard standing next to you. Damn it, Ziane! I *taught* you! I thought you were gonna fight with us! Not hop into bed with Carrion the moment you got a chance!"

In the face of his rage, Ziane struggles to come up with a good response, and she ends up pointing out, dazed and perplexed, "You never even wanted to teach me."

Lysander goes for the shot.

A split second before the laser pierces her skull, Carrion tackles her around the waist and shoves her to the ground. Bright light flashes before her as the beam cuts through Carrion instead, searing a red, torn-up line across their shoulder.

In the distance, she hears Essten yell, "We were told to capture her, not kill her!"

As if Lysander would ever listen to that while in the throes of bloodlust. Not ever, really, and she suspects even more so now, with Annie dead. Ziane recovers quickly, rolling onto her feet and coiling her body to move. Just as she was taught. And without a second to spare, as the air begins to screech with the sound of rifles being fired, the snipers having presumably been given the order from Jess.

Ziane and Carrion dash across the facility, shots blasting the floor as they run, the heat of the lasers kissing her heels.

Carrion practically shoves her behind a processing tank, using it as cover; their opponents are too smart to risk damaging one of the tanks and flooding the area with any of the toxic and flammable gasses that are processed here. Instead, there is the sound of boots slamming against the ground, of Jess barking out indistinct orders, of Leneat's gruff voice as she yells something at Lysander.

"Plan, uh… Plan D?" Carrion asks, not appearing nearly as concerned by all this as they should be. They roll their shoulder, and it's like the injury from the laser starts to fade away.

A well-aimed shot shines right past the edge of the tank, nearly hitting the tip of Ziane's foot.

"We aren't killing the Eoi," she states, in a way that tells Carrion she will not accept any negotiation on this front.

Carrion rolls their eyes in exasperation. "So many rules with you. Snipers first, then, I think."

"Can you deal with them?"

"Yeah." They reach into their coat and retrieve a handful of loose dirt and seeds. "I'll take the Vesperi, you deal with the Eoi."

"Go."

In a flurry of energy, Carrion leaps to the next protective tank and then makes a break for it, zig-zagging wildly across the facility in the direction of the snipers, their ratty coat flashing behind them. Ziane crouches, lying in wait as she hears Lysander get closer and closer. While she knows she can't defeat him, she doesn't have to. If their response is anything to go by, Essten and Leneat were under the impression that she wouldn't be killed. That makes Lysander the only real threat to her life. She can't beat him, but she can stall him. And maybe, just maybe, she can get Essten and Leneat to listen to her.

The muzzle of Lysander's rifle glints in the light, blade shining cold, as he steps around the tank. "End of the line, you—"

Ziane leaps to her feet, ducking under his reflexive shot, and shoves her hand not towards his weapon, as he would expect, but into the pack of dirt he carries on him at all times. Warm soil floods her senses, her cold fingers grasping for the first thing she can find and touching a single seed. Life blooms in accordance with her will.

White-pink oleander petals explode from Lysander's hip pouch as Ziane converts soil and seed to sapling.

In their natural state, oleander blossoms are not particularly poisonous, nor are they particularly fast acting, requiring prolonged contact or ingestion before they truly start to become lethal. But as Annie had once told her so long ago, the Eoi breed certain varieties for maximum potency, and it is those seeds that Lysander carries with him. Dozens and dozens of fresh, toxicant petals worm their way underneath his sleeves, settling onto his exposed forearms, and at her command they dissolve into that pure poison, sinking beneath his skin as the excess plant matter crumbles to the ground to return to drained soil.

Lysander opens his mouth to yell at her, and instead chokes. A groan of agony emanates from his throat. With a clatter, his rifle falls to the ground as he wraps his arms around his stomach and staggers backwards. His chest heaves as he gasps for breath, skin flushed, sweat beading on his forehead. A gurgling curse escapes his swelling lips before his legs wobble and he collapses onto his knees.

Ziane picks up his abandoned rifle, removes the battery pack, throws it away, and drops the rifle before kicking it across the floor.

"It won't kill you or permanently injure you," she promises him. "The abdominal pain and irregular heart rhythm are just going to slow you down." He's skilled enough that he should be able to counteract the toxins with time to spare. "Just listen, please. I'm not betraying the Eoi, I'm not betraying Queen Sef. This is bigger than you versus Carrion or the Vesperi versus you, this is about the whole *world*."

In response, Lysander doubles over and heaves, coughing up a mouthful of yellow bile. Ah yes, that would be the nausea, another possible symptom of *Nerium oleander* ingestion. It won't hurt him, she reminds herself. If anything, the indignity bruises his ego more than the poison could ever impact his physical flesh.

On the other side of the facility, she hears a scream that is suddenly cut off by a *thud*. One of the snipers is lying on the ground, limbs sprawled out, blood splattering the floor beneath them. Carrion whirls about on the balcony, kicking out at the second sniper and then dodging underneath a swing of their bayonet-rifle, their injured shoulder having put no dent in their frenetic skill. Jess is nowhere to be seen, but her vision is limited back here near the processing tank–

Her second of distraction costs her. Leneat skids in front of Lysander, rifle raised to protect her commander, her leader. There is fire in her hard eyes, her fingers gripping her weapon tightly enough for Ziane map the ridges of her knucklebones through her taut skin. Behind her, Essten kneels next to Lysander, putting a hand on the man's back and helping him through the pain, and stares straight at Ziane with pinched lips and creased eyes. The betrayal writ large across his features should hurt her, and it does – almost. It gets so close to hurting her, so close to stabbing something buried in her chest, but there is nothing there for the hurt to latch onto.

"You don't have to do this," Leneat says between gritted teeth. "Our queen ain't gonna kill you if you come quietly."

Ziane breathes in, slow and steady, and it does nothing to smooth out her twitching nerves. "I cannot."

Leneat spits on the ground. "Queen Sef may be heartless, but what you've done is cruel."

The words make Ziane flinch worse than a punch to the gut. "I have *always* done everything I can to protect the Bastion and the people who live here. That includes every single Astrosi, Eoi and Vesperi both. My purpose, my *true* purpose, is, was, and always will be the preservation of this world. I've gone beyond the Fringes, I went... *outside*. Outside the Bastion. I know it sounds insane, but there's so much out there, so much that we never knew about, and it..."

She trails off as Essten rises and holds out a small tablet before him like a talisman. "I'm sorry," he says, genuine contrition softening his words. "But if we can't reason with you, we've been authorized to command you back."

Command? Essten can't command her anywhere. And then Essten pushes a button and a hologram of Queen Sef is projected from the tablet, her flickering face blank and calm and emotionless. Lysander's ability to command Ziane in Sef's stead may have faded, but nothing, not time, not transformation, not loyalty, has removed the contract from Ziane's stomach. The recording opens its mouth, and Queen Sef orders:

"I, Queen Sef the Third, Guardian of the Eoi and Lady of the Deep, hereby command you on pain of death to lay down your weapons, surrender into the custody of the Eoi, and return to me with no further struggle."

Carrion had been right. They needed to break Ziane's contract, and she wishes she had insisted on doing so first. So many times now, Carrion has said that they cannot do this alone, and if Ziane is killed or imprisoned, they will go back to how they were. Even if they can carry on and be successful, they will kill so many to accomplish their goals. While they have no qualms about murder, they had resorted to non-lethal options with the assistant when Ziane had not been willing to let the man die. Without her, Carrion will continue to take lives as they please. With her, for whatever reason, they can be restrained.

She lowers her head and steels herself. "I won't."

Essten replays the recording. Sef's mechanical words echo even across the sound of distant conflict:

"...return to me with no further struggle."

Ziane does not move. If she can do nothing else, she will stay planted right where she is. Perhaps Carrion will deal with the Vesperi in time to save her. Perhaps she will die right on the spot once Lysander recovers from the poison and decides to simply kill her instead. Perhaps Essten and Leneat will let go of their hesitancy to use physical force against her and will drag her away.

A scratching sensation begins to emanate from the base of her esophagus.

"...command you on pain of death..."

There is no stopping the cough that claws its way past her tonsils and punches its way out of her jaw. She does not move; she refuses. They will not stop her from doing her duty.

"Please, Ziane," Essten whispers, his eyes shut, unable to look at her. "Just give up."

Sharp pain scours her stomach, minor at first but growing. Needles in her flesh, the iron of her lifeblood on the back of her tongue. Though she knew this was coming, had braced herself for it, that dizzy echo of panic fills her head and the pain rushes through her in an unstoppable tide. She gags. Blood mists on her palm when she covers her mouth and her stomach starts to constrict around herself. Her entire torso twitches, ribs and lungs and guts contracting, bones and muscles straining and finally failing to hold back the convulsions. She hits the ground hard, her knees banging against the cold surface, her fingernails scraping against the ground.

Something is lodged in her throat. A wrenching cough dislodges the thing, forcing it out of her, and once it is on her tongue, she tastes something else behind the blood. Rose.

A single, blood-splattered rose petal lies in front of her.

Ziane's cry of alarm gets cut off by another petal twisting out of her mouth. Then another, and then there are *thorns* scratching up her throat, and a whole flower blooms in her mouth, daintily tumbling from her lips. That contract seed in her stomach, that she swallowed so long ago, is finally unleashing its true potential.

It is difficult to hear beyond the rushing of her pulse, but she catches the faint sounds of Jess screaming insults. In the distance, she sees Carrion and Jess brawling, rolling on the ground and trading punches and kicks, weapons and skill discarded, and in Carrion's hand is the Vesperi scanner. They've gotten it.

Please let it not be for nothing.

Leneat lowers the tip of her rifle a single inch. She licks her lower lip. "Ziane. Seriously. Stop."

"I... I think it's gonna kill 'er," Essten whispers in disbelief, his grip tightening around the tablet and its unflinching hologram record.

"We've got our orders," Leneat replies, but she doesn't sound too sure herself.

With a ground-shaking roar, Lysander lunges forward, knocking Essten to the side and surging not towards Ziane but to Leneat. He rips her bayonet-rifle from her grasp, staggering as the toxin still courses through his veins. His motions are wild, without a shred of his usual precision and expertise, and when he jams his finger on the trigger, Ziane can already tell the shot won't land anywhere near her. She tries to scream regardless, because she can calculate the trajectory of the beam before it bursts into existence, and every instinct she has from her time as a First Responder is shrieking warnings in her mind.

The rifle's beam hits the hydrogen tank.

Everything happens so quickly, and yet every detail is so clear for one terrible second. Leneat falling from Lysander shoving her aside. Essten bringing his arms up to protect his face even as his eyes widen in fear, the veins in his sclera bright and sharp. Lysander's face contorted in fury, uncaring of what he has done, focused solely on destruction without concern for his own safety or that of those under his command. The menacing purl of the hydrogen escaping the tank into the heat of the laser beam.

Ziane collapses into the bed of flowers beneath her and the world is engulfed in fire as the hydrogen ignites.

CHAPTER THIRTY-FOUR

Everything burns.

All Ziane can see is pulsing red light. Her nerves whimper and plead as her skin blackens and chars, her flesh succumbing to the heat like melting plastic. Then mercy. Consciousness abandons her.

"Don't you dare die on me, love," she thinks she hears before she slips away.

She floats in blissful darkness, only to be cruelly interrupted by flickers of reality. The stench of her own scorched flesh crawls into her nostrils for a foul moment before she fades. Another brief flash, this time the sense of being carried, her body swaying in steady arms. Delirious, her mind conjures the image of a man holding her, somehow so familiar, like a brother to her... but it must be a hallucination, for she does not have one of those and never did, and then she is gone again and the illusion vanishes as well.

Then there is light – gentle, blue-gray light that kisses her forehead with grace and love. Blissfully cold as it seeps into her and fills her eyes with nothing but that pure brightness, chasing away the burning orange-red and the hungry darkness. An icy caress washes over her skin, permeating her flesh, settling into her bones. As the light blesses her, she catches a cloudy glimpse of Carrion leaning over her, of a lucent silver sphere that encompasses all else. She is cool as water, weightless as air, bones soft as mist. She is…

She does not know how long she sleeps after that. Time has no meaning, and though she's vaguely aware of drifting in and out of the waking world, she couldn't fathom a guess as to what is happening to or around her.

An eternity might have passed before she feels a calloused hand on her cheek and a voice says:

"There ya go. Easier the second time, ain't it?"

Ziane opens her eyes. She is greeted by the dingy ceiling of Carrion's nest, a few levels beneath the Office of the Administrator. To her right is Carrion, perched on the balls of their feet with their head cocked to one side, their customary smile oddly strained. Miraculously, there is no pain at all, and while her muscles ache and complain as she pushes herself into a sitting position, they don't actually hurt. The only strange thing is a peculiar numbness in her neck. She lightly probes the skin there but can't detect anything amiss.

Carrion holds out a piece of plexiglass mirror. "Sorry about your throat."

She cradles the mirror in her hands and stares at her reflection in… not shock. Not disbelief. All those things would be there, were she not devoting significant effort to shoving them aside and thinking critically about what she sees.

A twisted mess of lines, some elegant, some gnarled, cover every inch of her throat. As though her skin had shattered and the pieces been soldered back together with a silvered material. Liquid smoke curling up under her chin to the edge of her jawline and all the way down to peter out over her collarbones. Whatever it is, it's not killing her. It doesn't appear to be causing her any pain. When she hums, her vocal cords vibrate as they should.

"What is…" She gulps. Her voice is different. Lighter, yet resounding. A whisper of power that makes her drop the mirror and clutch her throat once again, fingers pressing against the markings until it hurts.

"Your throat was fucked anyway," Carrion tells her, an unexpected tenderness in their tone. "The fire, obviously, but it was torn to pieces by that shitty contract Sef shoved in you. I ain't anywhere near as good at this as Ari, so there was no damn way I would've been able to save it. And besides, I needed to trade *something* away. Might as well've been something you couldn't use anyways."

Something to trade away. Something that got replaced. She remembers that misty silver sphere above her, an impossible object that she had seen once before beneath the glass ceiling of King Ari's viewing room.

It takes her two tries before she can muster the courage to speak and face her altered voice. "I became… Vesperi?"

"Not exactly. I can't unmake you Eoi. And like I said, I ain't as good as Ari. But I know the gist – I've been through this song and dance more than anyone else." Carrion taps their chest with… not pride, perhaps. Solidarity. "You're the same as me now. Both."

"I don't know if I understand why…" She chokes, ignoring her sudden new state of being as more of the details of what happened resurface now that she's fully waking up. "The explosion! Essten and Leneat – did you see what happened to them? Are they all right? Are they alive? And Lysander, was he safe?"

They raise an eyebrow. "Lysander tried to *murder* you, sweetheart. Maybe don't be so concerned with his wellbeing."

"Please, just answer the question."

"Fine, fine. Answer is, I don't know for sure. The three of 'em were a bit further from the blast than you, and they seemed to be scrambling out when I got there, probably running back to the Deep. Didn't pay too much attention to 'em, honestly. I was just the littlest bit more focused on making sure you didn't kick it then and there. You're welcome, by the way," they add pointedly, and that's fair enough – she has been inexcusably rude. "I had to drag your unconscious body up to the Mists, manipulate an object in a way I ain't never done before to save you, and then drag you back down here before someone found us. It weren't easy."

"Thank you," she replies sincerely. "I…" Grateful doesn't cover it. Though it sounds a bit cliched and obvious, all she can think to say is, "I owe you my life."

"Sure do, but it ain't a debt I'll try to collect, I can promise you that. Oh, and as for Jess's scanner, I've got some good news there. I was able to stick my bug onto it while we were rolling around, and given that I've been able to see what it's up to on my own scanner, the guy clearly hasn't figured out what we've done yet." Carrion stands and goes to one of the supply crates stacked against the wall, fishing around in it before they pull out a dusty water canteen and toss it at her. "All in all, we got pretty lucky with the whole thing."

Ziane catches the canteen, but she doesn't drink. What if she cannot feel it run down her new throat? "Was this really the only way to save me?"

"Only way I could think of."

It took Essten a day to heal from a broken leg. It took Carrion barely any time at all to shrug off their shoulder injury. It didn't take her long either to heal from the burns. The more Astrosi a person is, the faster they heal. The less mortal they become.

"What does this mean? For me?"

"Means whatever you want it to mean," Carrion says frankly. "You're another new version of you. Aside from the physical, it's really up to you how you want to change from this. Change is a doozy, innit?"

Ziane takes a drink. The water feels the same as it always has, but when she turns her focus to it, she gets a flash of the same sensations she experiences when sticking her hands into soil to grasp roots. A faint sense of a map of atoms, of a responsiveness that's just out of reach. Her throat, her chest, her memories, her knowledge – so many parts of her have changed, it's a wonder than any of her has stayed the same.

Carrion kneels next to her, slinging an arm around her waist to help her get to her feet and keeping it there when she sways. After what happened, she would have expected her body to feel stiff, but instead there's a weightlessness in her bones that throws her off. It's faint, only a slight difference, yet still enough to require a long moment of adjustment as she clenches and unclenches her fists, stretching out her limbs and watching the way the air shifts. Though there's no doubt in her mind that she technically now has access to the same abilities that the Vesperi do, she has no idea how to use them. Will it be instinctive or will she need to be trained as she was with her Eoi skills? Whichever it is, she has no desire to use them until she gets a solid grasp of *how* to use them safely. She has no idea the damage she could do if she made an error.

"No idea what you're freaking out about right now, but maybe don't," Carrion suggests.

She blinks. "Excuse me?"

"You make a face when you're freaking out. Your eyes get all glazed over." They let her go once she stops wobbling and then continues, "Look, I know you've got a lot to adjust to, and I'd love to teach you all my tricks, but we ain't got the time for it."

"Before we continue with our plan," she decides, the words quiet and soft, "I want to find out if Essten and Leneat are all right. They were close to the explosion, and if they were as badly damaged as me, I can't imagine that they were brought to King Ari's terraforming sphere to receive the same treatment I was. You would have seen them there, for starters."

Carrion gapes at her in sheer bemusement. "And how in the fuck do you expect to do that? You thinking of just waltzing into the Deep through the front door and asking Sef very nicely if you can check in on some of her Eoi that, to be one hundred and fifty percent clear, were injured while *trying to capture you*? Absolutely the fuck not! We're going to the Deep all right, but it's to tear up your contract and link up their scanner to ours, not to play nurse to a couple people who were happy to let you choke to death."

"They're my *friends*."

"Choke to *death*."

Had Essten and Leneat really been so willing to let Ziane die? They had been faltering in the end, but that doesn't change the fact that Leneat aimed a rifle at her head and Essten activated the hologram recording that triggered her contract's kill switch. She doesn't want to believe that they would have actually let her die if it had progressed much further, only there's no evidence to support that theory one way or another, as everything had collapsed before it truly came to that eventuality.

"And," Carrion points out when she takes too long to respond, "you're even more like me now. If they were happy to kill you for working with me, they won't be any happier now that you're the same type of weird Astrosi as me."

She hangs her head. "Queen Sef might still be willing to listen. She didn't personally have the chance to hear me out."

"And they call *me* crazy," Carrion snickers, although it doesn't sound particularly insulting. Amused, almost. "Look, whether or not she is don't matter much if you've still got your contract. We break that. Everything else comes after. I…" Their pause is barely noticeable. "…can't risk losing you to that thing. Need my partner on this, eh?"

"Contract first," she agrees, "but my friends and Queen Sef afterwards."

They stare up at the ceiling. "Fine, fine. Come on, then. I can't imagine that Sef and Ari are gonna be any *less* aggressive about hunting us down after all that, so we'd best get a move on."

Once the two of them have packed up, they begin the journey back to the Deep.

The descent is far quicker than their ascent to the Mists. Many of the sharp drops and steep falls are nearly identical to Ziane's first trip down, all that time ago. Of course, the difference now is that, instead of following tracks left by Carrion, she is right alongside them.

When they approach the lowest levels of the Bastion, where the barriers between the realm of humans and the throneworld of Sef begin to waver and fade, Carrion takes her through a hidden passage that she never would have guessed existed – an air vent, one that runs right over the entirety of the great and green arboretum that Ziane has spent so many of her days in.

"How often do you take this path?" Ziane asks uncertainly as Carrion stops crawling through the vent ahead of her and begins prying open a panel. They get another screw out and remove the panel fully, exposing a sheer drop down onto a field of grass.

"Not often. Not in... not since the time I led you down here, I guess. It's hot in here, from the environmental lights and all that. Don't like it, don't normally need to get here. Not exactly the safest place in the world for me to be, if I'm ever caught." They shimmy their legs to hang out of the open vent. "Anyways, down we go!"

Once again, Ziane has no choice but to jump.

She plummets into a world filled with the bright daylights of the arboretum, as beautiful as they are unchanging, unblinking and blinding as she falls straight beneath them with no leafy boughs to shield her or distance to soften them. A whirlwind of color spins beneath her, bright purple wildflowers and gilt pitcher plants flashing in the corners of her eyes, and then, as she tips backwards, she sees rapidly approaching willows. She reaches out, skimming the edge of a branch as she fully falls into it, connecting with the spark of life inside the tree and bending it to her will.

The willow groans in obedience and, at her direction, a wide branch rises up to catch her, wrapping her in trailing leaves and gently setting her down onto the grassy floor.

Carrion is already waiting for her. "Nice work. Very neat."

"Thank you." She knows the section of the arboretum they are in quite well, and she makes a deliberate effort not to look in the direction of Annie's house. It isn't visible through the trees at the moment, but if she closed her eyes she would be able to walk there simply from memory. "How far do we need to go to... wherever it is we need to go?"

"Not far at all," Carrion says, and turns towards the heart of the arboretum. "You've been there before, actually."

"You can't mean…"

"Yep." Their smile is equal parts charming and lopsided. "Sef keeps all her secrets in the same place."

CHAPTER THIRTY-FIVE

Nothing has changed in Queen Sef's bower since Ziane was last here. The elegant bench near the rolling mound of brilliant green grass, the apple tree curving above with its roots entwining the mound and its branches bearing crimson fruit. And between those encircling roots still rests the pitch-black entrance to the lowest point of the Deep, to the room of night and its golden sphere, to the place where Ziane knows she became Eoi, even if she cannot remember what exactly she traded away. Where the sphere in the Mists had repelled her, now she is drawn in. It is as though a string lies beneath her breast, pulled taut by the darkness, beckoning her into the depths.

Even though Carrion stands right behind her, she doesn't need their encouragement to walk over that dark threshold.

It is just as dark in the heart of Sef's bower as it was when Ziane was last in here, her vague memory of that event having been nothing but darkness with the exception of the golden sphere. When she reaches the bottom of the stairs, she lingers three feet beyond that final step, the faintest sliver of the arboretum's light at her back, the void before her. Despite what Carrion may have said, she has no idea where contracts of any kind would be stored. There must be more to this place than just the darkness and the terraforming device.

Carrion steps down behind her and calls out, "Lights, activate!"

Bright cool light floods the bower with a smooth mechanical hum, briefly blinding Ziane with its radiance. When her eyes adjust she can finally see what's really been here the whole time. Overhead are the same kind of sleek light panels that cover every inch of the ceiling in the arboretum and Sef's throne room, these set not to a warm day frequency but instead to a cool, almost clinical tint of blue-white. A wide walkway leads to the center of the room, a circular platform with another circular indentation in the floor. She suspects it is the same as the hidden vault beneath Ari's viewing-glass room, where the terraforming device rests when not in use. Around that wide open center are towering stacks of what almost look like computer databanks, laid out in neat rows that stretch out further than Ziane can clearly identify.

While she takes in the newly revealed chamber, Carrion saunters forward. "This used to be a seed vault," they explain. "That's what the ship's original map shows. Someplace they stored seeds for just about every plant they had, so that once the ship landed somewhere and got set to terraforming, there'd be something for folks to start putting in the ground. Everything that grows in the Deep actually came from one of these bad boys. Well, at least originally. Eoi love to tinker with 'em. Every time I pop my head down here, they've got some weird new combination of genus kicking around."

"That is their calling. Not for me, of course, but..."

Without a shred of hesitation, Carrion replies, "Good. It'd be a waste if you were." They come to a sudden stop in front of one of the rows of databanks. "Here, this is probably it. There's an active computer that we can access here, and that'll be our best bet for finding your contract. Don't think either of us really want to search every single file here to find yours. There's been a *lot* of contracts over the years. It'd be a lot to sort through. But if we don't have your contract on hand, there's no way I'll be able to figure out how to break it. So... computer search it is."

Sure enough, there's a computer terminal at the end of the long stack of databanks. It's powered off, but there's a stand of sorts next to it, the same as the ones that Ziane had seen during her first trip to the Mists, when Lysander and Jess had dueled – the two stands that they'd placed locks of their hair into in exchange for ammunition in their rifles. Although there's no bayonet-rifle waiting to be loaded, Carrion goes to the stand, chews off part of their thumbnail, and drops that into the stand's receptacle.

With a hum, the nail vanishes and the computer screen turns on.

"It's just matter to energy," Carrion explains, leaning over the computer. "Eoi and Vesperi got it all ritualized out by now, but that's all it really is. Was designed as a backup source of emergency power for smaller systems."

"Everything changes, nothing dies," she murmurs to herself.

Carrion's fingers pause over the computer screen. Then they laugh, a shocked *HA* that takes Ziane entirely by surprise. "You really *have* learned Sef's tricks. I'd almost forgot she used to say that."

"Well, it's true, isn't it?" she asks, awkwardly looking away.

"Oh, sure. It's just such a silly little catchphrase of Sef's." They start messing with the computer again as they add, "Ari always called it 'the creation inherent in destruction'. Or at least he did when I was just Vesperi." With a snarl, they smack the screen. "Ugh! Where is it? Fucking system is locking me out, only giving me access to *my* old contracts."

Ziane nudges them aside to look at the screen. It's all a jumbled mess to her eyes, a stream of code and files with an esoteric labeling system. Computers were never her specialty, and certainly not Era One machines, but she had emergency computer training and knows the odd thing or two. "I think maybe..." She hesitates, her finger resting over a button with a confusing symbol on it, not unlike the image of soundwaves. "Let me just try..."

As soon as she presses the button, an alert flashes across the screen, a scan activates beneath her finger, and an electronic voice fills the hall:

"Biometric scan accepted. Welcome, citizen designated: Eoi."

Carrion grins. "The voice-prompt system! Now we're getting somewhere. Sef must have had my biometrics blocked after, well, everything." They give Ziane a little wave forward. "Go on. It seems to like you better."

Clearing her voice, she says, as clearly as she can, "I'm searching for contract records. Ones between Queen Sef and humans that became Acolytes."

"Voice print recognized." There's a pause, and then, *"Login credentials available. Please state your username."*

"My... username?" Her brow wrinkles as she tries to think if she has one. To access any of the Bastion's systems, she had always used her First Responder ID number, not any kind of set username. "I don't think I have a username?"

"Username not accepted. Please state your username," it repeats.

Carrion holds up a finger to shush her before she can ask again. "If you keep trying and failing, it'll lock you out. Just think. Your contract was entered into Sef's system, and you clearly have your voice identification of some kind on file, if it knows and accepts your voice print. Did you ever put in a username anywhere, even if it wasn't here? Or maybe you agreed to something verbally?"

"Just my contract. I mean, they needed my verbal confirmation to it, I think, but they never asked me for…" Everything from that time is so fuzzy, so unclear, and yet one detail sluggishly worms its way to the front of her mind.

Right at the very beginning, right before Lysander had started noting down all the details, Sef had said…

Use her name.

"Use her name…" Ziane murmurs to herself before gasping. "Not 'use her name' – she was saying *username*! That was when my username was set in the system, right before my contract got made and recorded."

"Yes!" Carrion leans forward, all aglow with excitement. "What was it?"

"It was 'use her name' and then Lysander asked me…" What had he asked? It was something important, something… And why can't she remember what she'd said in response either? Surely that had mattered at the time. "He asked me… He asked for my name. And I think I gave it to him." She turns her head up to where the voice is coming from and calls out, "Username is Ziane!"

"Username not accepted. Please state your username."

She doesn't have a heart, but if she did, the crestfallen look on Carrion's face might very well have broken it. "You really don't remember at all, do you?"

"I..." She swallows, her muscles tense. "I just gave them my name," she whispers, like if she says it quietly enough, it won't be real. There is that blankness in her memory still, a void where she had responded to Lysander, the memory of her mouth moving but no recollection of the words that came out. "I didn't mean to give it *away*."

"Oh, love..." Slowly, tenderly, Carrion cups her face in her hands and, their lips a scant inch away from hers, gleefully assures her, "Don't worry. They couldn't have taken your name even if you did tell them. You'd already given it to me *first*."

"Username not accepted. Please state your username."

Carrion leans forward and reverently whispers a name into Ziane's ear. Her lips form the shapes. The sounds vibrate in her throat.

"Username accepted. Three contracts on record."

A first name, middle initials, and a surname – the same as all other human names. Maybe she should feel more, some sense of wonder or a profound realization. None of that is there. It's just a thing she once owned, a thing returned to her at last, yet still a coat that no longer fits her body. "That isn't me," she tells Carrion softly. "Not anymore."

"I know," they reply, not surprised in the slightest. "But it's still yours. They don't get to have it."

Her old name as a possession. Something Carrion carried with them for so long while she had it taken from her, while she forgot it like she forgot so much. No, not quite simply forgot. Traded it away. And in the end it turns out it wasn't even hers to trade. Not anymore.

She clears her throat and eventually pulls away from Carrion. "The second contract... I think that was the informal one I made with Sef when I wanted to track you down, but

I can't remember what I traded for it. And the third would be when I became Eoi. The first one, though, that was the one where I swallowed the contract seed." She speaks to the disembodied computer: "Access the first contract, please."

"Contract accessed." A dense text file opens up on the computer screen. And then, *"Storage vault R-30 access approved. Please proceed to vault."*

Vault? What could possibly be in a vault? "I'll go to the vault," she decides, the curiosity outweighing the confusion. "Can you get to work on deciphering the contract?"

"Yeah." Carrion is already poring over the screen full of text. "This thing's dense. Sef clearly learned from the last time I wriggled out of a contract with her."

Ziane leaves them to it and walks off, examining the endless towers of databanks for any sort of marker that might indicate what she's looking for. When she looks closer at the databanks at the ends of each row, she sees a string of stamped letters. Perfect. They're in row G, so she hurries until she comes to row R and heads into the narrow corridor, checking each databank as she goes for any numerical signage. It turns out she doesn't need it, as one is open and stands out amidst the uniformity. It's not a databank at all, she discovers as she approaches. It's a small vault, the inside filled with a bright light and a faint mist emanating from within, like there's been some kind of temperature control.

Inside is a single object. A canister, approximately seven and a half inches tall and five inches in diameter. There's a temperature- and pressure-control unit attached to the top and bottom, keeping the bluish, transparent fluid within cold, cold enough that the plastic sides are dusted with condensation.

And within the canister floats a single human heart.

So that's where it went.

Ziane picks up the canister. It's not that heavy. Remarkably light, all things considered. A brief snippet of memory floats through her mind, of the golden sphere and the darkness of Sef's bower, and begging to make her heart stop hurting. The memories, the acute panic and fear and sorrow that have lingered as dull aches, as echoes of the memory of emotion, burned into her brain over the years but no longer resting within the emptiness of her chest. Had Annie known? she wonders out of the blue. Had Annie seen her wake up as Eoi and known right away that the trade had been the same one that Sef must have made, all those years ago? Not cruel. Just heartless.

When she returns to the computer, where Carrion is waiting, they don't look up at their approach, too busy furiously scrolling through the contract.

"Why in the fuck did you agree to this thing?" they complain, glaring at the screen. "I mean look at all this! You have options via arbitration, but oh wait, the Supreme Arbitrator is Sef. And if you want to get out of this by going to Ari, well – 'Judgment on the award rendered by the Supreme Arbitrator may be entered into any court having jurisdiction thereof.' You want to get out of this by something as simple as killing Sef? Too bad, there's a massive section on transferability of the contract to successors of one or both parties. And don't even get me *started* on what you gave up in the Right of Clawback..." They finally glance up at her and trail off. "Is that...?"

Ziane nods, staring down at the thing in her hands. "I suppose Queen Sef kept it."

"Probably something she's keeping in reserve. In case she needs to use it against you. There's a lot you can do with a heart." Carrion runs a finger along the condensation on the plastic container. "I bet we could find a way to put it back. If you wanted."

Does she want that? It's one thing to tell Essten that she's not interested in getting her old self back when it's abstract. Distant. Something that she couldn't really do even if she wanted to. When it's right in front of her, it's different. It might even be easy. She doesn't know how she'd shove her heart back into her chest, or what it would be replacing. Those golden rose petals, perhaps? Is that what's in there instead? Would it undo her transformation into an Eoi, would it really bring back her memories, or would it simply chase away the curtain of numbness that has been drawn between her and her strongest emotions?

"Aren't you a little tempted?" Carrion asks.

The longer she stares at the heart in her hands, the more certain she becomes. "No," she decides. "I'm not."

"Really?" They sound surprised. "Not even a bit?"

"I gave up my memories and my life as a human for a reason. I have to trust in myself, and trust that the past version of me knew what she wanted and knew what she was doing. I won't undo a bargain I wanted so badly that I gave up my heart for it."

"Not all knowledge is worth having?"

"If I didn't know better," she nervously remarks, "I'd say you sound like you *want* me to get my memories back."

"I don't," they reply right away, shrugging. "But... I can't say it wasn't fun. You chasing after me, that fire in your eyes when all you wanted was to see me dead or locked up. Is it really that bad to say I almost miss it?" They sigh. "I suppose it's better for me this way. And maybe better for you, too. We got an awful lot to do, and if you remembered all those little details you forgot... Well. You might just try to kill me for it, and then where would we be?"

"Was it really that bad? Whatever you did that you think I will hate you for?"

Their mouth twists into an unnamable expression. "Who's to say? I can't speak for you, and you can't speak for yourself."

And so all that stands between the two of them is a dead woman. Not insurmountable odds, all things considered.

"The contract," she says. "It's under my old name, made when I was human. That name no longer refers to me. I'm no longer human. I'm not really Eoi and I'm not really Vesperi either. The only thing left of the version of me that signed the contract is that heart, and it's nothing to me anymore."

Slowly, Carrion nods along. "We can argue that." They glance at the canister. "It'd probably make our case a lot stronger if we destroyed that."

She holds out the heart canister. The idea of destroying it herself makes her hesitate, even though she's committed to this course of action. But she doesn't have any issue with someone else ruining it. "I don't know if I can do this. Can you...?" she asks, half-bracing for them to say no, for them to insist that she be the one to end her own heart. "Could you please destroy my heart?"

Carrion stares at her, their pupils blown wide and dark, their lips slightly parted. They swallow, their throat bobbing. "I think that's the most romantic thing you've ever said to me," they admit, their voice low. "Of course I'll do it, love."

There is that true reverence painted on every inch of their face as they take the canister from her and cradle it in their hands. They caress the control unit at the top, lingering on each and every button that keeps the heart alive and healthy. With a final, anticipatory inhalation, they deactivate each button, one by one by one, the series of lights flicking off as the temperature regulation goes, then the pressure control, the fluid filtration, the artificial circulation, the glow within fading away and the condensation beginning to melt without anything to sustain it. Finally, the canister is flooded with liquid-nitrogen coolant.

When her heart fully dies, she does not feel it.

"We should split up," Ziane says once it's done. "Queen Sef will never listen to me if you're there as well. And we still need to plant your tracking device on the Eoi's scanner as well, and you're more likely to have success there if I'm drawing the queen's attention."

Carrion's attention is still on the dead heart. "Mm, yeah. Good point." At last they snap back to the matter at hand. "I'll snoop around, see what I can find. After that explosion, Lysander might not be carrying the scanner on him, depending on how bad his injuries might've been. Will you be fine trying this on your own?"

"Yes." Before saying it out loud, she hadn't been so certain, but she is now. "Queen Sef is reasonable. Heartless, not cruel, remember?"

"It's your shot to call," they agree. "I'm more than happy to follow your lead here."

Her face feels oddly warm. "Right. Well, let's get to it, then."

Together, the two of them depart the clinical databanks of Sef's bower, leaving her dead heart behind without a second thought.

CHAPTER THIRTY-SIX

Ziane walks into Queen Sef's throne room with her head held high. Whispers ripple out through the various Eoi who have crowded into the room, everyone ceasing their conversations and activities in order to stare. Two guards move to stop her before thinking better of it and allowing her to pass, sharing a confused murmur as if even they aren't certain what they should be doing. Both those guards are familiar to her, not ones she has worked with personally during her hunt for Carrion, but ones she has passed by dozens of times, exchanged friendly words with, bonded with distant and vague solidarity. They both look at the silver scarring over her neck and freeze on the spot. As she walks through the throne room, her footsteps muffled by the lush grass carpeting the floor, the crowd of her fellow Eoi parts before her, watching and muttering and then eventually falling silent.

And then there is Sef, sitting upon her throne of elegant wood, her hair filled with flowers and her bare feet buried in the grass. A stern, blank polish sits heavy on her eyes and Ziane is overcome with the sudden certainty that Sef has known she and Carrion were here from the moment they stepped into her bower. From the way her unnatural eyes flicker to it, the state of Ziane's neck is the only surprise.

The very first word from Sef smothers the last vestiges of whispers. "I did not expect you to return to my throneworld after recent events."

"Are Essten and Leneat all right?" Ziane asks, because that's the most important thing right now.

Sef inclines her head. "Resting and wounded, but they shall recover with all due haste and live without permanent injury."

"Thank you." She takes a deep breath and states, "I am here to break my contract."

Someone in the crowd gasps. Sef, however, remains unmoved, a rock standing tall in a sandstorm. "And why," Sef asks in that smooth, dispassionate voice of hers, "should I be swayed to grant you such a thing?"

"Because you made a contract with a person that no longer exists. You dealt with a human woman of a different name, with a different mind, with a different set of memories. I am Ziane, neither Eoi nor Vesperi but also both, and I cannot even remember what I traded my services as an Acolyte *for*. Not even the heart of that person remains, not anymore." She presses a hand to her abdomen. "The contract seed in my stomach was swallowed by a dead woman."

Sef's lips part to make her decree, but she does not get the chance.

"It's because you're a fucking traitor!"

Someone in the crowd cries out as they're shoved away. Another yells a protestation and a guard rushes to intercept, even though they're too late. Lysander pushes his fellows aside with total disregard as he stomps through the throne room to approach Ziane and his queen. Bandages wrap around his torso and there are remnants of shiny red burns licking the edges of his jaw and the corners of his eyes.

There's a drunken stagger in his steps, the same instability that comes with the potent opioid pain medications the medics of the Eoi use. Yet even that inebriation does nothing to cover the fiery fury in his eyes.

"Lysander..." That single word is a sharp warning from Sef, but it does no good.

"I'm sorry, my queen," Lysander growls, bodily pushing aside the last of the Eoi in his way. "But I ain't gonna stand around while this traitorous piece of shit wanders through the Deep like she still belongs here."

Confronted with such anger, Ziane stands her ground. She knows that she used to be more afraid of him, that his testiness had once frightened her to the bone, but now that fear is absent. Gone, along with everything else. "I know you might not approve of the methods I decided to take," she says carefully. "Everything I have done, regardless of who I've done it with, has been for the good of the Bastion, the Deep and the Mists included. If you would please just listen to me, if you would hear me out, then–"

"I'm not listening to a single fucking word from someone who decided to join up with Carrion." It would seem that Sef either does not disagree with this decision or is waiting for Lysander's rage to subside to the point where he will listen to her, at least, because she doesn't interrupt him and he continues, "You want out of your contract?" he snaps. "You want to slip our queen's leash? Prove the strength of your conviction and duel for it."

A duel? There's no way that either Sef or any of the assembled Eoi will listen to what she has to say if this resorts to a duel. "I don't really think that will achieve anything."

"Yeah, that's what you always fucking say, isn't it? You don't have the guts to face me in real combat without resorting to cheap tricks. You don't have the strength to take a shot at a Vesperi who wouldn't blink at killing you. You can't stand up for yourself or your stupid ideas to save your own skin. First time you ever darkened our door, you couldn't muster up the courage to fight, not even to save your–"

"I accept," Ziane says, before he can say anything that she doesn't want to hear.

Lysander pauses mid-vitriolic rant. Then his face contorts into a viciously satisfied snarl. "Finally, you step the fuck up."

Any remaining nearby Eoi vanish from the center of the throne room, clustering around the edges, waiting for further signal from their queen. Sef's posture had already been flawless, but somehow she manages to straighten up even further as she decrees, "Very well. If both parties consent, then we have no objections to the terms of this bargain. Ten paces from both of you and then you may make your wagers. They who draws first blood wins."

Ziane takes ten measured steps away from Lysander, and once she reaches the designated area, a piece of grassy floor slides back to allow a short pillar to rise up. It is the same as the ones in the Mists, with a receptacle at the top for hair – or, as Carrion had pointed out, matter of any kind. Beneath it, sheathed to the base of the pillar, is a bayonet-rifle, well-maintained despite how rare duels are in the Deep compared to the Mists. A matching pillar is already set up where Lysander has moved to, and he is clearly itching to grab the rifle.

Sef makes an elegant hand gesture and indicates the pillars. "Wager."

With one hand, Lysander draws a knife from his belt. With the other, he grabs his hair at the base of his neck. For Jess, he had wagered mere strands. For Ziane, he slices the blade through a massive swath of his long hair, left holding that great lock like a trophy while his remaining hair falls down only to his shoulders. Shocked gasps and murmurs fill the throne room as those watching struggle to believe what he has just done.

He drops the hair into the receptacle and the rifle lights up, not only with the main charge indicator fully illuminated but with three additional rows of backup power clustered beneath it. Roughly snatching it up, he then slings it over his shoulder and waits.

Ziane plucks a single hair from her head. A single sliver of a charge is spat out into her rifle. The bare minimum needed to let her duel.

"You smug motherfucker," Lysander snaps.

"It's not about arrogance," she tells him, picking up her rifle. "You asked me to prove the strength of my conviction. So I will."

Sef holds up her hand to stop Lysander from making another retort. "If the combatants have made their wagers, then we instruct them to prepare themselves. Observants, stand back. Raise barrier."

All the various Eoi ogling hustle away, allowing plenty of space around Ziane and Lysander. Someone must have activated a protective shield, as a shimmering, transparent energy barrier ascends from the ground to about fifteen feet up in the air. More elegant than the fighting pit in the Mists.

Sef gives one final glance at Ziane before declaring, with the finality and impassivity of a steel ball falling from great height, "Break."

Barely has the word left her mouth before Lysander is charging towards Ziane. He has paid a great price for the potency of his weapon, and he wastes no time in using it, opening fire almost immediately, the laser beam cutting through the air.

But there's no finesse to it, no clever angle, nothing beyond anger. As she had before, she can read the trajectory of the laser before it fires, all that training Lysander and Essten had put her through being funneled into dodging instead of fighting him in return. She runs across the arena circle, dropping to her knees and skidding through the grass when Lysander carves the beam around to chase her. That fall turns into a roll, and then she's dragging her fingers through the soil, raising up a wall of strong grass between her and Lysander. The next shot burns the grass to ash and she drops it, abandoning it the moment it's no longer useful as cover.

In a fair fight between the two of them, Lysander will win every time. And this time he'll be wise to her tricks. She won't be able to incapacitate him with oleander like she did before. But she doesn't need this to be a fair fight. All she needs is one well-placed shot.

Suddenly Lysander is right in front of her, using the same trick as her, digging into the soil and grabbing the matter for himself. Dozens of gnarled vines spring forth one by one, each stabbing towards her with the same ferocity he had employed when he'd severed his own hair. She ducks and weaves around them, using the bayonet to slice one particularly persistent vine in two and then grabbing onto another, enforcing her will onto it, wresting control from Lysander and turning it back into dirt. Though she's tempted to try to use a Vesperi trick on him, to catch him by surprise with a new skill, when she reaches out to touch her mind to the atoms in the air, it's so unfamiliar that it distracts her and she nearly gets shot.

It would seem Lysander is determined to make the sacrifice of his hair worth it. He fires at Ziane without any attempt to conserve the rifle's energy, cutting up the ground beneath her and tracking her as she runs, the laser beam always right behind her, close enough for her to feel the heat radiating from it. It's all she can do to keep out of reach, putting more distance between them when he gets close, narrowly avoiding getting sliced by his bayonet when he swings it at her.

Even with the stamina of both an Eoi and a Vesperi, there is too great a gap in experience between Ziane and Lysander. Her lungs begin to ache as her blood pounds through her veins, her muscles tiring rapidly. The training she has undergone since she became an Acolyte isn't enough to make up for the sheer number of years that stand between her and Lysander, and he must know it.

She rolls underneath his next shot, and this time when she plunges her hand into the grass, she grows thick roots, winding them around Lysander's ankles and up his calves. His legs flex as he fights the roots, easily starting to rip them out of the ground with just his own strength. But she didn't need to stop him permanently. She just needed a second. For the first time, she aims her rifle, calculating the laser's trajectory, and squeezes the trigger.

Her shot hits Lysander's rifle.

The metallic casing of his weapon cracks and melts beneath the heat of the laser and Ziane has just enough time to shield her face before the rifle explodes. All that power stored in it, all that energy, blasts outwards, ruining the weapon and turning it into two hunks of semi-molten slag, one held in Lysander's hand and the other scattering across the arena. His scream burns as hot as the beam itself as he drops the metal, shrapnel making dozens of tiny cuts all over his arm and cheek, tiny drops of bright red blood splattering every exposed inch of skin.

All Lysander can do is stand there, gaping at his wrecked weapon, uncaring of his burnt hand or nicked skin.

"That will be all." Sef's voice is booming over the quiet that fills the arena after the explosion. She makes a gesture and the energy barrier falls. "As Lysander is no longer able to continue by the rules of single combat, we have no choice but to declare the winner of this match–"

Lysander roars in anger and squares his shoulders, preparing to lunge at Ziane. "I'm not gonna let–!"

"Enough!"

With the swift grace of water, Sef rises from her throne. The thousand braids of her hair and the thousand vines entwined between them stab into the ground, lifting her up until she hovers in the air, suspended by her own braids in a halo of power. A single braid shoots forward and plunges into the dirt at Lysander's feet, and from that impact point a hundred tiny blades of grass burst forth, encircling him with a hundred razor-sharp sprigs aimed to pierce his body at Sef's will.

There is no give in the queen's voice, no mercy, no ease. Only the authority of a ruler in her domain. "The duel has been finished. Too long have we been lenient whilst you ignore our orders, Lysander. Your wager has been *lost*, and you shalt ne'er disobey our command again or may your head be severed from your shoulders as due penance for your transgression."

Only the condemnation of his queen could send Lysander to his knees. He drops to the ground as though every tendon holding his body upright has been cut, staring up at Sef with pleading eyes. "Forgive me, my queen. I never meant to fail you."

"Your loss of a single duel is insufficient to be marked as a failure. Nay, 'tis your disobedience of our word that betrays you." Sef turns her head full of deadly braids to face Ziane, looking down upon her and ignoring Lysander entirely. "The bargain struck has been fulfilled. You have been severed from the contracts signed in a life now past, and thus I, Queen Sef the Third, the representative of our Court, do hereby grant you leave from the ties and title of Acolyte. Henceforth, you have all due freedoms of an unbound Astrosi. For good or ill, you may do with them what you please."

Discomfort twists Ziane's stomach and she drops her rifle, doubling over to hack out a ragged cough. The small, smooth seed crawls up her throat until it sits on her tongue and she can expel it, spitting it out into the grass. It sits there, wet and glistening, and then turns to dirt.

"You may leave our throneworld," Sef grants, though it sounds less like an allowance and more like a command.

Ziane scrambles to her feet and bows, her head low and her back bent. For all that she wishes she had been able to properly speak with Sef, for all that she wishes Sef had been willing to listen all that time ago when she had first tried to talk about the world outside the Bastion, Sef was still her queen. Sef had still granted her leave to chase Carrion, still granted her the trade of her heart for becoming Eoi. In order to reign over so many for so long, to protect her throneworld from so many threats – Vesperi, Carrion, internal discord – it must be impossible to do so without becoming heartless in more ways than one. For that, Ziane cannot judge the queen.

In the end, there is not a trace of animosity in her as she turns from Sef and departs the throne room in the same way she first arrived, back when she was human: to the lift at the far end of the room. She steps up onto the platform and looks back on the world of the Deep, hoping, perhaps foolishly, that this will not be the last time she sets foot in this realm of greenery and life.

A figure wearing a ratty cloak hops onto the lift platform after her, and she sees Carrion's cheery and proud grin underneath the hood.

"*Very* well done," Carrion praises under their breath. "And damn, the look on Lysander's face was a thing of beauty."

Ziane's gaze nervously flickers back to Sef. "Did you get the tracker installed on the scanner?"

"Yeah. Lysander left it in a vault with, frankly, shit security."

"That's good. Let's... let's just leave. Quickly."

The platform has already begun to slide upwards, gliding towards the opening in the ceiling that will allow them to be carried all the way up and out of the Deep. Below them, the view of grass and flowers and Eoi gets smaller and smaller, and as it fades Sef raises her head, her too-sharp eyes locking on to Carrion. Then the doors shut beneath the lift, cutting Ziane and Carrion off from the throne room.

"Well," Carrion says, grabbing Ziane's hand. "Time to make a break for it, eh?"

CHAPTER THIRTY-SEVEN

Not even Ziane's previous flight from the Fringes, when unwanted echoes of terror had overcome her, compares to the speed with which she and Carrion flee from the Deep. Only Carrion's tricks and knowledge of the Bastion keep the two of them from being caught by the guards that they can constantly hear in the distance, chasing after them, shouting commands. For all the threat of imminent capture is right behind Ziane, she doesn't feel any of that fear. Not a trace of it. After defeating Lysander, breaking her contract, freeing herself from the constraints of that contract seed, an energy has filled her body, propelling her forward. Their goal is in sight.

Once the two of them are well and truly out of the Deep, they huddle in a maintenance tunnel beneath a lightrail station and examine the prize that she has twice risked her life for.

"Remotely activating the scanners now," Carrion says, their fingers flying over their scanner screen. "Time to find out if I'm really as good as I say I am, eh?"

Ziane's eyes are glued to the screen as she watches it calibrate. "If this doesn't work…"

"We'll burn that bridge when we get to it."

"I don't believe that's…"

"Got it!" They hold up the scanner in triumph, waving it in front of her so she can see the completed location data. "It's holding steady, too. The triangulation is keeping it on our sight. Here, wanna closer look?"

She takes it from them and starts to examine the location data that they worked so hard to get. Although she cannot immediately put her finger on why the information seems familiar, it soon comes to the forefront of her mind. She knows where this is. She has seen this combination of numbers before, or something close enough that she can do the math and figure out the logical place for the diamond to be.

"It's in the far-south-southeast of the central torus tunnel," she tells them.

"Right then! Off we go, I suppose. At least I know how to get there."

"No one can do everything entirely on their own," she reminds them quietly.

Their smile strikes her as not entirely genuine. "You're too nice to me."

Perhaps she is, considering all they've done. But she doesn't think it's as simple as nice or mean, of helping out of kindness or denying aid out of cruelty. She won't lie to Carrion just to have the barb hurt them, nor will she go out of her way to simper or flatter. All she says is the truth. From thanking them when she owes them to helping them when they are on the only viable path, she has told them nothing but the truth as she sees it. It occurs to her that Carrion has never once lied to her either.

Carrion leads her up through the Bastion until they're between the second and third levels, in the middle of the pressurization barriers that separate levels. The air is tense as a result, like it's too dry, too thin, unfinished. There is so little reason to come here that it's no wonder the place is intended for emergency maintenance crews and little else.

The tunnel entrance that Carrion leads her to is completely blocked off, and she cannot tell where it is even when they enthusiastically point it out to her. Only once they pry a solid sheet of steel off the wall of a maintenance shaft does she finally see a rusted hatch built behind the wall. A number of security locks are installed on it, but all are broken and useless, either by age or by Carrion's previous entrance. Carrion clambers through the hatch without a second thought. Ziane, however, pauses for a moment at the faded, peeled paint that had once been stamped onto the hatch – a hazardous-materials warning. It's old enough that it could have been Era One, but for all she knows it might have been the humans of the Bastion that blocked this area off to ensure no one wandered in.

It is cold inside the tunnel. Cold and dark. Only emergency lights stuck to the floor and rounded walls provide any kind of illumination, and even then it isn't much. Ziane cranes her head up to see the perfectly round roof of the tunnel, the smooth metallic walls around her sloping up and spreading out in both directions. From here, it looks almost as though the tunnel goes in a straight line, and she can only see where it starts to curve far in the distance. The tunnel is perhaps fifteen feet in diameter, and though she knows it's all in her imagination, she could swear that it's large enough and empty enough for even her breathing to echo.

Carrion circles the area with the scanner held before them until it gets a new lock on the diamond's location. They point to the right. "Still south-south-south eventual east or whatever you said. This way."

"Hopefully it won't take too long to get there."

"Shouldn't be bad," Carrion muses as they start to saunter off in the right direction. "Besides, waiting isn't what most people think it's like."

Ziane follows, her footsteps echoing off the metallic tunnel walls. "Better, or worse?"

"Both? It's less about better or worse than it is just different. The brain invents stuff to do while you wait. It settles, sorta. Finds ways to stay mentally busy. I'm kinda the foremost expert on waiting by now," they add cheerfully. Their every word is buzzing with energy. "Got loads of practice in it. If this doesn't work, I can show you all the ways to wait."

"I'd rather it not come to that, if it's all the same to you."

The scanner continues to guide them with a series of beeps as the screen keeps refreshing, the computer within chugging along as it keeps triangulating the diamond's position with the tenacity of an old man hobbling along on a bum leg. Given the tunnel's unwavering uniformity, only Ziane's diligent measuring of her own steps assures her that they're actually moving forward, as their surroundings don't change other than the occasional emergency light on the floor being broken and dimmed.

After some time, Ziane points up ahead and asks, "Is that a door?"

"Think so." Carrion's stride lengthens into a half-jog to hurry towards the vague indentation on the wall. "Yeah, looks like some kind of observation room, maybe. Hold on, lemme get it open."

They start prying the door open, examining the barely-there frame for any indication of a locking mechanism or other set of buttons. Ziane hurries to catch up with them, checking the wall as she goes to make sure that there isn't anything else they're missing, as she has no real idea of what to expect in this odd tunnel. For all she knows, all those hazardous materials that they have been warned about are right behind this door.

When Carrion cracks the door open an inch, nothing oozes out, or at least nothing Ziane can see or smell. They slip inside, leaving her no real choice other to follow them. This newly revealed room almost appears to be an observation room or monitoring station, as from this side she can clearly see that one of the walls is a one-way glass looking out into the tunnel that they were just walking through. Most of the large room is taken up by computer terminals. All are dead and black save one, which must be kept running only by the grace of the tower of power packs stacked next to it, half of which are already depleted.

Carrion heads right to the functional computer and starts poking at it until they get a hologram up and running. "It's the tunnel," they say, drawing a finger around the holographic torus. "And there, that moving dot – that must be the diamond. Slow thing, ain't it? Glad it won't crush us, at least."

The hologram only draws Ziane's attention for a minute before she catches sight of something on the back wall. It's the same sort of faded paint as the hazardous-materials warning from earlier, although it's survived the test of time a bit better, likely due to fewer people making it this far through the tunnel and into this room. She places her hand over the words, the paint smooth and soft beneath her hand. Beneath her fingers, in large letters, the sign proclaims:

DI-MOD

Dynamo-Interstellar Modifier Control Center

A slow breath escapes Ziane's lungs, drawn out by the words. "The diamond," she whispers, dragging her hand across the paint. Just like the Office of the Administrator. It's all the same story, forgotten and blurred over time. Louder this time, she calls out, "Carrion. Look at this."

They pause in their investigation of the computer and turn to see the sign. For a moment they just stare, and then they laugh, a sharp, "Hah! I shouldn't be surprised."

"I wonder what the others were called." Four of them, she thinks. Two forgotten, two barely understood. "Not just officially, although that too of course. But what Queen Sef and King Ari call their devices. What they know them as. If they know this only as the diamond, what else has become only half-remembered?"

"By now, I think anything that ain't half-remembered is totally forgotten." Carrion comes to stand next to her, splaying their palm over the sign, almost caressing the faded old paint and the metal wall it's stamped on. "We Astrosi love names, love taking 'em. Power in 'em, even if humans don't always think so. You've seen one form of that recently. But for all that power in names, they hide 'em, giving everyone and everything pseuds, and once they decide names are more valuable kept secret, then they eventually get lost. Maybe the last Queen Sef died before she could tell this one what she called that big gold orb in the bower. Maybe our King Ari never even bothered to name the one in his viewing room."

"I don't know if something can be *that* important to you for so many years without you naming it something, even if only in your own head," she remarks absently, tracing the lines of that one acronym over and over. DI-MOD. So simple. "They made those terraforming orbs their lives, in so many ways, from their own sources of power to the desire for the diamond. And all of it is based on a misunderstanding."

Carrion doesn't seem to share her melancholy. If anything, they're rather chipper at finding out this little tidbit. "Misunderstanding or no, it's a pretty decent take on the name, all things considered. Diamond sounds good, at least." They abandon the wall and its sign and go back to their work at the computer terminals. "DI-MOD or diamond, there's definitely some kind of control terminal here."

Reluctantly, Ziane removes her hand from the wall and goes to examine properly what Carrion is up to. There's still the tunnel hologram being displayed, and Carrion soon changes it to a much larger-scale image, one displaying all five of the torus-shaped tunnels in a neat stack throughout the Bastion's infrastructure. None of the others have the same glowing dot indicating a terraforming device that this one currently does, but there are two other dots present on the map. One is far down at the base of the accessible areas of the Bastion, and the other right at the top. It would seem that even though the terraforming devices the Astrosi use are trapped in a limbo of partial activation, they still register in the system.

She's about to mention this to Carrion, but before she can they apparently notice it themself and tap on those two dots, pulling up two files on the computer screen. While they read, she watches the dot of the DI-MOD move through this tunnel, making its way towards the control center at a leisurely pace. There's a notation on the hologram indicating stabilizers, and she wonders if the state of perpetual transit helps keep the DI-MOD in stasis. If the Astrosi terraforming devices got knocked out of that perpetual transit during the starship's crash, that would explain their current state.

"I think, and don't quote me on this," Carrion says, holding up a finger, "that the other two devices are still partially connected to the Bastion's original systems. They're in their own weird middle ground, unlike the diamond, but I can still access their data." They groan. "Ugh, yeesh. It's a whole fuckton of corrupted data in 'em. Guess that's what you get when you spend forever shoving massive amounts of transformative energy into human bodies."

Ziane stares at those three glowing dots until the light in the dim room makes her eyes begin to ache. "If they're still connected to the systems," she wonders, "can you control them from here? We could maybe... *maybe* activate all three terraforming devices at once. That would save us from having to go back to the Deep or the Mists eventually. Even after getting the diamond and its magnetosphere online, the other two will still be needed if we ever want to make the world outside anything other than actively hostile."

"I can sure as shit try," they say, a smile on their lips as they start typing on the computer's input screen.

While Carrion types away, Ziane returns to examining the control center. With her focus no longer solely drawn by the DI-MOD sign and the revelation accompanying it, she can pay attention to other aspects of the large room. Similar to some of the other places that have been sealed off since the starship's crash, there is no dust on any of the surfaces despite the obvious signs of age. Dust is mostly dead skin cells, and no one has been in here in who knows how many years. The place feels *cold*, even with her own dimmed body temperature.

"All right," Carrion mutters, cracking their knuckles. "I've got all the terraforming devices back online, they just need to calibrate. Figures, given how long they've been fucked up. Once they're all calibrated, then... well. It should work. The diamond should be coming around to the control center in a few minutes, and once it does, it'll grind to a halt and start the activation process. Guess you're gonna learn about waiting after all."

The hairs on Ziane's forearms stand up. Her skin pebbles. When she breathes in, the air tastes different on the back of her tongue, thicker as it goes down her throat, heavier as it sits in her lungs.

As if tugged along by an invisible force again, she finds herself taking one step and then another towards the door. "Carrion," she says, her body as tense as the air has become. "Something's wrong."

They glance at the calibrating screen, at the progress bar crawling its way towards completion. "Yeah. I feel it too, damn it."

Though every nerve in Ziane's body is screaming at her not to, it's as though her arm moves without her permission as she opens the door. The tunnel is just as cavernous and dim as always, except this time it isn't silent. Beyond the sound of her own breathing and the noise of Carrion tentatively stepping out of the control room behind her, she can hear the steady sound of confident footsteps. The hard echo of heavy boots against the metal floor. The unfaltering gait of someone who knows exactly where they are and exactly what they're here to do.

King Ari strides towards them, his face as blank and hard as the metal walls around him, his long dark hair glistening like a knife's edge in the low light.

CHAPTER THIRTY-EIGHT

Every muscle in Carrion's body goes taut as a fraying string, and they whisper, quiet and breathless, "Run."

Ziane is barely holding her ground as it is, but she doesn't have a choice. "We can't," she replies, too softly for Ari to hear. "The computer still needs to calibrate, and if we fail here then none of it mattered."

Carrion presses their eyes shut. "Damn it."

Between the tunnel's echo and the confidence in his voice, King Ari's words reverberate through the corridor. "Did you truly believe that your activities would go unnoticed?" He does not waver in his solid steps towards them. "Your interference with our scanner was detected nigh immediately, and from there it took me no effort at all to access your triangulation program and receive the diamond's location for myself. An audacious concept to be sure, but your ability to tie up loose ends leaves something to be desired."

"What can I say?" Carrion replies, somewhat weaker than their usual tone. "I got swept up in my own excitement."

Ziane holds up her hands in a gesture of peace. "King Ari, please, if you could listen to me for just a few minutes, I can explain. This doesn't need to be a fight. We might be here for the diamond, but it's not because either of us wants to use its power for ourselves. We're not trying to make it an arms race against the Eoi *or* the Vesperi, and we don't want to hurt anyone."

"I am not unreasonable," Ari allows. "As such, I will offer you this one chance to surrender. You will be taken into Vesperi custody, you will have the opportunity to provide whatever information you do or do not have at that time, and you will then await my decision."

Leaning down to whisper in her ear, Carrion mutters, "We go into a Vesperi cell, we ain't never coming out."

"We might," she whispers back. "I might not *want* to wait, but waiting in a cell while we convince Ari would be better than him killing you, or both of us."

"You said it yourself. The computer is already calibrating and I can probably stall for long enough. We won't get another shot."

And yet she doesn't want Carrion to die. Even though she knows they're so close to saving the Bastion, that they have no choice but to risk confrontation with Ari if it means buying time for the computer to calibrate and the diamond to come to a stop. She remembers yelling at Carrion, insisting that every life is a unique variable, that the mathematics of sacrificing one to save many are not so simple. She has her duty to the Bastion, the duty that she undertook years ago when she first started as a First Responder, to put the Bastion's safety at the top of her priority list. Even so, she does not want Carrion to die.

Ziane clenches her jaw and straightens her back. "How long can you stall Ari?"

"For you, love?" Carrion smiles one of their crooked smiles, and murmurs, "Long enough."

"Then keep him off me while I man the computer. As soon as it's calibrated and the diamond is in position, I can activate all three terraforming devices at once."

"Aight. And... then what?"

"We'll..." She tries and fails to return their smile, the expression false on her lips, the tugging on her cheeks detached. "We'll burn that bridge when we get to it."

They laugh and crack their knuckles. "Fine by me."

Ziane whirls around and makes a break for the control-room door, hoping to get inside and lock the door before Ari can stop her. It'll lock Carrion out too, but if the most important thing is to make sure that the terraforming devices are successfully activated, keeping Ari out matters more than preventing Carrion from entering.

Wind hits her out of nowhere. It crashes into her with the force of a sheet of metal, slamming into her body, sweeping her off her feet and throwing her five feet backwards, skidding and rolling across the ground, scraping her trousers and elbows. Her teeth rattle in her jaw, nicking the inside of her mouth. Groaning in pain, she spits out a gob of blood and saliva, wraps an arm around her shaken stomach, and then pushes herself onto her aching knees, vision briefly blurring at the movement.

Ari stands still, a single finger pointed at her. "Pity," he says. "I believed you more rational than this." His gaze flickers down to her scarred and silvered neck. "Even with your newfound vitality, 'twould seem that you've not found the time to adjust to the skills of the Vesperi."

"You don't have to do this," Ziane pleads, struggling to get up.

"It is my duty." Ari's gaze is heavy as his too-white eyes bore into Ziane. "And my burden."

The air contracts around him. The breath is pulled from her lungs and she braces for another blast, trying to cover her face, to reach out for the Vesperi skills she knows are somewhere within her. Wind roars in her ears but nothing hits her. When she risks cracking open her eyes, her vision is filled with Carrion's back and their ratty coat as they stand in front of her, arms outstretched as they cut through Ari's wind like a blade parting cloth. Her clothes whip around her, tugged to and fro as she finally gets to her feet, and by the time she is standing the wind has died, Ari no longer bothering to waste his strength on an attack that Carrion can block.

Carrion drops their arms, and she can see a dozen tiny nicks on their hands. "Come on, Ari. I thought you'd be more interested in a *real* fight. She ain't even armed."

"Neither am I," Ari states. "Rifles are mere distractions in combat."

"Oh, well." Carrion's throat bobs as they swallow. It's one thing to sneak around Ari's domain, but it's something else entirely to be confronted with him face to face, even for Ziane, who can only guess at Ari's strength. "Glad we're in agreement on that one."

Ziane runs right as Carrion moves to keep themself between her and Ari.

This time, Ari doesn't bother trying to knock her over. Instead he simply starts choking her, dragging the breath from her lungs with the simplest of gestures. She can tell what he's doing, she can *feel* it, but it's so different from what she knows of Eoi magic that it still makes her stumble, her hands wrapping around her throat as she tries to connect with the air molecules in her body, the atoms that have been torn from her trachea. Carrion reaches out, not to help her, instead gathering Vesperi winds in their palm, presumably to get a hit in on Ari while he's busy strangling her.

They never get the chance. Ari is *fast*. Too fast. Before Ziane can blink, the king crosses the gap between them in a single leap and kicks out, his boot impacting the side of Carrion's face with a crack of bone and the dead thud of smacked flesh.

Carrion goes flying, hitting the curved wall with a breathless scream. Trying and failing to call out to them, Ziane forces herself to remember what's at stake, what she has to do. Molecules of oxygen, eight buzzing electrons, so close to her and yet so far. She uses what little force her mind can muster to drag those drops of oxygen down her throat, counteracting the asphyxiation a little bit at a time. She puts one foot in front of the other, stumbling towards the control center, one hand around her neck and the other flailing for the metal door.

Before she can reach it, Ari grabs her shoulder and yanks her back harshly enough that her clavicle bends near to the point of breaking. He sweeps her legs out from under her in the same swift movement, the hard bone of his calf bashing the back of her knees and causing her to crumple. The pain of her back cracking against the metal ground is so acute that it takes a moment for her to feel it, and when it floods through her she cannot scream for lack of air in her lungs. Her eyes sting, fat tears rolling down her cheeks, her hands curling against the ground and achieving nothing beyond scraping her nails.

With her thus incapacitated, Ari turns to Carrion. "Get up," he demands.

"Workin' on it," Carrion wheezes, tenderly staggering to their feet, bracing themself against the metal wall.

The moment they get upright, Ari strikes again, aiming a brutal punch at Carrion's face. They barely manage to duck out of the way, moving with that same twisting fluidity that Ziane had seen previously, though this time they aren't toying with Lysander and random Eoi soldiers. Ari doesn't even bat an eyelash at missing the first hit, immediately following up by slamming his knee into Carrion's chest. Carrion doubles over with a gasping cough before letting themself fall to the side, turning the tumble into a smooth roll.

Groping for something in their pocket, they pull out a single match, preparing to strike it and cause another of those oxygen-fueled fireballs. Ari doesn't let them. He floods the area with something that's not oxygen, something that smells empty and cold, and as soon as the potential for fire is erased, he snatches Carrion's wrist, digging his fingers into their pulse point and making their fingers spasm, forcing them to drop the match. Carrion grits their teeth and squirms, wriggling out of the grip before Ari can break their wrist.

Something connects in Ziane's mind. An intuition. An understanding. She gasps the deepest breath she has ever filled her body with and scrambles to her feet, fueled by the sudden rush of air to her muscles and oxygen to her brain.

Ari turns to put her down again, but Carrion tackles him around the waist before he can toss her around like a ragdoll. The sudden rush isn't enough to hurt him, only enough for Carrion to buy Ziane a second of time. She jumps through the doorway and slams the door shut behind her, leaning her back against the solid metal and reasserting control over her shaking limbs and aching flesh. If she's lucky enough to survive this, she'll be black and blue from bruises.

She makes her way to the functional computer terminal, clinging to the walls to keep herself upright. The screen still displays that same progress bar, now far further towards completion. On the hologram, she watches as the dot of the diamond gets closer and closer, about to turn far enough in the tunnel that it should soon be visible to them, no longer just a marker on a hologram.

"Come on," she whispers to the computer. "Just a little bit further…"

Her skill with computers is nothing compared to Carrion's, but she has enough knowledge to find the menu controlling the diamond's speed. She accelerates it. A warning message appears and she dismisses it.

Through the one-way window, she can do nothing but watch as Carrion uses a handful of dirt to wrap thorns around their fist, and Ari in turn draws every drop of water out of the plant, turning it into a withered husk. Even as Carrion tries to punch them with their new weapon, Ari has disarmed them before they can get in that hit. Ari simply tilts his head back, and their fist misses by less than an inch.

Ari tosses Carrion across the tunnel by the scruff of their shirt and paces towards them before he stops in his tracks and turn his head to look at something outside of Ziane's field of view. Carrion, in the middle of getting back up onto unsteady legs, also pauses and turns to face the same direction.

Ziane shivers, the void in her chest yawning. She has a split second where her instincts scream at her to cover her face right before the window shatters into a thousand pieces.

Glittering glass shards fly through the control center in a torrent of flashing blades, slicing a hundred tiny cuts into her skin, cutting at her clothing and snicking off strands of her hair. When the final *clink* of glass hitting the ground fades, she lowers her arms to see a razor-sharp vine piercing the ground beneath her feet, and it's clear from its trajectory that it was the thing that broke the glass with a single thrust. If the resonance in her chest hadn't been enough to convince her before, this certainly is.

Carefully, she brushes the glass out of the way and clambers through the now-opened window. Carrion too has apparently been forced to dodge, as there is a gouge in the metal right where they had previously been standing, a waxy green residue left behind. To her dismay, Ari does not appear to have been attacked, let alone harmed.

A new figure has arrived. Queen Sef blocks the tunnel, those hundreds of braids of hers protruding from the metal ground like knives and keeping her aloft as though she is weightless. Unlike the austere efficiency of Ari's skill, Sef, with her bare feet and web of flower-woven hair, projects the illusion of ethereal grace. She descends with a smooth bow of her braids, her feet silent as they land on the metal, her hair gliding across the floor behind her, changing from strong as steel to light and flowing as water.

"'Tis a disappointment to see what you have done with our gift of clemency." Despite Sef's words, there is no disappointment on her face when she looks at Ziane, or indeed any emotion at all. "To continue such affiliation with Carrion is a poor choice."

Ari, having apparently judged Sef to be ally instead of threat, has returned the brunt of his attention to Carrion. "They have nearly reached the diamond," he tells Sef. "My priority is preventing them from getting hold of it – I imagine the same may be said of the Eoi. What say you? Shall we settle our own scores once this blight is cleansed?"

"An acceptable proposal." Sef inclines her head in agreement. "The final possession of the diamond is a matter that can wait."

Carrion groans. Their messy braid has almost completely unraveled after the beating they've taken from Ari, and they toss the loose clump of hair over their shoulder. "Oh, come on! It'd be so much simpler for me if the two of you would just stop being mature about this and fight each other." They huff, blowing a stray strand out of their eyes. "Never thought I'd find myself missing any aspect of Lysander's personality, and yet here we are…"

"From us, you shall find no quarter," Sef warns.

There's a glint in Carrion's eye. "It's funny, ya know. Even as strong as you both are, you've forgotten the pros and cons that come with that power. You're opposites. Just meeting with each other tires y'all out. In tag-teaming me, you've kinda given me an advantage."

Ari arches a cold eyebrow and scorns, "Have we?"

Behind Ziane, the computer terminal lets out a faint beep. She drops down into the tunnel, glass shards crunching beneath her boots. "This doesn't matter!" she calls out. "The diamond is–"

Bright light suddenly glows in the darkness. Not the dim shine of the tunnel's emergency lights or the flickering of the computer screens. Not the gilded light of the orb in Sef's bower or the silvered light of the orb in Ari's viewing room. Not the calculated wavelengths of the Bastion's daylamps under which all of them have spent their lives. True light. Day light. The warmth and radiance and distance and dispassion of the sun that illuminates every inch of the world outside the Bastion.

Sef's eyes are wide, glistening in the light, as she beholds what she has spent so long searching for. "The diamond…!"

The final terraforming device, the Dynamo-Interstellar Modifier, the diamond, glides down the tunnel towards them. Tiny vents or magnets of some kind are attached to the edges of its radiant sphere, moving it along with seamless grace. Warmth kisses Ziane's cheeks. Not enough to burn, just enough to settle in the void where her heart once was. All her bruises and cuts tingle like they've been freshly made, filled with a new life that she wishes she could block out.

"...Fuck me," Carrion mumbles as they stare at the diamond in stupor.

Ziane can do little besides stare as well. Even as she knows that the diamond will soon be halted in its tracks once it reaches the control center, even as she knows that she needs to be ready to activate the devices as soon as the computer is ready, even with all that in the back of her mind, it's impossible not to stop and gape at the aura of the diamond's majesty. It's beautiful. For all that the orb in the Deep had been rich as fertile soil and the orb in the Mists a puff of air on damp skin, she still hadn't been prepared for how disarmingly resplendent the diamond would be.

Only one of them isn't stunned into stasis by the diamond. Ziane tries to yell a warning, but her voice is slower than Ari. The king crosses the distance between himself and Carrion in a split second. It all happens so quickly. So clearly. He slides one foot between Carrion's legs, preventing them from wriggling out of his grip. His hands twist around Carrion's shoulders.

With a sickening *crack*, Ari snaps Carrion's neck.

CHAPTER THIRTY-NINE

A scream bursts from Ziane's lungs, too great to be contained within her body. She abandons the control room completely, rushing to Carrion's side only to be able to do nothing other than catch their body as Ari releases them. They fall into her arms, sagging in her embrace. *Please, no. Not them, not this, not again.*

Again? She can't–

The great nothingness in her chest rings like a stone being tossed into an empty shaft, clinking and clattering as it plummets, echoing all the while.

The memory of Sef's voice whispers in Ziane's mind: *I shall ensure that your heart never hurts again.*

Machinery creaks and whirrs as the decelerators activate and the diamond slows to a halt for the first time in an eternity. Carrion's eyes dart to and fro, fading but still there, still clinging to life, their neck at a wrong angle but their throat still contorting as they thread Vesperi air down their windpipe. They fix their panicked gaze on her and then release their final breath they had been stealing. The diamond's light drapes across their fading features and, for a moment, the lines that have been so deeply carved into their face smooth out.

"No!" Ziane chokes, desperately shaking her head. "You

led me into this to ease your loneliness. You don't get to die and leave me alone! You don't get to do this to me!"

Ari does not bother to watch his enemy die or Ziane weep for them. He simply turns his back on them and declares, "At last, my duty is done. Live, Eoi. If you so choose. If you interfere, I shall show you the same mercy I showed *them*."

Carrion's eyelids flutter and shut.

No no no! They're dying, after everything they've said and done, they mean to just *die* on her. As carefully as she can, she lays them down on the metal floor, straining her muscles in her determination to move as little as possible, to avoid jostling their head. She stands on trembling legs, the brilliance of the diamond casting her shadow over Carrion's limp body, shrouding them in her protection. If Carrion can save her, then maybe, just maybe, she can return that debt and save them.

Before she can think twice, she plunges her arm into the diamond.

It *burns*. Burns like ice, like fire, like the far-away glimmer of those stars that lit up the night sky. Pure energy seeps through her skin, crawling into her veins, making its home in the very marrow of her bones. Her teeth creak in the effort to avoid voicing her pain, and when she closes her eyes to block out the agony, the starlight is right there anyway, behind her eyelids, bright spots dancing and chasing away the darkness. Beneath her feet, the world turns. Everything rotates, tugged and pulled and spun, repelling and attracting.

With all her might, she closes her straining fist around *something* and yanks her hand out of the sphere of starlight. Rays of iridescence shine from between the cracks in her fingers as she stumbles backwards, holding something as weightless as a scrap of fabric and as heavy as a slab of steel. She falls to her knees before Carrion and, desperately, prays for this to work.

She drops the handful of starlight into Carrion's mouth. It slides past their lips like water, lighting them up from the inside out, making their jaw glow beneath their skin and the veins in their neck shine pure red-orange, the same hue as the burnt sky of the world outside. There is another *crack* as their spine snaps and shifts into place, each vertebra forced to conform into a neat, straight line. Nerves reconnecting, internal bleeding oozing back into capillaries. Hauling them out of the grave and back into the world of the living whether they like it or not.

They bolt upright with a gasp, eyes blown wide, clutching at their neck as she had not so long ago.

"What did you…?" They gape at her in sheer incredulity, and, perhaps, just the tiniest bit of resentment. "Your arm. You…"

A web of iridescent cracks spreads from the tips of her fingers all the way up to her elbow, vanishing beneath her sleeve. There's that same fire beneath her skin, that endless rotation settling into her muscles. "I had to save you," she insists, holding on to them even now that they live. "You might not have done the same, but I still had to."

"I would have," they swear.

They surge forward and their lips collide with her own. It's neither fire nor ice but that perfect match to her own temperature, and she cannot help leaning right back into it. Her cracked hands slide behind their new neck while their own fingers tangle in her hair, their body pressed as closely to hers as they can manage, their kiss greedy and possessive and reverent.

When they finally pull back, her lips brush against theirs as she admits, "I'm heartless."

They rest their forehead against her own and whisper, "You can share mine."

There is the slide of a boot against metal. Ari has ceased his retreat to once more turn to face Carrion. "I see you are more persistent than I anticipated. No matter. If I must put you down once more, then I shall."

"You will not harm them again," Ziane decries. "This ends. *Now*."

Both Ari and Sef tense for a return to combat, but Ziane won't give them that chance. Raising her mangled arm, she brings forth that sensation of rotation, of push and pull, of pure magnetism, the attraction and repulsion between atoms. It is everywhere here, with the diamond effulgent at her back and the pure metal above and beneath her. All she has to do is spin those atoms on their axes, turn neutrality into attraction, stasis into action. She flexes her fingers and expels the power in her bones.

Sheets of metal peel off the tunnel walls, slamming into each other with a screech of steel scraping against steel, layering and layering until a solid barrier stands between Ziane and the two Astrosi rulers.

"The computer must be finished calibrating." Despite everything, Ziane feels oddly calm. She knows what she has to do. "We need to activate the devices before Sef or Ari can make it through that wall." As if on cue, there is a loud banging against the metal blockade, like something solid crashed into it. "One last push?"

Carrion shuts their eyes and sighs. "One last push."

She supports their shoulders while they wrap an arm around her waist, and together the two of them sway like drunkards towards the control center. As the door is locked from the inside, they both have to clamber in through the broken window, sending fresh shards of glass clinking onto the floor as they go. Despite the tingling in her arm, it doesn't hurt, instead settling into something that, while not normal by any stretch of the imagination, is something she can live with.

Fortunately, it doesn't look like any of the computer equipment was damaged by Sef shattering the glass; when Carrion makes their way to the terminal, it's still in as good condition as it was when they first got here.

The calibration is complete. A happy little green confirmation hovers on the screen.

"Ready?" Carrion asks with a strained, lopsided smile.

She nods. "As I'll ever be."

"Want to do the honors?"

"I think," she replies, "that after all this time, you've more than earned it."

They don't linger on the activation button for more than a moment before pushing it with a firm tap, the tip of their finger turning white from the pressure against the screen, outlining their ragged nail and chewed cuticles. A quiet yet cheerful *beep* sounds in the control room. Another bang from behind the barrier. All the machines around them that have been sitting here, powered off and in the dark for eternity, suddenly whirr to life, filling the room with a satisfied hum as they, at long last, fulfill their final purpose.

Metal groans as a long vine, twisted with dark hair, wriggles between the plating of the barrier and pries it apart. Once one sheet of metal falls and the rest of the wall is swiftly shredded in much the same manner. Sef ascends through the now-opened tunnel, suspended by her hair once more as she prepares to strike, and standing before her is Ari, grim determination flattening his features.

A message pops up on the screen:

Activation complete.

Cracks form on the surface of the diamond. It does not shatter. It does not break or split open. It merely... sighs. An exhale. And then it fades away, dissolving into light and mist and flame, a wave rolling out through the tunnel, washing over the four of them without touching them, and then into nothingness.

Sef cries out, delicate yet shocked, and falls to the ground, her head tilted back as her eyes stare up at something only she can see. Ari too makes a grunt of pain, clutching at his chest and hunching in on himself, showing weakness for perhaps the first time in centuries. Though Ziane's chest does not hurt nor her throat burn, she can feel the slightest of absences, the connection to the two terraforming devices fading. Not enough to strip her of what she is, but enough that she can tell, with certainty, that they too have at last done what they were made to do. For Sef and Ari, who have spent their lives communing with their spheres and connecting so deeply to that power, the pain of severance must be far more acute.

"What have you done?" Ari growls, fingers clenching over his heart. Did he lose that too, or did he sacrifice something else to become what he is?

Ziane answers before Carrion can. "If either of you had listened to me, properly *listened*, then you would know exactly what I've done. The diamond is gone. The two spheres that create the Eoi and the Vesperi are gone. And as far as I know, there's no way to get any of them back, so please don't waste time trying to force us to undo this.

What's done is done. We were never trying to get hold of the diamond for the sake of gaining power. We wanted to use it, but not for ourselves."

Shouldering aside some of his shock, Ari makes his way towards the broken window to properly meet Ziane's eyes. "And why should I trust a single word you say? For all I know, the diamond dissolved because you took its power for yourself. Your arm and Carrion's healed neck stand as evidence against you."

She steps back, gesturing to the computer terminal so that both rulers have the opportunity to stand down and examine it if they so choose. "If you can't take me at my word, then look. *Please*, just look."

"And why should I not slay you where you stand?" Ari asks bluntly.

"What would that achieve? The diamond is gone. We're not attacking either of you. You already killed Carrion once today. You did your duty. How many more times do you need to satisfy your own personal bloodlust?"

Sef holds up a single dainty finger. "Shall we not cease, my friend? Our efforts to prevent them from seizing the diamond's power have... failed. Yet, we both have seen time and time again what it looks like when one merges with such a fount of power. The dispersal of the diamond did not appear to be such an event. I know not where its power went, nor do I comprehend how they were able to remove our own sources. However, 'tis a mystery that I sorely crave the answer to. Similarly, there is naught that can be gained by slaying either of them at this current moment. What more damage can they do?"

"With them involved?" Ari's voice is scathing as he stares down Carrion. "Quite a bit, I might imagine."

Much of the fire seems to have faded from Carrion as they reply, "Your opinion of my skills would be flattering if it weren't so bloody annoying."

Ziane shifts to put herself physically between Carrion and Ari. "When I first started to learn the truth of things," she says quietly to the king, "Carrion warned me that no one would listen. That they had tried to tell others before and no one listened to them, and that no one would listen to me. I tried. I tried to tell a friend, I tried to tell Queen Sef, I've tried to tell you. Will you prove Carrion wrong at last and *listen*?"

Ari does not stand down. But he doesn't attack either and Ziane once more indicates towards the computer terminal and waits for one of the two rulers to make a decision. Eventually, it is Sef that crosses into the control center and, keeping half her attention still firmly on Carrion, regards the computer screen out of the corner of her eye. She doesn't do much, not at first. Just looks at the *activation complete* message with the intense concentration of someone relearning how to read.

"Please," Ziane says quietly to the woman who was once her queen. "You know me. You know I'm not insane, or malicious, or a liar."

"I believed that I knew you," Sef admits. "Yet never could I have foreseen your alliance with Carrion."

"I tried to tell you. About what I'd seen. About what exists outside of the Bastion."

"Your holograms."

"No, that's... that's what I mean. There is no hologram outside the Bastion; there's an entire *world* out there." She gestures to where the diamond had once been. "The diamond, your sphere, Ari's sphere – they were never meant to be used to create Astrosi. They were designed to turn a world that can't sustain life into one that can. That's why the Astrosi are so much stronger than humans – they have all this energy inside them that was never meant to be inside a body. You've worked so closely with your sphere, you must have had your own questions, your own suspicions."

Sef still does not fully approach the computer. "My suspicions were meaningless when measured against the weight of my duty to my throneworld."

"And now that you no longer have your sphere of power? How much does that duty weigh now?" Ziane glances between Ari, who is still wound tight enough to throw punches, and Carrion, who looks like they'd prefer to slip away without anyone noticing. "If you did kill us, what good would it do? If you went back to the Deep and the Mists and just acted like nothing has changed, how long would that last? Neither of you can create any more Astrosi. The time delay between the Astrosi throneworlds and the human Bastion will fade away without the spheres maintaining it. Soon, your realms will begin to degrade at the same pace as the Bastion. What then?"

"Is that a threat?" Ari demands.

"No!" she replies with hasty shake of her head. "It's a warning. I don't want anyone harmed, human or Astrosi. That's the point of all this."

With the slightest twitch of a frown, Sef finally touches the computer screen, clearing out the completion message so that the screen once again displays the calibration and activation program. The three now-gone devices, all on the same network, with the noted absence where the first two terraforming devices once were, those that were properly activated so long ago and that are still remembered by the computer system. Even to Ziane, who knows the story from Carrion's explanations, the pure text of the computer is a bit esoteric. For Sef, who is devoid of the same level of context, it's impossible to say how much of it she truly understands.

Ziane clears her throat, trying to explain, "The various devices the system is talking about are what's used to make the world habitable. There were five of them. And the diamond was the last one. We have schematics, too, of the Bastion, that show where it ends, where the outside world starts. It all lines up with what we've been trying to tell you."

Ari watches Sef more than he watches the computer screen, as though there will be a hidden truth in what conclusion his counterpart comes to. "And how do we know that any of this is real? Carrion has always been *adept* at technological manipulation."

Pausing, Sef straightens up and abandons the computer. "That... is a fair concern."

"Really?" Carrion's puff of a laugh is as exasperated as it is exhausted. "I was just saying you don't need to keep stroking my ego like this."

"Enough of you." Ari watches Ziane. He closes his eyes for a second, tension creasing his face, his lips flat and pale. Then he exhales and asks her, "Have you any proof?"

Ziane asks, "Are you willing to walk for it?"

CHAPTER FORTY

After so many times walking this route, the path through the Fringes is a second home to Ziane. Well-trod, well-mapped. The oppressive darkness of the ruins is no longer so difficult to bear, the stale air no longer sickening enough to choke her. And beyond that, she now feels a sense of control, of power, of knowledge over this place that she didn't have before. Every time she has walked this path, she has done so in pursuit of mysteries or being led by Carrion, either via their words or with them at her side. This is the first time she has led another through these shadowed streets.

Queen Sef, despite her trailing braids and her bare feet, has yet to falter on the trek through the Fringes. Her head remains unburdened by the weight of her hair; the only time her neck bends is when she must duck underneath a collapsing doorway or fallen pipe. Next to her is King Ari, who has kept his keen, pale eyes fixed firmly on Carrion for the entire journey, never tiring or faltering, even though both rulers must surely be weakened, not only from the dissolution of their orbs and their prolonged absence from their realms, but also from remaining in one another's presence for so long a time. Not that either of them display any signs of such a shortcoming, of course.

"So this is where you fled to," Ari remarks after they pass one of Carrion's stashes.

For the entire duration of this venture, Carrion has so far remained as tense as Ziane has ever seen them. Even without the immediate threat of being slain by Ari, the distant possibility of it must still be right at the forefront of their thoughts. "Well, yeah. You knew that I kept hiding out here."

"I refer to your very first departure." There's almost a nostalgia to Ari's tone, albeit a bitter one. "After you first looked upon my viewing glass – this is where you fled to, is it not?"

"Where else would I go for answers? Not like any of the Astrosi knew nothing, and I knew there had to be something *else*. The end of the world seemed as good a place as any to find some truth. And I was right, too. Would've been a lot easier if I weren't and I could've just traipsed on back to the Mists, but…" They sigh. "Guess it worked out in the end. If you don't kill me after this, of course."

"If I did not know how tenaciously you have evaded our grasp, I would almost say that you seem *hopeful* for such an outcome."

Ziane glances at Carrion as she steps over a crack in the ground. They are not allowed to have a death wish. They're not allowed to succumb to their exhaustion and loneliness just because they've finally completed the work they have dedicated lifetimes to, and if they try, if they attempt to goad Ari into killing them after they show the two rulers definitive proof, then Ziane will simply have to drag them back to life once more.

"Eh." Carrion shifts uncomfortably when they catch the look Ziane is giving them. "I mean, what happens, happens, amiright?"

"You are not," Ari replies. "Learning now that your random acts of violence and subversion have been deliberately structured towards an ultimate goal, I no longer believe that you are someone who is content to simply let fate and happenstance sweep them away."

They fall silent at that, chewing their lips, presumably debating what snappy comeback to give and turning up empty.

Sef's stride lengthens until her pace matches Ziane's and she can speak without the other two hearing. "With all that has occurred," Sef says softly, "I cannot help but conceive of multitudinous scenarios in which you could have achieved this task that you pledged yourself to without aiding Carrion. The grief of your fellow Eoi was palpable upon my departure from the Deep. None suspected such an alliance from you, and all were sorrowed to hear of it. Had you attempted to deliver unto me this proof you claim to have prior to aligning with Carrion, then none of this violence need have occurred."

"You didn't listen the first time I tried to bring up the end of the world," Ziane reminds the woman who was once her queen. "I wanted to try to plead my case to you the whole time, but you didn't listen originally, and we needed to make sure that my contract was broken before I tried again. You saw what Lysander was like. Even if you had been willing to listen when I returned to the Deep, he would always have challenged me."

"Is the implication that I cannot command control of my own subjects?"

"No, it's... You only brought Lysander to heel after he lost the duel. You're not cruel – you wouldn't have struck him down so harshly right away, and even though it was counterproductive to my own goals," she admits, "I think you were right to do so. He deserved a chance to prove his own conviction, as he challenged me to."

Sef sighs, her voice like a leaf drifting to the forest floor. "My lenience with Lysander was an error." Her head droops barely half an inch, and Ziane notices that the pink cherry blossom from the tree over Annie's grave is still wound within her braids. What had the old woman meant to Sef, truly? Did she see Annie's life of service as a mistake, as a gift, as a burden? "Events may have unfolded more favorably had I not blundered so. But alas, 'tis naught I can change at this juncture. Thus all I can do is offer a single apology for that failure of mine."

"It's forgiven," Ziane immediately replies. "Like I said, I think you were right to let him challenge me. Though I suppose I might be forced to never see or speak with him again. He may just try to kill me on sight."

"An optimistic deliberation to consider," Sef points out, "as it implies that you will not only live through this proof of yours but will remain on terms that allow you entrance to the Deep or non-hostile confrontation with my people. Neither is guaranteed. The trust given to you has still been shattered by your actions, and there is much that you must do if you mean to regain it." She pauses for a moment before adding, "If that is your intent, of course."

"I want to see my friends again," Ziane admits quietly, wringing her hands together. "I want to apologize to them. They deserve an explanation, even if they don't forgive me for what I did."

Sef offers no commentary on that. After all, had she not forced Essten and Leneat to use that recording to bring Ziane back to the Deep, the two never would have been injured in the hydrogen explosion. Without those orders, they might have been willing to listen to Ziane's explanation, even if they wouldn't have been able to understand her alliance with Carrion. It's been just her and Carrion for what feels like an age at this point. The only two people who knew the truth, the only person she could rely on in this. She's almost forgotten what it felt like to have two friends at her side instead of one enemy who is the other half of her.

Carrion leads them around a corner and then there they are. There it is. The smooth wall that marks the final boundary of the Bastion, the door set into it with red sand scattered in front of it and caked into its frame. Hic Sunt Leones. Something buzzes inside Ziane's chest. Not an excitement. Not a worry, either. Anticipation. No matter what Sef or Ari decide upon seeing the outside world, this will be the final offering that she and Carrion can give them. The final forgotten truth.

She stands next to Carrion in front of the door, her throat dry as the sandstorms that may or may not rage beyond the door. "Do you think that the terraforming devices have made any impact yet?"

"I haven't a single clue." Carrion pauses. "Finally, something about the world that I don't know. Feels good."

"It could already look like the Deep," she tentatively suggests. "There could already be that water cycle set up. There could be plant life already starting to grow. The sunlight could look different with the magnetosphere."

The burnt and barren rock of the planet could already be replaced by soft grass and a blanket of mist. No deadly radiation overhead, no scorching temperatures during the day, no dry wasteland devoid of a single drop of water. No sandstorms. No danger. A true world of green paradise, not merely contained to the Deep and its little corner of the Bastion. A world that no longer makes her feel small and exposed beneath that eternal sky. A world that could maybe, just *maybe*, be as much a home to her as Annie's house in the Deep was.

"It's a very big world," Carrion reminds her. "Could be anything."

Ziane blindly reaches out and slips her hand into Carrion's. "Everything changes."

A sincere and shockingly gentle smile tugs at Carrion's cheeks and they hold on tight as though it is the most important thing in the entire world. "Nothing dies."

They open the door.

ACKNOWLEDGEMENTS

I'd like to thank *Star Trek: TNG*. I love you, you're incredible– yes that is a reference to Captain Jean-Luc Picard – and also sorry but *Deep Space Nine* is still better than you. All legal terminology is credited to Andrea, who actually knows things about legal fuckery and saved me from a lot of desperate stumbling around and grasping at search terms. Further thanks go to Mary Robinette Kowal, who helped me finally figure out what the heck the terraforming spheres did and stopped me from making the horribly embarrassing mistake of having concrete on a spaceship. As always, this whole thing could not be possible without my editor, Gemma Creffield, and the wonderful team at Angry Robot. And a final bit of infinite gratitude to my incredible agent, Lauren Spieller, and her equally amazing assistant, Hannah Teachout.